The Last Gig

Also by Norman Green

Dead Cat Bounce

Way Past Legal

The Angel of
Montague Street

Shooting Dr. Jack

The Last Gig

Norman Green

 Minotaur Books ⚐ New York

THE LAST GIG. Copyright © 2008 by Norman Green. All rights reserved. Printed in the United States of America. For information address St. Martin's Press, 175 Fifth Avenue, New York, N.Y. 10010.

www.minotaurbooks.com

ISBN-13: 978-0-312-38542-2
ISBN-10: 0-312-38542-0

First Edition: January 2009

10 9 8 7 6 5 4 3 2 1

In memory of Kathleen Mary Coolong
August 9, 1949–March 15, 2006

Flights of angels . . .

Acknowledgments

I would like to thank both Andy Markham and "Killer" Joe Delia, who shared with me the joys of making music and the pains of making it in the music business. Thanks also to Brian DeFiore, who is also well acquainted with the perils of serving a temperamental and occasionally ill-humored muse. Finally, thanks to Christine, for her patience and love, and to the Liberty Street Irregulars, to whom I owe a debt I cannot hope to repay.

The Last Gig

One

The things a girl's gotta do to turn a buck . . .

Alessandra Martillo leaned across the pool table and lined up her shot. Black hair fell forward across her face and hung down over one eye. She knew Marty Stiles, the fat dude at the bar, was staring at the gap in her V-neck sweater, but she also knew that he couldn't help himself. Her single unobscured eye flicked once in his direction, then back down at the table as she struck the cue ball softly. It rolled half the length of the table, knocked the last striped ball into a corner pocket, then caromed off the end bumper and rolled to a stop about a foot and a half behind the eight ball. She straightened back up, ignored Marty, tapped her stick on the other corner pocket. Her opponent, relegated to observer status since four shots after the break, stepped forward and laid a folded twenty on the table. "Forget it," he said. "You're out of my league."

She shook her hair back out of her face and winked at him. "If that's the way you feel about it, baby." The guy walked off shaking his head.

She walked around the table and sank the rest of the balls. Now that her game was over, she hammered them home one by one, almost violently. No one had yet come forward with the price of the next game. Stiles didn't reach into his pocket, either. Marty never played anything, anywhere, unless he had an edge. Besides, when Al was dressed for the club, the guy could never think straight; all he could do was waste his time admiring her ass.

She knew she was no cover girl, but she was tall, dark, lean, fine enough in her own way. If you wanted a Barbie doll, she wasn't for you, and she was comfortable with that. She was more like the kind of broad who could pitch a shutout against your softball team, hit one out herself, then drink you under the table after the game. There were certain guys who went crazy for that, and Marty Stiles was one of them. She knew it: when she stared at him she could turn his guts to water. Every time she wore a pair of low-rise jeans his tongue would hang out so far you could put a knot in it and call it a tie. He'd had it bad for her for a while. He'd given her his best shot: laid off the sauce, dropped about thirty pounds, got into some new clothes, sprang for a fifty-dollar haircut . . . But when he made his move, she laughed at him.

Not a chance, she told him.

He hadn't taken defeat easily. He had a certain kind of fat guy charm, she had to admit it, and he certainly had the green, but she wasn't interested. Angered and insulted, for a while he'd told everyone who would listen that she was a rug-muncher. She hadn't minded that, but when he began speculating, aloud, how unnatural it was for a Puerto Rican chick like her to be so cold, she'd had a short and pointed conversation with the man.

She watched a new victim come forward—guy looked like an off-duty cop, young, big guns, Republican haircut. Looked like the kind of guy who let his size win most of his arguments. He approached the table, quarters in his hand. "May I have the pleasure?" he asked her. She looked at him, nodded, and he stuck the coins into the slot. The balls grumbled down into the tray beneath the table.

"Carlo," he said, holding out his hand. "You mind if I rack?"

"Alessandra," she said, and she shook his hand. "And I'm feeling so good tonight, I'm gonna let you break. How about that?"

"Beautiful thing," he said.

He got lucky, sank a ball off the break, then two more in quick succession before faltering. "Left you tough," he told her, backing away. "I don't think you have a move."

She chuckled softly, chalked the end of her stick, and then she ran the table on him. Carlo leaned against a column and watched in silence until it was over. "Twenty bucks," he said, reaching into his pocket. "That the standard bet?"

She shook her head. "Don't want you feeling like you been hustled."

"No, no," Carlo said. "Call it a lesson. You do this for a living?"

"Strictly amateur," she said, watching him. Her habit of making direct eye contact, together with her looks, intimidated a lot of men. Not this one, though.

"Listen," he said. "If I buy you a drink, will you show me how you drew the cue ball back on that last corner shot? I thought you were gonna scratch for sure."

She looked past him, caught a glimpse of Marty Stiles over at the bar, a sour look on his face as he downed a shot and picked up the beer chaser. She knew what Marty really wanted.

He really wanted her to tell the guy to get lost, that she was taken, in love, going steady, head over heels crazy with this pudgy gentleman who—

"Cutty on the rocks," she said.

Carlo pulled a wad of bills out of his pocket, peeled off a twenty, and laid it on the table. "Right back," he said.

She felt Marty's eyes on her as she walked out of the place with Carlo about an hour later. Carlo's car was parked in two spots on the far side of the lot. She couldn't really blame him, it was a yellow Lamborghini Murcielago, a two-seat Italian sports car that optioned out for just north of three hundred grand, and it would be criminal, not to mention expensive, to find it with a ding from some meathead flinging his pickup door open.

"You like it?" he asked her.

"I love it," she told him. It was the truth.

"Climb in," he said. He put his hand on her butt and caressed her over to the passenger side door. "Let me take you for a ride."

They didn't get halfway across the lot before Marty Stiles stepped out from between two cars and stood directly in their path.

"Who is this guy?" Carlo said.

"Beats me," she said.

No one moved for about twenty seconds. Then Carlo blipped his throttle once. Twelve cylinders and five hundred and seventy-two horses murmured their impatience. Marty seemed to think it over for another ten seconds, then took a single step back, gave them just enough room to squeak by.

Carlo eased the car forward.

They passed by Stiles, his bellied shirt the only part of him visible, a hand-width away. He thumped his fist down on the car's roof as it passed.

Carlo stomped the brake. Marty backed away, groping for something under his jacket.

Carlo was cool, Al had to give him that. He didn't pop out of the car like an enraged prairie dog, he opened the door slowly and climbed out calmly. Marty walked unsteadily backward.

Carlo followed him five or six steps. "Exactly what," he said, his voice pitched low and hard, "is your fucking problem?"

Up ahead, a Pontiac GTO pulled up to the front door of the joint and stopped. The driver and his young female passenger got out, paused to watched the unfolding drama. "You oughta watch where the hell you're going," Marty snarled. "You almost ran over my foot!"

"You fat piece of shit." Carlo took another step in Marty's direction. "I am gonna—"

He was barely six feet away when Al made her move. Gripping the windowsill and the seat-back hard, she jack-knifed her legs up out of the footwell, and, butt in the air, knees in her face, she levered herself over into the driver's seat. Nice, she thought. But it's a damn good thing this baby isn't a quarter of an inch shorter . . . She didn't bother to close the driver's-side door, she just tapped the magnesium shift paddle, eased on the throttle, let the door close itself. The V-12 murmured sweet lies in her ear as she pulled away slowly. She could just make out Carlo's shout, looked in the mirror, saw him running madly after her, saw Marty Stiles, red-faced, bent over laughing in the background. She toyed with Carlo, kept the Lambo just out of his reach, slid past the GTO, past the long, pink, phallic club awning where the Pontiac's occupants stood watching in amusement. She eased on the gas a little more when she hit the street, left Carlo standing there, hands on knees, sucking wind.

Aw, come on, Al, an inner voice whispered. The guy had his hand all over your ass, you owe him . . . She toggled off the traction control, stood on the gas. The engine bellowed in finest Italian operatic tradition; the Lambo spun madly. She did not have to fight it, it was now a living thing, a coconspirator, something you did not steer, you pled with it, you urged it with your knees and your hips, you let it feel your desire . . . The acceleration pressed her back into the seat as the car exploded down the street. Carlo dived for the safety of the ditch on the far side of the sidewalk as Alessandra and her new friend ripped off two beautiful tire-shredding donuts right where he'd been standing.

And then she rocketed away.

God, it was almost like the thing breathed for her, as though she could feel the air pouring over her painted skin, feel the soles of her shoes sliding on the pavement.

You shouldn't have done that, she thought, and the car slowed.

It was pointless, she thought, and stupid. The Lambo took the next corner calmly, almost quietly.

Oh, please, the inner voice said. What's the point of stealing a supercar if you can't behave like Supergirl, if only for a minute or so? Pete, the tow driver, was parked up on the next block. With intense regret, she slid up behind the big flatbed. It was already tilted down to the ground, Pete standing behind it with a cable in his hand. He was an older guy, gray ponytail and goatee, couple days' growth of beard, balding on the top.

Good-bye, doll, she thought, and she caressed the steering wheel. I'm really sorry to walk out on you this way, but it never would have worked. I can't afford you, honey, you're way too hot for me. I know, I know, it's a lame and tired excuse, but it's the truth.

It wasn't you, baby. It was me.

She opened the door and climbed out. "Hook it up, Petey baby, and let's get the hell out of here."

Just then Pete's phone went off, and she could hear Marty Stiles's voice shouting, right on the edge of panic. "Mayday! Mayday!" he yelled. "The mark jacked that GTO and he's headed in your direction!" In the distance she heard the basso profundo roar of an American V-8, with cop sirens singing soprano harmony in the background.

Here we go, she thought, and she cracked her knuckles. Here we go . . . "Hook that mother, Petey, get that bitch onto the truck and she's ours. I'll deal with this guy . . ."

It was all over by the time Stiles got there. Alessandra leaned her butt against the fender of the cruiser, her arms crossed in front. She watched Stiles by the flashing lights of the police car and the ambulance. He horsed himself out of his car, looked at her and shook his head, but he kept his distance. She knew he was standing over there trying to figure a way to make this all her fault. It's your job, she told him silently, you're the guy who's supposed to give the mark the standard speech: "Nothing personal, my man, but you don't make the payments, Lambo takes their car back, so just chill, no point in anybody going to jail over this . . ."

The yellow Lamborghini sat up high on the flatbed. A blue-uniformed policeman watched two EMTs who were trying to attend to the Lambo's driver, but the guy couldn't hold still, he was down on his knees in the street, puking. He held his shaking right arm awkwardly away from his body. The cop's partner was over behind the cruiser, talking to Pete, who pitched his voice loud enough for her to hear.

"Well, Officer, she pulls up in the car, right, I get it hooked up, then we hear this yoyo one block over, he musta seen my flashers. So he comes screaming up, right, jumps out, but he don't care about the car anymore, he goes right for Martillo. He's gotta be twice her size, right, he makes a grab for her, I'm wondering how much of a pussy I am for not jumping in, then I hear this funny noise, sounds like when you bite a piece of celery, right, then the guy's fucking screaming. I mean, he's not yelling like a man, he's screaming like my wife after I track dog shit on the carpet. He had a piece, right, but when he tries to pull it out, she kicks him on the outside of his knee, he goes down, she takes the piece and tosses it under the truck. Which is where it still is. Whole thing took maybe ten seconds."

"She wasn't armed?"

"No, sir. I seen the whole thing. She done it just like I told you."

Another cruiser rolled up behind the tow. More lights, Al thought. Just in case someone wants to see us from the freakin' moon. Two cops got out, walked right past her, over to where the EMTs were trying to splint the Lambo driver's broken fingers. She shook her head. I do all the freakin' work, she thought, and what do I get? I get to stand here and wait while the big boys figure things out.

Same old shit.

Stiles stood over by his car. She ignored him, watched the EMTs. She knew he was staring, but the man just couldn't help himself.

Two

Marty Stiles, elbows on the table, watched the dancer at the other end of the stage. She didn't look half bad, at least not from that distance. Be careful, he thought. You've had too much to drink tonight to be able to think regular . . . He didn't look at Daniel Caughlan, the man sitting next to him. "I'd love to do it for you," he said. "Problem is, Al is the best man I got. I put her full time on this, I gotta hire another broad for the office, then I gotta find another guy to do what Al does out in the field. You know what I'm sayin'? So it ain't like I just gotta replace the one guy. An' I don't know where I would get somebody else like her. This business takes a special kinda person. Al has a real feel for it." He finally glanced in Caughlan's direction. Fucking guy, Marty thought, he's watching me like a cat watching a parakeet.

"I'll make it worth your trouble," Caughlan said.

Marty Stiles shivered. He had known Daniel "Mickey" Caughlan for years. Stiles had been a rookie cop when he'd first run across the guy. Caughlan had been one of the few to survive the immolation of the Irish gangs that had once haunted the neighborhood of Hell's Kitchen on Manhattan's west side. He had been just another body back then, just another face.

Perhaps smarter and without question luckier than his betters, he had survived, left alone at the reins of something called Pennsylvania Transfer Corporation when his silent partners all wound up dead or serving long prison sentences. The last of them, Patrick Donleavy, had disappeared without a trace. Donleavy had been Caughlan's friend and patron, but Rudolph Giuliani, then a prominent DA making his bones on the backs of the mobsters in New York City, had been hard on Donleavy's trail, and if Donleavy had fallen, Caughlan would have been next. After Donleavy's disappearance, the hounds had snapped at Caughlan's heels for the next six months or so, but the trail was cold, and eventually they wandered off to seek other amusements. Stiles had no direct evidence of what may have happened to Donleavy, but he knew what his gut told him. What he did know for a fact was that in the years since, Caughlan, using the ruthless tactics taught to him by Donleavy and his compatriots, had built Pennsylvania Transfer into a major interstate shipping firm.

Caughlan stared back at him, his face blank. "Look," he said, "I got a situation and I gotta do something about it, Marty, but I can't have you stomping around in my life with those big feet of yours. No offense, but you got the finesse of a hippopotamus with a bad case of hemorrhoids. I've heard about your girl Alessandra, and she's the one I want. Don't worry, you'll be working this, too. There are some elements to this that are gonna require your special talents. You got the contacts and you got the moves. And there might be some serious money in it."

Stiles could hardly hear him over the noise of the music and the shouted conversations going on around them. That's why he picked this place, Marty thought, his stomach turning over. The FBI could have a bug stuck right up Caughlan's ass, but they still couldn't hear a word, not over the roar in this place. Whatever Caughlan wants done, it can't be anything good. He thought for a second or two, wondering how bad he wanted Mickey Caughlan's money.

Caughlan put a hand on Stiles's shoulder, sending a chill all the way through him. Stiles tore his eyes away from the dancer, shifted in his seat, and took a long look at Mickey Caughlan. "How serious?"

Caughlan shrugged. "I'm thinking we're probably talking low six figures here."

Marty's eyes went wide. "No shit."

"Watch the girl, there." Caughlan gestured with his chin. "I think she likes you."

Stiles turned back to the stage. The dancer was still a long way off, but there was another one standing right next to him. Late twenties, he figured, blue eyes, dirty-blond hair, heavy breasts bursting out of a sequined bra. As he turned in her direction, he felt Caughlan press a folded piece of paper into his right hand. Glancing at it, he was astonished to see a hundred-dollar bill materialize in his fist. "Ben Franklin," he said to the girl. "My favorite president."

"Mine, too," she told him. She leaned up close, stuck her hand in his crotch. She whispered in his ear. "You like to dance, baby? Dead Benny always makes me feel like dancing." She massaged his growing erection through his pants.

Marty could hear a trace of the woman's Slavic origins. "Me, too," he told her. "But I prolly need some lessons."

She reached across with her other hand, plucked the bill out of his grasp, gave him one final squeeze. "Past the men's room door," she told him. "Go through the blue doorway. First room on the right. When you finish your business here, I'll be waiting for you." She leaned up close again, touched the tip of her tongue to his eyebrow, then released him. She stepped back slowly, turned her back, and walked away.

Marty swallowed, then looked back at Caughlan. "She come courtesy of you?" he said.

"Not me," Caughlan said. "Seen her coming, though. Man, I love this place."

"You kidding? You didn't pay her off?"

"All right," Caughlan said. "Maybe I tipped her on the way in. Maybe I told her about this lonesome and generous businessman I was meeting here tonight."

Stiles's head swam. "Just what is it you want me to do, Mickey?"

Caughlan glanced past Stiles at the departing blonde. "All right," he said again. "Listen up. Six, seven months ago, one of my trucks picked up a container off a ship down in Port Newark. No big deal, we do that all the time. According to the bill of lading, the thing was supposed to be a load of blue jeans headed for some discounter in Chicago. Okay? So the truck gets hijacked. We find it down by the river in Jersey City a couple days later. Container is empty, except for the driver; poor bastard was inside, deader than last year's Christmas goose."

"I didn't hear nothing about it," Marty said. "It musta not made the papers."

Caughlan shook his head. "We kept it quiet," he said. "There was some brown goo on the floor of the container."

"Goo?"

"Corn syrup, like. Thick and oily."

"Yeah." Marty Stiles felt the hair on the back of his neck rising. "What was it?"

"Chemist I sent it to said it was opium base," Caughlan said. "Stuff is like crude oil. Couple steps away from gasoline, but still damned expensive. You get me?"

"Yeah, I get you. What'd you do about it?"

Caughlan shook his head. "Nothing. Stuck our heads back in the sand. Hoped it would all go away."

Stiles stared at him. "For real, man. What did you do?"

"We waited. Figured whoever belonged to that shit would come looking for it, but they never showed."

"So you're off the hook."

"I don't think so. I got a tip, there's a secret grand jury looking into Penn Transfer. And into me."

"Over this? Over dope?"

"Don't know for sure," Caughlan said. "But I wouldn't want to bet against it."

I don't want to ask this question, Marty thought, but I have to, because Caughlan knows I should ask it. "You into dope? You get a piece of what moves through Port Newark?"

For a second, Caughlan looked like what Marty knew him to be: hard, cold, merciless. Then he looked away, caught a waitress's eye, waved his empty glass. He looked back at Stiles. "You and I go way back, Marty," he said. "You know I never been a altar boy. Joint like this one, maybe the cops think it's a brothel, and maybe it is, but I ask you: man can't get drunk and get his ashes hauled, what's the use in living? I ask you, where's the harm done? But the drug trade burns everyone it touches. I always kept my distance."

"So? You think someone's setting you up?"

"No. I think someone's using Penn Transfer to move their shit. I think they figure when the cops finally tumble to it, I'll be the one that swings, not them."

Marty nodded. What cop would bother looking past a man like Caughlan? "Smart," he said.

Caughlan leaned over and whispered in Stiles's ear. "Hundred large," he said, "you find out who's doing it. Buck and a half, you give me the score on the grand jury, too. A deuce if you get it all done before the end of the month."

It was too much money to even consider passing up, even if he was gonna have to walk through a few dark places to get it. "All right," he said. "But how do you want to work this? What is it that you want Al for?"

"I don't wanna tell you how to do your job," Caughlan said. "If I knew how to handle this, it'd be done already. But I figure you probably know every crooked cop and scumbag lawyer in Jersey. You chase the grand jury angle. Let Martillo loose, let her chase it from the other end."

Clever, Marty thought. Once I start turning over rocks, things will start to happen. Caughlan thinks it's someone close to him, and figures he'll have Al watching his back. "There's one problem with all of this," he said.

"Yeah? What's that?"

"Al. Al's the problem. She ain't great at following instructions. Matter of fact, she's prolly the single most annoying female I ever met. The bitch could find a white cat in a snowstorm, but she could never explain how she knew where to look. You get her going on this, she's gonna go where her nose tells her to go. You hear what I'm saying? You got some closets you don't want her looking in, that's your tough luck, she's gonna do what she wants to do. You better think about that before you pull the trigger here."

"I can handle her," Caughlan said. "Besides, I got too much at risk to worry about a few indiscretions coming to light."

Stiles watched the dancer. Caughlan thinks he knows Al, he thought, but the guy has no idea, not if he thinks he can handle her. Unless he figures he can just bury her once she gets to be too much of a pain in his ass. And good luck with that . . . But I might be putting Al in a tough spot with this, Stiles thought. His stomach rolled once, but the thought of two hundred grand in his bank account had a wonderfully restorative effect. "We need to talk money. I can't afford to go on spec. I'm gonna need fifty large up front and a guaranteed hundred, minimum, when we're done."

Caughlan stared at him for a moment. "Agreed," he said. "Set up a meeting—you, me, and Martillo. We can go over the details there."

"Okay," Stiles said.

Caughlan got off his stool. "The lady's waiting for you," he said. "Enjoy yourself, but watch that girl, she bites."

"She what? What did you say?"

Caughlan nodded. "Something wrong with her head. She bites. She'll want to blow you, but don't you let her. You knock her down and give it to her proper."

Three

"Your biggest problem is that you're a girl." That was the first thing he'd said to her back when they started, that first time she could remember him coming back home. Alessandra had been six years old at the time, a bit tall for her age and naturally athletic, but impossibly thin. He was back in Brooklyn after a tour of duty with the MPs on the Hong Kong waterfront. Tall, dark, and forbidding, that's how she remembered him; quick to anger, sensitive to any disrespect, intolerant of any lack of rectitude in matters of dress or speech or behavior.

She remembered standing in front of him, trembling, glancing over at her mother for support. Like a lot of project kids, Alessandra's mother had been her rock, her bodyguard, her ever-present protective shield, but right then her mother would not come past the kitchen doorway. "Beektor," her mother said, pleading, and her father reddened at the mispronunciation. "Beektor, she's so small. Are you sure . . ."

"How long do you want me to wait?" he snapped. "She's old enough. Go make dinner." He did not look in his wife's direction to see whether or not he would be obeyed. "Okay, Alessandra," he said. "Now you listen to me. You're a girl, and everyone is bigger than you. They think they can make you do what they want, you hear me? You have to learn to defend yourself. Do you understand me? You need to be able to stand up for yourself. Now pretend I'm a strange man, I walk up to you on the street, and I grab you. What do you do?" He approached her then, got down on one knee, wrapped a thick arm around her in slow motion. "I've got you now. What do you do?"

She had heard his voice on the phone many times, but this was the first time she had been confronted with the physical reality of the man. He was clearly in charge, and she was terrified of disappointing him. "I would scream," she said, after a minute. "I would scream for a policeman."

"That's good," he said, but he did not release her. "You should scream. But what if there's no policemen around? What if they're too far away to protect you? You need to be able to take care of yourself." She was afraid to look at him. "You have something to fight with. Tell me what it is."

She could smell the aftershave he used, feel the smooth warm skin of his arm. She considered his question. "I could hit you?"

"No, you can't hit me, you're too small and you don't know how yet. But you can poke my eye out."

She looked at her hand, resting on his arm. "Would that hurt?"

"Never mind that. I'm a strange man, remember? I just grabbed you, and bad things are going to happen unless you can make me let you go. Do you understand?"

She did not, but she sensed that he wanted her to say yes. "Yes, Papi."

"Good. Now we're going to try it. No, not like *The Three Stooges*." He released her then. He held his hand out in front of her, fingers straight and stiff. "Make your hand like this. No, hard, hard, feel mine. Just like that, hard. Now watch this." Still down on one knee, he pushed her back a half step. "Now you pretend you're the bad man, and you try to grab me."

She smiled at that, just slightly.

"No," he said, "just pretend. I'm the little girl, you're the bad man. You're way bigger than me, I can't hurt you. Try to grab me." She inhaled, took a half step, her hands raised, and quicker than anything she had ever seen, he jabbed at her face with his stiffened fingers. "Boom!" he said. "Now tell me what just happened."

"You poked me."

"I scratched your cornea. What that really means is if you were a bad man and I was a little girl, the bad man is hurting so much he can't see the little girl anymore, and she's running away. Do you understand?"

She did not. "Yes, Papi."

"Good. Now we're going to practice. First in slow motion. I grab you with this hand, slow, like that, and I'm going to hold up my other hand and you pretend it's my face, and you jab at it, slow, slow, hold your fingers stiff. Good. Now a little quicker." He reached for her again, holding up his other hand, and she poked at it. "No," he told her, "keep those fingers hard and stiff, and jab harder. As quick as you can. Ready? Okay, go. That's better. Let's do it again. Okay, good. Again."

That's how it started.

The bus let her out at the corner of White Plains Road and East Tremont in the Bronx, steps away from the building where her father lived now. White Plains Road had two traffic lanes in each direction, but only in theory because there were cars perpetually double-parked on both sides. She watched the bus pull away, shaking her head. Three years ago, when he'd finally gotten out of prison, he'd chosen not to go back to Brooklyn, moved up here to live in anonymous isolation. She stepped into the vestibule of his building, rang the bell next to his name, Victor Martillo. "It's me, Dad."

He buzzed her in without comment.

She climbed the steps to the third floor. The place always looked like a dark and dusty hole to her, although she knew he would never countenance dirt or disorder. He had a bedroom that also served as a sitting room, a bathroom, and a Pullman kitchen in what amounted to a closet. His front door was open. She knocked, pushed it open the rest of the way and stood in the doorway. "Hello, Dad."

"Hello." He sat on the other side of the room in a stiff-backed chair in the dim light of the single shaded window. "What brings you all the way up here?"

"I'm on my way to work," she said. "I wanna go to the hospital up on Eastchester Avenue to check on Tio Bobby. Tonight, after work." She stopped, knowing the answer to her question before she asked it. "I thought you might wanna come with me, just to say good-bye. The nurses don't think he's going to last much longer." Say it, she told herself, call him out, tell him about himself . . . But she didn't, because that would upset the delicate balance between the two of them. She had never been quite sure how she felt about him. He had betrayed her once, turned on her exactly at the point when she'd needed him the most. It still hurt her, if she let it, but she tried not to dwell on the past. Tried not to wonder how he felt about it, or if he felt anything at all.

"Maybe next time." He'd never talk about it, either. He never talked about anything real.

"All right. I gave you the chance."

"Yes, you did."

"Is there anything you need?" She knew the answer to that one, too. He had his job with the MTA, he had this cocoon of an apartment, and he had his buddies, the guys he played cards with at the social club a few blocks away. Those were the things he needed, and all he could cope with. He's pruned back his life this far, she thought. He's down to this.

"No, I'm fine, honey."

"All right. I'm gonna go. Let me say good-bye, first." She crossed the room, embraced him as he sat there. Time and ciga-rettes might have taken his wind, might have even slowed his reflexes some, but he was still the same hard man she remem-bered; she could feel it. He was still the wrong guy to mess with.

He accepted her embrace awkwardly, the way a man does when one of his friends has gotten suddenly and unexpectedly emotional. She held on for a few seconds, until he patted her on the back, letting her know.

Enough already.

"All right. Bye-bye, Dad." She could barely see his face in the gloom.

"Bye, now. You take care."

"I will." She looked around once, then headed for the door.

"Alessandra," he said, and she turned to look at him. "Thanks for coming," he said. He meant it, too, she knew that. He was always happy to see her come, and just as happy to see her go.

Outside, a group of young men were gathered around an old green Camaro parked by the curb with its hood up. They got a little raucous when they spotted her, voicing their appre-ciation of her form in English and in Spanish, glancing at one another for reinforcement. One of them, larger than the rest, blocked her way. "Hey, mami," he said. "Que pasa? You want a beer?"

She just stared at him. "You gonna move?" she said, adding silently, or should I move you? She didn't have much to fear from this guy, or from all of them together. Her father had seen to that.

The guy stood aside, hands raised in mock surrender. "Hey," he said. "Easy, baby. Just trying to be friendly . . ."

"Don't waste your time."

She walked past him, through the gate, and out onto the sidewalk. The guy's friends hooted, berating him loudly for his lack of success, all but one. He'd been leaning over the car, his hands in its internals, but he stood up and looked at her. "Forget her," he said to his friend. "That one looks good, but she's cold, man. She got nothing for you."

Yeah, well. That's just the way it was.

She stopped on the corner of East Tremont, looking for the bus, wondering if she ought to spend her lunch money on a cab.

Four

"Jesus, Mickey, I don't know where the hell she could be. I apologize."

"The name is Daniel. That nickname is old news. I wish you'd forget it."

"Yeah, sorry about that. Daniel." Marty Stiles, obviously nervous, wiped his red face with his napkin. Caughlan watched him gulp at his beer.

"The goddam bitch is supposed to be in at noon," Stiles said. "She works noon to eight. I'm telling ya, she didn't type so goddam fast, I'da fired her ass a long time ago." He swabbed his face again, then spotted someone just inside the bar entrance. "There she is! Goddam little—"

"Marty, shut up."

Stiles clamped his mouth closed, glanced at Caughlan. "Call her over," Caughlan told him. "I want you to introduce us, and then I want you to be quiet."

Stiles nodded, then waved at the woman standing by the door. Caughlan watched her walk across the room, noticed the way her eyes took in the entire place as she threaded her way through the throng of half-loaded bar patrons. Stiles rose unsteadily as she approached. "Goddammit, Al, where the hell you been? Ain't we talked about this? Of all the days you gotta show up late . . ."

Caughlan cleared his throat, and Stiles ate the rest of his tirade. "Daniel Caughlan," he said, "this is Alessandra Martillo. Al, Mr. Caughlan."

Caughlan stood, reached out, took her hand. "Very pleased to meet you," he told her. "I've heard about you."

She looked at him warily. Stiles sat back down, reached for his beer. "Al is the one—"

"Marty, I'm gonna ask you a favor."

"Anything, Mickey, you name it."

Caughlan grimaced at the sound of his old nickname. "I want to talk to Miss Martillo in private for a little while. I'm sure you have other things to do anyway, so why don't you go back to your office? I'll hook up with you later."

"Whatever you say, Mick," Stiles said, his face reddening. He glared once at Alessandra before draining his beer. He stood up. "Catch ya later."

"Yeah, okay." Caughlan watched Stiles walk away.

"He's gonna make me pay for this," Martillo told him. Caughlan turned and looked at her. She was staring at Stiles's departing back. Caughlan, a man who believed in doing his homework, had made inquiries about her. Rican, pale brown skin, black hair, good muscle tone, nails like talons. *Got a temper,* he'd been told. *Mouthy. Smart, but if you piss her off, she'll swing first and think later. Stubborn. Doesn't scare. And she can take a punch.* Jesus, what a piece! Another time, he'd have been interested. Very interested.

"You got nothing to worry about from Marty," he told her. "Please, Miss Martillo, have a seat."

"I need this job," she told him. She sat down.

"I know."

She sat with that for a minute. "So what else do you know?"

"I know you have trouble making your rent. I know you're better than this nickel-and-dime gig you got with Marty Stiles. I know that Marty goes out of his way to make sure nobody knows about you. And I know you're the one who dropped a dime on Gerald Baker."

A ghost of a smile played at her lips. "How'd you hear about that?"

"Stiles was bragging it up."

"I didn't do it for Stiles."

"Tell me about it," he said.

She watched him for a minute. "Gerald Baker pulled a home invasion on a couple who lived in my building," she said. "Seems he didn't terrorize them enough, and the husband went to the cops. Baker got bail—figure that one out—and as soon as he hit the street, he paid my neighbors another visit. Slit the man's throat. The wife asked if I would look into it. Can I ask you something?"

"Sure."

"No offense, Mr. Caughlan, but you look to me like a guy who knows how to get what he wants. Marty filled me in on the nature of your problem. I don't know what it is you want me to do that Marty can't handle. You need someone's neck broken, you don't need me to do it for you."

"No, Miss Martillo. I could probably manage that on my own."

"Al," she said.

"All right, Al. Look, I was told that the cops and the skip

tracers were looking for Baker for six months and they couldn't find shit. Then he shows up at the emergency room at King's County with a broken collarbone and a separated shoulder. The cops get an anonymous tip and they go pick his ass up. Baker is six four, about two and a half, he's got nothing to say about how he got injured, but the word I got was that some Puerto Rican female looks a lot like you tracked him down, dragged him out of his hole in Brooklyn, kicked his ass, and then dropped him off in the ER. I get all that straight?"

"Close enough," she said.

"So you're right, there's plenty of tough guys around. Not too many smart ones."

"I'm still not sure . . ."

He looked around, eyeing the crowd with distaste. "Let's take a walk."

She walked next to him down West Houston, headed for the river. Caughlan was not a tall man, but thick, heavy for his size, had the Irish boxer look: deformed nose, scar tissue around his eyes, big hands, solid chin. She knew that most men, if you hit them hard enough in the soft parts, laid down on the ground and cried, but there were some that got up grinning and came after you. She made Caughlan for one of those. You couldn't really hurt this guy, she thought. You'd have to kill him.

This one's like your father, she thought. Watch yourself.

He wasn't ready to talk about his problem yet. "What is it you do for Stiles?"

"The usual," she said. "Type up reports and invoices. Same line of crap, over and over again. 'The bartender wrote my order on a tab and ran it through the cash register. The waiter was

prompt and courteous. The food was tasty and well-prepared.'
On occasion I get to follow people around. Take pictures."

Usually people laughed when she told them that, but he
did not. "How come you ain't with the cops?"

"I tried that. Didn't make it through the academy."

"What happened?"

"I have problems with authority, Mr. Caughlan. When
people push me, I push back."

He nodded. They stopped at the corner of West Houston
and Greenwich. "Stiles gets a buck seventy-five an hour for
your time," he said. "What's he pay you?"

"Nothing close to that."

"Tell me what you think of Marty Stiles."

She made an effort to hide her distaste for the man. Stiles
might be using her like a paper towel but he knew his shit. If you
wanted to know how badly your bartenders were ripping you
off, Marty could give you names and numbers. If you suspected your wife of infidelity, Marty could get you pictures to
prove it. If you were tired of paying off a disability claim,
Marty would get you a video of the claimant in the act of having too much fun. If someone was trying to shake your business down for protection money, Marty could find out whether
your new friend should be paid off or frightened off, and provide you with a consultant to handle either contingency. If you
were a bondsman and one of your customers jumped bail, if
you needed to know where your ex-hubby hid his assets, if you
wanted your warehouse torched so you could collect, if someone had something of yours and you wanted it back, Marty
Stiles was your guy. "Marty's good at what he does," she said.

Caughlan nodded. "I'll give you that," he said. "But the
man has his limitations. I'm not after finding somebody lifting

ten-dollar bills out of my till. Someone is using me, and I think they've turned somebody close to me. Do you know what I'm saying? Someone that works for me, maybe even someone in my house. Ever since I got wind of this, I've wanted to kill them all."

"I see. How would you like to work this?"

"I'm having a party tomorrow," he told her. "Two hundred of my closest friends, at my house in Jersey. I want you there." He took a fat envelope out of his pocket. "Only a fool hires a surgeon and then stands over his shoulder telling him how to do his job," he said. "I'm giving you access to my business, my house, my life." He handed her the envelope. "I'm not expecting you to do this for the lousy crumbs that Stiles throws you," he said. "There's ten grand in there. You can use that for expenses, or you can put it in your pocket. I don't give a damn, I just want you to have whatever you need. When you need more, you let me know. All I care about is you find the son of a bitch that's got his dick up my arse, and you give me his name. You come out tomorrow, have a look around, how you take it from there is your business."

"Is this blood money you're giving me?"

"Look at it this way: you don't find out who it is, I'll start burying the candidates until I think I've got the son of a bitch, I swear to fucking Christ."

She was slightly ashamed of herself for being glad she'd missed Anthony. He and Tio Bobby had been together as long as she could remember, but she and Anthony had never really connected. There had always been a distance between them, a certain coldness, a mutual disapproval, something . . . She could never quite put her finger on it. But in the mad and riotous soap opera that was her family's life, Anthony and Tio Bobby together formed the one solid and reliable constant. And when Tio Bobby is gone, she thought, that will be gone, too. All the survivors, you included, will have no more connection to one another than a bunch of stray cats who happened, once upon a time, to inhabit the same alley.

You should go home now, Alessandra told herself. It had already been a long day. She didn't even want to think about the long train ride in front of her, from the hospital on Eastchester Avenue in the Bronx all the way back to her sanctuary on the top floor of a crumbling brownstone on Pineapple Street in Brooklyn. God, she thought, you'll probably sit on that platform for an hour, just waiting for the train back to Manhattan, then you gotta change to the A to get back to Brooklyn. Outside Tio Bobby's window, automotive headlights and brightly lit apartment windows speckled the Bronx night. You see? she thought. It's not empty. Everywhere you see light, there's life. Someone cooking dinner, someone watching television, someone waiting for someone else to come home.

She turned away from the window, looked across the room at the bed where Tio Bobby lay motionless under the sheet. His blood count is up, the nurses had been eager to tell her, his renal functions are almost back to normal . . . They had gone on and on, but she had been too tired to follow what they were saying. Is he getting better, she had asked them. Is he going to wake up? Ah, well, we don't know that, they'd told her, caution heavy in their voices. No one knows that. But these are encouraging signs! They give us reason to hope . . .

You've buried him, too, she told herself. You don't believe he can really get better.

She wondered if he knew she was there. One of the nurses

claimed that he did, that, on some level, he was conscious of everything that happened, that it was only a question of how much of that memory he could access once he made his way back to the living. Maybe so, she thought. But all you've done for the past two hours is sit here and stare out the window. Go, go give him something. Give him a memory. She got up, carried her chair over next to the bed. She groped for his hand under the bed linens, held it in both of hers, marveled that his skin was still so rough after all the time in the hospital.

"Hey, Bobby."

She could think of nothing else to say. Are you this vacant, she asked herself. What would you say to him if he were awake? "Victor says hello," she said, and then laughed ruefully. "But you know that's a lie, don't you. I stopped in to see him today. He lives in a room, Bobby. One room on White Plains Road. Not counting the bathroom. When he has nothing to do, I think he sits there in a chair in the dark without moving. They say reptiles are like that. You could have one for a pet for half your life, but it will never feel a thing for you." She felt guilty for putting that thought into words, but there was nobody around to reproach her for it.

"You knew him, Bobby, didn't you? Before he married my mother, you knew him. Was he always like this?"

Bobby didn't answer. She watched the slow rise and fall of his chest. Two men in the world you care about, she thought, and they couldn't be more different. Her father had joined the service, Bobby had joined a motorcycle gang. Bobby found out that he really didn't enjoy fighting all that much, and her father had become extremely adept at the art and science of controlling human beings through the judicious application of pain. Her father found that he didn't have the emotional vocabulary to deal with those who loved him. Bobby fell in love with Anthony. Her father, ten years retired from the military and three years out of the state pen, still wore his hair high and tight, kept his back straight and his shoes shined. Bobby still had the gang tattoo on the side of his neck, a green dagger right behind and below one ear. Why don't you have it taken off, she'd asked him once. It's good for me to see it, he'd told her. Reminds me how stupid I can be.

The room door, slightly ajar, swung halfway open. Someone stuck their head inside, saw her there, nodded once, and withdrew. They weren't too bad in this place. It was staffed by working-class people who knew firsthand how hard it could be to keep up with everything life threw at you. They wouldn't care how late she stayed.

She remembered like it was yesterday, Bobby kicking open the front door of the empty tenement building where she'd been sleeping. Nobody in the place even thought about standing up to him. You won't have to go back to school, that's what he'd told her. You can come stay with me and Anthony. I'll teach you how to fix motorcycles, and Anthony will teach you how to cook. She found herself wishing that she had learned either one of those two skills.

The day he'd come for her was about two and a half years after the day she'd found her mother on the kitchen floor. She'd spent the worst year and a half of her life living in her Aunt Magdalena's place, and then for another year she'd haunted the streets of Brownsville, working the Dumpsters, breaking into apartments when nobody was home, into shuttered businesses at night, looking for something she could turn into a few bucks, or for something to eat, or a warm place to spend a few hours. She'd been nothing memorable, not in that neighborhood, just another lost kid. Bobby had been long gone from gang life by then, but he'd had connections. Still, it had taken him months to find her. She remembered what he had looked like: shaved head, whiskered face, long thin braid hanging off his chin, tattoos, leather, black gloves with the fingers cut off, boots, thick silver jewelry, a bike that was loud enough to wake the dead. Not quite as heavy as he'd gotten, these last few years, but otherwise unchanged.

It'll be way better than this, he'd told her. And if you don't like it, you can leave. I promise. It was precisely because he looked so wild that she had believed him. Not long after that, he'd taken her to see the shrink. She hadn't wanted to go, but he had persuaded her. He's a nice man, he'd told her. I don't care, she'd said. He can't help me.

He'll help me, Bobby told her. So do it for me. Okay?

She was already falling under Bobby's spell.

Okay, she said.

Always an incurable snoop, she'd found the doctor's report a month or so later. Personality disorder, the report said. Attachment disorder. Borderline sociopathic tendencies. Short-tempered, hostile, reflexively violent.

Sugar and spice.

What the hell did they expect from her? But she hadn't tried to find out what an attachment disorder was, or any of the rest of it. She'd been too afraid, then. She still was.

It was just past one in the morning when she stopped in at Marty's office on West Houston in Manhattan. She fired up his computer, pushed his chair aside, dragged hers in from the other room, and shoved it in behind his desk. I am not sitting in his chair, she thought. Damn thing smells like crack . . . She did some quick searches on Daniel "Mickey" Caughlan and Pennsylvania Transfer. She didn't get much on him. He'd been arrested a few times back in his twenties, but then his name had faded from the newspapers. She did, however, find out that his son, Sean Caughlan, aged nineteen, had died six months ago. There wasn't a lot about it in the *Times,* but the *News* had covered it in a bit more detail. Sean, aka "Willy C," had been linked to Shine, the pop diva of the moment, and there were unconfirmed rumors of the existence of a sex tape featuring the two of them. Shine herself professed to be heartbroken at the loss, but refused comment otherwise. He'd been found inside his apartment in Tudor City, a small neighborhood in Manhattan. He'd been a student at Columbia and a guitar player in an up-and-coming rock band, BandX. A guitar that had once been owned by Stevie Ray Vaughn was missing from the apartment. The cause of death was an apparent overdose.

Guy like Daniel Caughlan, Al thought, he doesn't get over this in six months. This has got to be eating him up.

Five

The whole neighborhood of Brooklyn Heights had gone up-scale, all except the building Alessandra lived in, a five-story walk-up on Pineapple, which was still a dump. She was on her way back from morning practice when she saw the guy standing on her stoop. She slowed to a walk, stopped at the bottom of the steps, and looked up at him. He was tall and slender, mournful eyes that matched his curly black hair, skin a shade darker than the average white guy. He was probably in his mid to late twenties, but he wore the clothing of an older man, suit and tie, carried an old-fashioned trench coat folded over one arm. "Good morning," he said. His lips curled into a smile, but the rest of his face kept its somber air. "You must be Miss Martillo." He stepped down to the sidewalk with a dancer's grace, held out his hand. "My name is Gearoid O'Hagan." He pronounced his first name "G'road." "I work for Dan Caughlan. I'm his personal assistant. I sort of act as his liaison in what you might call, ah, delicate issues."

She hesitated for just a second, then she shook his hand. "Hello, Mr. O'Hagan," she said. His grip was surprisingly gentle. "Pardon the sweat."

"Oh, forget it," he said. "I should be doing a little more of that myself. And don't call me 'Mr. O'Hagan,' that's me fadder's name. Gearoid is tough for Americans, so you can call me Gerald, if that makes it easier."

Old-country Irish, she thought. Can't pronounce the "th" in anyt'ing. "Gearoid," she said, pronouncing it the way he had, feeling the strangeness of the foreign word on her tongue. "I can probably handle that." She wondered if he expected her to ask him up. She lived in a room on the top floor, and it was just as unimpressive as the building's exterior, one small room at the end of a long corridor, a tiny bathroom, a miniscule kitchen, no closets, one cranky steam radiator. She loved it, though—it was her independence, her refuge. Yeah, it was small and it was mean, cold in the winter and hot in the summer, but it was all she had and she fought hard to keep it. She had never once compromised it by having a stranger inside.

"I know this is a surprise, me dropping by like this," he said. "But there are a few things we should talk about. Know what I mean? How about we meet for breakfast? My treat. Would that be okay? There's a little joint right around the corner, on Henry Street. What do you say?"

This guy is surprising, she thought, sensitive to what I need in a situation where most guys wouldn't have a clue. Like a tap-dancing elephant, grace was something she never expected from the men in her life. "That would be fine, Gearoid. Give me twenty minutes."

He smiled at her. "Grand," he said.

He got up out of his chair when he saw her standing in the doorway, stood there until she made her way over. She watched him as he sat back down. "I ordered you coffee, Al," he said. "You do drink coffee, don't you?"

"Yeah," she said. "Thanks."

"Good." He looked around for the waitress. "Tell me, Al, do you like talking business while you eat? Because I hate it. If the food's any good, I like to give it the time and attention it deserves. You know what I mean? I hate to just swill it down while me mind's on something else."

"New York," she said. "You're always doing a couple things at once."

"No way to live," he said. "You miss out on the little pleasures in life that way. You pass them by, and then wonder what the hell happened."

"You might be right," she said, and she wondered why it was, when his mouth smiled, the rest of his face didn't.

She ordered an omelet, but he ordered the biggest breakfast on the menu, with a couple extra sides. "So tell me, Al," he said. "You grow up in the city?"

Normally she was guarded and paranoid, but O'Hagan was good, he got her talking about herself, and it wasn't until much later that she realized she had told him more than she might have, had he been less engaging. They talked about the Brownsville streets she had grown up on until the meal was done. She watched him mop his plate with his last piece of toast and stick it in his mouth.

"All right, Al," he said. "Down to business. The boss wasn't too forthcoming about the exact nature of his agreement with you. I don't think he really wants to talk about it. All I know, he wants me to make sure you've got everything you need."

"Very kind of him, but it's a little early for that. How can I get in touch with you if I do need something?"

"I'll give you my cell number," he said. "You can get me there anytime, day or night. Did Himself give you a retainer?"

"We have an informal arrangement," she said.

"All right," O'Hagan said. "Alessandra, your finances are none of my business, but I want to give you a short course on doing business with Daniel Caughlan. You go to Staples and you pick up one of those invoice books. Wednesday nights, you write up a bill for Pennsylvania Transfer, put down whatever he owes you for professional services rendered, and you put the dates for that week. Handwritten is fine. You give me the bill on Thursday morning, I'll get it to Himself on Friday, and I'll get you your check for Monday. It's important you do it this way. If you don't keep up with it, if you let him get into you for a couple of weeks, you could bring his son back from the dead, he'd love you until the day you died, but he'd never pay up. Know what I mean? He'll never give you the money. I been with Caughlan a while, I know how his mind works. You give him the bill every week, he won't care. Well, that's not true. He'll care. He's gonna call you Friday night or during the day on Saturday, he'll bust your chops like you won't believe, but at least you'll get paid."

"What do you mean, bring his son back from the dead?"

"Oh, shit," O'Hagan said. "He didn't tell you about Willy? I mean, I just assumed . . ."

"Never assume," Al said, leaning her elbows on the table. "Tell me about Willy."

"Ah, Jaysus. Well, it happened about six months ago. Sean William Caughlan, everyone called him Willy. He was a good kid, but, you know, I guess he had the problems rich kids have. His mudder give him everything he ever wanted, he never had to work for a thing, but I guess he warn't a bad kid for all that.

A couple of years ago he got into music. Not the shit kids listen to these days, though. Stuff the blacks did, back in the nineteen fifties, stuff I never heard of. Bought himself a guitar, spent days on end up in his room, copying this guy or that one. He got so he was pretty good, so his mudder said. Anyhow, he got hooked on this one guy a year or so back. Guitar player named TJ Conrad. Willy said Conrad was the second coming of Keith Richards. Of course, I know who Richards is, but I never thought he was any damn good, myself. A goddam dope fiend, just like every musician I ever met. Anyhow, Willy bought everything this guy Conrad ever recorded, went to every concert he played, even grew his hair out so he'd look like the son of a bitch—although there's no way, the kid would have had to hire someone to beat him with an ugly stick. But you get the idea. He even met Conrad a few times, I guess the guy was nice enough to the boy. Anyhow, what happened, Conrad was playing for this group called BandX, he got himself in a jam, wound up in rehab. The rest of the band knew Willy, knew he could play every song Conrad ever done, so they hired him. Nothing would do but he had to drop out of college and go move in with these dirtbags. They were all living in some hole they rented up in the Bronx."

"What did Caughlan think of that?"

"Oh, he had a bloody cow, ranted and raved, sixty grand a year he pays to send Willy off to Columbia and the ungrateful little sod drops out to get high and get laid, all of that. Made threats, I'll throw you out, cut you off without a nickel, but Willy had his mind made up, and he went."

"BandX," Al said. "Never heard of them. How'd it work out?"

"Well. You ever hear of this girl singer, calls herself Shine?"

Alessandra shook her head. "No."

"Are you kidding? Where you been, in a cave? She's all over the TV."

"I don't watch a lot of TV, Gro."

"She's the latest sensation. The next big thing. Her first album went platinum last year. She's got a movie in the works, and a cartoon show. Got reporters following her around every time she goes out. Famous picture of her on the Web, one of her tits fell out of this dress she wore to the MTV awards. Anyhow, she heard Willy playing somewhere, the next thing you know she signs BandX to open for her. She's doing six shows out at Jones Beach next month. That's all it took, now BandX has record companies offering them the world."

"So what happened to Willy?"

"The old man bought him a studio," he said. "Over on the east side. Four hundred grand the old man spends on this fookin' Manhattan shoebox, can you believe that? But he didn't want Willy living with a bunch of crack smokers. Anyhow, when Willy didn't show up for a gig, they went looking for him. Found him dead in the apartment. Nobody could believe it when the reports came back he overdosed."

"What did you think, Gearoid? He seem like he was using?"

"Ah, how the hell you gonna know? I thought he was a good kid, you know, maybe a bit spoiled, is all. But nowadays that shit is everywhere."

"I see. How did Caughlan take it?"

"Never said a thing about it. Him and Willy was never, you know . . ."

Fathers, Al thought. "I know."

"So that's the whole sad story. Will you be needin' a ride out to the party this afternoon?"

"No," she said. "Will I see you there?"

"Oh, absolutely," he said. "Jack of all trades, master of none. Nothing happens without me."

"Can I have a word with you?"

Alessandra tried not to look startled. It was Marty Stiles. He had stepped out of the shadows of the entrance to the St. George, the ancient hotel across the street from her building in Brooklyn Heights.

"Hello, Marty." The guy knew his business, she had to give him that. If someone held a championship for skulking, Marty would definitely be a contender. She wondered how long he'd been waiting for her.

"I know you're a busy woman." He smirked, not a great look for a red-faced fat guy. "Now that you're out on your own, with a big-shot client and all."

Al opened her eyes wide. "What are you talking about, Marty? I was under the impression I was on loan, here."

"Quit playing around. You're sharper than that. I'm just not so sure you're quite as smart as you think you are."

"I still work for you, Marty, until you tell me otherwise."

"Caughlan didn't hire you?"

"Quit fucking around, Marty. I know it goes against your nature, but square up with me here, okay?"

Stiles nodded. "Okay. I just needed to hear it from you."

"You're working the grand jury angle, am I right?"

"Among other things," he said. "But I just need to know where you stand."

"Like I said. Until I hear otherwise . . ."

"All right."

"That means you'll send my check to the house. Am I right?"

He looked like he smelled a fart. "Yeah, all right. But look, you got to be goddamn careful, here. Lemme buy you a cup of coffee."

He didn't actually pay for her coffee, he stood in front of her at the line at Starbucks, bought his, left her standing there. It irked her to pay four bucks for something she could make for herself, if she wanted it, and it irked her that Stiles would offer to pay and then conveniently forget. But that was Marty, that was the way he moved. You could never be sure Marty would pay off until you had the money in your hand.

The place was crowded, but Marty snagged a table inside the place, not out on the sidewalk. It was over in the corner, next to the side door. You could see up and down the block from there without being too noticeable yourself. And if you had to get out fast, you were right on the doorstep. No matter what you think of him, she thought, the man doesn't miss much.

"It's a dull life, over at West Houston Security," he said, his porcine eyes boring into her.

"So?"

"Lookit," he said. "I know corporate clients are not exciting. And I know you're not interested in catching barkeeps and waitresses, got their hands in the till. Well, it don't exactly thrill me, neither, but you know what? That kinda business keeps your door open. It's dependable, and it pays the overhead."

"You trying to keep me humble, Marty? You trying to make sure I don't get a fat head? 'Cause I appreciate that, really."

His eyes narrowed, and he leaned across the table at her.

She willed herself not to recoil. "I'm tryina help you, you silly little bitch," he hissed.

"That's better," she said. "That's the Marty I've grown to know and love."

"Listen to me! Daniel Caughlan would steal the pennies off his dead mother's eyes. I know that bastard for a long time. Longer than you been alive. Now, I seen you in action, Al, I know what you can do. But Caughlan has buried better men than you. And when he does it, they never see it coming. Never."

"Why would Daniel Caughlan wanna bury me, Marty?"

"Maybe he don't," he said. "Not yet, anyhow. You just take care that you don't wind up knowing more about him and his business than he's comfortable with."

"Come on, Marty. You know I can handle Caughlan." He didn't come out here because he was worried about me, she thought. She wondered what it was he really wanted.

"Yeah? You think so? Daniel Caughlan was hijacking trucks in the garment district when he was fourteen years old, okay? And he was breaking kneecaps for the loan sharks not long after that. There ain't a damn thing about hurting people that he don't know. He's so far from caring about anybody that he don't even know what that looks like anymore. You ever hear of the black Irish? Well, they don't come no blacker than Mickey Caughlan."

Mickey. Stiles had called Caughlan that before. Al had noticed how Caughlan stiffened when he heard it. "What's black Irish?"

"Ain't you listened to a goddamned word I said?"

"I heard you, Marty."

"All right. I don't wanna see nothing bad happen to you. Believe me, Al, I'm on your side in this one."

"I'll be careful."

"You do that. Listen, I gotta ask you a favor. When you're not too busy, take a run by the office for me, will ya? I hadda get a new girl, she can do a half-assed job of the invoices, okay, but apart from that, she don't know shit. You know I ain't no fucking good with paperwork. I just need you to show her the ropes a little bit. Can you do that for me?"

There it is, girl, she told herself, her stomach rolling. You really did it this time. "She just filling in while I'm out?"

"You ain't kidding, are you?"

"If you're gonna kick me to the curb, Marty, man up and tell me about it."

He leaned back, picked up the oversized pecan roll he'd bought, and bit into it. She watched his face change as he chewed. "All right," he said. "All right. If you're still on the payroll, I'm gonna bill that son of a bitch for your hours. And you call me, you keep me up to speed on what you're doing. I don't wanna hear about you flying off somewhere, chasing a ghost."

"Did you know about Caughlan's son, Willy? Is that what you're talking about?"

"Yeah, I know about him. But the kid ain't got nothing to do with us. Leave it alone, 'cause Mickey's touchy as hell about it. Leave it be. You and I are looking for someone who's moving opium base into the country using Caughlan's trucking company. Do yourself a favor and remember that."

"All right," she said.

He looked at her, doubt in his eyes. "I mean it," he said.

"I said okay, didn't I?"

"Yeah. Just like last time. And don't forget, swing by the office and talk to the new girl."

"Yeah," she said, thinking that she ought to tell him to go shove his paperwork up his ass. "Yeah, sure, Marty. No problem. I'll get over there in a day or so."

Six

She held her cell phone in her hand, regarding it with mixed emotions. It's senseless to hate the telephone, she told herself. It's a connection. You can't go through your entire life keeping everyone at arm's length. You push them all away and then bitch because you're alone . . . How stupid is that? She flipped the thing open and dialed Tio Bobby's home number.

"Hello." It was Anthony. She had expected to get the answering machine, but he surprised her by picking up. She was slightly disappointed not to hear her uncle's voice on the recording.

"Hi, Anthony. How are you?"

"I'm tired," he told her. Anthony had little regard for rhetorical questions. You asked him how he was doing, he told you. "I haven't had to spend this much time on the subway in ages. I think I'd sleep in the chair in Roberto's room if they'd let me. And my back is killing me. I think it's those damned plastic seats on the train. I've got half a mind to sue the MTA."

"Well, why not?" she said. "Maybe they'd give you some money if you promised not to ride on their trains anymore.

Why don't you take a room up there somewhere? I could ask my father if he knows—"

"Heaven forbid," Anthony said. "Leave us not trouble your father with our little difficulties. Besides, I'm just complaining. I do think sleeping in some strange bed would only make things worse."

"I understand. Listen, do you think it would be all right if I borrowed Tio Bobby's van?"

"Of course you can have the van. You know the only thing I hate worse than being seen riding in that thing is being seen driving it. And Roberto would have wanted you to have it anyhow."

She wasn't ready to start down that road yet. "I just need it for a day or so, Anthony."

"It's all right," he said. "As far as I'm concerned, it's yours."

"Thanks. Listen, Ant, I know that you and I haven't always—"

"Nonsense, darling," he said. "In my own sick way, I have come to appreciate the value of your company. But it does go against my nature, sweetie, to confess to a woman that I feel something for her."

"I'm not like all those other girls, Ant."

He laughed at that, and she thought she could hear sorrow in it, but she couldn't be sure. "You know something, Al?" he finally said. "You're right about that. You are nothing like the other girls."

Tio Bobby belonged to the "Drive 'em till they drop" school of automotive theory, and Alessandra stood with the keys in her hand looking at her uncle's battered Chevy Astro. The thing had spent its first lifetime in the service of the phone company. Bobby had acquired it at auction, and in the years he had owned it, he had personalized it in accord with his own whimsy. It still looked plain-jane on the outside, but on the inside, the cargo compartment had dark purple fur on the floor, walls, and ceiling. There was a fridge, a television with a DVD player, and a black couch that could be taken out when Bobby needed the van to pick up or deliver a motorcycle. The windows Bobby had cut in either side were so dark you could barely see out, and nobody could see in. The thing had more horsepower than any truck its size needed. In a strange way, the van was the complete opposite of her uncle. It looked normal enough on the exterior, it kept its weirdness hidden out of sight. Tio Bobby, on the other hand, with his tattoos, his jewelry, and the beads and other assorted junk he wove into the braid on his chin, wanted you to know right up front that he was no ordinary cat. Al had never completely figured Tio Bobby out, but no matter where she went, it seemed that he had already been there, and had thought more deeply about the trip than she.

Problem was, Tio Bobby could generally fix anything, so he didn't pay much attention to the niceties of vehicle maintenance. You gotta know that this van is gonna stick it to you somewhere, probably in the middle of an intersection . . .

She got into the Astro and fired it up. She gave it a minute to warm up. The fat Italian guy who owned the lot where Tio Bobby kept the van stood smiling at her the way that guys do when their heads have stayed fifteen long after their asses have turned fifty. She waved to him, goosed the accelerator, thought the thing sounded all right. She said a silent prayer as she dropped it into drive. Please, God, you know I don't know anything about cars . . .

Typical, Al thought, rich people don't want ten-year-old Toyota Camrys full of Puerto Ricans driving through their neighborhood, so they lay the streets out in such a convoluted way, nobody comes through unless they live here. You tried to take a shortcut through this place, you could drive around for an hour trying to find your way back out. Shit. You've got to be the first Latina driving down this road who isn't a maid, a cook, or a nanny.

She'd already passed by Caughlan's house twice, took a look at the imposing façade and the cars parked out front, and kept on going. Friggin' place looked like a hotel, or a ritzy corporate office center. Glass, stone, and heavy timber; red tile walkway curving up past the stand of weeping birch; the koi pond and the waterfall; and on up to the heavy black wooden front doors, looked like they were designed to resist battering rams.

A Porsche 911 passed her going the other way, probably another one of Caughlan's friends, she told herself. More Porsches around here than Fords. Earlier in the day she'd thought about washing the van. Yeah, she thought, like that's gonna help. Lipstick on a pig. She figured she had done slightly better on herself. She owned one outfit that she kept for those rare occasions when jeans and a T-shirt wouldn't do. It was a pinstriped suit, jacket and pants, and she'd worn it with a plain white blouse. It's good enough, she told herself. She'd splurged on a new pair of shoes, not that she was going to impress anyone, but if you're going to be standing around all afternoon, you might as well be comfortable.

She turned down Caughlan's street again. Come on, Martillo, she thought, where's your guts? You have to do this, he's paying you for it. She pulled the van into Caughlan's circular driveway, opened the door and got out, grabbed the camera bag she used for a purse out of the backseat. A short dark-skinned young man wearing a black suit walked over, tore a red ticket in half, held his hand out for her key. Mexican, she thought, or Central American. "Señorita," he whispered softly, smiling. Country boy, she thought, up here in the cold north, probably trying to send money home to feed a family he'll be lucky if he ever sees again. She wondered how much money Caughlan was paying him. Guy wasn't much more than a boy.

"Señor," she said. "You work for Caughlan?"

He nodded his head.

"How is he to work for?"

The kid shrugged. "You give him what he wan'," he said, "he take care of you. You don't give him what he wan', he go craze."

"What's your name?" she asked him.

He looked at her face for the first time. "Epiphanio Neves," he said.

"Alessandra Martillo," she said, holding out her hand.

He shook her hand softly. "You born here," he said.

She nodded. "Brooklyn. My parents are from Puerto Rico."

"Lucky," he told her. She knew what he was talking about. She didn't have to worry about Immigration.

"Yeah," she said. "I am. Be careful with my uncle's van, okay, Eppi?" She handed him the key.

He bowed slightly as he accepted it from her. "Of course," he said, and he smiled. She knew the look: he was smitten. "I take good care."

"Thank you."

She watched him climb into Tio Bobby's van and drive it away, and she wondered where he was taking it. The kid is right, she told herself, you are lucky. No matter how bad you got it, there's always someone around who has it worse. She stuck the claim ticket in her pocket and undid the top three buttons of her blouse. Loosen up, she told herself. Show 'em a little brown skin. The man asked you to come, so you got as much right to be here as anybody. You ain't nobody's goddamn maid, not yet.

She stepped through the front doors and looked around. My God, she thought. The place was beyond elegant, it was beyond opulent, it was beyond anything she'd ever seen. You give me a million dollars, she thought, I could never decorate a space to look like this, no matter how hard I tried.

A young woman swept into the entryway where Al stood, held out a manicured hand. Al tried not to stare at the rings on the woman's fingers. She was a few inches shorter than Alessandra, but she was stunning, with heavy blond hair framing the sort of face guys went to war over. She wore a strapless peach gown that was suspended, contrary to the laws of physics, from the bottom half of her bosom. Creamy white skin, sparkling green eyes, and a perfect smile—the woman was flawless, she looked good enough to eat. Alessandra wanted to button up her shirt and run away, but it was too late. "I don't believe we've met," the woman said, her voice carrying a trace of a Southern accent. "I'm Helen Caughlan, Daniel's wife. And you are?"

God, Al thought, she's even more gorgeous than the house. She's everything you will never be . . . Stop it, she told herself. Bitch probably can't even do one chin-up. She took Helen's hand. Probably break all of her fingers if you tried, she thought. "Alessandra Martillo," she said. "Very nice to meet you, Mrs. Caughlan."

"Alessandra Martillo." Helen said it as though she were tasting something. There was a hint of something in the back of those green eyes, a trace of fear, maybe, or doubt. "What a beautiful name. Are you a friend of Dan's?"

She's wondering if I'm sleeping with him, Al thought. She's wondering if I'm the one that will get her booted out of this house. "Business associate," she said.

"Ah," Helen said, and she held onto Al's hand a second longer. "But no business today."

"Scout's honor," Al said, and she tried to smile. Tried not to dislike Helen Caughlan.

"Excellent," Helen said. "Come with me, I'll show you around."

Alessandra's phone went off just as Helen ushered her across the marbled bridge that connected the two halves of the second floor. They paused while she fished it out of her camera bag. Below them on one side was the entrance she'd come through moments earlier, and on the other side they looked down on what might, in a humbler dwelling, have been called the den. Soft yellow walls, rough-hewn stone fireplace, leather couches scattered around the perimeter. A glass wall formed the fourth side of the room, and through it could be seen a sort of greenhouse structure that housed another waterfall, some small evergreen trees, and an indoor swimming pool. A short Italian man stood in the center of a knot of people and expounded. "Excuse me," Al said, and she turned the phone off. "I really hate telephones."

"I know exactly what you mean," Helen said. "You can never really have a moment to yourself anymore. You can't be indisposed, you can't be out of reach, ever. Lord, Daniel gets positively incensed if he should happen to call me and I don't answer. It's a small thing, I suppose, but it does wear, knowing that one can never be truly alone."

"Who is that guy?" Al said, pointing down at the short Italian.

"Jerry Tomasino," Helen said. "He was once the mayor of Union City. I'm not quite sure what he does these days, something in real estate, I think. Daniel seems to have dealings with him from time to time."

"I see."

Below them, one of the younger female guests had shed her clothes and was wading into the pool. Alessandra watched Helen watch the girl. "There," Helen said. "Just what I was saying. We've lost all sense of privacy." She looked up from the nude girl in the pool to Alessandra. "There's your proof," she said. "Everyone is an open book. There are no secrets anymore. I could understand if she were four or five years old, but she's twenty if she's a day."

"I could never do that," Al said. "Not that I'm ashamed of how I look or anything, but I'd be too worried about who was going through my stuff while I was in the water. I guess I still need to hang onto my secrets."

Helen had a strange laugh—she sounded almost as though she were choking—but then she cut it off abruptly. "Well, I wish I could say that," she said, turning her attention back to the pool, where the girl was out in deeper water, trying not to get her hair wet. "But I can never quite convince myself that it's true. I feel eyes on me constantly, whether or not they're really there."

"Look at it this way," Al said. "For the rest of the afternoon, all of the eyes in the place will be watching her, not you or me."

"Yes," Helen said, and she laughed that strange strangled honk again. "The men will all be hoping she'll take her clothes off again, and their women will be trying to catch them looking."

Alessandra caught sight of Gearoid O'Hagan, who was standing off to one side of the room below them. He was looking up at her and Helen, not at the girl, and when he caught her eyes, his somber face lit up. He's smiling with all of himself this time, she thought, not just his teeth . . . He seemed genuinely glad to see her, even in the presence of such a compelling distraction. Al felt the impact of that smile, felt herself flush as she wondered what might be behind it. She glanced at Helen, but her escort was staring down at the girl in the swimming pool. Al turned back to O'Hagan, but Gearoid's face had clouded over as he watched Daniel Caughlan stroll across the floor, a bath towel in his hand. The girl swam back to the shallow end and climbed out to a smattering of applause. Caughlan wrapped her in the towel and smacked her on the rear end.

"End of the show," Al said.

Helen shook her head. "Never," she said. "Just the end of the episode. Shall we continue?"

It was numbing after a while: media room, kitchen easily twice the size of Al's apartment, maid's quarters, library, game room, guest rooms, his and her master suites. Helen even took Al through the garage so they could ogle Caughlan's new Bentley Continental GT. "He won't even sit in it yet, let alone drive it," Helen said. "I don't know why he even bought it."

"You ever think about taking it for a joyride?" Al asked.

"I've considered it," Helen told her. "Not that I care anything for the car, but it would be easy enough. Daniel keeps the keys in the top drawer of the workbench over there. The gardener will get to drive it before I do—he's supposed to take it back to the dealer in a week or so to get the alarms installed." She shook her head. "Men," she said. "But I suppose Daniel deserves it, if that's what he wants."

"There are worse preoccupations," Alessandra said.

"Yes," Helen said dryly. "You're right about that." Al followed her out of the garage, followed her past a room filled with model trains, down a hallway, and into the large central room that was dominated by a bar and a wooden dance floor. "There'll be music down here," Helen said. "A bit later." There was a door on the far side of the room, diagonally opposite the bar.

"What's over there?" Al asked.

Helen held her breath for a second before she answered. "That was Willy's room when he stayed with us. He liked being down here in the basement, all by himself."

"It must have been a terrible loss," Al said. She looked at Helen when she said it, watched as the woman's face seemed to age a dozen years.

Helen glanced at her watch. "I really must be getting back upstairs," she said.

"Thanks for the tour," Al said.

"My pleasure. If you need anything at all," Helen said, and she turned and walked out of the room. Alessandra stared after her, wondering if she ought to feel guilty for making Helen feel bad, bringing up the subject of Willy, if her interest in him had chased Helen off. It was possible that the woman had genuinely cared about her stepson, that she was sensitive of her memories of him, but that was a kind-hearted assumption, and therefore not the smart money bet. But Helen had looked absolutely haunted . . .

Al's mental file on Willy Caughlan was getting fatter.

She walked across the dance floor and stepped into Willy's room.

There didn't seem to be much of him left there. The room was more about the parents than the kid, it was filled with the kind of stuff kids discard and bereaved parents gather up and squirrel away. There was a boom box on the desk in the far corner of the room. It had a cassette and CD player, both formats outdated. The other stuff in the room was of the same flavor: either it was out of style, too small, or too nineties to be anything Willy had cared about recently.

She walked over and sat down at Willy's desk, leaned back in his chair. A short time later, Daniel Caughlan filled the doorway. "Thought I might find you here," he said. He sat on the end of the bed, between her and the only exit.

Alarm bells went off in Alessandra's head. *He's got you boxed in,* she thought, *and he's a man who's used to getting what he wants. There might not even be anyone else down on this level.* She could hear her father's voice. *Men always have the same thing on their minds.* He'd told her that many times. *There's only one thing they really care about. Do you hear me? I don't give a damn what they tell you. And don't go thinking one of them is different from the rest.* Al glanced at Caughlan with as much cool as she could muster. "How much you pay her?"

"Her who?"

"The girl in the swimming pool."

"Two large," Caughlan said. Al could sense him reappraising her. "How did you know? Did O'Hagan tell you?"

"I haven't talked to O'Hagan yet," she said. "I just had a gut feeling."

"Based on what?" he said. "I don't know that I care to be so transparent."

"I figure you like your parties to be memorable," she told him. "Any woman doing that for real would probably be fat, forty, and fucked up."

Caughlan shook his head. "Maybe," he said. "You got one out of three, though, she's flying on something. Her and her two friends was supposed to do it later tonight. More toward the end of everything, but she got messed up and jumped the gun. Just as well, I suppose. Fucking O'Hagan hates it when I do stuff like this."

"Why is that?"

"He's funny that way."

Al kept her voice low. "How come you never told me about Willy?"

His face, human one moment, seemed set in plaster the next. Al watched him as he fought to compose himself. After a few moments he swallowed and glanced over at her. "Stiles told me you'd never leave it alone."

"Forget Stiles," she said. "Nobody here but you and me. Why didn't you tell me?"

He shook his head. "Have you ever lost someone?" he asked.

"Yes."

"Then you should know."

"Why don't you just tell me about your son," she said. "Do it now, and then we can be done with it."

Caughlan sighed. "Not a hell of a lot to tell. We didn't talk much, he and I." He stared down at his shoes. "My old man never talked to me, neither. I don't know if I did the right thing by Willy. I didn't want him in the business, I wanted him to go to school. Be a lawyer or an accountant or some damn thing. So I let him alone, you know what I mean? I let his mother do his raising. But when he bought his goddam guitar . . . It was the end. I should have taken it away from him, I should have broken it over his feckin' head."

"He had nothing to do with Penn Transfer."

Caughlan shook his head. "Willy was an airhead. He didn't have nothing to do with nothing. When he was a little kid, all he could think about was trucks. You believe that? I'm trying to get him to go to Harvard, and he wants to be a goddamned truck driver. Then he picks up a guitar, from that moment on the only thing he gives a damn for is music." He paused, looked at the floor between his feet. "I wanted him to have everything I didn't."

"You wanted him to be different from you."

He turned and stared at her. "Maybe. But that goddam guitar poisoned the water between the two of us, I can tell you that."

"All right," she said. "I have to ask this, okay? Did you know he was into dope?"

Caughlan shook his head. "No."

"I'm sorry about Willy."

Caughlan sat silent for a minute. "Thank you," he finally said. "She's twenty-four."

"Who's twenty-four?"

He nodded at the ceiling. "That one upstairs. In the pool."

"Whatever," Al said. "Not my business."

"Oh, but it's all right," he said.

He doesn't want me to think he's a dirtbag, Al thought, surprised.

Caughlan sighed again, then stood up. "I'll close the door behind me here. No one will bother you. I expect you'll have to go through his things. Just put it all back when you're done. And leave me alone about it." He walked out, shutting her in.

She opened the top drawer of Willy's desk.

This is supposed to be a drug case, she told herself. Why are you so interested in Caughlan's kid? Funny, though, how Willy checked out just as his father's problems had gotten started. Must have been a bad month, she thought. Someone uses your company to smuggle dope into the country, a grand jury starts looking into your business, and your son dies.

He's in heaven. That's what Alessandra's mother would have said. In her mother's cosmology, everyone went to heaven when they died, God being too nice to really put the screws to anybody. In the end, he forgave you and let you in. We make up these bits of hopeful dream because they make us feel better, she thought, and then we forget that we, or someone like us, invented them, and they harden into dogma, they become carved in granite, accepted as the revealed wisdom of our betters, passed down to our children as truth. And though the hopeful notions of her mother had not been enough to sustain her, they were as valid as anyone else's opinions. They lacked only the unquestioning acceptance of a few learned-sounding adherents to let them congeal into canon. Maybe it's better this way, Al thought. Maybe it's better that the old ways are dying, that now everyone seems to need to make up her own mind. What else can you do? Swallowing someone else's pre-chewed conclusions is the lazy way out.

In Al's own mind, God was a half-mad amalgam of her mother, Tio Bobby, and Tito Puente, with lesser parts of everyone else thrown in, from Jim Morrison to Lenny Bruce. She mentally added Sean Willy Caughlan to that list. She went through the stuff he'd left behind, found nothing useful or particularly informative.

She found herself back on the second-floor walkway, the only part of the house she really liked. She supposed it was the voyeur in her. She leaned on the railing, looked down on the scene below. It felt like sitting in the front row of the balcony in a theater: the performers didn't make eye contact with you, they were more conscious of the faces on their own level, but you were close enough to watch and hear everything that went on.

Helen Caughlan stood with a group of women in the foyer below. "Cars!" the woman said, her voice a little too loud. "God, could I tell you stories." Her Southern accent was gone, now she just sounded like another chick from Jersey. Her perfection had developed a crack . . . Alessandra felt small for taking pleasure in that. "Drunk," to Al, had always meant you were too messed up to go get yourself another one. Helen was not that far gone, but she was on the way. "Fuckin' bastards," Helen went on, her voice a touch lower. "If it's something that they want, oh, sure, it's a classic, it's an investment, five more years and it'll be worth whatever-the-hell. What a load of bullshit. But if I need something, you can bet he's putting the brakes on, he's thinking of all the reasons I can't have it. Men." Her hair had broken free of whatever constraints she'd had it under, but the dress maintained its grip on her bosom. "They don't even make good house pets."

"Jerry was a nice pet, up until last year," one of the others chimed in. She was another one, another too-young and too-perfect blonde. Talk about house pets, Alessandra thought. "Then his doctor gave him a prescription for Cialis," the woman went on, "and ever since then he's been a pain in the ass. Or should I say . . ." Al wondered if the Jerry in question was Jerry Tomasino.

They all laughed, all except Helen Caughlan, who laid a hand on the speaker's arm. "He'll get a girlfriend soon, honey, they all do. You just need to make sure—" She couldn't continue, though, she lost her audience when the lawn sprinklers just outside went on prematurely, spritzing about a dozen guests who'd been hanging around in front of the house.

They all seemed to take it well enough. The men trooped in through the front door, laughing it off. The women followed them, pretending not to care, but they made their way, one by one, into the powder room to check on hair and makeup. Al watched them emerge, repainted, looking a touch younger and fresher than when they'd gone in. It was an art that she'd never really mastered; her mother had died too soon to teach her, and there had been no one else. She supposed it was too late now, she was used to looking the way she looked and it was hard for her to picture what she ought to change. You can take the girl outta Brownsville, she thought . . .

Daniel Caughlan didn't weather the sprinkler incident as well as his guests. One of the sprinkler heads was malfunctioning, and instead of a gentle shower, the thing was shooting a jet of water thirty feet straight up in the air. Caughlan stood in the grass staring at it, his jaw clamped shut, face red, visibly angry and growing steadily wetter. His wife stood inside one of the enormous windows flanking the entrance, watching him, but her back was to Alessandra. After a while someone got the water shut off. Probably O'Hagan, Al thought. Al watched from her seat in the balcony as Caughlan kicked the dirt and grass away from the offending sprinkler head. Someone, she thought, is going to hear some shit about that . . . To her left was the master suite where Caughlan slept, and where, presumably, he would soon repair for a change of clothes. She walked away, down the stairs, and out into the backyard. She took refuge on a park bench down by Caughlan's garden.

Strange thing, she thought, for a man like him to grow vegetables. You would never refuse him if he wanted to give you tomatoes, she thought, but you'd probably think twice about eating them. About a quarter of the garden was ripped out. Whatever had been growing there had either lived out its useful life or had failed to please Caughlan, and now that corner was raw black earth. The rest, though, was thick and green. Al didn't recognize all of the plants, but some of them were easy to identify: the tomatoes were staked to a wire trellis, the carrots had orange heads poking through the dirt, and a low, dark, densely growing vine produced either cucumbers or green zucchini, Al wasn't quite sure which.

Daniel Caughlan found her there a while later.

He sat down on the bench beside her. "So?" he said. He looked at her, not the garden. "You have a good time?"

She nodded, mostly out of reflex. She chewed on her lower lip. "Keep asking myself why, though."

"Why I asked you?"

"No." Her father had drummed it into her: there was only one major motivation for men, it was why they did almost everything. "A house is your refuge, isn't it? It's the place you hole up, where you can shut the world out. I mean, look at this place. It's beautiful, it's more than I could imagine ever wanting, but you've got all of these characters here." She looked at him. "You don't seem like you're enjoying yourself. This afternoon had to be a production, even for you. This couldn't have all been for my benefit. Why put yourself through it?"

He shrugged. "Some of it's business. You gotta show 'em you still got it. And when you grow up as poor as I did . . ." He stopped, looked at her. "Can't use that line on you, I suppose."

"No," she said. "I never pictured you in a place like this, though. I had you figured more for a west side penthouse. This place has got to be an enormous pain in the ass. I bet the sprinkler system is the least of your problems."

"You don't know the half of it," he said with a sudden heat. "Feckin' sprinkler, the landscape guy is gonna get a good kick in the arse about that, you can bet on it. I've thought about the other, though, I've thought about goin' down that road. But I'll never move back into Manhattan. I'll never sell this house." He glanced out at the square of raw dirt in front of the two of them. "If the missus is still around when I die, she can do what she likes with it, I suppose I don't give a damn. Till then, I'm keeping it."

"You're dug in."

"This is it for me, I'm not going anywhere new."

"I couldn't pay the light bill for this place."

"Not to mention the housekeepers, the feckin' interior designer, the property taxes, the contractors, the pool guys, the gardeners . . . It never stops."

"Gardeners? I thought you planted this garden."

"No." Caughlan snickered. "I have planted a thing or two here, meself, but I've got men doing most of the work."

"Your personal finances," she said, and she watched as his

eyes came around and met hers. She stared at him evenly. "Do you use an accountant or do you tend to them yourself?"

"I got a guy," he said, "but I sign the checks meself."

"You keep all your records here?"

He nodded. "Upstairs, in the office."

"All right," she said. "Monday, I'll come back out and go through what you've got going on."

"I suppose it's necessary," he said, "but that don't make it feel any better."

"Maybe not," she said. "Probably feel better than being in jail, though."

"Good point. Listen, I've got a favor to ask of you."

"Okay."

"Stick around a while longer, then give O'Hagan a ride back to Brooklyn. He's been drinking steady all afternoon. I already lifted his keys. I can't have him killing himself on the drive home."

"All right," she said. "My pleasure."

"You learn anything today?"

"Yes."

He eyed her. "You wanna talk about it?"

"Not just yet."

He nodded. "I tend to be a straight-line thinker," he said. "A plus B equals C. Works well enough, most of the time. I used to think it was a male thing, and that women's heads was foreign territory. Well, that may be, but I don't think it's that simple. Some people don't bother too much with A, B, and C, they just watch, they keep taking in what they see, and then they make the leap. They reach right across the bog the rest of us are stuck in, all the way across to the answer that's been staring at us all." He looked over at her. "I'm thinking that's the way your mind works. I hope I'm not wrong."

Al shrugged. "Hard to say."

Caughlan was right, Gearoid O'Hagan had drank enough so that the anger that lay beneath his morose exterior was showing through. Alessandra, sorry she'd promised to stay, ran into him when she wandered into Caughlan's kitchen. She was growing tired of the place. There were empty glasses on almost every available surface, there were dirty plates shoved into potted plants, and the crowd that remained was deteriorating. This could get ugly, she thought, before it's over. O'Hagan was leaning on the island in the center of the kitchen. Al rested her elbows on the side opposite him, and the two of them listened to a loud argument coming from the foyer about who was, and was not, going to drive home. The woman was the blonde who'd been complaining about her husband's Cialis. Al took a step, peered down the hall to see the combatants. The man was Jerry Tomasino.

"How drunk are those two," Al said.

"She's drunker'n me," O'Hagan said, "but not by a lot. Course, I've probably had a lot more practice at it than her. It's these feckin' amateurs, givin' honnes drunks a bad name. But that bassard Tomasino, he's as sober as when he walked in here."

"Doesn't drink?"

"He drinks, all right. But you'll never see him show it. Part of his deal with the divil."

"What's he do?"

O'Hagan shrugged. "Chemicals. Real estate. Used to be a

politician. Mayor of Union feckin' City, twenty years back. Didn't go to jail when he was done being mayor, neither."

"How would he know Caughlan?"

"D'ese guys are all the same, Al. If there's a buck, they're all over it." He looked around carefully, then glanced back at Al. "Himself owns a couple acres down on the Husson River. In Hoboken. Used to be a warehouse, back when the whole feckin' waterfront wasn't nothing but a unflushed toilet. Now, though, that empty buildin' and the dirt it's on is worth millions."

"Serious?"

He nodded slowly, looked at her through half-lidded eyes. He looked like he was falling asleep on his feet. "Twenny million. Give or take. But firs', you know, Tomasino has ta change the zoning for 'im. Thass the way of it in Jersey."

"So? Won't Caughlan just pay him off?"

O'Hagan inhaled and tried to stand up straighter. "Yeah, course. But fer how much, thass the question. There'll be a lot of arse-sniffin' and growlin' and bared teeth before they settle it."

"You're working here, am I right?"

He grimaced. "Makin' the attempt." He looked at her. "You talk to Himself?"

She nodded. "He caught me snooping in his son's room."

"He'd be disappointed if you didn't look. Be disappointed in himself if he missed you doin' it."

"You think he's a shark."

"You ain't met the real Daniel Caughlan," he said. "Back him into a corner, he turns into Dracula."

"Maybe so."

"No maybe about it. So now you've seen 'em in their native habitat, all of these flaming arseholes he's got crowded around. What do you think?"

Before she had a chance to answer, she heard Helen Caughlan, her voice strident, yelling at one of the waitstaff. O'Hagan wiped his face with both hands. "Better go," he said.

Seven

It wasn't a big thing. Maybe the car's driver wasn't even aware of it, but the guy had a headlight loose. Alessandra would feel the Astro go over a rut, and four or five seconds later, the light on the driver's side of one of the cars behind her would flicker in her mirrors. She drove south, through the affluent little towns clustered on the Jersey side of the George Washington Bridge, and the guy stayed with her, a few cars back. Gearoid O'Hagan was slumped in the passenger seat beside her, floating in that creamy dreamworld halfway between consciousness and oblivion.

"Gro, where do you live?"

"Huh?" He rolled his head in her direction, tried to focus.

"Your address. Where do you live?"

"Brooklyn," he said.

"I know that. Where in Brooklyn?"

"Red Hook," he said. "Right offa the BQE." His head rolled back and his eyes closed.

She knew the neighborhood. It was in a state of flux, clawing its way back to respectability, but it was still a dicey place at night, half-industrial and too deserted for her taste. Even if she knew few of the inhabitants, she felt more comfortable living in Brooklyn Heights, a crowded place. There was comfort, for some reason, in the middle of the swarm. Plus, if the people in the car following them knew that Al and Gearoid were going to Red Hook, they might have a welcoming committee set up. Being too predictable would be a mistake. She glanced over at O'Hagan. The guy looked like he was too far gone to be a lot of help. She piloted the Astro through the streets of Englewood, New Jersey, past the dark and shuttered windows of the downtown stores. Fancy handbags, expensive dresses, fur coats . . . She couldn't imagine herself shopping in any of them. They'd take one look at you, she thought, they'd hear your voice, see the color of your skin, and they'd write you off. What you doin' in here, girl? This shit ain't for you . . . "Hey, Gro," she said, glancing in his direction.

He didn't look like he'd heard her.

"I ever tell you where my father lives?" The entrance ramp to Route 4 was on her right, and she got on. It was a couple miles up the hill to the toll booths at the George Washington Bridge. She watched her mirrors, trying to see what kind of car it was that was following, but it was too dark and the guy stayed too far back. Couldn't count heads. No way to tell how many in the car. Big sedan, though, she could see that much. We ought to be safe for the moment, she thought. If they didn't try anything on the quiet streets of the Jersey suburbs, they're not likely to make a move on the highway. Too many eyes. They'll wait until we get to Brooklyn . . .

"Hey, Gro."

"Hmmph."

"You ever been to the Bronx?"

His chin came up off his chest. "Bronx?" He stared at her stupidly. "Wass in the Bronx?"

"My father. Wanna meet him?"

He seemed to come out of it a bit more. "Takin' me home to meet the folks? I ain't even kissed you yet."

"No, you haven't." The guy didn't lack for confidence. She remembered when she'd caught his eyes, back at Caughlan's house, remembered seeing his face light up. "What are you waiting for?"

He swallowed once, blinked, squinted at her, then looked around. "Ahhh . . ."

Talking to a drunk, she told herself, is like talking to a child. "You wanna see the Bronx?" She glanced in her mirror, watched until she picked up the car. It was still back there. Gearoid's head rolled back, rested against the seat.

"Whatever you wan'," he said.

She eyed the mirror. You guys want to play poker with me, she thought, we're going to play by my rules . . . "We'll show 'em a card," she said. "See how bad they want it."

Gearoid's eyes were closed again. "Mmm."

Manhattan is just a sharp, narrow sliver of an island where the George Washington Bridge hits it, only seven blocks wide. Alessandra stayed on the highway and the Astro was across in an eyeblink, from the Hudson River, which separates Jersey from Manhattan, and then over the Harlem River, which separates Manhattan from the Bronx. On the far side of the Harlem River, Route 95 becomes the Cross-Bronx Expressway. It is a place where you do not stop unless you are forced to do so, you do not leave the highway unless you are sure of your ground. Al passed by the first three exits. She got off at the fourth, Webster Avenue, a wide, four-lane road. She caught the green light at the end of the ramp and turned right, headed deeper into the South Bronx. The car behind her, trailing by about two hundred feet, ran the yellow light and fell in behind them. She eyed the side streets as they drove past, looking for the right one. "Gearoid," she said. She reached over, grabbed his shoulder and shook him. "Hey, Gro, wake up."

"I'm awake," he said. He sounded like himself for the first time in a while. "Where are we?"

"South Bronx."

He looked around, his face clenched into a frown. He looked like a man who knew he'd forgotten something important. "What the hell are we doing here?"

"We're gonna step on a cockroach. Put your seat belt on."

He looked at her, steadied himself, then complied. He stared at her then, black eyes in a dark face. "What's up?"

"We're being followed," she said. There were no other cars moving on Webster Avenue, just the Astro and the car following. The traffic lights began turning yellow, then red. Al ran the first light, pulled to a stop at the next, her eyes on the rearview mirror.

"G'wan," Gearoid said, sounding almost sober. "Go away out of that."

"Two blocks back," she told him. "Sitting at the light."

"Caughlan," he said, breathing a world of distaste into the word. "Or someone wanting to mess with him." He kicked himself a little more erect. "What the hell'd you come down here for? You've played right into their hands. You should have went to a police station. That would have scared them off."

"What good would that do?" she asked him.

He stared at her. "You're crazy," he said.

"Maybe," she said. "You sounded, just now, like you hated

Caughlan. Why? Is it the religious thing? Him Catholic and you Protestant? Something like that?"

"Could be," he said. He was sounding progressively more awake. He turned to look at the car behind them again. "Maybe it's that he's my boss, maybe it's that he's married to a beautiful woman and he treats her like dirt. Or maybe it's just in my blood to hate everyone that's got a little more than me. Martillo, what the hell are you going to do?"

The light turned green. Alessandra winked at him. "Hang on," she said, and she turned the wheel all the way to the left, then stomped on the gas. The Astro's rear wheels howled, then caught, and the van spun 180 degrees and rocketed back north. It was a gypsy cab, Chevy, red and black. Three guys inside. The one in the backseat gesticulated wildly as the driver fought the steering wheel, turning the big sedan to give chase.

"We're trying to get away. Right?" Gearoid's voice was incredulous, uncomprehending.

"Hell, no. We are gonna have a conversation with those guys before we let them go. How far back are they?"

Gearoid turned to look. "About three blocks. There's three of them, you know."

"Tell you something that most guys don't understand," she said. "There are plenty of equalizers in the world. Anyhow, don't worry, we'll be fine. Here's what's gonna happen: I'm gonna turn up one of these side streets, and a block or so in, I'm gonna stop and get out. You jump behind the wheel and drive straight up about two blocks, park this thing, and walk back for me. Got it?"

"Yeah," Gearoid said, "but what—"

"Don't worry. Just get behind the wheel, drive up two blocks, park, walk back. No big thing."

"All right."

"Great," she said.

"Oh, yeah, grand," he said.

She found the side street she'd been looking for, jerked the Astro into a skidding right turn, and stood on the gas. Only one or two of the streetlights on the side street were lit, leaving most of the first few blocks in gloom. Cars were parked thick and close on both sides of the street, which ran sharply uphill. Whatever had been built on the left side was gone, razed to a large, brick-littered empty lot behind a chain-link fence. Up ahead, at the top of the hill, dark on dark, some empty and deserted project buildings rose straight up into the night. Jesus, she thought. How bad must they have gotten? She jammed on the brakes, shoved the gearshift into park, and got out. Gearoid leaped out, ran around the front of the Astro, got in, and took off up the hill.

Five seconds later, the van's brake lights lit up just as the gypsy cab rounded the corner of Webster Avenue. She could hear the cab's engine moan as it accelerated up the hill. There was a heavy metal trash can on the curb—she'd seen it on her way up the hill, it was the reason she'd picked this particular spot . . . She grabbed it, swung it high over her head, stepped out, and planted it in the windshield of the cab as it screamed past. The sound of exploding glass was followed closely by the noise of the cab sideswiping the row of cars on the far side of the street. Two of them had alarms that began hooting mindlessly into the uncaring Bronx night. The cab had hit the last car hard enough to climb up onto its trunk in grotesque metallic coitus, and its headlights were now pointing more or less skyward. The metal garbage can was still embedded in what was left of the cab's windshield. Al walked across the street to survey the damage.

The driver's side airbag had gone off, punching the driver unconscious. The front passenger had apparently planted his face on the inside of the windshield, because there was a head-sized impression in what was left of the glass, and the man lay back in the seat, just beginning to stir, blood seeping down out of his nose. One of the back doors was open, and the third guy was hanging out of the car, semiconscious. Al grabbed him by the collar and dragged him out, headed for the opposite side-walk.

She heard Gearoid's heels clicking on the pavement as he stumbled down the hill and skidded to a stop behind her. "Holy shit!" he said. "Holy mudder a Christ!" She ignored him and kept going, and he followed her between two of the buildings, down into a pitch-black alleyway lined with stinking garbage cans. There was a wrought-iron fence at the front of the alley with a gate hanging from one hinge. Al pushed her way past the gate and into the darkness. She dropped the guy when they were halfway up the alley and began patting him down. "No wallet," she said. "No keys, no money. Got a piece, though." She came up with it. It was a small gun, black, fit neatly into her hand with just the barrel sticking out. She could barely make it out, down in that unlit space.

"What is it?" Gearoid asked her.

She squinted at the pistol. "Throwaway, looks like a thirty-eight. Bet your house the serial number's filed off. This guy was planning to hose one or both of us, drop this thing down a sewer, and then go home." She bent down over the prone man. "Hey, asshole. C'mon, wake up." She grabbed the guy by the hair and slapped his face, to no effect. "C'mon, dickhead. Wake up. Wake up, buddy." She glanced back down the alley toward the street, her eyes adjusting to the gloom.

After a few more seconds, the guy rolled over on his side and groaned. Alessandra gave the guy a minute longer to come around, then stuck the pistol in his ear.

"All right, asshole. Who are you? What do you want?"

The guy looked up then, first at Al, then at Gearoid, then at the gun. His face twisted into a sneer. "Fock you."

"Yeah, maricon? You think I won't shoot you? How about I pop you with your own piece, you dumb bastard. How about I stick this up your ass and pull the trigger? They paying you enough for that, chica? Who you working for?"

"None of your focking business," the guy said. He glanced at Gearoid again.

"Forget him," she said. "He ain't gonna help you. It's you and me, baby. Tell me who you're working for."

"Fock you," the guy said. His face still showed nothing but contempt.

"Yeah? How much did you get paid for this gig? Not enough to die for, am I right?"

"You ain't gonna do shit. You gonna stand there talking all night."

"Yeah, you think so? You don't give me a name, and I mean right now, I am gonna shoot you right in the head." She grabbed the guy by his collar and pulled him up onto his knees, stuck the gun back in the guy's ear. "What you gonna tell them when you get to hell? You gonna admit you got wasted by a girl? Huh? Last chance, my friend."

The guy's face twisted into a sneer, and his eyes glittered. "Go ahead."

"Don't do it," Gearoid croaked.

"Why not? Friend of yours?"

"No. But don't do it. It's not worth it."

"No? How about I just shoot his dick off?" She pulled the pistol back, pointed it at the guy's crotch. His eyes went wide then, and he swallowed, glanced at Gearoid one more time, his face showing, at last, a touch of fear. Alessandra cocked her head, listening to the sound of a distant siren. "Too late now," she said. She turned back to the guy. "Your lucky night."

They went out through the back end of the alley, through a dimly lit courtyard and into a building on the far side, then exited onto the sidewalk a block away from the car crash. Al had stripped their assailant, left him crouched naked in the reeking alley. She stuffed the guy's clothes and his pistol into a trash can as she and Gearoid went up the hill. They turned the corner and headed toward the van just in time to see a police cruiser come down the hill and stop on the corner. Two cops got out of the car. One of them went down to look at the accident, the other one stopped Al and Gearoid when they got to the corner. He looked from one face to the other. "Who are you two?" he said. "And what are you doing here?"

Gearoid took a step forward, holding his hand out. "Hello, Officer," he said. "We're Jehovah's Witnesses. We was just having a Bible study with a family right around the corner. We're parked up the hill, there." The cop didn't shake Gearoid's hand.

"You people are fucking crazy, you know that? I don't even come down here in the daytime without a gun. You see what happened here?"

"No," Gearoid said. "We heard the noise, though."

The cop shook his head. "You two should really do this, like, during the day."

"God will protect us," Gearoid said.

"Sure he will," the cop said. "Get outta here, both of you."

"Have a blessed day, Officer."

"Didn't I already tell you to get lost?"

Gearoid collapsed in the car seat, sick with relief. Al looked over at him and laughed. Gearoid shook his head. "That cop was right, you are crazy. Do you know that?"

"Me? You didn't do so bad yourself. Bible study, that was priceless. Where'd you come up with that?"

"I don't know." Gearoid wiped his face and tried to sit up a little straighter. "Would you have really killed that man?"

"I wanted him to think I would."

"He wasn't going to tell you anything."

"No. I think he was actually going to take a bullet."

"God."

"Yeah. I hate to say it, but he wasn't posing, he was for real." Another siren sounded somewhere in the distance, but it was the whine of an ambulance and not the racket of a police cruiser. "You recognize him?"

Gearoid shook his head. "Never saw him before in my life."

Eight

Isn't that just like you, she thought. You finally get up enough nerve to have a guy over and he's unconscious the whole time . . . O'Hagan lay on the daybed, unmoving, in exactly the same position he'd been in when she left for morning practice two hours ago. She had considered blowing off the class, but it bothered her, losing something she'd already paid for. Besides, it was not something she could let go that easily. It wasn't like she enjoyed the class, it was hard, it was early, and the sensei drove her like she was the world's worst student. She'd felt, right from the beginning, that he disapproved of her, thought her previous training unorthodox and dangerous. For her part, she wondered how much real application there was for what she was learning. How well does this stuff work when you cross that door and get into the real world? She was too proud to ask, just as the sensei was too proud to ask who her previous teacher had been. She could feel it, though, he wanted her to place herself entirely in his hands.

She could think of a hundred reasons why she could never do it. She flexed her arm, made a fist, looked at it. It's the only thing your father ever gave you. How could you let it go?

She stopped for breakfast on her way back. She sat alone at a table, listened to the messages on her voice mail. One of them was the call she'd ignored when she'd been with Helen Caughlan. It was from someone who identified himself as a reporter. She called the number he'd left.

"Rod Benson," the voice said.

Al decided to mess with the guy. "What kind of a mother," she said, "would saddle a poor helpless infant with a name like 'Rod'?"

Benson had that smoker's laugh that ended with a cough, sounded like someone tearing a piece of rotten canvas in half. She could hear his breath rattle deep in his lungs. "Oh, now that's a subject I could get lost in," he said. "But it's a boring story, when you get right down to it. I do think 'Rod' is a distinct improvement over 'Rodney,' which is what she called me right up to the instant I pushed her wheelchair off that balcony. So call me anything you like, as long as it isn't 'Rodney.' Miss Martillo, I presume."

"How did you hear about me? Can I ask how you got my number?"

"Well, I'm only as good as my sources. But thank you for returning my call. I thought perhaps the name of my employer had frightened you off."

She couldn't picture Marty telling Benson about her. Must have been someone on Caughlan's end, she thought. "*The So-Cal Insider?* Not so far."

"That's probably a good thing. Let me get right to it, Miss Martillo. Did you know that Willy Caughlan was, ahh, intimate with Shine before he died?"

"Heard the rumor," Al said. "I haven't confirmed it, though. All I've got is hearsay."

"Well, if it's good strong hearsay, we'll print it. I'm just kidding, Miss Martillo. Sort of. I do actually have eyewitnesses who have verified the nature of the relationship between Willy Caughlan and Shine."

"You have people claiming they saw what, exactly? Are these the same people who give you pictures of that three-hundred-pound baby?"

"That's in the past, Miss Martillo. We have evolved since that story last ran. My sources may not have seen actual coitus, but they did observe plenty of face-sucking and general fondling. And where there's fondling, I say there's fire. But what I heard was that Willy actually filmed the two of them. En flagrante."

"Tacky," Al said.

"You're only young once, Miss Martillo. But I do agree that one should exercise caution when it comes to the ways and means by which one chooses to immortalize oneself."

"So you're after the tape."

"Darling, the world is after that tape. Mind you, I can't say for a fact that it exists, but Shine's camp has been singing all the usual songs."

"What would those be?"

"Oh, you know. 'Unconscionable invasion of privacy,' and so on and so forth. Seeking injunctions to prevent the public display of something that apparently no one has seen yet. That is to say, they've been acting very guilty."

"How about that? You suppose they're worried about the effect this will have on her career?"

"Well now, that all depends on how good she looks naked, doesn't it? If her people are very smart, and I am betting that they are, they might be banking on reverse psychology. Trying your damnedest to bottle something up is the best way to make sure everybody wants to see it."

"Why would Shine want to appear in a porn tape? How much money could she make off that?"

"Miss Martillo, please. It isn't the royalties from the tape, as considerable as they might be. What we're talking about here is ink. Publicity. The lifeblood of the entertainment industry. It's everything. Ever since word of this tape leaked out, Shine has been all over the news. I'm talking about print, television, and the Internet. She's gotten weeks over this! I heard she's on Larry King's most-wanted list. Name recognition and market penetration are the only things that matter here. If she could string this out for, say, another month or so, and then have the tape come out, it would vault her into a higher tier of celebrity. She'd be right up there with Pamela Anderson. As a matter of fact, having the tape go missing might be the worst that could happen, from her point of view."

"Wow."

"Exactly. So I want to make something clear to you: if, in the course of your, ahh, activities, you happen to stumble across such an item, I'm guessing it would be worth something in the neighborhood of half a million."

"Dollars? Are you kidding?"

"I'm completely serious."

"Why don't you hire someone to go look for it?"

"Someone such as yourself?"

"I'm already booked. But I'm sure that there are plenty of talented people . . ."

"Miss Martillo, you surmise correctly, we do employ a number of your compatriots. And we have, in fact, tasked one or two of them to pursue the item in question through the usual channels. But we have a unique situation here. Somewhat of a problem. First of all, the person who would have been in possession of the video is unfortunately deceased. And second, his father is, ahh, how shall I put this? Formidable. And not without assets. He caught one of our reporters going through his trash recently, and the man was beaten severely. Quite frankly, no one on staff wants to tangle with him."

"You think I do?"

"Miss Martillo, you'd have to solve that equation on your own. If, however, certain things or certain information were to, quietly, come into your possession, then you might consider passing them, quietly, along. I assure you, we can guarantee your anonymity. For whatever it's worth, we do quite a bit of business in this fashion."

"You sound as though you're proud of that."

He laughed, and again she winced at the sound. "Ah, well, listen, Miss Martillo, I don't pretend to be the reincarnation of Edward R. Murrow, or even Hedda Hopper. But Americans love celebrities, and I make a fine living airing the soiled linens of the famous and semifamous. I assure you, there isn't a journalist alive who wouldn't strangle his own mother to get his hands on that video, even if he had to turn around and sell it to someone like me. Ethics, Miss Martillo, are far more popular when the price tag attached isn't too hard to swallow. Anything over, say, a month's pay, they become inconvenient."

"I can't argue with you, Mr. Benson."

"I do hope you won't forget me, Miss Martillo."

"Not a chance," she said. "I'll call you if I find what you're looking for."

This is probably just another case of insufficient paranoia, Al thought as she ended the call. The girl had probably done it in innocence. She probably had fully intended to destroy the thing after she and Willy looked at it. Maybe she'd been confident that no one else would ever see it.

And maybe Rod Benson was right.

First, she made the video, assume that much. Second, someone leaked word of its existence. Third, her management team had denied the whole thing. Fourth, her lawyers had gone to court, giving everyone the impression that she was fighting to keep the thing off the market. Those were the steps that had already been taken. If the objective really had been to keep Shine's name and face in the news, it had, according to Benson, succeeded admirably. So fifth, just as the next news cycle gets off the ground, the video hits the Internet, and Shine's lawyers, surrendering to the inevitable, would demand a cut of the profits for their client. And if Shine were cold-blooded enough, she would tearfully and publicly cop to it all, mourning the loss of the love of her life, the late, great guitarist, Sean Willy Caughlan.

And if her next album was at all competent, it would hit like an atomic bomb.

Half a million bucks. What a thought! She couldn't even imagine what that would feel like.

She wondered if Daniel Caughlan knew about the video.

She brought a large container of coffee home with her, left it, open and steaming, on the floor next to O'Hagan. She sat in a chair in the opposite corner and waited. It took a few minutes, but the smell brought him around. He stirred, then put his hands up to his head. She looked past him at the two posters she had pinned to the far wall. The Aegean Sea, sky and ocean impossibly blue, bright white buildings on a hill sloping down to the water's edge. I'll go one day, she told herself often, but she didn't believe it. Anyhow, it was the colors she really loved. They made her feel warm, almost peaceful.

"Mudder a Christ." His voice was soft, muffled.

"So you're alive after all." What is it about this guy, she asked herself. In this unguarded moment, his hair all crazy, unshaven, a pained look on his face, he looked more like a man to her than anyone she could think of. Except Victor, maybe. Except her father.

"Don't jump to conclusions." Gearoid opened one eye and peered at her, moving his head carefully. "Al," he said. "Al, is that you?"

"In the flesh."

He rolled over slowly. "Ah, God, coffee. Martillo, you're an angel of bleedin' mercy."

"I bet you say that to all the girls."

He pushed himself into a sitting position, bent down for the coffee. "God," he said. "I'm drier than a cork leg. This your place, then?"

"Yep."

He looked around. "Well, t'anks for not leaving me down there in Hotel Chevrolet." He stared at her. "Last night really happened, didn't it? Up in the Bronx."

"How much do you remember?"

"I remember seeing you take out one car and three good men, all by yourself," he said.

Great, she thought. Now whenever this guy sees you, all he's going to think of is a Mutant Ninja Turtle. "And I remember you sweet-talking some cop into letting us walk."

"Ah, well, I suppose we all have our uses," he said. "You didn't want to go down to Red Hook last night, am I right?

Not after what happened. You thought it'd be safer to come here instead."

"If I thought those guys had been after me, coming here would have been just as risky," she said. "But compared to you and Caughlan, I'm pretty small potatoes. I figured some-one's probably trying to get to Caughlan through you. Or else, someone from your past wants to remind you how much they love you."

"Your potatoes," O'Hagan said, "take a backseat to nobody. Which way to the bat'room?"

"Straight down the hall," she told him.

"If I'm not back in a day or so," he said, "send for an ambulance."

"If what you drank yesterday didn't kill you," she said, "you're probably gonna live forever."

He stood up carefully, straightening his legs first, then his back, then his neck, then he tottered off down the hall. Al stared across the room at the Aegean as the sound of running water temporarily drowned out the other noises in the building. You could go, she told herself. A week on a beach, somewhere in Greece. Maybe two weeks.

Yeah. By yourself.

Bad enough, being all alone on your home turf.

Gearoid was back a few minutes later. "You didn't tell me," she said. "What's your take on last night?"

"Well, I don't know how many enemies you've got," he said. "I've got a few meself, but it's a safe bet Caughlan has us both beat in that department. You talk to him yet?"

She hadn't thought of that. "No."

"All right," he said. "I'll make the call. I'll have some of his people meet me down by my place. If someone's laying in the weeds, we'll turn them up. I'll give you a call after, let you know what happened."

"All right," she said. She remembered something Stiles had said. "Gearoid, tell me something. What's the black Irish?"

"You know, I never heard of that until I got over here," he said. "What is it about Americans, everybody needs to know what color you are? Like baseball. They all want to know what team you root for."

Alessandra didn't know what to say to that, so she kept silent.

"The story goes, when the feckin' Brits sunk the Spanish Armada, some of the Spanish sailors made it to shore. They say it was the mixing of them with the natives that started the black Irish."

"You believe that?"

"Makes for a good story, don't it? But there's no telling if it's real or not."

"I guess I heard it wrong. I was under the impression it was a class thing."

He gave her a sidelong glance. "Well, if a man has one pig and his neighbor has two, that makes his neighbor a rich man, don't it? Ireland is a desperate poor country. Them that survives is the ones who bit and scratched the hardest."

"No different anywhere else," she said.

"I suppose not," he said. "We got no monopoly on misery or hardship. But maybe we been at it longer, you know what I mean? It's like when you leave your stewpot on the stove too long, there's a lot that boils off and is lost, and in the end all you got left are the hard lumps on the bottom."

Al thought about survival on the streets of Brownsville.

Don't turn this into a contest, she thought. There's no prize if you win. "So you come from a long line of hard lumps, is that what you're telling me?"

He laughed at that, then winced at the pain in his head. "I don't know too much about what I come from. Me mum was a long-sufferin' woman, I know that much, and me stepdad was a flinty old bogtrotter. I can count on one hand the times I seen him smile."

"You lost me," she said. "What's a bogtrotter?"

"Farmer," he told her. "Cow shit on his boots, you'd say over here." He looked at her, then over at the Aegean. "And one hard lump he was."

"He's gone, then."

"Yeah. Him and me half-brother, both."

"I'm sorry to hear that," she said. "Do you miss them? I never had a brother or sister. My father's almost all I have left." And I get precious little of him . . . But at least he's there. At least he's still alive.

"Ah, I don't know if I miss the old bastard, exactly. Me and him never got on. I was never what he wanted. I t'ink I spent half my life trying to impress him and the other half trying to piss him off."

"Did you ever do it?"

"Piss him off? Royally."

"No, impress him."

"Never came close." He looked uncomfortable, glanced at his watch. "I really need to get going. T'anks, Al, for looking out for me last night. Hadn't been for you, I'd have been a dead duck."

"My pleasure," she said. "There's a car service one block over, on Clark."

"Thanks again, Alessandra Martillo."

"You're welcome, Gearoid O'Hagan."

The male nurse on Tio Bobby's ward was just the sort of guy her uncle loved: anglo, thin and fussy, blond and blue. She stood in the doorway of her uncle's room, looking at the empty chairs around the bed, her uncle's still form under the blanket. He had lost sixty or seventy pounds since he'd been in this place, but he was still far from small, and of course the rest of his persona was firmly in place. The tattoos, the beads woven into his beard, the heavy silver jewelry he wore on his fingers, they were all unchanged. He had a quarter inch of iron-gray stubble growing out of his skull, though she still couldn't get used to that. She turned to see the floor nurse floating in her direction.

"Where's Anthony?" she asked him.

The nurse peered past her into the room. Alessandra barely felt the hand he laid across her shoulders, but she allowed the man to steer her away from the door, over to the duty station. "Roberto's family came," he said, and suddenly he had tears in his eyes. "They said Anthony has no legal standing. Can you believe that? He and Roberto have been companions for twenty-eight years, but now they want him to leave. They say he has no right to be here."

"Nothing those people can do would surprise me," she said. "Where are they?"

"A whole conglomeration of them took over the day-room," he told her. "They've got Anthony in there now, they're browbeating the poor thing unmercifully. They want him out of the hospital, and they want him out of Roberto's house. They're telling him the house is in Roberto's name. Anthony hasn't got any rights at all, and they're going to get a lawyer, and, and . . ."

"Calm down," she told him. "You got any papers anywhere?"

"What kind of papers?"

"Anything. Give me something with a lot of text on it."

He fished around on the desk and in the trash, came up with a half dozen sheets of white paper covered with type. "Will these do?"

"Perfect," she said. "Stack them up neat, put a staple in the corner. Now fold them up nice and stick them in an envelope."

He did as she requested, then handed her the envelope. "What are you going to do?"

"Run them off."

"How do you propose to do that?"

"You ever see those little dogs they use to keep the geese off the golf courses? All they do is run around barking."

He looked at her, doubt plain on his face. "I'll be in the kitchenette," he said. "I can hear everything from there."

She could hear them, louder as she walked down the hall. She opened the heavy wooden door and looked into the room. There were eight of them, some she recognized and some she did not, but they had Anthony backed into the far corner of the room, over by the window. They look just like crocodiles, she thought, waiting for him to try and cross the river. She took one step forward, then stopped and slammed the door shut as hard as she could. The impact and the noise stunned them all into momentary silence, then they turned to face this new threat, leaving Anthony forgotten on his window ledge.

Her father's sister Magdalena was the first to speak. Alessandra considered her a repulsive human being, not just because she was short, fat, and ill-tempered, but because she used a series of imagined illnesses and ailments to manipulate her brood and to avoid contributing anything to the world other than the sound of her complaining. "Alec," the woman said, spitting out the word. "You got no bidness here, you—"

"Shut your ass up," Alessandra said. She did not even glance at the woman, she stared at Magdalena's husband. As always, she was surprised that he had not killed himself by now. His capacity to absorb abuse was truly impressive.

A young man she did not recognize crossed the room. "Don't you speak to my aunt that way," he said, and he grabbed her by the elbow and yanked her toward him. She did not resist the motion, instead she went with it, pivoting on one foot and using her momentum to drive her knee into the man's midsection, just above his belt. She could hear Magdalena shrieking in the background as she continued the move, spinning up close, but she pulled her elbow back. She'd been ready to hammer it into his jaw, but she saw that it was not necessary, he was already done. He released her, staggered back, went down hard on the concrete floor.

"And he's down," she said, mostly to herself. "Didn't last the first round." Magdalena was still squalling, and Alessandra turned on her. "I told you to shut your dripping hole!" she shouted, and then she turned and looked at her silent uncle, Magdalena's husband. She knew that what few active brain cells the family possessed were in his keeping. She held her envelope aloft. "You see this? This is a will. Tio Bobby gave it to me before he got sick. He's leaving everything to me. The house in Queens, the motorcycle shop, all the bikes. You hear me? You wanna know what he left you? The sweat off his balls." They all gaped at her, and she stared back. Where were you, she wanted to ask them, where have you been all of this time? Why is it the only times I ever see you, you've got your hands empty and your mouths open? But then the pain she kept hidden threatened to break loose, the anger and the sorrow over all the years of isolation and rejection wanted to spill over into the room, and she could not allow it. She would never give them that. She turned away, faced the door.

"We gonna go get a lawyer," Magdalena said. "We gonna take you to court, you'll see. We gonna—"

"You do what you want." She still wasn't ready to look at them. "But any lawyer who would take your pathetic ass for a client must be an idiot."

"Al?" It was her uncle. "Al?"

She turned to face him. "I will consider splitting the estate with you," she told him. "But if you let that bruja go to a lawyer, I will fight you until there's nothing left. The abogados will get it all." The two of them stared at each other. "Half for you, half for me. You wanna give something to the rest of these pigs, you take it out of your share. But you get them out of this hospital right now, and you leave Anthony alone, or else nobody gets a thing. Nobody but the lawyers." She nodded at Magdalena. "And you keep her goddam mouth shut."

He looked at her, thought about it, then nodded once. "Come on, everybody, we're leaving now." Alessandra watched them shuffle out of the room. Her uncle was the last to go.

"You could have waited until he was dead before you started digging the grave."

"It ain't like that, Al. Mag just gets upset. She's afraid . . ."

"You need to give her the strap," she told him. It was their private little joke, they had been passing it back and forth for years. "That woman needs a good beating."

He surprised her. "Maybe she does." He turned to go, then paused, his hand holding the door open. "I'm sorry about Roberto. I know you loved him."

She was surprised at how much that hurt. He loved me first, she wanted to throw it in his face. He's so much more than all the rest of you . . . She couldn't, though, she still wasn't sure of her grip on her emotions. "Thank you," she said. When the door closed behind him, she turned and looked at Anthony, a finger to her lips. He nodded his understanding. The two of them sat down at one of the tables.

Anthony could have been father to the nurse she'd met out on the floor, the two of them looked that much alike. He leaned across the table, took her hands in his. "You're shaking," he whispered to her. "My God, you must be human after all." He cocked his head, eyed her doubtfully. "Roberto never said anything to me about a will."

She shook her head and whispered back. "They're just papers from the garbage." Anthony's pale and drawn face opened up and cracked into a smile, his eyes went wide, he leaned back in his chair and laughed silently. "Just a bluff," she told him, keeping her voice low. "It'll never hold up. They know me too well."

"I don't care about the house." Anthony was telling her the truth, he always did. She had never understood the man, never thought he cared much for her, but the two of them had declared a truce long ago, mostly because each of them knew Tio Bobby loved the other. "If all you've done is buy me some time with him, that's enough."

"I'd hate to see them put you out on the sidewalk."

"Well, thank you. But don't worry about me. I'll be fine."

The door opened and the nurse came in, glowing, and he sailed across the floor. Alessandra rose to meet him and he threw his arms around her. "Good Lord, what a performance," he said, squeezing her. "That was wonderful." He released her, and they both sat down. "Well, they're all gone. I watched them go down the elevator." He and Anthony began competing for the right to tell her all about the new and experimental medicine the doctors were giving Roberto, and how it was going to strangle the thing that was growing in his stomach before it could finish killing him. She swallowed her sorrow one more time and tried to listen.

She didn't really understand it, wasn't sure if it was fueled by sorrow or loneliness or deprivation or maybe just adrenaline left over from earlier that evening. She preferred to think of it as simply the stirring of one of her inner demons, one that she resisted well enough most of the time. Occasionally, though, something broke free, and then it wasn't a matter of yielding to temptation or giving in, it felt more like she was overwhelmed, swept under, carried off.

The place was a dump, a little hole-in-the-wall joint in Hackensack, just yards away from where the railroad tracks spanned busy River Road over a crumbling concrete overpass. The place had a pool table, though, and just enough light to shoot. She ignored the loser smell of stale beer and sweat.

She played a couple of games, abandoning her usual finesse and control. The game was not the point, not tonight, and she didn't care how hard she slammed the balls home. She drank Bloody Marys as she played, felt the alcohol feeding the beast, dissolving the adhesions that normally kept her in her place.

And is that a crime, she wondered. Is it necessary to keep yourself under such tight control all the time?

There were eight guys in the joint, not counting the bartender, and they all came up and had a go at her. She dispatched them easily, even playing as carelessly as she did. There was one guy who could shoot a little bit—he might have been decent if he'd worked on his game, and if he were sober . . . He was a white guy, wore a white shirt with the sleeves rolled up, tie unknotted, still threaded through the button-down collar, sport coat thrown across one of the chairs in the back. He looked like he worked in one of the big office buildings a block away on Main Street. He came back for a second game; she let him break. He was trying hard, she could tell, she watched him sink a few balls, and then she walked past him, brushed up against him as he lined up a shot.

"Excuse me," she said. "Sorry."

He turned to look at her. He was maybe thirty, junior exec type, decent shape, sculpted goatee on his chin. Starting to sweat. "No problem," he said. He turned back to his shot, but she had rattled him and he missed badly. She laughed softy, walked past him again, close, again, but not making contact. She leaned over the table, pretended to look for a shot. She felt his hand on her ass, warm, not quite steady. Afraid, she thought. Hungry.

We're perfect for each other.

She stood up slowly, toyed with the cue as she looked over her shoulder at him. His face was pale. He swallowed, then smiled uncertainly as he let his hand fall away, but he didn't retreat. She felt her skin burn where he'd touched her. Like a male spider, she thought, he has to dare to be killed, and eaten. He has to want it that badly . . .

She laid her stick on the table. "Let's take a walk," she said. She tugged once on the loose end of his tie, turned her back on him, and walked out.

He followed her into the night.

"My car's over here," he said, trotting to catch up, jerking a thumb at the half-lit parking lot. She ignored him, walked up to the railroad tracks, turned, and followed them onto the overpass. She stopped right in the middle of the bridge over River Road.

"You like the danger," he said, one eye on the cars roaring past beneath them. She leaned her butt against the pipe railing, her back to the traffic, avoided his lips as he leaned in to kiss her. He was up close, though, and he pinned her against the rail, his hands on her hip and her chest. She grabbed his shirt and yanked it out of his pants. "Oh my God," he said, and he pulled her dress up around her waist, found nothing under it but her. "Oh my God," he said again, husky. "Jesus."

She writhed in his grasp, then she pushed him back off of her and ripped at his belt, tore it out of the loops and flung it away. She bent down swiftly and jerked his pants and underwear down around his ankles. His penis popped out, hard, bobbed up and down in her face. She stood up again, pulled her dress back up, hopped up onto the railing. She wrapped her legs around his waist as he entered her, gave in to it, rode the wave until it threatened to crest. Then, gripping him tightly, she lowered her feet to the ground and stood up to him, face to face. He continued thrusting, but slower now, easier, because his penis was bent at an uncomfortable angle.

"What," he said, his breath ragged. "What do you want to do . . ."

She turned him around, put his back against the railing. He

was still hard, but he stood still as she rode him. After a moment she grabbed a handful of his shirt, pushed him back until his upper body was out over the rail, in empty space above River Road. His feet came up as he struggled for balance, his pants inverted as his legs flew apart, she heard the tinkle of car keys and change from his pocket as it rained down on the street below.

"Yaahhhhh!" he bellowed, skewered on the twin spears of pain and pleasure. She held him there, slamming into him. "Aaaaaaghh! You're killing me!" He flailed, finally grabbed a handful of her hair. "Goddammit!"

She shifted her grip from his shirt to his throat, squeezed until he let go of her hair and grabbed her wrists. "Please!" he rasped, when she gave him air. "Please! I have kids! I have . . . I got a wife . . ."

She came then, one long shivering burst, and then she pulled herself off him, dragged him back off the railing. Her dress fell back down around her thighs. She let him go, stepped back, looked at him standing there, quivering. "Crazy bitch," he said, but there was still fear in his voice. "Don't just leave me here. Finish me, at least. Finish me off."

"Do it yourself," she said, and she walked off into the darkness without looking back.

Nine

The sun burned through the dirty windows of the offices of Creative Data Recovery, Inc, casting a glare on the computer screen that made it hard to see. The kid working the computer didn't seem to notice, though. He was one of the best hackers in the business, and Al had hired him to set up a pipeline into the Pennsylvania Transfer Corporation's server. And half of what Caughlan wanted was right there, it was just a matter of looking for it. But Caughlan's in the shipping business, Al thought, he's worried about how much he's paying for fuel, he's worried about his accounts receivable, he's trying to decide how many legs he's gonna have to break to get his next labor agreement done, he doesn't have time to pore through piles of paperwork.

Alessandra had the time. All you gotta do, she told herself, is ignore that pounding hangover, and quit replaying last night over and over again. He was a big boy, he walked into it with his eyes open. Pay attention to business.

Still . . .

Anyway, thank God for computers, because it meant she could sit in the relative safety of this office and sift through the documents generated by Caughlan's freight company. And she could do it anonymously. She hadn't told anyone about this, so whoever the turncoat at Penn Transfer was, they'd have no way of knowing what she was looking at.

It was a simple system, once you figured it out. Call up a shipping contract, it was tied to a customer number. The customer number was tied to a bill of lading, which was tied to a delivery confirmation, which was tied to an invoice, which was tied to an entry in Caughlan's accounts receivable file. When a check covering the invoice came in, it was tagged to a specific invoice or group of invoices and dropped out of accounts receivable and into old business. Beautiful system.

Anyhow, that's how the hacker explained it. "Look, babe, it's simple. All of their customer numbers have six digits, okay? But every so often there's one with seven. The seventh digit is always a zero, and that zero triggers a subroutine in their program that buries the transaction. So what happens is the bill of lading prints out, the driver gets his orders, but there's no contract, no invoice, no tag to accounts receivable. After the bill of lading prints out, the file drops out of memory, so there's no record of delivery, and there's no address, not on the hard drive. There might be a paper copy of the original bill of lading sitting in a box somewhere, but there's no real reason to dig through all the paper after the freight has been moved. Even if there's some kinda audit, nobody's gonna find this unless they know exactly what they're looking for."

Alessandra was more interested in the human side of the equation. "So if I understand this correctly, someone inside Penn Trans had to modify the program to set this up, am I right? And someone on the inside, probably the same person, is entering these seven-digit customer numbers to generate these phantom transactions." And that's how the morphine base moves out of

Port Newark, onto Caughlan's trucks, and off to the next stop in the chain, probably a lab or a warehouse.

"Not necessarily. Nobody capable of this kind of hack is going to sit in some shipping office. They could have done it remotely, the same way we're doing this now." The kid scowled. "These phantom shipments, do you know how valuable they are? Do you know what the actual freight is? Is it worth a lot of money?"

Al nodded. "Yeah." She didn't want to say more than that, and the kid probably didn't want to know.

"Then it's a good bet they won't just generate the bill of lading and hope it gets where it's supposed to go. Too many things could go wrong with that. They probably have an inside guy to babysit the transaction. Could be anybody in the place, could be one of the office girls who answer the phones—all she'd have to do is grab the bill of lading and walk it over to the right driver. If we're talking a lot of money here, there's no way they'd take the chance their merchandise could wind up sitting on a loading dock someplace. Know what I'm saying?"

"Yeah." Office girls, she thought, what are you, the Boy Wonder? Just then the pain in her head spiked. Leave it alone, she told herself. It means nothing. "Listen, can you make this thing send me a copy of the bill of lading the next time it sees one of these seven-digit customer numbers?"

The kid looked up at her. "You sure you want your e-mail address sitting on this server? They'd follow it right back to you, man. But I can get you what you want." He turned back to his keyboard. "Take me a couple of hours to put it together. Okay, we'll make the seventh digit of the customer number trigger two things: it'll post a copy of the bill of lading on the Web, and it'll activate a spam program. We'll buy a list of, like, ten thousand addresses, and we'll spam them all, including you, with what? Frederick's of Hollywood? That sound okay?"

"Why not," Al told him. She gave him Marty's e-mail address.

"Okay. We better make it a hundred thousand addresses. So when you see the e-mail from Fred's Poon and Titty Emporium, just go to this address I'll give you, and you'll see the bill of lading. Ought to give you the freight pickup and the destination. That work?"

"Beautiful thing," Al said.

She was a compact woman, almost a head shorter than Al, but she had an undeniable presence, she took over the room when she walked through the door. Her fiery red hair was streaked with blond, her face movie-star perfect, her teeth porcelain white. She didn't smile, though, when Al rose to shake her hand.

"Alessandra Martillo."

"Thank you for coming, Alessandra." Shine didn't introduce herself. When you are the pop diva of the moment, Al thought, there's really no need. They were in the sitting room of a suite at the Lucerne, an upscale Upper West Side Manhattan hotel. Shine glanced around the room. "Relax," she said to Alessandra. "Have a seat. Can I get something sent up for you? You want a drink or something?"

"No, I'm fine," Al told her. Irish, she thought. Shine still had a pretty good accent, it came through in her speech much stronger than in her singing. Al watched as Shine paced across the room, stopping to close the blinds, shutting out the million-dollar view of the Hudson River. She picked up the remote and clicked on the television.

"Background noise," she said.

"You okay? You seem nervous."

Shine shook her head. "Nah, I'm all right," she said. "I just got a lot on my mind. Last week we caught one of my assistants photocopying some of my private papers. Legal shit, itineraries, scripts, contracts, stuff like that. I had to let her go. But now I can't stop thinking about bugs and camcorders and all the people I thought were on my side. Especially when I wanna have a private conversation. Like now."

"Your assistant. Who was she feeding stuff to?"

"I think it was that son of a bitch, Benson."

"Rod Benson? The guy from the *SoCal Insider*?"

Shine nodded. "He swears it wasn't him, but that's exactly how he operates. Look through your trash, pay off your driver, any slimy, scummy thing he can think of."

"But you still talk to the guy."

"Yeah. Yeah, I know. Stupid, right? But it discourages the rest of them if they think they can't get anything on me that Benson doesn't already have. Look, I don't like doing it, and I don't like him, but it's the cost of doing business." She continued her circuit around the room. She stopped, picked up the house phone, stared at it, put it back down.

"You're not gonna be able to talk in here, are you?"

Shine shook her head. "I'm about to 'what-if' myself right into the nuthouse."

Al stood up. "Come with me," she said.

Shine looked at her for a moment, then nodded. "All right," she said.

"The roof! What made you think of it?" The two of them climbed up the ladder at the top of the stairwell, stepped through a hatch, and out onto the black rubber surface.

"When I was thirteen," Al told her, "there was this old factory building in Brownsville. I used to sneak in through the loading dock when nobody was watching and climb the stairs all the way up. They had a machine room up on top of the building—it was where the freight elevator motors and stuff were. The walls and the ceiling were all glass." They walked across the roof, leaned on the parapet wall, looked south over the hazy Manhattan sky. "It stayed pretty warm in there, too, even in the winter. You could see all the way out to the East River bridges." She could see them now, antiquated spidery creatures of stone and steel, way off in the distance.

"Your mom didn't worry about you going places like that?"

Al turned and looked at Shine, remembered her mother's gray and lifeless face pressed to the kitchen floor. "No," she said. "What can I do for you?"

"For me? Nothing."

"What, then?"

Shine's face went dark. "I wanna talk about Willy Caughlan."

Willy again, Al thought. This kid's name just keeps coming up . . . "Okay."

"I know you're working for his father."

"Rod Benson tell you that?"

She nodded. "He gave me your phone number."

"I should just post it on the Web somewhere."

"You might as well. Listen, it's none of my business what you're doing for Willy's dad, okay? But I'm here to tell you that Willy did not OD. He was not a user. He didn't even drink beer, for crissake. Somebody killed him."

"Someone held him down and shot him up?"

"Hey, I didn't say I knew how they did it!" Shine flared in sudden anger. "But I swear to God, Willy did not knowingly put a drug into his body!" She turned away, heaved a deep breath, wiped at her face. "Someone killed him, I don't care what anybody says."

"You don't know how they did it. Fair enough. Any idea why?"

Shine turned to face Al. Her hands were shaking. "No," she said.

"You sure? You think it might have had something to do with that video the two of you made?"

"I don't give a damn about that video, okay? And I don't know if Willy kept a copy, either. But Willy was a good kid, and if I ever find out who killed him, I swear to God I'll see them bleed for it."

"Gotcha." Al watched Shine's face for a moment. "Did you talk to the police about this?"

"Yes. They weren't interested."

"And you can't think of anybody who would want to hurt Willy? He didn't have any enemies?"

Shine thought for a moment. "Willy didn't have it like that," she said. "He wasn't a guy that you hated." She glanced at Alessandra. "I don't know anything about what you do. But to my mind, anybody who would kill another person has got to be pretty sick, and if you want to look for sick people, the industry is a pretty good place to start."

"The music industry?"

"Yes."

"Technically," Al said, "I'm not really supposed to be looking into Willy Caughlan at all. I mean, I suppose I have a certain amount of leeway, but . . ."

"Quit," Shine said. "Come and work for me. I can make it worth your while."

"I can't do that. Not in the middle of a job."

Shine stared at the ground. "Willy was a good boy," she said after a minute. "He never . . . He didn't have anybody to stand up for him, he never had anybody to watch out for him." She swallowed noisily. "I never thought I'd lose him so quick. We were just starting, he and I . . . Look, I understand if you don't wanna, you know, drop everything and come do this for me. But can you—" She stopped, stared at Al. "Willy wasn't like everybody else. He was good. Couldn't you just . . ."

"I can't promise you anything."

"I'm not asking for promises. It's just that Willy . . . he was . . ." Al watched as Shine's face crumpled. Shine turned away, covered her face with her hands, and seemed to withdraw into herself, becoming smaller as her whole body began to shake. After a minute or two, she pulled herself together. She stood more erect, but didn't turn to face Alessandra. "I tried to talk to his father, but he was too mad. He called me a drug addict and hung up on me. But once he's in his right mind, wouldn't he want to know what really happened to his own son?"

"You would think so," Al said.

"BandX is playing this club tonight up in Boston," Shine said. "You could go and talk to them. You could tell them you work for me—they'd kiss your ass, believe me. It would only take a day . . ."

The kid's life ought to be worth a day, Al thought. "All right."

Shine exhaled as though she'd been holding her breath during the entire conversation. "Thank you," she said. "Let's go back downstairs. I'll have my assistant give you the club address and time and all that. My new assistant . . ." She still didn't look at Al, she just walked over to the open roof hatch and climbed down.

"Goddammit, Al, how come you never answer your fuckin' phone?" Stiles was definitely cranked.

"I don't leave it on all the time. All you hadda do was leave a message."

"Yeah, sure, and you'd ignore it until you felt good and ready to call me back. Dammit, Al, if you're still working for me, you gotta stay in touch. I was about ready . . ."

"Relax, Marty. I been working here."

"Oh really? Gimme what you got."

Yeah, sure . . . "All right." She told him how someone had hacked Penn Transfer's computer to set up the dummy pick-ups. "So, theoretically, all we gotta do is wait until the next pickup, then follow the truck. That sounds like something in your department."

"Oh, what is this? Now I'm working for you? You giving me orders now?"

"Okay, forget it, Marty, I'll do everything."

"All right, all right. Frederick's of Hollywood. And all I gotta do is click on the link?"

"Yeah. If you have any problems with it, just give me a call. Oh, and one other thing."

"What?"

"Someone had a go at Gearoid and me the other night."

"Who? You and who?"

"Gearoid O'Hagan. He's kinda like Caughlan's boy Friday. He's this Irish guy . . ."

"No shit. Really?"

"You wanna hear about this or not?"

"Go on, Jesus Christ, don't be so goddamn touchy."

Alessandra took a breath, counted to ten. "Okay. Three guys in a gypsy cab . . ." She told him about the assault and the aftermath.

"So you didn't find out who they were working for?"

"No. What bothers me is that they were onto me so fast."

"Yeah. Well, whoever's behind this, they ain't gonna give up now, so watch your back. And next time, see if you can find out something useful, how about that?"

"Not my fault the cops showed up so quick."

"Yeah." He didn't sound convinced. "I know some guys on the job in the Bronx. I'll make a few calls. Maybe they'll know who those guys were. Sounds like at least one of those mutts hadda go to the hospital. Plus, there's gotta be an accident report."

"While you're getting police reports . . ."

"Yeah? Now what?"

"Why don't you see what you can get me on Sean William Caughlan's death?"

"You're wasting your time."

"How can you be sure?"

"Okay, you're wasting my time, how about that? And you're gonna piss off my client. Leave it the fuck alone."

"Tell you what. I want the tox reports on what they found in his blood. You get me what you can, we'll sit down and look at it together. You still think there's nothing there, I'll drop it."

He knows I'm lying, she thought, but she waited him out. "All right," he finally said. "Just don't bring it up with Mickey, all right? The guy feels bad enough about this as it is."

"You think so? I'm not sure about that. Seems to me he just wants to turn the page and forget about Willy altogether."

"Whatever. Don't bring it up around Mickey."

"All right."

"What's next?"

A club date in Boston, but Al was not about to tell him that. "I gotta take the afternoon off. My cousin up in Massachusetts just had a baby."

"Jesus Christ, Martillo! You are unfuckingbelievable! Do you gotta go right now? The fuckin' kid ain't going anywhere, am I right? This isn't the time . . ."

"Calm down. I'm just gonna drive up this afternoon, see the baby, drive right back. One day, what the hell's the difference?"

"Goddammit, Martillo, last time you said you were taking a day off, you wound up staying in Puerto Rico for two fuckin' weeks!"

"That was different. I'll be back tomorrow, I promise."

"I don't know how anybody could be more annoying than my goddamn ex-wife, but you're coming damn close, you know that?"

"You're a really sweet guy, Stiles."

He hung up on her.

She decided to stop in Manhattan and take a look at Willy Caughlan's apartment. It took a half hour to find a parking spot on the street, but no way was she going to spring twenty-five bucks to put the van in a garage.

Tudor City is a tiny enclave on the East River, just south of the United Nations. The buildings there are all done in Tudor style, hence the name, but the real interesting thing about the place is how it feels cut off from the rest of the island of Manhattan. You walk in here, Al thought, it's like you've taken a step out of time, somehow, and put yourself in some quieter and more civilized New York City than the one you're used to.

Imagine that, she thought, feeling a pang of jealousy as she stuck Willy's key in the front door of his building. What must it be like to have an old man who would get you an apartment in a place like this, just to be sure you had a safe place to sleep? She wondered what her father would do if he had Caughlan's money. Probably nothing, she thought. Probably let it molder away in some bank, probably go on and live the exact same life. She did not understand the man. You're not going to figure him out, she told herself for possibly the millionth time. Leave him alone.

Anyhow, she thought, you couldn't just change one thing, you'd have to take the whole package. What would it be like to have a father like Daniel Caughlan? Could you stand to have someone like him looking over your shoulder? It did seem a shame, though, how willing he was to bury his son and move on. Families aren't supposed to be like this, she thought. They're supposed to be on your side. Aren't they?

She rang the super's bell, told him she was Caughlan's real estate agent and needed a key to the apartment. He looked doubtful until a fifty-dollar bill reassured him.

A little old lady was struggling down the hallway, wrestling with an aluminum walker. "Let me get out of your way," she said when she noticed Alessandra behind her. "You go ahead. Are you new here? I haven't seen you before. Or have I? I don't remember so good anymore."

"Take your time," Al told her. "I don't live here. I work for Mr. Caughlan, the guy that owns 4D." The words tasted strange in her mouth, made stranger still by the fact that they were true.

"Willy's father?" The old lady stopped and turned to look

up at Al, her face gray. "My God. He was just a boy. He didn't even shave regular yet. I used to tease him about it. I used to tell him he could put some cream on his chin and let my cat lick his whiskers off."

"Did you know Willy?"

"He was just a boy. I don't think he was even twenty yet. My God . . ."

"Did he have a lot of people over? Make a lot of noise? Things like that?"

"Honey, when I turn off my hearing aids, you could play the tuba in my kitchen and I'd never hear it. But no, he never gave no trouble. When he practiced his music, he had a gizmo with headphones. I could never hear him. He used to play for me sometimes, though. Can you believe that? A boy like him, hanging around an old lady like me. But he didn't have no friends. Not that I ever seen."

"Didn't have people over?"

"No. Well, once in a while this man would come by, but he tried to boss Willy around. You could hear it in his voice. My second husband was like that, he thought he knew what everybody should do, every minute of the day. The son of a bitch. Pardon my French, honey. But men can be like that. You tell yourself how good they are, but they generally turn out to be nothing but a pain in the ass."

"That sounds like the voice of experience. Do you remember what this guy looked like? The one who used to visit Willy."

"Tall," the old lady told her, one hand fluttering in the air up over her head. "That's all I remember."

"Oh. Well, thank you very much. Willy's father will be glad to hear that Willy was happy here."

"I never said he was happy. You should have heard the stuff he played on that guitar. So sad, it would make you cry. He would never play nothing regular. I offered him fifty bucks once if he would play 'Won't You Come Home, Bill Bailey,' but he wouldn't do it." She took a couple of steps down the hall. "You wanna know what Willy's problem was? He didn't have nobody. All he had was that guitar. And it wasn't enough."

It was a beautiful studio, but it was a boy's room. It seemed to have been left untouched since the police finished their investigation. Dirty clothes were strewn across a hardwood floor. There was a tall loft bed with a built-in desk and bookcase underneath, piled with comic books and *Playboy* magazines. The stainless steel appliances in the modern kitchen looked like they had never been cleaned, and the sink was piled with dirty dishes, dry, now, and dusty. The spot on the floor where they'd found Willy was outlined with black tape. A Gibson semi-acoustic and a Fender Strat leaned in a corner. A Martin acoustic lay on the floor nearby. There was a black carry-on suitcase–sized amplifier near the guitars, a snarl of wires attached.

Spoiled kid, Al thought. She could hear her father's voice in her head, yapping about messiness indicating a lack of character. It was a grating voice and a familiar speech, usually delivered via long-distance telephone, but she didn't know if she really disagreed with it.

Printer on a shelf, blank spot on the desk below where the laptop had been. She wondered if the cops had taken it. She looked carefully at the old wooden double-hung windows. The one in the bath looked like someone had tried to pry it open, but that must have been a generation ago, and the scars in the wood were thick with paint. The front door and the jamb were solid, too, showing little of the damage inflicted on the apartment doors Al had grown up behind.

Suppose Shine is right, she thought. If someone did kill Willy Caughlan, they walked right into this place. Either they had a key, or Willy let them in.

Al called O'Hagan's cell.

"It's Alessandra," she said when he answered.

"I know," he said. "You think I'd be after forgetting you already?"

"Do the police have Willy's computer?"

Silence for a moment, then: "I don't know. You want it?"

"Yeah," she said. "Can you get it back?"

"I'll get right on it," he said.

"Did Willy have a cleaning lady?"

"No. Not unless he paid her himself, which ain't likely. You making any progress?"

"Hard to tell. But do me a favor, okay? I don't want to have to answer a lot of asshole questions about why I'm interested in Willy, so keep this between you and me if you can."

"Not a problem. But can I ask? Why are you interested in Willy?"

Because he didn't have anyone to look out for him . . . "I don't know," she said. "Call it a hunch."

"Ah. Woman's intuition, huh? Well, don't worry, I know how to keep me mouth shut."

"That's a useful skill," she told him. "Thanks."

Ten

The place looked like a slightly overgrown movie theater from the days before multiplexes, with a broad stage where there would have been one big screen. It had a big balcony, room for about six or seven hundred seats. Al parked the Astro around the corner and stretched the kinks out of her back. It had been a four and a half hour drive, and the Astro's front seat had only been comfortable for about half of that. The front door was open, there didn't seem to be any security, so she wandered in. The interior was dark except for some dim lighting on the stage, the red EXIT signs in the corners, and the daylight filtering in through the open entrance behind her. She walked about a third of the way down one of the aisles and took a seat. She guessed the members of BandX were doing a sound check, although the only sounds she heard were the bickering voices of the guys on the stage. A tall, athletic-looking guy with long orange-blond hair sounded particularly upset. He unclipped the strap that suspended his guitar from his shoulders and let the instrument drop to the floor with a loud clang. "No way, man," he said, after the electrically amplified protest from the guitar faded away. "I don't wanna fuckin' hear it. Where was you, huh?

Where was you when we needed you?" He advanced on a shorter, thinner, dark-haired guy who was holding a guitar. "You was fuckin' wasted, man, you hung the rest of us out to fuckin' dry. So now you don't like the new shit, that's too bad, fuck you, 'cause when we was writing it, you was locked up in Shaky Acres or some shit, drying out. So don't fuckin' start, okay?"

"Trent." A third man put a hand on the orange-blond guitarist, holding him back. Al assumed the new guy was the singer, because he wasn't carrying an instrument, and he was better looking than the other two, with chiseled features and theatrically curly blond hair. "I thought we talked about this, Trent."

"He needs to hear this, Cliff. He's back pulling the same shit just like nothing ever happened."

"Excuse me." A guy stood in the aisle next to Alessandra, bent over, his voice low.

"S'up?" She ignored the guy, trying to concentrate on the argument up on stage. The dark-haired guitar player's sand-papered voice was harder to hear than the other two. "You asked me," he said. "You want me to lie? Fine, I'll lie to you. It's a great riff, man. It's classic. It's gonna make you rich. Okay? You happy now?"

"Excuse me." Al finally looked over at the guy in the aisle. He was young, maybe early twenties, clean shaven, short black hair, watery blue eyes, minty breath. His suede jacket looked like it cost more than her entire wardrobe. "Ahh, who are you, please? 'Cause I'm not sure you're supposed to be here? This session is not open to the public."

"Throw me out," Al told him. Cliff, the singer, was still trying to reason with Trent, who seemed to have a limited appetite for it. Al decided not to use Shine's name. She wanted to keep a lower profile. "I'm with Knight Ridder."

"The newspaper chain?" The guy's demeanor changed immediately. "Really? No kidding?" He took a step and sat down in the seat in front of Alessandra, half-turned so that he could keep one eye on the stage and one on her. "I'm Sandy Ellison, A&R for Gemini Records." He stuck a hand over the seat at her. She shook it briefly, sensing the tremor in Ellison's grip. He was bobbing up and down in the seat, and one of his knees twitched spasmodically. Coke-head, she thought.

"Hi," she said, not giving him a name, guessing that he wouldn't care. She was right, he didn't appear to notice. If the dude ran into you tomorrow, she thought, he'd never remember you at all.

"Knight Ridder." He repeated the words to himself. "Wow. You a stringer or you on staff?"

"I was on staff, Sandy, I wouldn't be sitting here. My ass would be in a nice comfy chair in an office somewhere, and we'd be having this conversation on the phone."

Ellison snorted. "I hear ya, baby. I hear ya. Ya wanna make the big time, ya gotta do the footwork. How'd you hear about us? From me to you, okay, BandX is gonna hit it, and soon. We ain't talking flavor of the week, either. These guys are gonna be huge."

"That's what I hear, Sandy. They fight like this all the time?"

"This is nothing." He dismissed the current disagreement with a wave of his hand. "Creative differences. Great ideas germinate best in the midst of chaos, under pressure. Take away the pressure and the chaos, these guys would sound just like every other band out there trying to make it. But they don't, okay? These guys are unbelievable. And what you're seeing down there is a necessary part of the process. Don't hold it against them."

This kid's a natural, she thought, except for that Jimmy

Swaggart thing he gets in his voice when he's trying to sell you. He loses that, he'll be great.

"No matter what anybody else tells you," he said, "just remember this one thing, okay? It's all about the music. Nothing else matters. It's all about the sound. So, what have you got in mind here? How can I help you?"

How about shutting the hell up and letting me listen, Al thought, but she didn't say it. Talk like a reporter, give this guy the same line of shit he'd give you, she told herself, if your positions were reversed. "Well, Sandy, this might be old news to you, but I think there's a story here. Maybe you see it all the time, but to my readers, this is a snapshot of the New American Dream. A bunch of very talented people bucking the odds, chasing the big one, and paying a big price for it. Hanging in there, fighting obscurity while lesser artists make it. And you know, the arbitrary nature of success, the struggle to be heard—let alone appreciated—all of that, but still knowing all along that one phone call or one gig at the right time can change everything. You with me?"

"Yeah, oh, absolutely."

"It's gotta be hell, thinking you could catch on fire tomorrow, or you could waste away like a million other bands. I can't imagine paying dues like these guys do." A dozen rows down, a guy Alessandra hadn't noticed was sitting at a darkened console. He was wearing headphones, but he must have overheard the conversation, because she could just make out his face in profile as he turned and looked her way. "BandX has a huge opportunity coming up, did I hear that right? And look at what they've been through in the last year. Discord threatening to tear the band apart. Death of a young and promising artist, then the return of the prodigal guitar player. How many years have these guys been riding in buses, trying to make this happen? Working dead-end jobs, living in dumps, playing club dates all over the place, not even making gas money. And then maybe, just maybe, they catch the right break, they play in front of the right crowd, or maybe even just that one right person—it could all pay off. So tell me: do you think they can make it?"

"Oh, hell yes." It sounded like real conviction. "Wait until you hear these guys. God, they've got a sound, I'm telling you, it's what rock and roll has always been about. It's like, stripped, it's like, skin and bones, babe. These guys are the shit, man. Like, if you brought back a caveman from a hundred thousand years ago, okay, and he caught BandX on a good night, okay, he would dig it. He would get it, you know what I mean, he would fucking feel it. That's what these guys have got. It's the music, babe, it's all about the music. When you hear them, you'll understand, believe me. Sometimes I think you could take a deaf man, never heard a sound in his life, you could stand him in front of the amps and he'd be able to, like, just feel the shit coming up through the floor, he could sense it coming at him through the air . . ." His voice drifted off as he contemplated the profundity of the concept.

"So which one of them is the guy?"

He closed his mouth, came back down to earth, and looked back at her. "Which one of them is what guy?"

"Come on, you know what I mean. Which one of those guys down there gives BandX that elemental sound? That raw, naked edge? Because there are musicians, right, then there are the guys who just have it. You know what I'm saying."

He turned away from her, stared down at the stage for a minute. "You must know the answer to that already," he said, "or else you wouldn't have asked the question."

"Should I ask about their favorite colors instead? Come on, Ellison, give it up. I wanna hear it from you."

He nodded. "It's TJ," he said.

"TJ Conrad. The prodigal guitarist."

"Yeah."

"He's the one who was in rehab. How was the kid who was standing in for him?"

"He was okay. I mean, it was tragic and everything, and the kid could play, okay, but TJ's like, I don't know, he's like the fucking Rosetta Stone." A distant sound of coughing filtered up from the guy at the console, but Ellison ignored it. "Everything gets filtered through him. What makes it tough is that the other guys don't always understand what TJ's doing. Because he doesn't write much. He doesn't put a lot in. He takes things out. His favorite thing is, like, 'too many notes.' And then he like, peels it away, he strips it back until they've got that thing you were talking about, that raw, naked thing that everybody on this planet can feel. I mean, I was all broken up about that other kid, believe me. But BandX needs TJ. He's what makes them special."

Down below them on the stage, the voices were getting louder and more strident. The guy at the console took off his headphones, stood up and stretched, then leaned over and spoke into a microphone. "Take five, everybody," he said, his amplified voice booming throughout the nearly empty theater, and he walked up the aisle, past Ellison and Alessandra, and out through the door. The musicians resumed their argument in somewhat softer tones. Ellison watched them, his knee bouncing.

"I gotta go," he said. "I gotta go say something. Listen, I'll get you backstage, I'll get everyone to talk to you. I mean, I'll take care of you, I'll get you hooked up, okay? Anything you need." He stood up and jittered down the aisle. "Guys . . ."

Alessandra had been hearing lines like that just about as far back as she could remember. Another guy, promising to watch out for her. *Oh, yeah, baby, don't you worry about anything, you just give me what I want and I'll make everything go down so good . . .* It made the hair stand up on the back of her neck. She stood up and walked out.

"You buying that bullshit Ellison was peddling?" He was a thin, pale bone of a man, medium height, long gray hair parted in the middle and hanging down over both sides of his face, making his sharp beak of a nose seem even larger than it was. Looked like Jeff Beck, or maybe Cousin Itt. Alessandra had been thinking about a cup of coffee. The guy was leaning against a column, smoking a cigarette. She stopped, regarded him without expression.

"I'm sorry?"

"Come on," he said. "I had a nickel for every time I heard a line of shit like that, I could retire. Makes me want to hurl." He pushed himself away from the column, held out a knobby hand. The back of it was veined and spotted. "Luke Rushton," he said.

"Nice to meet you, Luke," she said, shaking his hand. "You were the guy inside, right? With the headphones."

"That was me," he said. "Soundman extraordinaire. Not that anyone gives a shit about sound anymore. At your service."

"I was gonna get some coffee, Luke. You want?"

"No," he said. "But you can buy me a bourbon. I know just the place."

Rushton held the door for Alessandra, waved her in with a gallant flourish, then chuckled to himself as she preceded him inside. It was a dark place, pseudo-Spanish décor, heavy wood, wrought iron, crimson vinyl booths along one wall, bar along the other, empty tables in between. There was a restaurant attached. Al could hear voices, the clink of cutlery, and the reek of stale pastrami was inescapable. The bar, however, was empty. She picked a table in the middle of the floor, her survivor's instinct fully alert. Rushton left her there and went off to order drinks. He brought them back, set her coffee down in front of her, cradled his bourbon lovingly. He shook the hair back out of his face and in the dim light, the folds, creases, and lines bracketing his mouth gave him the arid and bitter look of a man facing too much ill-tasting medicine. He drank his bourbon at the same speed and to the same apparent effect as she drank her coffee, which is to say, none at all.

"So?" she said.

"The biggest lie," he said, "is a good place to start." Even his half-smile was acrid, with a touch of anger. "'It's all about the music,' isn't that what Ellison kept saying? That's so pathetic, it's almost funny. What is going on with BandX has, really, nothing to do with their 'sound.' Nothing at all. At this point, it makes no difference to anyone what they 'sound' like."

"Apparently they got enough talent to fill that theater tonight. So if it isn't talent that's gotten them this far, what is it?"

"I didn't say they weren't talented," he said. "I just said that their 'sound' had nothing to do with their success. Listen, let me tell you how this business really works, okay? It's a little like baseball. You take the Yankees, or the Red Sox. God only knows how much money those teams pull in, even after paying million-dollar salaries to the GM and the manager and the guys on the field. But they have to keep it going, right? They have to keep looking for the next Manny Ramirez and Mariano Rivera, because they're using up the ones they got as fast as they can. So they have this minor league system, which they lose money on, but they don't care about that. They'll employ hundreds of ballplayers just so they can find the two or three that will make the whole thing pay off. Because it isn't about the game, you know what I mean? It's never about the game."

"You don't have to be able to sing," she said. "Or play an instrument."

"Please," he said, pity heavy in his voice. "Do you honestly think that what you hear coming out of your radio has anything more than a distant relationship to what musicians actually do?"

"Well," she said, "I know that there are things you can do in a studio . . ."

He was shaking his head. "It's all technology," he said. "None of it is any more real than a video game. For every sound, okay, for every instrument, for every chord, tinkle, thump, cough, and fart you hear on a recording, there's an engineer running a program. You don't need a drummer, you haven't needed a drummer in, Christ, twenty-five years, you don't even need a drum machine anymore. For years now, drummers have just been guys who like to hang with musicians. But now you don't need the rest of them, either. Every possible sound that a guitar can make—or a piano or an organ, or a human throat—every one of them has been digitized, cataloged, stored, bought, sold, racked up like books in a library. You want to use one, you find it, you make a copy of the part you want, and you plug it in."

"Has it really gone that far? When I hear my favorite singer . . ."

"Maybe she sat in a studio for an afternoon," he said. "Okay, yeah, she sang the tune. But her voice didn't wind up on a tape. It wound up stored in a computer. On a screen, it's represented by a graph." His fingers danced in the air, following an imaginary chart. "You can pinpoint exactly where your singer was off-key, or late, or shrill, or whatever, right there on the screen. So the only person whose talent actually counts for anything, which would be the recording engineer, he runs Auto-Tune, or one of a dozen programs just like it, and he repositions the graph. For lack of a better term, he moves the notes around on the screen until they're all exactly where he thinks they ought to be. And when he's done, the singer is dead-on, the guitar player bends the note just so, the drummer and the base player and everybody else nails it clean and perfect before a single one of them has even done their first line of coke for the day, let alone showed up and actually played something."

"So when they go up on stage . . ."

"They play behind recordings," he said. "Or sometimes they've actually learned to play an approximation of what the engineers have manufactured for them."

"So BandX," Al said. "Is that what they do? Because all that technology and engineering sounds expensive as hell, and they don't look like they've got the money."

"Ah, but they're under contract now," he said. "They might not know it yet, but they've become part of the machine. They've been signed up for the full treatment, and baby, they're gonna get it. It ain't gonna be about five guys kicking it, not anymore. It'll be all about the fucking producers, the fucking hit doctors, the fucking computers, the fucking A&R douche bags like Ellison, the fucking publicity men, and all that shit. And it won't have a goddamn thing to do with what you'll hear these guys doing tonight."

"Well, if that's true, why did BandX get picked? What's the criteria?"

"Criteria?" he snorted. "There isn't any criteria. The record company just keeps throwing shit against the wall, hoping that some of it will stick. They make so much money off of one *Don Henley's Greatest Hits* or some goddamn thing, they can afford to bankroll a thousand acts like BandX, and you can bet your last nickel that nobody at corporate has listened to ten seconds of music from any of them. There's a hundred guys like Ellison, arrogant little pricks with an MBA from Wharton and a coke habit, and every one of them is out here hustling."

"Looking for the next Manny Ramirez."

"You got it. Nobody gets a recording contract because they're any good. They get it because Ellison's boss owes him a favor, or because it's his turn, or maybe the guy wants to give Ellison enough rope to hang himself. So BandX becomes a part of this season's bucketload, and they'll get thrown up against the wall along with the other fortunate few. And maybe they'll stick and maybe they won't, but either way, it won't have a goddamn thing to do with whether or not they're any good. Success in this business is a crapshoot, nothing more. Nothing ain't got nothing to do with nothing."

"Okay. I don't quite know how to ask this, Luke, I mean, it seems like an obvious question . . ."

He looked at her. "What am I doing here?"

She nodded. "Yeah."

He shook his head. "I ask myself that almost every day. But I been in this business ever since I was in high school, and believe me, that was a lotta years ago. This is all I know. Shit, I remember back when it really was all about the music." He glanced over at her. "Back before you were born. It was great for a while. I was in a lot of bands you never heard of. A couple of times, I came close, Jesus, we almost . . ." He shook his head. "Almost don't count."

"You could do something else if you really wanted to," she said.

"Maybe," he said. "But not for long. No matter how much this sucks, no matter how lousy the money gets, I still can't see myself anywhere else."

"Back to BandX," she said. "Is it true, what I hear about them opening for Shine, at her concerts in Jones Beach?"

He nodded. "So far. I thought that was gonna go by the wayside when Willy C got whacked, but as far as I know it's still on."

"Is that a big deal? Could it do something for BandX?"

"Ahh, who knows. It ain't gonna make them any money, that's for goddamn sure."

"Why not?"

"Well, God's manager . . ."

"You lost me. God? Who's God?"

He looked up from his bourbon and grinned. "Shine, aka God. You don't think she's a mere mortal, do you? She lives in a different universe than you and me. Anyhow, her manager cuts a deal with whoever is gonna do the openers. I mean, it ain't just him, that's the way these things usually work. He'll say, 'Look, you guys can open if you pick up tour expenses,' or something like that."

"So it's 'pay to play.' "

"Same old shit. God makes a hundred and fifty, two hundred grand per show, BandX makes five hundred bucks. But they get to play for a whole new audience that never heard of them before, and maybe they'll hawk some T-shirts and CDs and shit. If they're lucky, they'll break even. That's the theory, anyhow. In practice, half the audience will be out in the parking lot smoking dope until BandX finishes their set."

"So if I get this right, Shine's manager calls up BandX's manager, and . . ."

"Usually. That ain't how it went down this time, though."

"No? How did it happen this time?"

"Well, what I was told was that Willy C was sleeping with God, and God decided she was gonna take care of Willy C, and by extension, BandX."

"Is that true?"

He shrugged. "That was the rumor. Willy would never say. He even got some love from the tabs, but he would never give them anything. Didn't matter, they just took his picture and printed what they wanted. Anyhow, that was what was supposedly behind the Jones Beach gigs, and all the buzz about BandX."

"You mean it really wasn't all about the music?"

He laughed, sounding unnaturally loud in the empty room. "Shit," he said. "I gotta get back. Come on back and hang out, I'll get you a good ticket and a backstage pass. I might not be good for much, but I can still swing that. That douche bag Ellison has probably forgotten all about you already."

"Story of my life," she said. "Thanks, Luke."

He shook his head. "Nothing to it."

BandX was actually playing when she got back, making music. She had expected generic white-boy rock and roll—overproduced, overamped, and overwrought—but BandX was much better than that. Ellison, it seemed, had not been entirely full of shit. The band was doing more with less than just about any other act she could think of. She couldn't make out any of the vocals at all, but that probably didn't matter a hell of a lot. Cliff, the lead singer, had a voice with enough weight and timbre to reach right past her logical mind and deliver its emotional freight to the most primitive parts of her brain, the parts that didn't need words. Maybe she couldn't hear what he was saying, but she knew what he meant . . .

She found herself liking Willy Caughlan a little better. Maybe he had been a spoiled rich white boy, but he had tagged the diva of the moment and he'd kept his mouth shut about it. He'd had some class. But had Willy gotten too close to the fierce heat of celebrity? The potentially toxic mixture of sex, money, and notoriety had a long list of deadly side effects. When you already have your hands on everything in life that Madison Avenue teaches you to want, how hard would it be to run across someone who would lash out at you, either from envy or greed?

The song they were playing faded away. Sandy Ellison stood down at the stage apron, applauding loudly. "Goddamn!" he shouted. "God, that was hot! Goddamn!" Cliff, the lead singer, glanced at Ellison, then turned his back as the drummer counted off and BandX launched into their next tune. Maybe these guys will make it, Alessandra thought. If the music counts for anything . . .

Eleven

The radio in the van didn't work.

Maybe it's just as well, Al told herself. You've had enough music for a while. She was still rattled from the sensory overload that was BandX in full cry. They had played at a volume just short of her pain threshold, but it had been as good a show as she'd ever heard. The music, almost a physical sensation, had washed over her in waves. Her seat had been about twenty rows back, just left of center. The people around her had risen to their feet almost as soon as the concert began, and had remained standing the rest of the night. She stood as well, peering around taller bodies to try to get a sense of what was happening on the stage. TJ Conrad was obviously the band's leader, even though he tended to stay out of center stage, letting Trent, the second guitarist, take most of the flashier solos.

She ignored the reek of marijuana and the chemical stink of crack that floated past. She herself was far too paranoid to surrender even partial control of herself, particularly in a public space, surrounded by people she didn't know. She shook her head at the courage or foolhardiness of those who chose to do so. As if, she thought, the sheer volume of BandX was not stupefying enough.

She'd thought about leaving for at least half of the three hours BandX was on stage, but she couldn't, they held her there, rapt. About halfway through, the band ripped into a bunch of old R&B covers, some of them classics, some of them obscure, all of them rendered with enough verve, soul, and cool to rival the originals. God, Al thought, these guys really are something else.

Toward the end of the concert, the crowd and the band went into their ritual mating dance, the musicians walking offstage, the people standing, clapping, and screaming until the band came back out, okay, a couple more, all right, this is it, really, okay, one more and then we really have to go . . . The house lights came up, finally, and that signaled the end of the show.

The ringing in Alessandra's ears was actually more of a hiss, but it was clearly audible over the drone of the Astro's engine and the waves of sound from the other cars and trucks as she drove south. A soft rain pebbled the windshield, smeared away rhythmically by the wipers. Funny, she thought, you put those five guys up on stage and they approached transcendence. See them afterward, what a bunch of jerks. It had taken her a while to make her way backstage after the show, just to find that the term "backstage" was a misnomer. Three of them, Cliff, the singer, Trent, the guitar player, and the drummer, whose name she did not know, were already in the tour bus, which was in the alley out back. It was a big, shiny chrome behemoth parked under a streetlight, lights out, big diesel grumbling. A guy stood on the bottom step of the bus, his hands held out for quiet. A group of maybe thirty females was gathered close, and the guy on the bus shook long blond hair back out of his face and thrust his chin forward. Dude looked like a soprano getting ready for her solo. "Ladies," he said, and they all fell silent at his feet. "Ladies . . ."

None of them had looked like ladies to Alessandra. To her, they looked like a bunch of fourteen- to sixteen-year-old suburban schoolgirls with a few older aunts mixed in. They were all what her father would call "dressed for the corner." It wasn't true—most of the streetwalkers Al had seen dressed far more modestly than these.

"Ladies," the man continued. "Nobody gets on the bus without ID. Okay? If you don't have ID, thanks for coming, have a great night, see ya. Next, if you don't want to have sex with the musicians, thanks for coming, have a great night, go on home. We're clear on this, right? Third, the carriage turns back into a pumpkin at one in the morning. That's when the bus leaves, so make sure you have transport home, because if you didn't get here on the bus, you aren't leaving on the bus. Okay?"

Al sensed a presence behind her, and she turned to see Rushton, the sound guy, at her elbow. He grimaced. "You believe they pay that creep more than they pay me?"

Al took a step back, putting a bit more distance between the scene at the bus door and herself. "This a normal occurrence?"

Rushton looked at the women. "BandX has played here a lot," he said, a little defensive. "They've got a following."

"This is like the zoo during rutting season," she told him. "I'm not gonna get anything here tonight."

"I should have warned you," he told her. "You probably could have went home hours ago. Except TJ and Doc, they ain't on the bus. I can get you in to see them." He grimaced.

"Doc won't be good for much, he's always bummed after a show. And TJ, well, he's TJ. But you can probably talk to him."

They actually had part of the place roped off.

It was a couple of steps up from the joint Rushton had taken her to earlier. This place was what was once called a nightclub, small stage on one side of the room, dove gray and pink décor, lots of tiny tables, mirrors everywhere, annoying lights that danced and flickered at odd angles. It was crowded and noisy, but there were only about a dozen characters behind the thick velvet rope. The only two that Alessandra recognized were TJ Conrad and Doc Jamison, the bass player. Doc, a black guy with a shaved head and dark glasses, was elbows down on a table in the far corner, and TJ was sitting across from him. A bouncer stepped up on the inside of the barricade when Rushton and Al approached. "Evening, Luke," the guy said. "She with you?"

"Hah," Rushton said, as though that were not even a remote possibility. "No, she's a reporter. TJ and Doc are gonna want to talk to her, believe me."

The bouncer shrugged. "Whatever you say." He stepped to one side, holding the barrier aside so the two of them could pass. TJ looked up as they approached his table, while Doc continued to stare into his drink. TJ shook his head.

"Beat it," he said. "Take her out to the bus. They're out in the alley. Nothing happening here." For a moment, Al thought about kicking TJ's chair out from beneath him, but she didn't. And why is it, she asked herself, why can't you be attracted to some nice, normal guy with a job? Why are you always drawn to jerks like this?

"Dude, she's a reporter. She's doing a story on the band. You need all the ink you can get."

TJ rocked back on the rear legs of his chair, then stood up, bowed slightly, held his hand out. The expression on his face never changed. "My apologies," he said. "I thought . . . ahh, well, anyhow, lemme make it up to you. Have a seat. I'll buy you a drink, Doc and me will answer all your questions."

There was nowhere to sit. Alessandra looked at TJ for a couple seconds. "All right," she said.

"Dude," TJ said, looking at Rushton, "why don't you go find another chair for the lady." Rushton looked around, found the bouncer, then he and the bouncer unseated someone at another table. Rushton brought the chair back, held it for Al.

"Thanks, Luke," she said.

"I can't stay," Rushton said. "I still got equipment to get stowed." TJ ignored him. Rushton looked at TJ once, then turned and departed.

This guy acts like he's royalty, Al thought. He doesn't need to be polite. She had no problem imagining his picture in the newspaper, above a story about imported morphine or a murdered guitar player. Or both. "So," she said. "How come you two aren't out on the bus?"

"Pressing the flesh? Doc here is a seriously married man, and I ain't into it just now."

"I see. Tell me, how do you think you guys did tonight?"

Doc looked up for the first time, and TJ glanced once in his direction. "It was an okay night," TJ said. "We did mostly new shit for the first hour, and we're not all the way there with a lot of that, but once we got past that, we had our moments. Don't you take notes, or use a tape recorder?"

"Don't need to," Al said. "Everybody tells me you guys have a shot at the big time. How does that feel?"

Doc was shaking his head. "Everybody wants to be a millionaire," he said. "Everybody thinks they gonna die rich."

"Pay no mind to him," TJ said. "Doc's a melancholy drunk."

"It doesn't sound like you guys care a whole lot about making the big time," Al said.

TJ shrugged. "Hey, nobody's gonna say no to the money," he said. "Not even Doc."

Al looked from one to the other. "But?"

"You tell her, Doc."

Doc looked up at her. "For me," he said, "for myself, okay, tonight was as good as it's ever gonna get. No matter what happens after tonight, it's all downhill from here."

"Why?"

"Told you he was a melancholy drunk," TJ said.

"Six hundred and fifty seats," Doc said, his voice rising to override TJ's interruption. "Almost everyone in the house is a fan. They seen us before, they're all on our side. We got nobody telling us what to play, or how long. We mix the sound the way we want it. We play until we're ready to quit. It's a beautiful thing, man." He didn't look like he'd enjoyed it at all. "But if we make it, if we hit, the record company talent will be all over us. They ain't gonna sit still for us playing like we did tonight. They got hit doctors and they got producers and they got engineers. If the company wants a blue band, they'll paint us blue; they want a green band, they'll paint us green; they want a yellow band, they'll paint us yellow. And we'll never have another night like this one. We'll never play here again."

"And what if you don't hit?"

"Year from now, we'll be playing bar mitzvahs."

Doc seemed to be done. Al looked at TJ. "Is he right?"

TJ shrugged. "One way to look at it," he said. "But that's

the way Doc looks at most things. And you know how it is, you got shit on your upper lip, the whole world stinks."

"So what do you think?"

TJ shrugged. "I try not to think," he said. "I'm a guitar player. If I was any good at thinking, I'd probably be a dentist." He shifted in his chair, ran his fingers through his hair.

"So you don't care about the record company's money."

He shook his head. "They haven't offered me shit. It's the band they want to buy, and the band has to pay the house, and the promoter, and the manager, and the roadies. We got to pay what's-his-name to do the sound, we got lawyers and accountants and security, Jesus. You got any idea how many fingers a dollar has to dance past before it gets to me? Forget about it. Listen, lemme tell you something, in this business, you can be broke on your ass or you can be fat. Mostly, you're gonna be broke on your ass. But it's impossible to be anything in between. You know what I'm saying? So if some asshole shows up with a wheelbarrow full of money, yeah, I'll take it. But I ain't holding my breath, honey, record company contract or not." He looked at Doc's empty glass. "I promised you a drink, didn't I?" He twisted in his chair, waved for the waiter, but couldn't catch the man's eye. TJ grimaced, put two fingers to his lips and blew a piercing whistle. The noise level in the place dropped by half, and everyone present stared at TJ. "Hey!" he shouted. "Who you gotta schtup to get a little service around here?"

A guy in a white shirt, black pants, and a bow tie hurried over. TJ hollered at the guy before he could open his mouth. "Another round," TJ said. Gradually the noise rose back to where it had been. "Bourbon for Doc, gin on the rocks for me, and whatever the lady wants."

"Cutty," she said. "On the rocks."

"Damn straight," TJ said. "None of those weenie drinks for you reporter types."

"So if you're not making any money with BandX, how do you pay the bills?"

He looked at her, shrugged. "You do what you gotta do."

He fits, she thought. Two motives: money and jealousy. He knew Willy and he knows the drug scene. "You wanna talk about your recent, ahh, difficulties?"

"You mean rehab? I copped a plea, it was either rehab or do time for felony possession." He scowled. "It was a bullshit rap. I was holding some shit for a friend of mine. If they had got her with it, she'd have gone away, they would have taken her kids, the whole bit. You see what happens? I try to be a stand-up guy, okay, and I get nothing but shit for it."

Al looked over at Doc, who was wearing a wry smile, then back at TJ. "So you don't consider yourself a drug addict or an alcoholic?"

"Hell, no. I can put this shit down any time I want."

She looked at his glass. "Don't you have to pass a drip test?"

His lined face split into a grin. "Don't print this, okay? We cool with that?" Al nodded. "I got the shit covered, man. Place where I go to get tested, okay, one of the nurses there takes care of me. You know what I'm saying? I could piss gasoline and it wouldn't matter."

She changed gears. "Do you have any idea what might have happened to Willy Caughlan?"

TJ's face went dark. "No, man, I don't."

"What did you think of him?"

He shrugged. "Nice kid."

"As a musician, I mean."

"Hadn't found his groove yet. Everybody has to go through that, when they're trying to sound like Hendrix or Knopfler or whatever. Willy had soul, though, and he knew it. He would have been all right, if he'd had time."

"You think the band would have kept him, and let you go?"

"Not a fucking chance," TJ told her. "It's my gig. You can print this if you want, I don't give a fuck, okay? But these guys are nowhere without me."

"That guitar that Willy Caughlan had, the one that got stolen. Any idea how much that would be worth?"

"You know something?" Conrad's voice was angry and hard. "Stevie Ray Vaughn couldn't fucking buy a decent review when he was alive. Some mentally defective douche bag of a reviewer trashed him in *Rolling Stone* just before he died. 'I don't mind the voice that much,' the piece of shit says, 'but the slavish imitation of Hendrix gets old in a hurry.' You fucking believe that?" He seemed genuinely angry. "How would you like it? You're the most influential guitar player in a generation, and the slimeballs in the press shit all over you because they're too stupid or too tone-deaf or too fucked up to understand what you're doing. And then, before he's even cold in the grave, they canonize the son of a bitch. Unbelievable."

"So how much would the guitar be worth?"

"Oh, shit," Conrad said. "You're the press . . ."

"It's all right," she told him. "How much?"

He shook his head. "Collectors," he said. "That's another disease. Who the hell knows? You get a couple rich half-wits in the same room bidding against each other, shit, man, you might get a couple hundred thou for it. Maybe more." He shifted in his seat. "Hey, Doc! We should do it! Buy a beat up old Strat, dummy it up to look like Vaughn's, throw a set of double-ought strings on it, I bet we could score an easy half million! What do you say?"

Doc slid his sunglasses down to the end of his nose and peered at Conrad over them. "You never give up, do you?"

Alessandra held the Astro steady in the center lane, fighting its tendency to wander and her own tendency to zone out, put herself on cruise control, and let her attention stray. She rolled her window partway down to see if the cool, wet night air would keep her more alert. Here you are, she thought, looking around at the other drivers, just like always, you're surrounded by people, you can't reach them and they can't reach you. All you've got to keep you company is the noise in your own head. Same old story.

You could have gotten a ride on the tour bus, she thought, and she laughed out loud. Like there'd be somewhere to sit on that bus that wasn't already smeared with someone else's DNA . . . At least you get a couple days off before you have to see any of them again, she told herself. The band had a recording session somewhere in Queens in three days, and Rushton had promised to get her in. "Observe and report," he'd said. "But time is money, okay, so you can't be asking a lot of questions." Yeah, she thought. Like I wanna sit right down and have another heart-to-heart with TJ Conrad. Christ.

Maybe Conrad was essential to the success of BandX. Maybe he really did have the touch, maybe he was what lifted them out of the ordinary. He certainly thought so, that was clear, but it wasn't clear that he cared all that much about BandX, or the record company money that was dancing just out of his reach. Would he kill an innocent kid to protect that?

You forget, she told herself, these guys have already spent years working just to get to this place, just to have this one shot. She wondered if Doc's pessimism and TJ's blasé attitude might just be defensive, so that they could tell themselves they didn't care if everything fell apart. But people had committed murder over matters much more trivial than this. She had seen real envy on the face of Luke Rushton, a man who had spent his entire life chasing the dream—it had to be killing him to be so close to it and still have no chance. Rushton looked sick with the desire, the outright need to be up there on that stage and not behind the console. But she could not see any way that Rushton would benefit from the death of Willy Caughlan.

Sandy Ellison, the A&R guy, was a possibility. Would his career survive if BandX fell apart? Did he need this shot badly enough to murder for it? And Conrad—God only knew what he'd be doing if he didn't have a band to play in. And would the other members of BandX feel the same way? Suppose two or three members of the band wanted to keep Willy and let TJ slide? Would one of the other musicians resort to murder to get what he thought the band needed? How far would any of them go to protect the experience of a night like this? If the money wasn't motive enough, what about fame? What about the music? What about the girls on the bus?

If you don't want to have sex with the musicians, don't get on the bus . . . Jesus, what a class act that guy was. She wondered what his job title was. Bitch wrangler? Pussmaster? And all of those females stood there and listened to that drivel, each one eager to outdo her sisters for the privilege of spreading for one of the musicians. Maybe you're getting old before your time, she told herself, then laughed out loud at the absurdity of the idea. God, she told herself, you can't be old, you're just getting started. She couldn't imagine it, though, couldn't wrap her mind around wanting any man badly enough to debase herself to that degree. Oh, yeah, I might be hot for some guy, she thought, sure, but I am not going to roll around in the dirt at anyone's feet . . .

The van's temperature needle had crept close to the red zone. Oh, Bobby, she thought, why couldn't you have, like, tuned this thing up or something? This is all I need, getting stuck out here on the highway with a broken van and about eighty bucks in my pocket . . .

You could have ridden on the tour bus, she told herself.

Yeah, right.

She rolled the windows the rest of the way down and turned the heat on, and that seemed to help for a while, but then the needle headed back north again. Oh, God, please, Al thought, you gotta be kidding me. She'd seen a sign for the next rest area, but it was still thirteen or fourteen miles away, and she could smell antifreeze. Damn, she thought. This thing has got to be boiling over. I'll never make the rest area. There was an exit ramp ahead, and she pulled over to the side of the road by the ramp, as far away from the highway as she could get. At least there's lights here, she told herself, and a little more distance between me and the traffic.

She turned the van's lights off and pulled the hood release lever. Nothing happened. She felt her own temperature begin to rise. Goddammit, Bobby, why didn't you take better care of this thing? And why did you have to go and get sick and leave me all alone? Without you I've got nobody . . . She gripped the wheel, squeezing hard, gritting her teeth, waited until it passed. She mentally reviewed her assets. She'd allocated two hundred bucks for the trip, and she had about eighty of that left. Nobody's gonna fix this piece of shit for eighty bucks, she told herself, they won't even tow it for that much. She had one Visa credit card, limit of five grand. The card was for emergencies, but there'd been too many of those lately and she didn't know what her balance was, she'd been afraid to look for some time. She had the little silver cell phone, she could use that to call someone.

Yeah? Like who? Caughlan? O'Hagan? Stiles? Wouldn't that be great. *Hello? I'm having this little girl moment, wouldn't one of you big strong men please come and rescue me?*

Be a cold day in hell.

How about Anthony? Anthony could tell her if her black jeans clashed with the van's purple shag interior, but he wouldn't be much help with an ailing motor vehicle.

She yanked on the hood release lever again. Still nothing. "Pendejo!" she yelled. "Son of a bitch!" She jerked her door handle and kicked the door open. It flew all the way open to its stop, rebounded, and slammed shut again. "Goddammit!" She jerked on the handle again, then slammed her elbow into the door, regretting it almost immediately. It's a metal door, she reminded herself. It can't feel pain. Unlike, say, you . . .

A truck flew down the exit ramp, the wind of its passing rocking the van. Al got out into the rain. What would happen, she wondered, if you just left this thing here? She walked around to the front of the van and looked at the hood. Was it possible that Tio Bobby had the thing chained shut? He might do it to keep someone from stealing the battery. All right, maybe he would, but wouldn't there be a click when you pulled the hood release? And when the hood popped open a couple of inches, you'd have to reach in to unlock the chain. Tio Bobby would never make you lie down on the ground and reach up inside to unlock a chain, because that would mean he'd have to do it himself. But you never knew, Bobby might have taken it into his head to rig the hood to open backward, just for the hell of it, or sideways, and then hide the button you pushed to operate it somewhere nobody would ever look for it. She looked around the front of the van for some kind of button or lever, but there was nothing.

The rain dripping off her face was doing nothing to cool her down. She stuck her fingers into the crack under the leading edge of the hood and pried up. It seemed to give a little, so she pried harder, and then harder yet, straining muscle against metal, but it was no use. "Son of a bitch!" She lost it then, slammed her fists down on top of the hood, and it popped, jumped open several inches. "God," she said, relieved, and then she laughed at herself. There was still something mechanical that kept the hood from opening all the way, but she felt around underneath until she found the lever she had to push.

She felt the heat rising in waves out of the engine compartment, heard water boiling somewhere down inside. She stepped back, looked off into the night, felt the cool rain wetting down her hair. She remembered that first night, the one after she'd run away from her Aunt Magdelena's. It had been a cruel realization: her mother was truly gone for good, her father was not around, and that left no one to watch over her. She was on her own. Her twelve-year-old self had accepted the truth of that. She wanted to dispute it now, she wanted to believe otherwise, even though she could not marshal any evidence to the cause.

Well, she told herself, just for tonight, why don't you see if you can nurse this piece of shit back to Brooklyn? She waited, and eventually the engine cooled. She took the cap off the radiator. That would lower the pressure, even she knew that, and wherever the fluids were leaking, they would leak more slowly.

Just do it, she told herself. There's no one here to help you. She got back in the truck, wiped her face off, started it up.

Twelve

They met for breakfast in a coffee shop on Third Ave. Stiles stared across the table at Alessandra. "Al, honey," he said, his fat face etched with concern. "You promised. You said you'd drop this if there was nothing in the police reports."

Stiles had been thorough, she had to give him that. He had copies of all the police reports, plus news articles dealing with Willy's death, and even some older stuff covering Daniel Caughlan's early years. Al looked up from the papers, watched Stiles stick a piece of bacon into his face and chew slowly. Bad enough I got to watch the guy eat, but it's taking him forever to finish. Like watching someone with a dull razor at his wrist, she thought, sawing at himself in slow motion. "I said we'd talk about it."

He leaned back in his chair. "So talk," he said. "I looked at everything there. There's nothing to indicate that Willy's death was anything more than what it looks like, another musician that got his dosage wrong."

"Maybe not. But think about this, Marty. Six months ago, one of Caughlan's trucks gets hijacked. Had dope in it. Right?"

"So?"

"And you're telling me six months ago, this grand jury starts meeting, looking at Caughlan and Penn Trans. Right?"

"Yeah."

"And six months ago, Willy Caughlan turns up dead, and nobody bothers to look past the surface."

"The kid overdosed," Stiles said. He sounded stubborn.

"Oh, come on, Marty, gimme a break. Doesn't the timing here strike you as a little suspicious? And what about the laptop and the guitar that were missing from his apartment?"

"What about 'em? Could've been the cops. You think guys on the job don't grab shit from a DOA scene, you're dreaming."

"Okay, maybe it was cops. But maybe Willy knew something, maybe he had something in that laptop. Maybe someone thought it was worth killing him for it."

Stiles's mouth turned down at the corners. Means he's thinking, Al told herself.

"People I talked to say Willy never touched drugs. Said he didn't even drink."

Stiles still looked unconvinced.

"Listen," Al told him. "What's at the core of this whole business?"

"Dope," Marty said.

"Wrong. Dope's the product, but what makes this work is the hack. The key to this thing is the job someone did on Penn Trans's bookkeeping system."

"What's that got to do with Willy Caughlan?"

"Willy was a musician. That means he was a techie. He was into computers, he had to be, or else he couldn't function as a musician."

"You saying you think he hacked into his own father's . . ."

"No. I don't think that at all. But Willy loved trucks, Marty, his own father told me so. And I'll bet you he wanted what almost every other guy his age secretly wants."

"What's that?"

"He wanted to be like his father."

"Mickey tried to keep him away from the business. Wanted him to be a schoolteacher or some shit."

"Yeah, no kidding. So what do you want to bet he hung out down at Penn Trans with the truck drivers every chance he got? Probably without his father knowing, if he could manage it."

"So what if he did?"

"Maybe he was sharp enough to figure out what was going on."

Stiles was shaking his head. "Too much of a stretch," he said.

"Maybe. But there's one more thing."

"Yeah? What's that?"

She would have preferred to hold it back, but she told him about the sex tape featuring Willy Caughlan and Shine. Then she told him about the reporter who'd taken the trouble to learn her cell number, and who called to offer her a half million for the video.

"Holy shit," Marty said. "You find this video, we split. Fifty-fifty."

Very easy to split money you don't have, Al thought. "Sure. But the point is, I think Willy's laptop has something more than that video on it. I think he was onto whoever sold out Daniel Caughlan and Penn Trans. And I think he was killed just to keep his mouth shut."

"I still think it's a stretch," Marty said. "I'll give you another couple of days on it. I'm not buying your theory, okay, but the tape makes it worth the time. Half a mil is a big chunk of change."

"Quarter million," Al told him. "Half for you, half for me."

"Oh, yeah," Marty said. "Right. Absolutely. But listen, if this fixation with Willy Caughlan is all you got, you ain't got much."

"You forget about those three guys in the Bronx?"

"The ones that took a swing at you? No, I didn't forget." But it seemed obvious that he had.

"I seem to be making somebody very nervous, Marty. I mean, it's classic. If he kept his head down, odds are he'd be pretty safe, but he went for me once, he's gonna do it again. All we gotta do is wait for him to make a mistake, and we got him."

"Unless he gets you first," he said. "What are you gonna do next?"

"I'm gonna go talk to your new office girl," she said. "And then I'm gonna start looking for that laptop."

Sarah Waters was her name, the little plastic sign on the desk said so. She occupied the outer office at West Houston Security, the company owned and operated by Marty Stiles. Sarah Waters sat behind the desk that Alessandra had recently vacated. She was on the short side, mid-thirties, a little plump, round face, dark hair that didn't quite reach her shoulders. Despite her last name, she looked Italian. Howard Beach, Al thought, or Bayside. Some neighborhood where her father and her brothers knew where she was at all hours of the day and night. Probably married to a guy named Angelo, or Vito. Probably has the two-point-five kids, and the dog, too. Coming in to work on Houston Street, Al thought, must feel, to her, like she's taking the train to hell. The woman looked up from her computer screen and regarded Al over half-glasses. "Hello," she said, soft-voiced. "Can I help you?"

"You're in my chair," Al said.

If Sarah Waters was intimidated, she didn't show it. "You must be Miss Martillo," she said, keeping her behind firmly in her seat. "Mr. Stiles talks about you all the time."

"I'll bet he does."

"Only good things, so far," she said. "If you'll wait here, I'll go get another chair for you." She said it without any change of expression. Al watched her get up and walk away. We're like a pair of stray cats, Al thought. We haven't quite decided whether or not to claw each other's eyes out.

Sarah came back carrying the chair, put it down, and held it for Al like a teenager out on his first date. "Thanks," Al said.

Sarah reoccupied her station behind the desk. She leaned on her elbows and peered at Al over her glasses. "Mr. Stiles told me you quit on him. That's exactly how he put it. 'She just up and quit.' He must have told me that a dozen times. Reminds me of my oldest son when he's lying to me."

I knew it, Al thought. Should ask her if the kid's name is Vito Jr? "How old is your son?"

"Twelve," Sarah said.

"You treat Marty like he's about twelve, you won't go too far wrong."

"I figured as much. Well, Miss Martillo, let me be up front about this. If you don't want to help me with Mr. Stiles's bookkeeping and so on, I'll understand. It's really his problem, not mine. I'll just do the best I can. I don't see how he can expect more than that."

"I don't like to think I'm that small-minded," Al said. Yeah, so maybe the guy is a dirtbag, but it's a job. It pays the bills.

Almost. She refocused on the woman in front of her. "Marty isn't the worst guy in the world, I guess. I mean, he'll use you like a paper towel and still convince himself he's done you a great big favor, but he's all right. As long as you don't expect too much out of him."

"It doesn't matter," Sarah told her. "I need this job."

"I know the feeling. It's a long story, and a boring one, but technically, I still work for Marty. Just not in the office. At least not at the moment."

"Oh, great. Dammit all to hell. Mr. Stiles told me this was gonna be a steady gig, he said you left, and now it sounds like he'll just dump me when you get done with whatever you're doing. Son of a bitch . . ."

"Don't worry about it yet, a lot of things could happen before that time comes."

"I suppose. But I wish he'd just have told me the truth."

"Oh, come on. What fun would that be?"

"I suppose. Well, Mr. Stiles tried to explain his bookkeeping system to me," Sarah said.

"System?" Al snorted. "He doesn't have a system. The only system in this place is the one I came up with. It might not be the best, but it worked okay for me."

"You have it very securely password-protected."

"Dumont," Al said. "All lowercase."

"Dumont?"

"From Dumont Avenue. I used to live there. In Brooklyn. That's the password."

Sarah brightened. "Brooklyn? I don't think I ever heard of Dumont Avenue. Where is it?"

"Brownsville Houses," Al said. "The projects."

"Oh." The light went back out. They didn't have much in common, after all . . .

"You?"

"Bensonhurst."

Bull's-eye, Al thought. You could ride the subway from one neighborhood to the other, but they were worlds apart. She probably sees Hulk Hogan when she looks at me. Probably thinks I got a box cutter hidden in my panties. And here I am looking at her, all I see is Sister Immaculata. "Scootch over," Al said, standing up and picking up her chair. "I'll show you how I set it up . . ."

"Well," Sarah said, when they were done, "I can't tell you how much I appreciate this." She said it with something like relief. "You've saved me loads of aggravation. After this, my biggest problem will be keeping myself from getting too bored. Mr. Stiles will be so happy when I show him . . ."

"Word of advice?"

Sarah nodded. "Go ahead."

"Don't show Marty anything. There are things he's very good at, but paperwork is not one of them. As long as he doesn't understand how you do what you do, you're a life-saver and a magician. If he starts thinking he can do it himself, or explain how to the next person, you're a peon and a drain on his pocketbook."

Sarah sat there considering that. "I guess I've been out of the corporate world too long," she said.

"Don't worry," Al told her. "Computers and the Internet are not that—"

"Oh, I didn't mean that. I have a degree in library science,

I'm actually pretty good at finding information. I meant, you know, the personalities and all."

Sharks, Al thought. Like me. But I'm not a shark, I'm just another scared fish, trying to find my way home. "You'll get used to it," she said.

The woman was an older version of the current Mrs. Daniel Caughlan. She had those same green eyes, that same heavy blond hair, but that aura of physical perfection was, in her case, tempered by time. Her eyes looked lost and the skin of her face had begun to sag, like a balloon that has lost much of its air. She rubbed a hand through her hair. "Hello? Did I talk to you on the phone? Because if you're a reporter, I, ahh, I don't think . . ."

"I'm not a reporter, Mrs. Caughlan—"

"Moran," she said, shaking her head. "My name is Judith Moran."

"I'm sorry—"

"Daniel thinks everything in the world belongs to him. He can't understand why I wanted my own name back." She looked at Al, seemed to focus with an effort. "Are you one of Daniel's new tomatoes?"

Alessandra could feel the steam rising. Moran looked stoned, and her voice had a faraway and dreamy quality to it, but still, she had found a sore spot. "I am nobody's tomato, Miss Moran. I just happen to work for your ex-husband."

"Well, all right." Moran stood just inside the door to her Greenwich Village apartment, and Alessandra stood just outside, in the hallway. "What can I do for you?"

"I'd like to talk to you about your son."

Moran's face looked like someone had just let some more air out of the balloon. She stood in the doorway, stared off into space, but then she seemed to notice Al again. "All right," she said, and she stood aside. "Come in."

Moran's living room resembled a knickknack museum that had just relocated from much larger quarters. There was a smell about the place, too. Al couldn't quite place it, but it reminded her of Tio Bobby's hospital room. Get on with it, Al told herself. "Did your son speak with you often, Miss Moran?"

"Willy and I were very close," Moran said. Her eyes were unfocused and her voice so soft Al had to lean in to hear her.

"Did you ever know Willy to experiment with drugs?"

"No," Moran said, drawing out that single syllable. "No, Willy . . . Willy never got high. He was too busy, he had too many things he wanted to do. That's what he always said, anyhow."

"Did you notice any changes in his personality after he got involved with BandX?"

"He smiled more," Moran said, and her voice seemed a bit sharper. "He was happier. He was doing something creative, something he loved. It seemed that he'd found himself. And the other musicians in the band appreciated his gift. It was probably the first time in his life that other men paid him any significant attention."

"Didn't he hang out at Penn Transfer when he was younger?"

"Yes. He was a beautiful child. The truck drivers used to let him ride along . . ."

"How much did the other band members know about Willy's father?"

Moran thought about it, then shrugged. "Who knows," she said. "I didn't have that much contact with them. Musicians are all very self-involved. If you don't play something, they don't notice you."

"Did Willy seem close to any of the other guys in BandX?"

"I don't think so. Willy idolized the one guitar player, the one who went off to jail, or whatever . . ." Her hand fluttered uncertainly in the air. "CJ, or something . . . He knew CJ was going to come back. He told me once he was just keeping the seat warm."

"Was he all right with that?"

"I think so. Willy was just a boy, he didn't care about anything beyond the day after tomorrow. If they let him play for a while, he was happy."

"Were you aware of Willy's relationship with a singer who calls herself Shine?"

Moran sighed. "Willy had a lot of girlfriends. He was very personable . . . None of his relationships lasted very long. I think Willy enjoyed being around women, but I don't think he ever really knew what it was to love any one particular girl. He always seemed so puzzled when some girl he'd walked away from got angry about it." She was staring at Al for the first time. "He was like his father, in that way."

"Did Willy leave any personal stuff here, Miss Moran?"

"No."

"Are you sure? Willy seemed like a pretty tech-savvy kid. Did he leave any discs here, or maybe a memory stick?"

"I know what you're looking for, Miss Martillo. I haven't seen it. I sincerely hope no one ever does."

"Miss Moran, I am not interested in pictures of Willy having sex. But there are two things missing from Willy's studio. One was a guitar allegedly once owned by Stevie Ray Vaughn, and the other was Willy's laptop. The guitar, I can't really figure, but I wonder if Willy had something on his computer that might have led to his death. If Willy backed up his data, he'd probably leave it somewhere other than his apartment. That's what I'm looking for. It would most likely be on a CD or a memory stick or some floppys."

"Willy's gone," Moran said, looking and sounding unfocused again. "We were very close, you know. He talked to me all the time . . . But he didn't leave anything here with me . . ."

This woman is so wrecked, Al thought, if Willy's petrified body were standing in her front hall, she probably wouldn't notice it. "Thanks for all your help," she said.

Thirteen

The house was in the upper reaches of the Bronx in a neighborhood so suburban in nature that it hardly looked like part of the city at all. It was big, square, redbrick, red tile roof, green gutters, lots of windows. It was set well back from the road, behind a ragged fringe of bushes and a ratty lawn. The driveway was buttressed by six-foot brick columns. Alessandra checked the address in the predawn gloom, then found a parking spot down the street and settled in to wait. This was the day the band was supposed to begin recording their album, and Al had assumed that they would get started early, but she was wrong. The sun rose, rush hour came and went, but there were still no signs of life in the brick house. Finally, a little after ten, a Toyota minivan with a BABY ON BOARD sticker in its back window rolled down the street, turned into the driveway, and pulled up near the house. The driver did not get out at first, he sat there and honked his horn, but when that did not work, he got out, walked up to the front door, and began pounding on it with a fist. Al, peering through her long lens, recognized Doc Jamison, BandX's bassist. He kept it up for another minute or so until someone finally opened up. Ten minutes later, the rest of the band members joined Jamison in the van, all but TJ, who apparently did not live with them anymore.

Al watched them back out of the driveway and pull away. She followed at a discreet distance until she was sure they were really leaving the neighborhood, then she turned back and parked the Astro back where she'd had it. She crawled into the back of the van and changed quickly: tight blue pants, blue jacket with the gas company logo on it, shades, a plastic ID card on a chain around her neck, and a toolbox.

She walked down the driveway. Briskly, she told herself, but not too fast. Don't run. She pounded on the door just as Jamison had. She couldn't hear anyone stirring inside, but that didn't guarantee the place was empty. She had her cover story ready—sorry to bother you, ma'am, we've had reports of a gas leak in the area, you're going to have to vacate the premises. Not too elaborate, but she figured the odds were pretty good that any woman sleeping in this place with one of these guys had to be dumber than a box of rocks.

No answer.

She tried again, got the same result. The door had a dead bolt, but she could see from the outside that they hadn't locked it. She popped the other lock with a Slim Jim, stepped inside, kicked the door closed behind her. She put her toolbox on the floor, slipped on a pair of clear plastic gloves, and looked around. No bars on the windows, no alarm, and they hadn't bothered with the dead bolt. Didn't even have a dog.

They had a cat, though, maybe more than one. She could smell cat shit and ammonia over a faint sweet trace of herb. She left her toolbox where it was and took a quick tour of the first floor. It was more or less what she'd expected. The house must have been something back in its younger days, hardwood floors, ornate wainscoting, a library with french doors, fancy moldings. Someone had started to strip the layers of paint from the moldings, exposing and refinishing the wood. The effect was striking, but whoever had made the attempt had run out of gas after doing most of one room, and the rest of the stuff was still painted. The house had steam heat, and the heavy metal radiators had embedded themselves into the wooden floors. The radiators were painted, too, along with the valves and pipes.

The walls were plaster, crumbling here and there, rippled the way plaster gets after about a century. The house had fallen into that state a lot of guys seemed able to tolerate: if something died in the middle of the floor, someone would eventually get rid of it, but nobody was going to run a vacuum or actually wash anything.

There was a drum kit set up in one corner of the living room, and the rest of the room was packed with all of the other tools of the trade: keyboards, amps, guitars, and a piano. Alessandra paid particular attention to the guitars, but none of them matched the description of the Stevie Ray Vaughn guitar, the one that had gone missing from Willy Caughlan's studio.

Upstairs, it got worse. This smell is not just from a cat, Al thought. The walls were painted blue, and there was a beat-down wall-to-wall shag carpet, also blue, and dirty white woodwork. Al paused to take a look through one of the windows at the street out front. A long-haired guy in a raincoat walking by had most of the street to himself. Al picked a bedroom, started in.

Jesus, what a hole.

Just get it over with, she told herself, and get out. Dirty clothes in one corner, clean ones in another, an iPod on the floor next to the bed, no books or printed matter aside from a foot-high pile of sheet music. Plastic liter-sized bottle of vodka, half empty, on the floor next to the bed. Ashtray on the nightstand, overflowing with butts and roaches. Two shoe boxes full of junk, the kind of personal stuff people accumulate and can't bring themselves to discard: pictures, old pennies, cuff links, a couple of watches that weren't running, an expired passport. There was a laptop on a small desk, already up and running. Al sat down at the computer, plugged in a memory stick and started looking, downloading anything that piqued her curiosity. Most of the stuff she found was of little or no interest: music, sound editors, porn. The room she was in belonged to Cliff, the lead singer, and he seemed to favor two distinct types—Asian women, and the more traditional Hugh Hefner fare: corn-fed, big-breasted, all-American.

No Puerto Ricans, Al thought. She mentally compared herself to the pictures. God never gave breasts that size to a woman without the behind that went with them . . . Not much muscle tone, she thought, nobody who looks like she's in any kind of shape. And why does it always come back to that, she wondered. Yeah, she might be beautiful, but I can probably kick her ass . . . Is that all you've got?

The other bedrooms were similar. One held a desktop instead of a laptop, and she had to boot it up. It asked her for a password, but she'd been ready for that. *Passwords and locks only keep out the honest people.* Tio Bobby had told her that a hundred times. Working for Marty Stiles had proved the truth of it.

There was another room on the second floor which seemed to be a repository for broken or rejected equipment, mostly keyboards and some outdated recording apparatus. No guitars, though. Maybe guitars don't change that much, Al thought, or maybe they look cool enough, even silent and disconnected, so they never got thrown away. You could pick one at random, stand it in the corner of a room, and it would look at least as interesting as just about any other piece of art or sculpture.

She found the stairs that led up to the attic behind a door at one end of the second-floor central hallway. She hesitated before going up. She walked back and checked the street out front again, looking through one of the bedroom windows for a few minutes. Nothing out there, she told herself. But if you were on the first floor and somebody started to come in, you could always run out back. On the second floor, you could climb out onto the porch roof, or maybe jump from a window, but if you were on the third floor you were probably screwed. You've always got to have an escape hatch, she told herself. If you start feeling boxed in, even just a tiny little bit, you start feeling uncomfortable. Not happy unless you're damned sure you can run away . . . You ought to go see a therapist about it. She wondered how much money therapists charged, and how you went about finding one. She went and checked through a window at the back of the house, too. Seeing nothing unusual, she hit the stairs and went up into the attic.

Most of the attic space was uninsulated and unfinished, but one small bedroom, along with a tiny bathroom, was framed off in one corner. Both were empty, looked like they had been so for some time. They were dusty, but seemed to hold none of the squalid aura of the other two floors. She stood looking at a Hendrix poster thumbtacked to one wall. Willy lived in this room before he moved to that studio, she thought. She didn't know how she knew that, but she was sure she was right.

She stood in the middle of the floor in the empty room, caught a glimpse of the long-haired guy on the street out front.

He was standing on the sidewalk, right at the property line between the brick house and the place next door. He was half-obscured by the hedges, but as she watched him, he twisted his head to one side, looked like he was talking to an invisible companion. Radio, Alessandra thought, her heart accelerating. The only reason I can see this guy now is because I'm up here on the top floor, high enough to see over those bushes. She ducked back out of his line of sight, took one last quick look around the empty attic room, then ran down the stairs. There was nothing of hers on the second floor, the memory sticks she'd used to pirate computer files were hanging around her neck. She risked one quick peek out a front window. She couldn't see the guy from this level, but she thought she could just make out the color of his raincoat behind the bushes. She took another few seconds and checked out a back window. There was a guy in the backyard of one of the houses that fronted on the next street behind, watering his grass. She didn't see anybody else. One for sure, she thought. But if he really had been talking into a mike, there had to be more somewhere.

She was a little more cautious as she descended to the first floor. There were no coverings on the windows down there, which meant she was much more exposed. She got as low as she could when she hit the bottom of the stairs. There was a black man walking up the driveway, big guy, jeans, sweatshirt, running shoes, one hand shading his eyes as he peered at the upper floors of the house. Al dropped to the floor and slithered to the front hall, grabbed her toolbox, then scrabbled on hands and knees back to the kitchen, which was at the rear of the house. She was barely through the door into the kitchen when she heard the crunch of a footstep on the concrete stairs out back. Without pausing, she changed direction and headed into the hallway to her left. There was a door slightly ajar in the hallway, and before she could think about it she was through, into the relative gloom of what had to be the cellar steps. It was an ancient wooden staircase, and it made what sounded to her like a frightfully loud chorus of creaking noises as she went down. She stopped at the foot of the stairs. Two guys, one at the front door, one at the back. Could she really hear them both, or was her imagination in overdrive?

You're in a hole in the ground, she told herself.

Get out.

Dim light filtered through the few small cellar windows. They were below ground level, sunk in small metal-lined pits next to the house. Pick one, she thought, and she headed for the far end of the basement, where there was an old wooden workbench under the window farthest from the driveway. The window was covered with dust and cobwebs, looked like it hadn't been opened in years, but when she pushed back the sliding bolts that held it shut, it creaked open readily enough. She climbed up onto the workbench, shoved her toolbox out into the leaf-lined pit. She was about to slide through herself when she heard the voices.

". . . we gonna explain this?" Male voice, sounded like a brother.

"Reports of a prowler," another voice answered, also male, probably white. "We'll just say the door was open. That's probable cause."

"The hell it is . . ."

"It's close enough."

"Look, man, suppose we find something here. Okay? What then? We won't be able to use it. A flimsy excuse like 'the door was open' ain't never gonna hold up."

"Relax. We find what we're looking for, we leave it right where it is and we go work on getting a warrant. No big deal."

Cops, Alessandra thought. Maybe they hadn't written Willy off after all. Or maybe there was a tie between BandX and the dope filtering into the country through Penn Trans. Maybe it was Willy himself, using his father's business to do a little business of his own . . . She stuck her arms out through the open window, then her head and shoulders. It was a tight fit, she'd have to jackknife her body out and up to get through the window. She squeezed through the opening a little farther, but then her foot slipped. There was a big coffee can filled with nails and screws. It had been sitting on one end of the workbench, but she kicked it off onto the floor, where it landed with a loud metallic crash.

Al, you clod, she thought, you really stepped in it now.

She could hear hurried clomping footsteps as the two men on the floor above her reacted. Looking for the steps down here, she thought. She jerked her body the rest of the way through the window, gouging her hip on the window frame in the process, but then she was through, and the window slammed shut behind her.

She crouched down in the hole just outside the window, grabbed her toolbox, then jumped out and ran as hard as she could for the hedges along the property line about fifteen feet away. She thrust herself through the bushes into the neighboring yard. Nobody outside, she thought, at least there's that . . . She heard an angry shout behind her.

"Hey! Police! Stop right where you are!"

Command voice, just like they teach you in the academy. She turned and glanced back at the house. No way, she thought, no way either one of those two gorillas is gonna fit through that window. That probably buys me thirty seconds . . . She sprinted the length of the hedge, heading for the street, but not the one out front. She headed for the street one block back. One more hedge and she was behind the garage that went with the house just to the rear of the brick house. She slipped along the back of the garage and up the far side, out of sight of the men who had to be hitting the yard right about . . . now.

The window on the far side of the garage was broken, smashed out, and the garage roof had collapsed inward. Al reached through the opening where the window had once been, put her toolbox on a beam inside, down low and out of sight. It was a possibility that the cops might find it there, but maybe not a likelihood. If they found her on the street with it, though, it would be "possession of burglary tools" for sure. She looked down at her side, pulled her jacket and shirt up and the waistband of her pants down to see a red oozing gash. Not horrible, she thought, doesn't even hurt much. But you left a little bit of yourself back there on that window frame . . .

She walked past the garage, down the long driveway and out onto the street.

The main avenue of the neighborhood was two blocks away, and as she walked down the hill to the avenue she heard a siren. Stay calm, she told herself, don't look around, just go down the hill.

She found a place around the corner, a storefront that contained an enterprise named Lucky Nail. She went inside, reviewed her finances, decided to go for the full spa treatment— pedicure, manicure, massage, and a wax job. Normally she didn't much care to be touched or fussed over, but she told herself that it beat the hell out of sitting in a police station and answering a lot of questions. It killed most of the next two and a half hours. She walked out of Lucky Nail a hundred and seventy-five bucks poorer and a little bit sore. She stuffed her blue jacket into a trash can behind Lucky Nail, tucked the memory sticks into a pocket, and hoofed it back up the hill to Tio Bobby's Astro.

No sweat, she told herself. Don't be looking around, you're just another Puerto Rican broad out for a stroll, the city is lousy with 'em. Who'd look twice at another one?

D.

N.

A.

Damn.

She drove Bobby's ragged little Astro through the streets of the Bronx, trying to concentrate on where she was going. Jail was not something Alessandra spent much time thinking about. In the Brooklyn neighborhoods where she grew up, everyone seemed to have an uncle or a brother or a cousin doing time. Nobody made too big a deal out of it. Maybe it was to be expected, given the nature of job opportunities in the inner reaches of the outer boroughs. Should you fight for that job in the straight life? Six bucks an hour, yo, or an easy tax-free G a week wholesalin' . . . It always amused her that people from middle America—that strange and foreign place from whence all the loudest complaints about drugs and crime originated— were the weekend warriors, they were the people who drove their cars over the bridge after the sun went down, who came in and cruised the side streets past the atrophy and decay. She'd been watching them all her life. Man, we live here, how can you waltz in here and show us your ass? As a child she'd wanted to say it, but they would have paid her no attention, they were zoned, man, they were locked in. Privately, they were looking for what they publicly condemned so heartily: weed or blow or rock or a piece of strange. And when they'd gotten what they wanted, they'd drive their SUVs back home to their four-bedroom three-bath splits in Limbaugh-land, thinking, *Eew. How can people live in those places?*

The scratch on her side nagged at her. Hey, she thought, it was just a break-in, happens every day, all over the city. No cop is going to waste time and energy chasing a burglar. It was a fact of life that burglars generally got caught by mistake. Unless you were stupid enough to get yourself a nickname in the press, nobody was going to chase you too hard. The *Post* starts calling you "The Park Avenue Bandit," the cops will be annoyed enough to come after you. Otherwise, unless you had the bad luck to bump into a policeman on your way out, the way Alessandra very nearly had, you were probably pretty safe, because it was too much work for too little chance of catching you. And DNA tests were still too expensive to waste on a lousy B&E.

But it wasn't just a B&E, was it? There was still the drug connection to consider, along with a dead musician and a missing guitar once owned by Stevie Ray Vaughn, not to mention a porn tape whose current value was pegged right around a half million bucks. Any one of those factors could provide the motivation for a much more thorough look at the evidence, including but not limited to the blood and tissue sample generously provided by the recent perpetrator of an unauthorized entry into a domicile occupied by three quarters of the members of BandX.

It's a hell of a lot more likely, she told herself, that they'll find your stupid toolbox and backtrack you from that, somehow.

All in all, not a great performance, she told herself.

She got sick of looking for a parking spot, wound up putting the Astro in a lot a couple blocks from Marty's office. He wasn't in when she got there, but Sarah Waters was. "You look bored," Al told her.

Sarah shrugged. "I finished all the stuff he left me this morning," she said. "I'm gonna have to get a TV or something."

"You wanna give me a hand?" Al showed her the flash drives. "I need to go through all the files on these things."

Sarah held out her hand. "Why not," she said. "Gimme one. What am I looking for?"

"Any files that contain the name 'Sean Caughlan,' or 'Willy Caughlan,' or any combination thereof. Also a video, probably homemade, that shows a young guy having sex with Shine. You know who she is?"

"Of course I do. Did she make a sex tape?"

"Don't know for sure. I'm gonna go use the PC in Marty's office."

Al came back out a couple of hours later. "You find anything?"

"Yeah," Sarah said.

"What?"

"Guys are pigs," she said.

"I meant, anything new and useful," Al said.

"No. Sorry."

"Me, neither. If Marty asks, BandX is in a recording studio over in Queens, and I got an invite of sorts to watch them work. It's probably a waste of time, but it'll kill the afternoon."

"See ya."

Fourteen

They were in full crisis mode by the time she got there.

Sandy Ellison, the A&R guy, had TJ Conrad pigeonholed in a corridor of the old converted warehouse currently housing Astoria Studios and seemed to be lecturing him sternly, poking his finger into the guitarist's chest for emphasis. TJ, a cigarette smoldering in his mouth, took it silently until he saw Alessandra watching them from the end of the corridor, and then he exhaled smoke into Ellison's face and pushed past him. Ellison stared at TJ's departing back, angry. "Goddammit, TJ . . ."

TJ stopped about ten feet away from Ellison. "Tell you what," he said, his voice pitched so that Alessandra could hear. "How about this? You tell Trent I said he could go fuck himself. Okay? I'm not getting up on another stage with that asshole."

"TJ, you're blowing this out of proportion! You want to risk everything we've worked for?" He held up his right hand, thumb and forefinger half an inch apart. "We're this close! If we can just get these tracks laid down over the next couple of days, the fucking album is done, and you won't have to see any of these motherfuckers until the Jones Beach shows. And by that time, the buzz will already be starting. You haven't heard any of the finished tracks yet, but I'm telling you, this is going to be your *Tommy!*"

TJ looked at Ellison and snorted. "*Tommy?* Gimme a fucking break. The Who is a joke. They made one half-decent album in thirty fucking years, and it wasn't *Tommy.* Let me tell you something." He took a step in Ellison's direction, and Ellison retreated a step. "If I thought the best thing I ever did wasn't any better than fucking *Tommy,* I would go climb up to the top of the Empire State Building and jump the fuck off."

"Are you crazy?" Ellison shouted, red-faced. "The Who is one of the largest selling acts in the history of the fucking universe! Every one of those guys is a multizillionaire!"

TJ shook his head. "You don't get it, do you?"

"I don't get what?"

"Look," TJ said. "Here's what you do: you go tell Cliff, you go tell Doc, you go tell the rest of those guys it's fucking Trent or it's me. Got it? Because you know as well as I do, a second-banana guitar player is a hell of a lot easier to come by than a musical genius." He turned, looked in Alessandra's direction, and winked. "Give 'em a half hour to think it over," he said, walking in Al's direction. "Then come find me, I'll be hanging."

"Goddamn you, TJ, don't do this to me!"

TJ held up a one-finger salute without slowing down or looking back.

"Don't do it to yourself, TJ! This could be the best shot you'll ever have!"

TJ continued in Al's direction. He smiled at her when he got close. "Can I buy you lunch? I know it's a little late . . ."

She nodded. "Sure. Since you just blew up this gig, I should accept while you've still got a buck in your pocket."

He put a hand on her shoulder, turned her to walk next to him. "Hey," he said, "one of the many things I excel at is being broke. Come with me, I know a nice Greek place right around the corner. Cheap, too."

"So you don't sing." He seemed astonished at that; it was the third time he'd asked her.

"Not even in the shower," she told him. They were sitting in a small hole-in-the-wall eatery a block from Astoria Studios. The cooking was done at an open charcoal grill in the front of the place, giving the restaurant a smoky, garlicky aura. "I hope the food here is as good as it smells."

"You won't be disappointed," he said. "But listen, I'm having a hard time letting this go. You don't sing, you don't play any kind of instrument? What if I told you I could get you a backup-singer gig with a band I was sitting in with this morning? What would you do?"

"Run," she said. "My theory, there's a performer's gene, you know what I mean? Everybody's got an aunt, you get a couple of margaritas in her and she gets up to sing with the guitar player in the Mexican restaurant, right? She's got the performer's gene. She might not have anything to go with it, like the voice or the face or the legs, but she doesn't care, because she's got the gene. I don't have it. Standing up in front of a bunch of people and doing anything—speaking, reading, telling jokes, forget about singing—that's my idea of Hell. I would rather have my toenails pulled out."

"Wow," he said, shaking his head. "You're not kidding, are you?"

"No. Why? You know somebody who needs a backup singer?"

"I do, as a matter of fact. But you've got to be the first person I've met in about ten years who'd turn it down. In the business, you know, everyone you meet, every engineer, every sound guy, every groupie, band manager, roadie, and bus driver, what they really want is to be in my shoes. They want to be up on the stage."

"Must be oppressive, after a while. Every person who talks to you wants your job."

"I always thought of it like hitting the lottery," he said. "Not that I've ever done that. But imagine it, you buy a ticket, the next day you wake up rich. But all your so-called friends, right, the first thought that comes into their head when they see you is, *that fucking bastard. That son of a bitch, that no-good, no-talent, no-voice, ham-fisted hack of a guitar player, how the hell could he hit when I can play circles around him and I can't get arrested? God hates me, that's what it is, God must fucking hate me.* And all the time, right, they're in your face, they're telling you how much they love your stuff, they got all your records, they been to see you play so many times, all of that. But you can see it in their eyes: all they want is what you've got, they want it so bad they'd kill you if they thought that would get it for them. And what happens, after a while, it kind of turns you into an asshole, which is what I acted like when I met you up in Boston. I apologize."

"Not necessary," she said. "What happened this morning? I think I missed out on all the fun. Were you serious, what you said to Sandy, back there? Would you really quit BandX over what's-his-name? The guitar player."

"Trent? He's no guitar player, he's a poser. No, hey, listen, couple things you got to know about musicians: we're drama queens, every freaking one of us. I can't just say, 'Back off, Trent, you're giving me a pain in my ass,' I have to throw a tantrum or he won't take me serious. If I don't break something and threaten to quit, he won't hear me at all."

"So what did you do? Break your guitar?"

"No," TJ said, laughing. "I broke his."

"You're kidding. No offense, but he's a much bigger guy than you. Weren't you afraid he'd do something to you?"

TJ shook his head. "Trent's all noise. Now Doc, he's a different story. Doc will throw down on you in a second, but Trent gets by on bluster, and when that don't work, he don't know what to do."

"So what got all this started? Were you late or something?"

"Not me, not when you're paying for studio time. They were the ones who were late. Doc usually rides herd on them, gets their sorry asses to the church on time, but he didn't get it done this morning. No big thing, you understand, it ain't Doc's fault, it's got to get old after a while, being the designated adult. But I'm sitting around, right, I see a couple of guys I know, they're having trouble with one of the tracks they're working on. Sometimes you try too hard, you get so close to something you can't hear it anymore. So I'm not doing anything, right, I sit in, they play me what they got, right away I see what's missing. Not that I'm that smart, I'm not trying to sound like that, but you call a plumber, he's gonna see what you got wrong with your plumbing. Right? I'm a guitar player, I hear a guitar-shaped hole in their cut, and what they need is a riff." His fingers played it in midair and he whistled it for her: a mournful plaint, six or seven seconds long. "I pick up a guitar and I do it. They think about it for maybe ten seconds, next thing you know I'm in the sound booth ripping it off, over and over, and then another one, a little variation, sort of a coda for the end of the piece. Doesn't sound like much, right, but it takes like two and a half, three hours before we get it down, and of course right away they want to change it and I got to fight them off. So by the time I come back out, BandX has been cooling their heels for a while, and I'm the bad guy. Well, they were the ones that were late, so screw them, right? And it kinda went downhill from there."

"Who was it for? The piece you worked on this morning."

"I told you, couple guys I know. One's an engineer and the other's a producer."

"Yeah, but who's the artist? Who's the singer?"

He shrugged. "I dunno. They didn't play me the vocal."

"So how do you get paid for what you did?"

"Please. Anyhow, they were friends, I was just helping out. No, listen, I love this shit. I would pay them to let me do it. To me, there's nothing better. I hear what you got, and I give it something, right? I take it to the next level. Even if nobody else hears it, even if it never sees the light of day, doesn't matter. It's doing it. It's sitting those two hours in the studio just to get eight or ten seconds of sound that turns something ordinary into something beautiful. That's why I'm here."

She'd been looking at his face as he talked, saw him now as he caught her watching and went a little red. "You're not kidding," she said.

"No," he said. "I really would do it for free."

"You said there was a couple of things about musicians, but you only told me the one thing, that you were all drama queens. What's the other thing?"

He tilted his head back. "Fear."

"What do you mean?"

"Fear. Musicians are all driven by fear. Let me put it this way. I am goddamn good with a guitar, and I know it. Okay? But here's something else I know: there's maybe ten guys on the planet who can play most of the shit I can play, but there's ten thousand who can fake it, and most people don't know enough about music to tell the difference. So you know what the real difference is between me and them? I got the gig, they don't. Clarence Clemons and Bill Clinton, they both play the sax, okay? Clarence ain't half bad, and neither is Bill. But Clarence has the gig. So Bill plays in his garage. You know what I'm saying? And Clarence knows in his gut, if The Boss hears some new horn player and he likes the guy better, Clarence could show up for work tomorrow and find some other guy parked in his spot, security won't even let him into the building. Hey, don't look at me like that, shit like that happens all the time. Those guys in the Tonight Show Band, they're all happy and shit, they live in the big house and they drive the Corniche or whatever the fuck. But the only difference between them and half the dudes playing in bars? They got the gig. They're not better musicians, they don't work any harder, they're not any smarter or more virtuous or anything like that. They got the gig, the other guy don't. End of story. So every working musician wakes up with this one fear, and he goes to bed with it, every day: what if this is the last gig I ever get? What if Jay Leno wakes up and decides to shitcan the whole band? Which he ought to do, by the way. Those guys are a joke. What if Springsteen decides to do *Nebraska* again? What if this is the last time I make a real paycheck playing my music?"

"So you're not afraid the guys will pick Trent over you?"

"Never happen. It ain't about that, anyhow, I don't mind Trent that much. Here's how it will play: they'll yell at Trent for the rest of the afternoon, then tonight or tomorrow morning they'll yell at me for a while, then we'll get back together. He'll stay out of my face and I'll try not to make him look stupid. At least until the next time."

"You're not afraid this is the last good gig you'll ever have?"

He inhaled, started to answer, then laughed and shook his head. "I been making a living with my guitar for almost twenty years, okay? So part of my brain knows I can find something else if this falls apart. But I won't lie to you. If they go find another guy, I'm gonna be suicidal until I find the next thing."

She looked at him. Why can't you fall for some nice guy with a job and a pension, she asked herself. Why you gotta flip over some dude five minutes out of friggin' rehab? The only reason you're even talking to this guy is because you think he might be involved with the enterprise that's moving product through Daniel Caughlan's business . . . And what if he's the one who killed Willy? But there was something compelling about him. She didn't know if it was his outlaw aura or maybe just the way he seemed to speak whatever was on his mind, but she felt an undeniable attraction. Tall, dark, and fucked up, she thought, just the way you like 'em . . . So what are you gonna do, hold a knife to his throat while you hijack his dick for ten minutes? You gonna hold him out over a balcony, shove a gun in his face, what? Because you know you'll never trust him enough to let him come to you the way normal people do it . . .

The waiter had just cleared the plates away and they were waiting for coffees when she showed up. She had long, straight brown hair that went with her tall, thin frame, she wore a pair of bell-bottom jeans and a Radiohead T-shirt with no bra underneath it. She came through the front door of the restaurant and looked around. When she saw Alessandra and TJ looking back at her she broke eye contact, but she walked across the floor and stood by their table. "Hi, guys."

"Hi, Laurie. Al, did you ever meet Laurie?" TJ said.

"No," Al said. It took an effort to bring her mind back around to the present. "But I've seen you before, right?" She remembered the hair and the nipples, sharp under an old T-shirt. "You were at the show up in Boston."

"Yeah." Laurie looked at the floor. "I, um, I'm supposed to give TJ a message."

"Go ahead, Laurie," TJ said. "She's with us."

"Um, Mr. Ellison says, um, he bitched everyone out, especially Trent, and um, can you, you know, come back tomorrow, and everybody will try to be cool and stuff."

"Tomorrow? What about this afternoon? What about all the complaining about studio time costing Ellison half his budget?"

"Um, we got bumped, so it doesn't matter."

"What do you mean, we got bumped?"

"Um, Shine, um, showed up, and they're, like, giving her your slot."

"You're kidding. Is that what they told you?"

"No, I saw her, she's really there."

"Serious? You saw God?"

Laurie glanced up at him. "I've met Shine before. She's actually very nice."

"Unlike certain other . . ."

She turned red. "I never said that."

"I love you, Laurie, you know that. When are you going to come away with me?" He was earnestly phony.

"Of course you do. Do I tell Mr. Ellison you'll come back in the morning?"

"I'll be there. Tell him the rest of those assholes better be on time."

"Okay." She looked at Alessandra, then quickly away. "You were the one who was asking about Willy Caughlan. The other night, up in Boston."

"That was me," Al said.

"Call me sometime," she said. "I'm in the book."

TJ's mouth fell open as Laurie turned to go. "What's your last name, Laurie?" Al asked her.

"Villereal," she said. "I'm in Queens."

TJ closed his mouth and swallowed. "How can you leave me like this, Laurie? You're breaking my heart."

"Breaking your heart?" She scowled at him. "How can I break something you haven't got? Now that would really be something." She turned and walked out of the restaurant.

TJ looked at Alessandra. "I'm in shock," he said.

"Why?"

"She's so shy, but she actually asked you to call her. I've never known her to be so brave."

"Brave? She's a pussycat."

"She's a mouse. Listen, it seems my calendar for this afternoon is suddenly open. Whaddaya say we blow this joint? There's a big Impressionist exhibit at the Met, I was gonna go Saturday, but it'll be much less crowded today. You interested?"

Her answer at times like this was so automatic it was almost out of her mouth before she could think about it, but she reeled it back in. It was always "no," no to the movies, no to dinner, no to a good-night kiss, no, now and forever, either no

or hell, no. But she'd never been to the Met, never known anyone other than Anthony who'd go there.

And besides, she liked the guy.

"Why not," she said.

He restrained himself when he saw the Astro, just looked at her
once with eyebrows raised and that was it. Maybe the guy is
used to a certain amount of weirdness, Alessandra thought,
maybe it's no big deal to him. Anyhow, she was tired of apolo-
gizing for the van, so she didn't comment, she just let it ride. TJ
climbed into the passenger seat and belted himself in.

How old is this cat? The voices started up as soon as she got
behind the wheel. The voices were ageless and without gender,
but the questions they asked sounded suspiciously like the ones
her father would ask. *So what is he, thirty? Sixty? And he's on pro-
bation for some kind of drug rap, did you forget about that? Does he
have a real job? Has he ever had a real job? And his face looks like it
was sewed together out of old shoes, do you actually find that attrac-
tive? And where are you gonna go with this anyhow? You really think
you got that kind of courage?* "So," she said, pulling away from the
curb. "What do you do when you're not playing for BandX?"

He shrugged. "There's a couple of other bands I work with.
I do a little bit of session work, although there ain't much of that
anymore. I buy and sell guitars, and I do some custom work for
players who are looking for a specific sound or a certain look.
There's a few sound guys and composers who call me in for this
and that. And if worse comes to worst, I can always paint."

"Paint? As in oil on canvas?"

"Hah. Latex on walls, babe. I got an uncle in the business,
and whenever things get bad enough, he puts me to work for a
while until it picks up again. I mean, it ain't my favorite thing,

you know what I mean? I always feel, like, 'how bad did you fuck things up to wind up back doing this?' But I refuse to do fucking weddings and bar mitzvahs, and the gig with my uncle pays the bills when there's nothing else going on."

"Nothing worse than frustrated genius," she said, curious to see how he'd take it.

"Unless it's a frustrated moron," he said, grinning. "Hey, listen, like the man says, you can't always get what you want."

"I've heard that," she said. "Truthfully, I think I have to respect someone who's willing to support his art. I guess I have that prejudice that musicians are a bunch of rich, lazy, spoiled, womanizing, coke-addled prima donnas."

He laughed. "Subtract the 'rich' part," he said, "and you're not that far off."

"Is it worth it?"

"You asked that before," he said. "Up in Boston."

"Did I? Sorry."

"That's all right. I don't remember what I told you last time. But you know what I think, really? It's just me. It's what I do. If I gotta paint or whatever, you know, shovel shit for a while just to keep it going, then that's just my tough luck. But I found my thing, I found my groove. This is what I want. So I don't suffer from that trip where you sit around second-guessing yourself, 'oh, I shoulda went to school for this or that,' or whatever. Maybe I am wasting my life, I don't know, but I'm just trying to hang on to what I want." He looked at her. "What about you? How'd you come to do what you do?"

Careful, she told herself. "I don't think life equipped me for anything else. I'm no good at any of the traditional female things. I don't like being around sick people, I hate school, I'm not very maternal—about a half hour with somebody's kid is enough to last me for a month—and I have a low tolerance for bullshit. So I can't be a nurse or a teacher or a librarian or a mom or a nanny. I'm like you, in a way." She surprised herself, saying that. "I found something I think I'm good at, so, yeah. I'm trying to hang onto it."

The thought struck her as they climbed the stone steps to the museum. Is this a date? Is that what this is? Are you actually going out with this guy? Alessandra Martillo don't go on dates, are you kidding me? Have you lost your freakin' mind? Alessandra Martillo finds a guy she can stand for ten minutes, she drags him into the bushes and she takes what she wants. Besides, you're supposed to be looking into the possibility that the guy is a murderer. Isn't he the common denominator here? He knew Willy, he's into recreational pharmaceuticals, and he's a hustler. If he had a key to Willy's place, it very well could have been him. And anyway, even if you could manage to have something normal with this guy, how can you expect to compete with a bus full of naked sixteen-year-old girls? TJ Conrad going out with you must be the rough equivalent to a regular guy going out with his grandmother.

The dude knew his way around the Met, though. She got turned around after about five minutes, she wasn't sure she could find her way back to the main entrance without stopping to ask for directions, but she followed Conrad as he wandered through the rooms. The guy's got no focus, she thought, he's got no goal, he stops and stares at whatever catches his eye, a painting or a statue or even just a kid admiring something. He didn't try to explain anything to her, though, which was a large point in his favor. And when they finally got to the rooms that housed what they'd come to look at, works by Manet and Monet and Degas, he got lost in the paintings. He stood silent, open-mouthed, transported, and then after a while he'd bring himself back, shake his head slightly, and move on to the next. She lost track of time, for a while she just watched him, but ultimately she found herself wondering how anyone could, through the application of spots of paint on rough fabric, capture anything as ethereal as luminescence, as evanescent as human spirit.

They finally made it out, into the next gallery, which was occupied with more contemporary works, which Conrad ignored. "Whew," he said, and he headed for a stone bench next to a window. "Man, I gotta sit down. What did you think?"

I think I need to open my eyes wider, she thought. "I'm glad I came. Thanks for asking me."

"You feel like walking?" he asked her. "It's a sin to come this close to Central Park without at least sticking your head inside."

"Why is that?" Alessandra had spent her life in New York City, but hadn't been to Central Park twice that she could remember. Her childhood had been about survival, not about going to the park.

"It's like the city's backyard," he told her. "It's where we all come out to play. It's the best place in the world to watch people."

"All right," she said.

"You want my jacket?" It had gotten chilly as the afternoon wore on, and she wasn't dressed for it.

"No," she said. "I'm fine."

"You sure? You look frozen . . ." He put an arm around her shoulder, pulled her close to himself, and just like that she knew her mind was made up. And how can it be, she wondered, why is it, at the key moments in my life, the buried primitive mind makes its choice while the rational part of me swallows its tongue? How can I be afraid of what I think this man might be and yet want him so badly at the same time? She felt his hand rough against the bare skin of her upper arm. She quaked at the very idea, her letting him get past the razor wire and up next to who she really was. "You *are* frozen," he said.

She stopped. Fuck it, she thought. You can't risk this, your life is gonna suck beyond belief. He turned to face her. "I am not," she said, her voice emphatic, "frozen." She stepped into him then, wrapped herself around him, felt his arms folding her in, and she kissed him, kissed him with as much of herself as she could manage, and then she did it again, holding him harder, as though she could squeeze their two separate selves into one new thing. She did it to shut her inner critic's mouth, she did it so that the choice could be made once and for all, and not reconsidered later, weighed, doubted, debated. And she did it because she wanted to.

But that inner voice of fear is never really defeated. She broke free, buried her face in the side of his neck. You can't back out now, she told herself, you run away from this guy you'll never get this close to real ever again.

He didn't let her go. "Okay," he said, after a moment. "You're not cold."

"No."

"All right," he said. "But I think we should go."

Her pulse jackhammered as the beast inside her exulted, but she had wrested the tiller back out of its grasp. "Okay," she said, as they separated. "God," she said. "It is kinda chilly out here."

They didn't speak until she drove the van onto the FDR. "How do we do this? Do I ride you home?" she asked him. She wondered if he could hear her voice shivering. She glanced at him, saw in his eyes that he knew how afraid she was.

"We do whatever you say we do," he said. "We go where you wanna go."

"We can go to my place," she said, her voice shaking.

"Well all right," he said. "Drive this love wagon back to wherever you hide it, and I'll walk you home. Just like in the movies."

"You know what? I think I would like that. But it's like a half-hour's walk from the lot back to my place."

"Tell you what," he said. "I'll drop you home, then I'll go park this thing and walk the keys back to you. Okay?"

"Are you sure?"

"Absolutely."

He's trying to be nice to you, she thought. Why don't you let him? "Okay. Thanks."

Fifteen

The door to the apartment directly under hers on the fourth floor opened when she climbed up the stairs. The Korean guy who lived there came out, stared at Alessandra's chest. "There were some guys here earlier. I think they were waiting for you."

"Are you serious? What did they look like?"

"One of them looked like a football player. Might have been Hispanic, I don't know. Dark hair, dark eyes. Pockmarked face. Wore one of those green fatigue jackets. I didn't get a good look at the second guy. He might have had blond hair."

"Have you seen them around since then?"

"I was working," he said. "I don't know if they came back or not. Maybe they left you a note."

"Maybe they did. Thanks." She turned, looked back down the stairs behind her, then craned her neck to see if there was anyone on the landing above. Nobody there, or at least no one in sight. She turned back to catch the Korean guy staring at her ass.

So? My best feature, she thought. If I got breast implants, I could be the Wet Dream of the Month. Alessandra Martillo in all her naked, airbrushed, surgically enhanced glory. Miss April loves children and reading the Bible, she's saving herself for her soul mate, oh, and for you, too, of course, and you can talk to her direct by dialing 1-900-Miss April, please have your major credit card ready.

Her neighbor went back inside, closed his door. She wondered if he even knew what her face looked like.

Concentrate, Martillo. Someone has shown an unhealthy interest in your whereabouts. You can still get out of here. Take the cell phone off your belt and call Anthony. You know he'd let you sleep in your old room for a couple of days . . . Or you might even have enough courage to let TJ take you home to his place.

But it had been a long day. She didn't want to call Anthony, she didn't want to sleep in her old room, she wanted to be in her own space where she could think about what had happened in the park. She walked down the hallway, turned, and looked up the stairs. She could see the door to her apartment. Nobody around, she thought. Go for it.

She sat on the floor in her studio, leaned back against her daybed. She looked at her watch. You've got at least a half hour before he gets back, she thought. Probably more like forty-five minutes . . . She had the news articles and police reports she'd gotten from Marty spread around her. She tried to wrestle her mind back to her job. She read through the newspapers, which were more succinct than the police reports. *Promising young musician found dead in east side studio. Sean William Caughlan, aka Willy C, was discovered in his apartment by the other members of BandX, the musical group in which he played lead guitar. They came looking for him after he failed to show up for a performance. Cause of death was an apparent overdose.*

It was the same story in the police reports, told in convoluted copspeak. No sign of forced entry. No marks on the body. Body temperature indicating a time of death eight to ten hours prior to discovery. Various officers filed reports after interviewing neighbors, who had collectively heard and seen nothing unusual. There were signed affidavits by each of the band members which stated, among other things, the whereabouts of said individuals ten hours before discovery of the body. Cliff Davis and Trent Wegman had been at the home of a Miss Charlotte Rae Peters, corroborating statement signed by Miss Peters and by the two other women present attached. Timothy "Doc" Jamison had been home with his family, was observed mowing his lawn by his next-door neighbor, corroborating statement attached. Theodore James Conrad had been confined in a court-mandated inpatient treatment facility, corroborating statements attached. Missing from the victim's studio was a guitar alleged to have once belonged to Stevie Ray Vaughn, description and pictures attached.

And so on. No big deal, just another dead druggie.

The NYPD sometimes suffers from a short attention span. Each new day brings its crop of victims who must be attended to. The press has an even shorter focus. The next batch of stories elbowed its way in: a Democratic congressman from Queens indignantly denied the outrageous charges against him and his campaign finance committee, the federal DA was confident of a conviction of the congressman and several key aides; two ex-cops were charged with carrying out executions in the service of a well-known organized crime figure; the New York Mets traded away two starting pitchers for a minor league starting pitcher, a reliever, and a bucket of warm spit. The passing of

Sean William Caughlan faded from public view. So much for the record.

They buried the kid. After that, no one seemed to have given him much thought.

She called Caughlan's cell number. He answered on the first ring. "Al," he said. "I been meaning to call you back. Things have been a little bit crazy out here."

She could hear voices in the background. "Can you talk?"

"Not really." She heard some muffled noises, as though he had shifted the phone from one hand to the other. "I can listen, though, if you're quick about it."

"Okay," she said. "Number one, have you heard about a video your son supposedly shot of himself doing the wild thing with Shine, the singer?"

Caughlan was silent for a moment. She was beginning to think he wasn't going to answer. "I can't be mad at him for that," he finally said. "If he was still alive, maybe I would be. Maybe I wouldn't."

"Regardless," she said. "The video has gone missing. I was offered a half a million bucks if I could turn it up."

"Holy Christ," Caughlan said. The voices in the background went silent. She listened to him breathing into the phone. "Is that . . . How real is that number?"

"Sounded real enough to me. Someone from the West Coast entertainment industry made the offer. We can go over the details later, if you want. My opinion, a half million was just the opening bid."

"Lot of money," he said.

"You grow up as poor as I did," she said, feeling him out.

"Yeah, yeah. Anything else?"

"Gearoid say anything to you about three mutts who tried

to make a grab for us the other night? On the way home from your party?"

"He did not. They after you or him?"

"Good question. How bad would it be for your business if someone sat O'Hagan down on a hard chair in a small room and shined a light in his eyes?"

"Bad enough."

"You think he just forgot to mention it to you? Slipped his mind, maybe? I'm not trying to get anybody in hot water here. Nobody likes a rat."

"He's an independent cuss," Caughlan said. "Don't care for anyone messing about in his life."

"Which you're about to do."

"No choice," Caughlan said. "I can't have him running around loose. Not if what you say is true."

"Is it possible it's him they're after? That they don't really care about you?"

He chewed on that for a moment. "Doubt it," he finally said. "But there is one other possibility. And if you catch my drift, you'd better watch your arse, Miss M."

"You think they may have been after me?"

"Add it up," he said. "You're the one who's been going around asking questions. Look, I really gotta go. I'll call you later. You watch your step, you hear me?"

"Yeah," she said. "I do."

"Sorry," Caughlan said, and he stuck the phone back in his jacket pocket. "Go ahead."

"The grand jury's been meeting every Thursday for about six months," Marty Stiles told him. They were walking west on Fourteenth Street in Manhattan. The city had just finished paving it, and now, for whatever reason, they were tearing it up again. "So far, they got shit. Bunch of icky-picky stuff, some interstate shipping rules violations, some labor law bullshit, nothing anybody cares about."

"So they don't know about the opium base," Caughlan said.

"I don't think so. Maybe they got a little sniff, but they don't got anything in the way of evidence, or even hearsay. That's probably why they been dragging this thing out so long. I mean, you look guilty as hell, Mick. You fit all the stereotypes."

"Maybe I ought to hire a bunch more illegal Mexicans," Caughlan said. "Let them catch me at that, I can pay a fine and everybody goes home happy."

"Nice theory," Stiles told him, "but no way you want these guys up your ass. We gotta figure out who's using you to move that product, first."

"Any progress on that front?"

Stiles shook his head. "Nothing concrete. Couple things I gotta check into, though."

"Yeah? Like what?"

"Little birdie told me about this chemist, guy's up in Rockland County, just over the New York State line from Jersey. The boy was in trouble last year, the FDA banged him for some hair regrowth formula he was selling on the Net. He got fined something like seven hundred fifty thou, but he's been livin' large. Just bought his girlfriend a new Jag."

"It fits," Caughlan said. "They gotta process that shit someplace. Stupid to do it in New York State, though. Bring it in through Jersey, then up across the state line, that makes it federal. Who is this guy? And who was the little birdie? Who ratted him out to you?"

"His lawyer," Stiles told him. "Never stiff your lawyer out

of his fee. But have a little patience, okay? I don't want you stomping on the guy, not yet. At least lemme make sure he's our guy first."

"Can you find out who he's connected with? You trace him back to whoever he works for, we've probably got our guy."

"That's the plan."

"Okay. Sounds good. And you're telling me I don't need to sweat this grand jury thing."

"Not yet. Anyway, drug busts have went out of vogue this year. Listen, the indictment don't mean shit. They can get that any time they want it. Doesn't mean a fucking thing. What you gotta worry about is what they can convince a jury that you done. Besides." Marty waved his hand at the crowd on Fourteenth Street. "Half the people out here are walking around whacked, and the other half don't give a fuck. You gotta figure, it would cost the state of New Jersey, what, five million to prosecute? Ten? And for that, the DA gets his picture on page four of the fucking *Bergen Record,* maybe once. Twice if they convict. So about eight people see it. Who gives a fuck? Nah, that's going nowhere. Now, you was the mayor of Jersey City and you had your hand in the cookie jar, you'd be dead meat. That's what's hot this year. Everybody wants to be seen 'cleaning up corruption.' Drug busts are yesterday's news."

"Glad to hear it," Caughlan said, "even if I ain't done shit. You let me know if there's anything I can do to help with your chemist."

"Will do. Listen, speaking of crooked politicians, I hadda promise this guy fifty large for his reelection committee. That's how I got the dope on the grand jury."

"Grand," Caughlan said, shaking his head. "Terrific. Can I send it direct or do I have to go through you?"

"No, we gotta bury it," Stiles told him, a little too quickly. "We can't have it look like you paid him off."

"Of course not," Caughlan said. "What a terrible thing that would be. Let me know how you want it."

"I already got it set up," Marty told him, pulling a piece of paper out of his pocket.

Her kitchen was too small to sit in, you had to stand up while you were in it, so she sat on a chair just outside. She had the top apartment in the rear of the building, but she had a sidelong view of a slice of Pineapple Street through the kitchen window. A Brooklyn Union Gas Company truck was parked on the far side of the street, and three guys in BUG uniforms stood around behind the truck. Where the hell could TJ be, she wondered. Maybe Tio Bobby's van did it to him, maybe he got lost, maybe he stopped in somewhere for a few . . .

What made me ever think I wanted to do this job, she asked herself. Maybe you were trying to impress your father, she thought. She remembered what Gearoid had said about that, trying equally hard to impress his old man and to piss him off, and having success only at the latter.

Maybe you should consider a career change, she thought. It's not too late, you could still get those implants . . .

There had been something real between her and her father, she remembered thinking that, back in the old days. Maybe it had been more of a drill sergeant–recruit thing than a father-daughter thing. He'd treated it like a job, one more obligation to be discharged.

She could still hear his voice.

Do it the same way, every time. Don't ever let your technique get sloppy. Do you hear me? Let the other guy get sloppy, that's how you beat him, especially if he's bigger and stronger than you. You absorb the punishment, you take the pain, you survive, and you wait for your opening. When you see your opportunity, you drive right through it. Then he had turned against her, sided with Magdelena. She wanted to let go of that, but it kept coming back up.

She watched the three guys standing next to the gas company truck. There is an art to looking busy while doing nothing, and most hardhats are masters of it. These three, though, seemed to be working way too hard at occupying the space in front of her building. She focused on them for the next five minutes as they studiously ignored her side of the street, but then all at once all three of them turned and stared in the direction of the front entrance of her building.

Maybe somebody came out. Maybe something on the stoop attracted their attention. There was a young girl on the third floor who was pretty hot, maybe she came out and flashed them or something . . .

Right.

It was discouraging.

I just want to go to sleep, she thought. I want to get the keys back from TJ, and I want to go to bed. Can't they come back for me in the morning? But three was too many, this wasn't surveillance. This was something more serious. One of them looked directly at her kitchen window, but she had the lights off inside. There was no way he made actual eye contact, but for a second it did feel like that. She could sense him willing her to come out.

She waited.

They waited.

You could call someone, she thought. You could call the cops. You could call your father, who would probably call the local precinct and get a couple of blueshirts to come and roust these guys. And then he'd come himself, wouldn't he? She didn't know. But it was a good forty-five minutes from where he lived, up in the Bronx, down to her Brooklyn street, even in a car, even if there's no traffic. There's always traffic . . . She didn't feel like calling him.

And there'd be plenty of questions later. Most of them would come from the local cops, who would be incredibly aggravated by her lack of cooperation. Her father would sit back in silent judgment. It's what he had done, years ago, when she'd left her aunt's house and hit the streets. He'd reacted the same way when he found out she'd moved in with Tio Bobby. Her father was the kind of man who'd spent his entire life waiting for God to smite the wicked, and who had been consistently disappointed when it didn't happen.

I don't need that, she thought. I don't need to see that look on his face again.

Overhead, the ancient timbers that made up the roof of the building creaked, and then a second later creaked again. Someone up there, she thought. Sitting or standing in one position too long, had to move.

She was willing to bet there was another guy outside, down at the bottom of her fire escape, cutting off the obvious escape route. Probably another one inside, waiting somewhere in the stairwell, hoping she'd show her face. You go down the stairwell, she thought, the guy waiting at the bottom hears you coming, no matter how careful you are. He calls his buddy on the roof, they've got you boxed in. Maybe you can immobilize the guy on the ground before his buddy can get down to you, and maybe you can't. And that's assuming they aren't armed, and that they don't just put a bullet in your sorry behind . . .

The guy on the roof moved again. Getting restless.

Same story on the inside. You march down those stairs, you're caught in the stairwell, they've got a man above and below you. They'll grab you, toss you into the back of that truck, nobody ever sees you again.

Fuck it, she thought. I can handle this.

She gathered up the paperwork, stuck it back in the envelope, shoved the whole mess into her oven and shut the door. What guy would ever look in there? She unlocked her rear window, the one that fronted the fire escape, and eased it open a millimeter at a time. It was already dark inside, so nobody could see her take down the curtain she'd improvised out of an Indian-print sheet and lay it aside. Clear path, she thought. But for them or for you?

She tried to maintain her grip on her emotions. Stay calm, she told herself. Your temper is your greatest weakness . . . She couldn't do it. She felt herself beginning to boil as she headed for her front door. Five, six guys, she thought. Six guys for one skinny little broad. Somebody must want you real bad. Plus the gas company truck, somebody is laying out a nice piece of change to stage this little exercise.

Bastards.

She opened her front door, stuck her head out, and looked around. Nobody in sight. If there was a guy in the stairwell, he must be down a couple of floors. She slithered out, left her door ajar, crept up the final flight of stairs, the ones that led up to the roof. The steel door at the top, contrary to the fire code, was generally chained and locked closed in a lame attempt to make the building somewhat secure. The chain and lock were both missing, but there were two large dead bolts on the inside of the door, and they would do. They made a clear and distinct sound when she slapped them shut.

Four seconds to get back down the stairs. Two more to get back inside her apartment, yanking the door shut behind her, where it locked automatically. Four more seconds to get to the open window. As she traversed the space, she heard footsteps on the roof above. Human nature, you hear somebody lock your ass out, you have to go and yank on the door handle . . .

Five more seconds and she was looking over the edge of the roof. The guy was standing over by his side of the steel door, still jerking on the doorknob. He fumbled for something on his belt. She got ready to duck, but it was a Nextel, not a gun; she heard the thing beep as he held it up to his face. "Goddammit, Ramon," he said. "Quit fucking around. You know I don't like heights to begin with . . ."

She stepped up onto the roof while the guy's attention was compromised, crossed the space between the two of them at a dead run, slammed into the middle of his back with her shoulder, pinned him against the door as she grabbed the hand holding the phone, and jerked it behind his back. She twisted his wrist and arm into a shape God had not intended. The guy lost the phone, it skittered across the roof and over the edge. A couple of seconds later she heard it crash into the weeds of the empty lot next door. Meanwhile, the guy's body had taken over, overwhelming him with the imperative to escape the sudden wracking pain that flooded his consciousness. Like a bumper car stuck in a corner, the guy slammed himself into the steel door over and over as Alessandra used his own strength to hold him there. It was a good feeling, knowing she didn't have to be bigger or stronger than he was, she just had to be better. It actually took very little of her own strength to control him. The guy was squalling, sounded like a munchkin with a sore throat. She eased the pressure off his wrist and elbow slightly, enough for him stop moving and shut off the noise. She leaned up close and whispered in his ear. "You've got fifteen seconds to convince me not to give you a flying lesson," she said.

"Anything you want." His voice was guttural, harsh with pain. "We was supposed to work you over. Warn you off Willy Caughlan."

"Who do you work for?"

"Jerry Tomasino."

She'd heard the name, couldn't remember when or where. Plenty of time for him later . . . "Why does Tomasino give a shit about Willy Caughlan?"

"He don't. He say he owe some guy a favor."

She didn't answer, she just ratcheted up the pressure on his arm.

"Ahhhhhhh! Jesuchristo, lady! It's the troo, I swear! We wasn't gonna hurt you too much, we was jus' gonna have a lille fun . . ."

Cuban accent, she thought. Born there, most likely he learned his English here, on the street. "I bet you were. How many guys?"

"Tree in the truck, one out back, and me."

"Nobody in the stairwell?"

"No. We got the fron' cover, why would we—"

She tweaked his arm again just to shut him up. The thought of him and his friends having some fun with her made her so mad she thought she was going to crack a tooth. "Who was Tomasino doing this for?"

"How the hell should I know? He don' esplain shit to me, he jus' say, 'go do this,' an' I go do it."

Pretty soon this guy's arm will go numb, Al told herself, and when he can't feel it anymore, you won't be able to control him. She wrapped her free arm around his neck, just under his chin, got the right grip, and squeezed. The guy didn't react because he didn't understand: she wasn't trying to shut his wind off. The pressure of her forearm on his neck pinched off his carotid artery, cutting the flow of blood to his brain—what he had of one . . . It took about forty-five seconds for him to lose consciousness.

She released him and he slumped down to the tar paper surface of the roof. It took an act of will to keep from damaging the guy further. She patted him down quickly, relieved him of the .38 in a holster strapped to his ankle. He had pissed his pants. Another time she might have been amused.

She stood up, sucked in a breath of cool night air, looked at the windows of the St. George Hotel across the street. If I could just jump over there, she thought, if I could fly across that space, somehow . . .

The mortar in the top of the brick chimney next to the door to the stairwell had long since eroded away, and the chimney was not much more than a squarish pile of bricks. Al peeled four of the bricks off the top of the pile and eased up near the front of the building. The BUG truck was still there. Two cars passed by, pausing at the intersection of Henry Street before moving on. Al waited until they were gone. Nobody on the sidewalk. She wondered if the goons standing behind the truck were half hard already, anticipating the games they were going to play with her in the back of that truck. Well, she thought, I know a different game . . .

She lofted the four bricks out into the night air in quick succession. They picked up speed as they sailed down through the five-story space between her and the street. The first two exploded harmlessly on the sidewalk behind the truck. Adrenaline, she thought, you threw them too hard . . . The third brick hit the bull's-eye, though, it took out the truck windshield with a satisfying crash. The fourth caught one of the phony hardhats, hit him on the top of a shoulder as he flinched away from the flying glass. He flopped down to the street, lay there without moving as his two compatriots ran for the front of her building.

As she dropped down onto the top level of the fire escape attached to the front of the building, she wondered how long it would be before they realized their mistake and one of them came back out. She flew down the iron stairs, hit the sidewalk, turned to walk away. Henry Street was just steps away. She didn't sense the man stepping out of the alley between her building and the next until it was too late. She only got a glimpse of the guy before she felt the cold steel barrel of his pistol on her neck.

"Don't move," he said. "Don't breathe, don't think." He grabbed her hair with his other hand and backed her into the dark space between the buildings. "You know," he said, his voice soft and low, "you are making some important people very angry."

"Who are you?" she said. She matched her tone to his.

He jabbed at her neck with his pistol. " 'For the living are conscious that they will die, but the dead are conscious of nothing at all, for there is neither wisdom nor work nor devising nor knowledge nor anything at all in Sheol, whither thou art hastening.' Don't be in such a hurry to meet your maker,

Martillo. Don't make me shoot you. I'd hate to do that without getting paid for it."

"Who are you?"

"You're thinking you can come back on me." She thought she could hear amusement in his voice. "Listen to me. You're good, but you're not immortal. You can die from lead poisoning just as quickly as the next guy. Do not turn around, I thought I made that clear."

"Sorry." She tried to place his accent. English? Maybe, but definitely not street. An educated man, she thought. "You've got a couple of guys down. Shouldn't you be getting them some medical attention?"

"All in due time." She heard some noise coming from the front of her building, then the sound of feet coming down the alley. Two sets of footsteps, two guys. One of them breathed out a sigh of relief.

"Good, you got her. I think Ivan's arm is broken, and Angelo is—"

"Shut up, you idiot." The pressure of the steel against her neck never wavered. "The two of you, get the other two loaded up into that truck. Get them the hell out of here. And you," he said, apparently addressing the second man, "you come back here and help me with her. We'll do what we have to do, right here."

"Just the two of us," another voice said. "That's too bad."

"Mova la culo," the man with the gun said. "Shake your ass, we don't have all night."

They softened her up, first.

The Brit pushed her face-first up against the alley wall, held her there in almost the same fashion she'd held the one they called Ivan against the steel roof door, only this time it was the pressure of his pistol in the back of her neck that kept her compliant. When the second man returned, he slipped something over her head. It was made out of a coarse, rough fabric and it smelled of dust. There were some mumbled instructions from the first guy, but she did not quite hear his words. Pay attention, she told herself. Calm down. Try to remember everything they say . . .

She felt her arms pinioned behind her back. Rope was looped around her wrists, drawn tight. She tried to sense the man's presence, tried to feel where his face might be, then jackknifed her body as hard as she could, striking out with her head. She felt her resolve turn to disappointment as she connected with something soft, heard someone grunt as the air went out of him. "Pendeja," the man muttered. "Bitch. Can't you hold her still?" The other guy grabbed her then, got her by the throat, yanked her erect, held her up on her toes. It was then that she felt the first blow, a savage shot to her sternum. She recoiled in pain, heard herself make a noise like she'd never made before, lost her balance as the guy holding her let her go. She collapsed to the ground, unable to break her fall with her arms, cracked her head on something hard. Stars pinwheeled behind closed eyelids as she rolled herself into a ball. The two of them began kicking her then, hurriedly, as though they had a plane to catch. Or maybe this particular alley wasn't quite as dark or secluded as they may have wanted . . . It went on for what seemed an eternity, but probably was only a few minutes. She took a lot of shots to her legs and thighs, which, though painful, didn't worry her too much. It was the hits to her stomach and rib cage that scared her, and the ones to her head, because she knew there were things there that once broken might never mend. By the time they were done, she could barely move from the pain. She almost passed out when they dragged her out of her protective fetal curl. She went cold all over when she felt one of them stripping her pants off, but she had no strength to resist. Her heart thundered in her chest. You had to know this was coming, she told herself. They rolled her facedown on the ground, one of them sat on her head and neck. The pain was so intense she hardly felt the other one kick her legs apart.

"Hey! Hey!" Another voice, affronted, irate, coming from the end of the alleyway. "What the fuck are you guys doing?"

"Bugger off!" It was the Brit, the guy sitting on her neck—she felt as well as heard his words.

"Oh, yeah? Fuck you, asshole, I've got your picture, I've got you and your friend, douche bag, right here on my cell phone, and I'm going for the cops!" Alessandra's mind reeled. It was TJ's voice, she was sure of it, he'd finally made it back from the parking lot. He had more balls than brains, but she couldn't fault his timing.

Thank you, God . . .

"Ramon, go get that bloody phone!"

"Yeah? Come on, motherfucker . . ."

Run, TJ, she thought, you're a musician, not a fighter . . . More feet, then, one man fleeing, another chasing. The pressure on her head eased as her assailant got to his feet. She heard his shoe leather creak, heard the slight snapping sound of his knee as he got down to whisper in her ear. "It seems I have to go, but I trust our message has been delivered. You do understand? Back off. Nod if you heard me."

She didn't nod, a tiny gesture of defiance. "I heard."

"I'm going to untie your wrists, and I'm going to take the

covering off your head. You keep your eyes closed, or I will shoot you."

"Yeah."

He jerked at the rope, pulled it off roughly. Every movement now seemed to cause her head to explode. He yanked the covering from her head, taking some of her hair with it. "We can do this anytime we want," he said. "And more. You were lucky tonight. Don't forget that."

He stood back up. She heard him walk back down the alley, the sound of his footsteps receding as he reached the end of it. She lifted her head, looked in his direction just as he turned the corner. A short man, blond, stiff, erect posture to go with the accent. She didn't get a good look at his face. Slowly, by degrees, almost involuntarily, her body rolled itself back into a ball.

Get up, she told herself. Get up, you've got to get your pants back on, if someone finds you here like this, they'll probably pick up where Ramon left off. She couldn't, though, it hurt too much to move. She faded out for a while.

Later, she awoke with a start. She was cold, everything that hurt before was still hurting now, and she was beginning to stiffen up as well. She felt a spasm every time she inhaled. Breathing in shallow gasps, she rolled herself up into a sitting position, her back against the alley wall. Everything went dark for a couple of seconds, the world spun on a strange new eccentric orbit, but she steadied herself, her hands on the ground, and rode it out. Her pants were just a few feet away, but for a long time she could only sit there and look at them. Go, she told herself, the sun will be coming up soon, people will start walking by, they'll see you here like this. That thought might have sent her scrambling for cover just hours ago, but now it didn't seem to matter all that much. She stared down at her bruised thighs. No matter how bad this is, she told herself, it was very nearly a lot worse. Silently she thanked whoever it was who had interrupted her assailants, hoped that he got away. Had it really been TJ? She couldn't say for sure, it was too hard to reach back through the haze of pain to relive that moment. Later, she told herself. You can find that out later. She gathered her strength and her courage, fell over onto her side, reached over, caught one leg of her pants, and dragged them over to her. She took the phone off the belt, dropped the pants on the ground next to her, and snapped the phone open, praying that it still worked. She made the call.

"Ant," she said when he answered, groggy. Then she spoke the single phrase she hated more than anything in life.

"I need help."

Sixteen

It was an ordinary house in a neighborhood of ordinary houses, an unremarkable structure of bricks and plaster built back in the thirties, a dark basement, two stories, an unused attic, a detached one-car garage, small square of grass out front and in back. It was and had always been, as far back as Alessandra could remember, Anthony's refuge. No motorcycles, except for the one Tio Bobby rode back and forth to work, no loud parties, no raucous music, nothing to annoy the neighbors. It was a comfortable place, hardwood floors, painted and papered walls, furniture you might find in your mother's house, a kitchen from *Leave It to Beaver*, big steam radiators that hissed in the night. It smelled the way she remembered it, baskets of potpourri and scented candles burning here and there. The sound of Tio Bobby's voice echoed in her mind, grumbling that Anthony was going to burn the place down. She relived the sensation of unearthly silence that she'd felt when Tio Bobby first brought her into his home. It was an illusion, really, the subdued racket of suburban America was quiet only in contrast to the streets and back alleys of Brooklyn.

The room she woke up in seemed smaller than she remembered. It had been her bedroom. Anthony hadn't changed it much since she'd moved out, just enough to make it feel like a guest bedroom, a space that was no longer hers. It had seemed enormous once, an entire room devoid of relatives, empty of her mother's sister's strident progeny and their urgent, sharp-elbowed needs. She hadn't needed to compete, here, to fight for her share of the meager resources of an economically marginal household, always too little to be divided among too many. And yet, the worst privation had been the poverty of spirit: we have nothing to give you, nothing more than shelter and food, and we expect nothing from you. Half of a bed and a plate of rice and beans had proved insufficient. Even the street had been more hospitable than that.

Someone on the next block fired up a leaf-blower; she lay listening to its muted burr. She lay in the bed in a narcotic haze, under heavy bedclothes. She half-remembered being given something to help her sleep, but she was coming out of it now. She stirred, felt the sudden ache in her rib cage, her legs, and her head, and something returned, something snapped into place, and she struggled to a sitting position.

"Anthony!" God, it even hurt to talk. Was that pathetic squeak really her voice? "Hey, Ant, are you here?"

She heard stirring from the floor below, and a few seconds later he was climbing the creaking stairs and poking his head into the room. "Good morning, Alessandra," he said. "Or rather, good afternoon. How are you feeling?"

"I feel terrible, Ant. Listen, I have a problem."

"You have a few problems, dear, not the least of which is you're not supposed to be moving. Or even awake yet. I told Rachel you have the metabolism of a linebacker, but she didn't believe me."

"Who's Rachel?"

"She's the doctor. She came here late last night to have a look at you. You were pretty out of it. She said you've got some fractured ribs, some contusions, and some pretty serious bruising. Said you've had a concussion. According to her, I am an idiot for listening to you, I should have taken you straight to a hospital."

"Thanks, Anthony."

"She says you should stay in this bed for at least a week, to give your body time to heal itself. Of course, she doesn't know you like I do."

"Ant, listen to me. The guys who did this got interrupted last night. I can't be sure, but I think the man who kept this from being a hell of a lot worse was a guy named TJ Conrad. Theodore James. I don't have his phone number, Ant, I don't even know where he lives. I think he said something about Greenpoint, but I have to find out if he's all right."

"What else do you know about him?"

"Not a hell of a lot. He plays the guitar for BandX, if that helps at all."

"Not to worry," he told her. "I didn't work for the public library for twenty-five years for nothing. If he has a credit card or a driver's license, I can find him."

She lay back, somewhat relieved. "Thanks, Ant."

He stared at her, an odd look on his face. "My pleasure," he said. He turned to go, hesitated. "You know," he said, "I think this is the first time you've ever allowed me to help you with something."

"No," she said. "Maybe I didn't come out and ask, but . . ."

"First time I remember," he said.

"I'm sorry," she said. "You must think I'm a pretty cold fish."

He shook his head. "I didn't grow up where you did."

"I suppose not," she said. "How long can I use that excuse?"

"Al, your childhood isn't a bruise or cramp that you can walk off. You might spend your life trying to comprehend where and what you are." He took a step toward the door. "You hungry?"

"Ravenous," she said.

"I thought so. I'll be back up in a few minutes with your breakfast."

"I'll meet you at the kitchen table," she said, and she hitched herself up higher, ignoring the sharp pain in her side and the thundering in her head.

"Don't you dare get out of that bed," he said, hands on hips, "or I'll kick your behind myself."

"I have to get moving, Ant."

"Not yet, you don't. You stay right there."

She listened to him walking back down the stairs. The memories of the night before flooded in on her, unsummoned, unwelcome. Anthony had reacted like a maiden aunt when he first saw her. *My God, Alessandra, what happened? Who did this to you? We have to get you to a hospital, my God, why didn't you call an ambulance? We should call the police before we move you, shouldn't we? But we can't wait for them, we have to . . .* She remained still, on the ground, her back to the wall, waiting him out.

"No cops," she said, when he finally stopped.

He calmed down, she could see him reeling himself back in. He sat down on his haunches next to her, reached out for her hand. "All right," he said, after a minute. "It's your choice." He looked over his shoulder, back down the alley toward the street. "Do you think you can walk? How bad is it?"

She pictured the words in her mind first, then summoned the energy to use them. "Got kicked in the chest," she said. "Got whacked in the head. Everything hurts, but . . . I think I'll be all right."

"You always think that." He shook his head, looked down at her bare legs, then over at her jeans.

She watched him formulate the obvious question. She decided to save him the embarrassment of asking. "They just kicked the shit out of me," she said. "They got sidetracked before they got around to anything else."

He thought about that before he answered her. "I am glad you didn't get hurt any worse than you did," he said. "I had my friend Roger drive me over. We should get you dressed before we try to move you."

She looked at her jeans, in a heap on the ground beside Anthony. "Not those. Too tight. I'll die trying to get back into them."

He nodded. "All right." He grabbed the jeans, stood up with them. He went through the pockets quickly, fished out her keys and the money she'd had in a front pocket, wadded up the jeans, and flicked them away like he tossed the butts of the short, skinny cigars he sometimes affected. "Wait right here." He must have realized how ridiculous that sounded. "I mean, you know, I'll be right back."

"Ant."

"Yes?"

"My bag . . ."

"I'll get it."

"Paperwork. In the oven."

He didn't bother to look surprised at that. "Okay. Anything else?"

"No."

Of course, Anthony being Anthony, he didn't stop with her bag and some paperwork. He was back in about ten minutes, carrying a big black garbage bag stuffed with her belongings. "Sorry about the choice of luggage," he said, plopping the bag down beside her. "I was in a hurry." He pulled a blanket out of the bag. She recognized it, he'd taken it off her daybed. "Let me wrap you up in this, honey." She recognized his tone—he had gone back to the way he'd spoken to her when Tio Bobby had first brought her home all those years ago. "Roger's waiting with the car," he said, and leaning down, he picked her up with surprising ease. "I'm going to put you in the car, then I'll come back for your things."

Anthony returned to the bedroom with a number written on a little yellow stickie note. "This is your friend's cell," he said. He had a cordless phone in his hand. He was wearing a pair of loose, flowered pants, a long-sleeved striped shirt, purple clogs, and a disapproving look on his face. Al looked at him, wondering how she'd failed to notice his getup before. "I got it from his record company. I hope you don't mind my asking," he said. "How much do you know about this person?"

She'd have bridled at that once, taken offense at the presumption. God, you're touchy, she thought. "I know, Ant. Thank you for worrying."

He looked relieved. He was waiting for me to bite his head off, she thought. "As long as you know what you're getting into," he said. "I'm probably the last person who should try to give you advice. You never listen, anyhow."

"I know."

He waited there a second, giving her the opportunity to ask his opinion. When she didn't, he laid the phone beside her on the bed. "Breakfast in twenty minutes," he said.

"Thank you, Ant."

She cradled the phone in her hand. She lay that way for a while, waiting for something. Courage, maybe, or inspiration. God, she thought, if he's hurt, alter the laws of physics for me, just this one time, please, I promise I won't ask ever again . . . I never wanted to get anyone hurt . . . She dialed the number.

"Hello?"

"TJ," she said, and the air went out of her. He was alive, at least. "Are you okay?"

"Jesus, Martillo," he said. "Goddamn, what the fuck happened to you? Are you hurt? When I got back to that alley, you were gone. I didn't know what to do. The cops thought I was crazy, but then they found the window on your fire escape open. Man, I thought they were gonna toss my ass in the can just for being there. Are you all right? What the hell happened?"

Oh shit, she thought, he called the police. "Those guys were waiting for me when I got home," she said. "I saw them on the way in, but . . ."

"Yeah? But what?"

She shook her head. "Overconfident," she said. "Stupid."

He was quiet for a minute. "So you're all right," he finally said.

"They worked me over pretty good," she said. "I'm gonna be laid up a few days."

"No kidding." The tone of his voice had changed. "You got a place to hole up?"

"Yes."

He was quiet again for a few seconds. "This kind of shit happen to you reporter types a lot? What'd you do, write a nasty article about someone's mother?"

"TJ, I'm not a reporter." It had only been a matter of hours since she'd kissed him for the first time, but it felt like years had passed.

"Yeah, you know something, Al? I think I finally figured that out."

"I'm sorry, TJ."

"'S okay," he said. "Usually it's me, lying to the woman. Guess I had it coming."

"At least tell me if you're all right," she said. "Did that guy catch you?"

"No," he said. "Man, I ran like a little girl. A very quick little girl. Left you lying there. I been feeling lousy about it ever since."

"Don't," she said. "You did exactly the right thing. If you hadn't run, those two would have killed you. Did you really get pictures of them on your camera phone?"

"No," he said. "It's just a phone. I always thought those camera things were stupid. Sorry."

Don't worry, she thought. You'll get them anyway. "Listen," she said. "You really bailed me out. I don't know what to say, I don't know how I could ever repay you."

"You think? You think maybe you owe me the truth? About yourself. Who you are, what you do."

She felt her stomach heave. "Maybe even that."

"Good," he said. "'Cause my parole officer is gonna want to

hear it. I'm supposed to stay out of trouble, no contact with cops at all. When she gets the police report from last night, she's gonna barbeque my ass. She don't believe a thing I tell her as it is."

"She can come see me if she wants. My face looks pretty convincing. I won't be able to get out for a couple of days yet."

"Sorry to hear it. Yeah, she's gonna need to see you. And your face. Are you okay, for real?"

"Bruised up. Nothing that won't heal, I hope," she said. "Listen, TJ. You mad at me?"

He laughed first, then took his time answering. "Martillo," he finally said. "That is your real name, isn't it?"

"It is."

"Martillo, you are the strangest female I've ever met, and I've met some real honeys. No, listen, I wanted to be pissed off, but I was too worried. You're not gonna tell my parole officer the truth, are you?"

"Don't worry. I'll make her happy."

"I don't doubt that. But I'd like to see you again. You know what I'm saying? You, ahh, I don't know how to say this. I feel like I fell asleep during a movie, and you woke me up. You and I, we clicked back there. Didn't we? I'd like to find out what I been missing."

She exhaled, felt like she'd been holding her breath since she'd dialed his number. She could feel her hands shaking. So hard to tell exhilaration from fear, she thought. Do you really dare to let this guy get up next to you? "TJ, I'd like that, too, but give me a few days, okay?"

"Whatever you need," he said.

"Are you Rachel?" Alessandra asked. "You look too young to be a doctor."

"You're very kind." Rachel was Jewish, early thirties, five foot six, long brown hair, brown eyes, soft round face, glasses. She dragged a chair over next to the bed and sat down in it, watched Al taking shallow breaths. "Why don't you tell me what happened?"

"This guy stepped out of an alley." Alessandra gave her an abbreviated account of the assault.

"Are you sure that's it?" Rachel took one of Al's hands in both of hers. "You can tell me. Did they rape you? I can understand why you wouldn't want to talk about it, but it's nothing you should feel any shame over. You wouldn't be the first woman it's happened to." She leaned in, stared into Al's face. "You won't be the last."

Al sighed. "They were going to. They got interrupted." She burned, remembering them yanking her out of her protective fetal curl, ripping her jeans off, kicking her legs apart.

"Men who do this shouldn't be allowed to get away with it," Rachel told her. "They shouldn't be allowed to assault another woman. And they will, believe me, if something isn't done to stop them. I realize it will take incredible strength on your part, but I do wish you'd let me take this to the police."

Alessandra squeezed Rachel's hands. "They're not going to get away with anything, Doc."

Rachel winced. Al eased her grip. "Sorry."

"It's all right. But I'm not sure I understand. Do you think you can . . . Surely the police are better equipped . . ."

Al shook her head. "This isn't about me," she said. "I should have expected something like this." And I didn't. It was a rookie mistake. "Someone wants me to go away."

"And you're not going to do it."

She shook her head. "All they've done is make my job easier."

"How is that?"

"I only had theories before. Now I have something real." She thought about her assailants. "Flesh and bone." And some names . . .

"I see." Rachel sighed. "Okay, Alessandra. Let's get started." She stood up, pulled the covers down to the foot of the bed. She paused, looking at the dark bruises. "I'm going to cut that shirt off you," she said. "I don't want you raising your arms over your shoulders . . ."

Rachel's voice and manner changed once she started her exam. She prodded with soft hands, listened to Al's body as it breathed, pumping air in and out, circulating her blood, doing the body's business. "Any blood in your urine?" Rachel asked, sounding slightly distracted.

"Yes." It felt strange, lying naked and hurting in front of another woman.

"How much? Like a period, or little spots?"

"Little spots."

"Okay. How long since you last saw your gynecologist?"

"I don't have one."

Rachel gave her a look. "You have to have one. I can recommend someone for you. You'll need to see her at least once a year, especially if you're sexually active. Are you?"

Alessandra sighed, thought about the guy down at the bar in Hackensack. Was that what you called "sexually active"? "Been a while," she said. She looked at the gold band Rachel wore on her ring finger. Someone's wife, Al thought. Maybe even someone's mother. She looked up, into Rachel's face, but the doctor had already moved on. Al lay back on her pillows as the process continued: cough, inhale, hold it, exhale, does this hurt, how about this, look straight ahead, not at the light . . .

When she was done, Rachel pulled Al's covers back up and sat down in the chair. "Do you know what your BMI is?"

Body Mass Index, Al thought. The new statistical tool to tell you how fat you are. "No."

"I suppose it doesn't matter. I dated a guy when I was in pre-med. He was a soccer player. He ran miles every morning. Worked out every day, ate measured amounts of protein and complex carbs, did 'rhoid cycles twice a year. He was out of shape and dumpy, next to you."

"I've always been this way."

Rachel nodded. "You haven't got the muscle mass of a juicer."

"Mass does not equal strength," Al said. "Bruce Lee was a skinny guy. Didn't have the biceps everybody loves."

"Genetics is a fascinating subject. Did you know that you carry within you the entire history of your race? It's in your DNA, everything we ever were, all the way back. We're only just beginning to learn how to read it. At one time, our ancestors needed to be much stronger and quicker than we do, just to survive. Those traits are still there, but they're carried by recessive genes. That means if both your parents have a particular gene, they pass on the trait it carries to their child. That's why you have the physical gifts you do. It probably happens about once in five or ten thousand births."

"I'm a freak, you mean."

"If you want to look at it that way. Alessandra, I couldn't get to where you are, physically, not if I left my family, quit my job, and worked out with a personal trainer every day for the next five years. I'll bet you're stronger than most men. Better coordinated, too."

"Maybe."

"Accept it," Rachel told her. "Stop trying to prove it. It's a shallow way to measure yourself anyway. I think you're probably better than that." She looked away. "End of lecture. The rest of this is medical fact. You are going to have to spend the next few weeks right where you are. Your body needs time to heal itself. You don't have anything broken, but you've got bone bruises and cracked ribs. There isn't a lot we can do for that, you're just going to have to let them heal. I'm going to leave two prescriptions with Anthony, one for the pain and one to help you sleep. The only other thing you need is time."

"Okay."

"If you start pushing yourself too soon, you'll only delay the process. When all the discoloration from the bruises has gone away, you can start some mild exercises."

"Okay, Doc."

"Good. Now how about we get you into the shower?"

"I can make it."

"No, you can't. You were in enough discomfort just going through an examination. Honey, I went to school for this. It's what I do. Let me help you. Please. What if you slipped in the tub?"

Irritated, Alessandra inhaled a little deeper than she had intended, ready to tell Rachel where to go, felt the sharp pang in her side. Okay, God, she thought. I get the message. "All right."

Her cell phone warbled. Alessandra opened her eyes, looked at the thing with distaste. May as well answer it, she thought. "Hello."

"I heard you got roughed up." It was Caughlan, and he sounded agitated.

"That right?" How could he have known? She tried to rouse herself out of the half-sleep she'd been in. "Who told you that?"

"What difference does it make?" he said. "I thought you were the best. I thought this kinda shit didn't happen to you. I thought—"

"Yeah," Al butted in. "I'm fine, thanks."

"Hey," Caughlan said. "I thought you were the one who was gonna kick ass, not the other way around. What the hell happened?"

"Lighten up, Caughlan. Even Ali lost once in a while. How well do you know Jerry Tomasino?"

"I know him." Caughlan's voice was a little calmer. "We do a little business. What of it?"

"He a friend of yours?"

"Friend?" Caughlan said the word like he'd never heard it before. "He's a guy. What about him?"

"Tell me about him."

"What do you wanna know?" Caughlan was starting to get loud. "He's got money and he's got connections. Used to be mayor of Union City. You need to get something done in New Jersey, the guy to go to is Tomasino. He can get you permits, he can get you variances, and he can also get you put in a box and buried in the swamp if you piss him off. That what you needed to know?"

"Keep going."

"What? What, keep going? What the fuck do you want from me?" She could hear the steam building in his voice. "He's a douche bag and a fucking pain in my crotch, but I live and do business in Jersey, so Tomasino has got to get his. Okay? Why you so goddamn interested in Tomasino? You telling me he's the guy behind this morphine running through my trucking company?"

"Tell me exactly how you heard I got beat up."

"Tomasino, Christ, you better be goddamn sure. I need this like I need a fucking hemorrhoid . . ."

She allowed herself the luxury of yelling, put up with the pain in the ribs that it caused. "Goddamn you, Caughlan, quit whining and suck it up! I need to know. How did you hear I got beat up?"

There was a sudden silence on the line, and Alessandra began to wonder if she'd pushed him too far. "They were talking about it in the office this morning," he said finally. "O'Hagan and them. I didn't ask how they'd heard. I should have done that. Should have . . ."

"Leave it alone," Al told him.

"Is it him? Is it Tomasino?" Caughlan's voice was flat and hard.

"Maybe. I don't know for sure yet."

"Look, you go stepping on Tomasino's dick, you're doing it on your own account, not mine. You hear me? You go up against a guy like Tomasino, you can't just knock him down. You gotta put a knife in his throat. Anything short of that, you're just signing your own death warrant."

"Thanks for the call," she told him. "You been a lot of help."

He hung up.

It only took a half hour for Stiles to get to her.

"What are you doing?" He was both scared and indignant; she could hear it in his voice.

"Hiya, Marty."

"What are you doing? What are you thinking? What makes you think you can go after a guy like Tomasino? Do you got any idea . . ."

"I didn't go after anybody, Marty. He came after me." She told him about the assault.

"All right. All right, Al, you did good." She could still hear the fear in his voice. "This might not be as bad as I thought. You stay in bed, okay, and you let me take it from here. You remember that thing you did with Caughlan's computer? Yesterday afternoon I got the spam from Frederick's, okay, and I followed the truck to a warehouse in Jersey, up in Norwood."

"And you were gonna tell me all about this, right? Next time you saw me?"

"Yeah, come on, I was gonna tell you . . ."

"Gimme the place, Marty, I want a name and an address."

He was silent for a moment, but then he gave it to her. "Anyway, the warehouse don't matter, it's just a blind drop. Fuckin' place is leased by some offshore corporation, I couldn't trace it. But there's a lab in New York, just up over the Jersey border. I think that's where they're cooking this shit. What we gotta do is connect the lab to Tomasino. We find a link between any of this and Tomasino, that'll be enough. I can give that much to Mickey, and what he does with it is his business. But you stay down, you hear me? You stay out of sight. This shit is out of your league."

"What about Tomasino's inside guy?"

"We ain't even sure he's got one. Let Mickey worry about—"

"What about Willy?"

"What about him?" Stiles was on the verge of losing it.

"What are you, the Spotless Avenger, for crissake? You wanna worry about saving some kid, why don't you find one that's still alive? We got this just about wrapped up, Martillo, so don't you go and blow it. You hear me? You let me tie Tomasino to the dope so I can collect and we can walk away from this. You get out of that bed, you're fired, and I mean it."

"Okay, Marty."

"Goddamn you, Martillo, I ain't kidding."

"Stop worrying, Marty, I can't get out of bed, it hurts too much."

"Good!" He sounded relieved. "I mean, you know——"

"Good-bye, Marty." She snapped the phone shut and lay back on her pillows. The thought came, unbidden: they're walking away, Willy, and they want me to walk away, too. She sat back up, swung her legs down to the floor. She went dizzy and her head began to throb. She could feel every nerve ending in every spot where they'd kicked her. The pain was almost a physical assault. After a few minutes, it seemed to coalesce and settle in the front part of her head. The bathroom seemed a lot farther away than it had just seconds ago. How bad do you need to do this, she wondered.

The hell with that, she thought, and she stood up. She held onto the bed to steady herself. Move, she told herself. Take the first step.

Seventeen

Two days of inactivity were all she could stand. Her body wasn't ready, but she was. She took her time getting ready, took a cab to the lot where she kept the van, stopped to take a rest whenever she needed it. Pretend you're rich, she told herself. Pretend you've got all the time in the world.

She drove the van to Dumont Avenue in Brooklyn, found a parking spot. She shut the van off but made no move to get out. She was behind the Brownsville Houses. She wore shades and heavy makeup to hide her bruises. She was sure her presence had been duly noted, what would come next would be the assessment: is she weak? Is she vulnerable? Is she good to eat? Is she a cop, a customer, or just a nutbag? They would need to know.

You could hate the hyenas for what they did, but it was pointless. It was their function to eliminate the weak and the sick, and if you had a problem with that, you probably needed to take it up with the system architect, because the hyenas, ignorant beasts that they are, just follow their programming. They were hungry, they fed themselves the best way they knew how.

This was where she'd spent the first twelve years of her life, but the place had no nostalgic pull. She had no sense that she'd ever belonged here. Her life then had been lived under the wing and watchful eye of her mother. Her mother had been there to walk her to school, to walk her back home when school let out; she had accompanied Alessandra virtually everywhere she went. That's how it had been in this place. Maybe it still is, she thought, looking out her window. Maybe the predation level here is still so high that the only way to see your children safely grown up is to guard them every moment. Other than that, the only memories she had of life in the projects were sensory: the noise level, smells of cooking, oppressive heat of summer, occasional gunfire, the strong urine smell of the elevator unless her mother or one of the other ladies expected company, in which case the elevator would smell like Pine-Sol for a day or so.

They used a kid to make the approach. He was maybe twelve or thirteen, and he wore the uniform of the day: cornrows, baggy jeans low on his waist, boxer shorts, muscle-T. He sauntered out of one of the buildings and rolled up to the driver's side of the van. Al, resting her arm out the window, did not look at him. "Hey," the kid said. "Wassup."

"Looking for someone."

"Who you wan'? I could, you know, expedite."

She turned her head slightly in his direction. "That what you do?"

He shrugged. "You want sum'in?"

"Guy used to live up on fourteen. Dealt in hardware. He still around?"

The kid straightened up, looked a bit more cautious. He probably thought he was going to make a drug sale, Al thought. This was a bit more unusual. "I 'ont know," he said.

She rolled her fingers, and a C-note materialized in her hand. "Suppose you go find out."

He looked at the money, took a step back. "You keep it," he said. "I be back." He turned away, walked back inside the building.

It took a while. Alessandra sat where she was, feeling the heat of the late afternoon sun coming through the windshield, watching the people come and go. Brownsville was one of those places that put pressure on everyone who lived there, but it was hardest on the men. There were mothers with their children, grandmothers with their grandkids, young girls and young boys, but not as many young men walked the sidewalks and even fewer mature males. Al watched the boys with a sort of resigned sadness. We put you in a place where you can't succeed, she thought, and then we punish you for failing.

When she had been a child down here, the gangs that ran life in the projects had tolerated the presence of the arms dealer on the fourteenth floor. They got a cut of his gross and a professional discount, and in return, they were the crocodiles in his moat. It had been a while, though, and maybe things had changed. Maybe the guy is gone, Al thought. Maybe he's out of business, maybe he's dead. Maybe the kids inside the projects had more pressing matters to attend before they'd get around to her. In the meantime life flowed by and Al sat watching it, wishing Brownsville were something other than what it was. Every four years a succession of earnest-looking men would appear on television and promise, in exchange for your vote, to rescue the next generation of children but day followed night in Brownsville and nothing much ever seemed to change.

The kid came back out about forty minutes later. "Yo,

Martillo," he said. Someone had remembered her. "You can go on up. Fourteen C. You could leave the van here."

"All right," she said. She opened her door, gathered herself. It was important, from now until she got back to the van, not to show any weakness. No limp, no hesitation, no fear. The kid was already walking away when she swung down out of the Astro. Doesn't matter, she told herself, you've got eyes on you and you know it. She gritted her teeth at the pain her movements caused, but otherwise gave no sign of her discomfort. She slammed the door shut, stuck her hands in her pockets, strolled across the courtyard in what she hoped was her best unhurried strut.

"Damn," the guy said. "You sure you gotta have clips? Most shotguns use a tube mag under the barrel, carry seven or eight rounds."

Al shook her head. "No good," she said. "Too long, and I don't want to have to bother with reloading something like that."

"Babe, listen to me. You can't clear the room with six or eight rounds from a twelve-gauge, you ain't in the right business."

"Are you telling me," she said, hands on her hips, "that nobody has what I want? Or are you saying that you can't get it?"

"Easy, easy," he said. "There's one piece like that I know of. Made in Italy. SWAT teams in LA carry it. Nice weapon, but kinda rare."

"I can't wait around while you get it from LA."

"Goddamn, you're in a hurry." He shook his head. "I got a source," he said. "But I got to send someone down there to make the pickup. In person. You're talking five- or six-hour drive, each way, and that's if my source has one he can lay his hands on. Figure, ten grand for the piece, another ten to transport it. You make the pickup, right here."

She shook her head. "For twenty large, you gotta bring it to me, where I say. And I want four extra magazines, loaded and ready to go. You interested in taking a car in trade?"

He sneered. "Ain't no used car dealer, babe."

"Bentley," she said, and watched the change wash over his face. She had him now. "Continental GT, still got the new car smell on it. Ain't got fifty miles on it, never seen rain. Still got the sticker in the window, hundred and fifteen grand."

The guy watched her for a moment. "Clean," he finally said. "No LoJack or none of that shit."

"They ain't had time to install it yet."

"Done. But you can't bring it down here, you got to drop it out on the island."

"No way. You give me a driver, out in Jersey. Where you take it from there is your business. And you ain't getting the Bent for one lousy shotgun. There's a few other things I'm gonna need . . ."

If they catch you now, you can't even run . . .

She changed her clothes in the van, then dropped it back at the parking lot, took her time walking back to where her apartment was. You should have gone back to Anthony's, she told herself, you should have gone back to bed, you could have done this tomorrow . . . Her impatience had overruled her common sense, and she knew it, but she was still stubborn enough to push her luck.

She stopped when she could find a place to sit. Fear itched at the back of her mind, rolled in her stomach, twitched at her hands. All right, so maybe this wasn't such a great idea, she thought, waiting to catch her breath. But fear is only natural, it's a necessary component. You need it, she told herself, maybe it will keep you from making any more stupid mistakes . . . Don't fight it.

She wore a green corduroy dress, a voluminous black canvas jacket, a knit hat, and sunglasses to hide her bruised face. She'd found the jacket and dress in a Goodwill store in Anthony's neighborhood, paid four bucks for the dress, fifteen for the coat. She felt absolutely bizarre in the outfit, but maybe it would make it a little more difficult for anyone watching to spot her. She stood up to go, appalled at the effort it took to get up.

"Hey, lady, you okay?" It was a kid, coming up the sidewalk behind her.

"I'm fine."

"Are you sure? You need a hand, I could—"

"Buzz off, pal. I told you, I'm fine." No way, she thought. No way I'm that far gone.

"Okay, okay," he said, and he passed her by. "Sheesh. Suit yourself."

She watched him go. I don't need you, buddy. I've been making it on my own too long to start taking help from some yutz on the street . . . That had always been the way it was. You get nothing from nobody, not unless you take it away from them. She took a step, felt the pain in her side.

Maybe that's not exactly true anymore, she thought.

Maybe it never was.

Cadman Plaza was a wide street, two lanes in each direction, an empty park on one side, a broad, brick-paved walkway on the other. The streetlights of Cadman Plaza and the light coming out of the buildings on Henry Street, one block over, kept the darkness at bay. Her apartment was directly across from the subway stairs, where Pineapple Street ended at Henry. Alessandra turned her back, slowly walked the three blocks down Cadman to the beginning of Henry Street, then turned and headed up Henry.

It was odd how the neighborhood people seemed to step out around her. Brooklyn Heights was mostly middle and upper-middle class, but in New York City, the less fortunate are not always content in the spaces reserved for them, and some of them make their presences felt whenever and wherever they've a mind to. The suited gentry on their ways home gave her a generous berth, their eyes averted. They must have accepted me before, she thought. They must have thought I was one of them. How come I couldn't tell? I always felt like the kid outside the window, with her nose pressed up against the glass, staring in at all the things she couldn't have. And it was almost funny, if her heart hadn't been halfway up her throat she'd have laughed, because homeless loony wasn't the effect she'd been going for. You should have asked Anthony to go with you, she thought, he'd have known what you should wear. And he'd have been happy to help.

She walked past the intersection of Pineapple and Henry, stood on the sidewalk on the far side of Henry Street and stared down Pineapple, past the entrance to her building. She felt curiously disconnected, alien, she couldn't find that sensation of home in this place either. You have to let this place go, she thought. All you had here was a one-room rat hole with your name on it. And now anytime anybody's looking for you, all they have to do is camp out here and wait for you to show up. You can't come back here again.

Her stomach turned over, and she felt a wave of sadness wash over her. At least it was my rat hole, she thought. Finally got the rent paid up, even had a couple months' cushion . . . The place was mine, I wasn't there on anyone else's sufferance. But she'd lost it. Maybe she'd already known that, but the impact of the realization hit her as she stood on the sidewalk. She shrugged herself deeper into the canvas jacket, pulled the collar high up around her ears. You're really doing great, Martillo, she told herself. No home, lousy job you're barely hanging onto, and you got your ass kicked. Hell of a week.

The Brooklyn Union Gas truck was gone, of course. Cars were parked down one side of Pineapple Street, complying with New York City's complex, arcane, and profitable alternate side of the street parking code. Traffic crawled slowly past her on Henry Street, creeping up to the light on the next block. A few big drops of rain spattered down out of the night sky. They hit her, the sidewalk, and the cars parked on Henry Street, contributing a hollow metallic mutter to the background noise.

Terrific, she told herself. Now it's gonna rain, too. What else can go wrong? She stepped off the curb, stood between two parked cars and looked across the street at the St. George Hotel. There was a subway stop down under the building. You went through street-level doors into an arcade just inside where there were some tiny shops and an elevator that took you down underground to the Clark Street station. You can go in there, she told herself. You can go hang with all of the other tragic figures who, whether through birth or misadventure, no longer possess either the resources or the intestinal fortitude to provide for themselves . . .

There was a guy sitting behind the wheel of the car she

stood in front of. He had a phone to his ear. He stared at her and she stared at him, and a second later her self-pity was gone, replaced by that white-hot rage that had been her downfall so many times. She wanted to drag the guy out of his car and bounce his head off the hood. "What are you looking at?" She shouted it, louder than she needed to, and the guy broke eye contact, pretended to fiddle with his car radio while he continued talking on the phone. Al clamped her teeth shut, steaming. Knock it off, she told herself. The shape you're in, this guy could kick your ass. Hell, his grandmother could probably kick your ass right about now. A panel truck came to a stop in front of her, and she stepped out, walked around behind the truck and crossed the street.

She could feel the guy's eyes on her. She glanced back when she reached the opposite sidewalk. The panel truck had crept forward, and the guy's face stood out white in the driver's side window of his car. Screw him, she thought, why do you care what he thinks? But she walked past the entrance to the subway arcade, continued up to the corner, and turned right. There was another entrance to the subway arcade just up ahead, out of the guy's line of sight, and she went in there.

The arcade was a large, L-shaped corridor. The air was heavy with that old-building smell, musty and damp, with a faint touch of ozone from the subway mixed with the essence of too many humans in too small a space. A Korean guy stood outside the flower kiosk and stared at her as she walked by, as did the Indian guy behind the newsstand counter. She knew why, she understood how hard they worked for what they took home, how much every bit of stolen merchandise impacted their lives, but it was hard not to hate them for their careful watchfulness. You get sick of it, this idea people have that they know something about you just from looking at you. She went all the way through, back around to the Henry Street entrance, the one she'd passed by, stood just inside the doors and looked out. The guy she'd yelled at was out of his car, standing on the street. He was still yakking on the phone, a little more animated now, gesticulating at whoever he was talking to, but then he snapped the phone shut, shook his head disgustedly, crossed the street, and headed in the direction Al had taken.

Whoever he'd been talking to must have told him to shake his butt, Al thought.

Oh, shit. They had someone waiting to see if you'd come back.

You've got to be kidding me.

She opened the arcade door, stuck her head out, looked up the street in time to see him turn the corner, just as she had.

Get out now, she told herself, go, get lost. She stood still for an extra moment, though. You better be smart about this, she told herself. They put on the full-court press last time you were here, so they might have the exits covered. That means you should forget about the subway. And taxis don't spend a lot of time cruising the Brooklyn streets—the money is all in Manhattan. You could try to walk out of here, she thought, but you'd really be rolling the dice.

Go to ground, she told herself. Find a place to hide. But Brooklyn Heights wasn't that kind of neighborhood. There were no empty buildings, no dark and fragrant barrooms, every available storefront housed a boutique or an expensive wine shop or a chichi little restaurant, places she'd be lucky to get into, where she'd stand out even if she did get past the front door. And the only empty lot was the one right next door to her building. It was hemmed in by brick walls on each side, and by tall fences front and back. Weeds and sumac bushes grew high there, obscuring decades' worth of accumulated trash. It'd be stupid to try to hide in there, she thought, it's too close and too obvious.

But she was out of time. She took one glance back over her shoulder and headed on out.

You couldn't get into the empty lot by way of Pineapple Street, the fence was too high and too tight. If you went down the alley behind the deli on Henry Street, though, you could squeeze through a gap in the fence. Alessandra could feel her heart accelerate as she went down the alley. Every step takes you farther out of sight, she thought, farther from public view. There won't be any passersby to save you, not this time. And the way you're feeling right now, a schoolgirl could beat you to death with her bookbag. But it was too late to reconsider, too late for a plan B. Her hand shook as she reached for the metal post where the metal links of the fence were pulled back. She had to stoop down and twist herself sideways to get through the opening, and the pain took her breath away. She gritted her teeth, blinked the tears back. Suck it up, Martillo, she told herself. You're in too far to back out now. You have to do this.

Once through, she was in a clump of sumac bushes. She found a spot on the ground to sit down, gathering the folds of green corduroy beneath her. It's only dirt, she told herself, and you don't care about this dress, anyhow. But it was hard, just then, being afraid, being hurt, being alone. Sixty seconds, she told herself. You've got one minute to sit here and feel sorry for yourself. She waited as long as she dared, until the pain in her side abated enough to allow movement once again. She got up, then, carefully, rolling over onto her hands and knees, rocking back on her feet, rising slowly.

She looked up. She could make out the roofline of her building in the dark night sky overhead, black on black, five stories above. We were about in the center of the roof, she thought, right about in the middle when that guy's phone went over the edge. It was a Nextel phone, one of the tough ones they made for blue-collar guys. It just might have survived the fall, if she were lucky it might have landed in the weeds and not on any of the junk littering the empty lot. She made her way to the center of the lot, looking up to judge her progress, feeling her way in the dark.

She heard them back at the fence. One of them made too much noise, grunted as he got through the opening. Probably the head guy, Al thought, either old or fat. There was some whispering, then, and footsteps moving, fanning out. They're gonna make a line, she thought, work their way across the lot, see if they can turn me up.

Something crashed in the bushes then, behind her and off to the far side of the lot. "This way!" someone shouted, and her pursuers converged noisily on the sounds. Al ignored her reflexes, held her ground and listened as hard as she could.

"Ah, shit!" came a second voice. Then someone screamed. It was a high, thin scream, quavery, an old person's scream.

"Shut up," someone said, but the screaming went on. Al heard the unmistakable sound of a slap then, the sharp crack of a hand against skin, and then another one, but that didn't stop the screamer, it just aroused them further.

"Police! Police! Help! Help!" Whoever it was, they went on for another thirty seconds or so, but seemed to lose their intensity then, and faded off to nothing.

"Forget it," one of the voices said. "We're wasting our time here."

"Sammy said he seen her."

"We're wasting our time," the voice repeated. "Who knows what Sam really saw. We're out of here."

"Jesus. You mean we can go home? I thought Jerry T said—"

"Tomasino said to give it a shot, he didn't say we had to camp out here for a week. I've had enough. Come on, let's go."

Al listened to them make their way back to the fence and out of the lot. She didn't quite believe they were leaving, though. *That last bit of conversation might have been for my benefit*, she thought. *They followed me in here, they're probably waiting for me to come back out.* She settled down in the brush, arranged her skirt beneath her in the dirt. She concentrated on slowing her breath, waited for her heart rate to come back down to something like normal, focused on the noises around her. Whoever the screamer had been, they were still on the far side of the lot, maybe thirty feet away, but Al could hear sounds of cautious movement in the brush. She sat still in the dark as the sounds got closer and closer. Then they stopped, and she smelled a sharp feral stink. "Did they hurt you?" she said, keeping her voice down to a whisper. "I heard the slaps."

"Wasn't nothing," a voice whispered back, startlingly close. Al looked for the speaker, but it was too dark for her to make out anything. She couldn't even tell if the speaker was male or female. Old, though, with the whisper of missing teeth. Al decided to assume the voice was female. "Just a couple love taps. Was it you they was after?"

"Yeah," Al said.

"I know you. You live in the building next door. Never seen you in a dress before, though."

She hasn't decided to trust you yet, Al thought. "They

came the other night," Al said. "That was the first time. They took me up on the roof. They said they were going to throw me off, but they didn't. They just threw my phone instead." She waited, listening intently, heard nothing. "It's not worth any money," she said. "It's only a telephone."

"You come here to look for it?"

"No," Al said. "I just wanted to go home." Stupid, she thought. What were you thinking? "They were waiting for me."

"I got the phone."

Alessandra could feel the sweat on her forehead. You're running hot, she told herself. You probably do belong in bed. If you catch something out here, Rachel's going to have a fit next time she sees you. "Can I . . . um, can I buy it from you? I could use the numbers in it."

She was silent then, and Al wondered if she had insulted the woman by offering to pay for the phone. You never knew, with crazy people, what would set them off.

"You let me into the building once, last winter, when it was snowing."

She couldn't remember doing it. "Cold, in the winter."

"I don't mind cold. Cold's fine, long's I stay dry. It's the snow that's bad, 'cause it melts inside my shoes, and then it freezes my feet."

"I been on the street," Al said. "I know how it is."

"Did you ast too many questions?"

"What's that? Did I what?"

"Ast too many questions. You get too nosy, they'll come after you. That's why I'm here. I know things. They find me, they'll lock me away."

"Who will?"

"Guvmint," she said. "CIA. They don't like people that astses too many questions."

"I think you must be right," Al whispered. "I probably did ask too many questions."

"You got to lay low, like me." The other voice was still quiet, but harsh, as if from too many cigarettes. "They can't see you, they can't get you. I tried suin' 'em, you know, the CIA, LBJ, the city, the welfare people, tried to sue the police for harassment, I took 'em all to court, but that don't work no more. You got to hide, that's the only way to get by."

"That's good advice. I'll try to be quiet for a while." She found herself wishing she could go to sleep. You have to get back, she thought, you have to get back before you pass out.

The rustling in the bushes started up again, farther away, then very close. She felt something pressed into her hand, solid, rectangular, cold. A telephone. "Thank you," she said, overwhelmed with fatigue. "Thank you. You want my coat?"

"Summertime. Don't need a coat. If I last 'till winter, though, you might come look for me."

"I promise."

"Just chuck it over the fence. No need to come inside."

"All right. I'm going to go, in a minute. When I do, I'll leave twenty bucks on the ground here, right where I'm sitting." There was no answer to that. Maybe she is insulted, Al thought. But she'll pick up the twenty.

It was all she could do to start moving again. She made her way back out through the fence and down the alley. She stood, unsteady, on Henry Street. No one looked at her twice, no one made eye contact. This is my impression of a homeless bag lady, she thought, but nobody laughed. She waited, she didn't have the juice for anything else. A yellow taxi passed her by, but about a half hour later, a gypsy cab pulled over at her signal. She gave the guy Anthony's address, and he took off. He was an island guy, spoke Spanish with a Dominican accent. He told her he had been a doctor back in his country, told her she looked like shit. He had to wake her when they got there.

Eighteen

"Jesus Christ, Martillo, are you all right?" It was Gearoid O'Hagan. Al had been half asleep, even though it was almost noon. She was still recovering from her exertions of the previous night. The phone had startled her awake, and she'd answered it out of reflex.

"I'm fine," she said, and she exhaled, sagged back down into her pillows.

"T'ain't what I heard," O'Hagan said. "I heard you was damn near killed. I heard—"

"Relax, Gro. I'm fine."

"It's a lie, then? You weren't set upon outside of your apartment? You didn't get beat half to death? And why don't you answer your goddamn phone? I been half out of my mind, worrying about you."

"That's very nice of you," she said. "I got knocked around a little bit, but I'll be all right in a couple of days. Where did you hear about all this?"

"Himself told me. Al, why don't you lay low for a while? It's plain you've gone and kicked over the hornet's nest. First there was that t'ing up in the Bronx, and now this. Nothing you're doing can be worth this. It ain't worth getting killed over."

"Why would anyone want to kill me?"

"Oh, hell, I don't know," he said. "But does the why of it really matter? There'll be other opportunities for you, Al. There's other t'ings coming your way. Where are you, anyway? You have a safe place to stay?"

She was still half asleep, and she answered without thinking. "I'm home, Gro."

"Are you out of yer feckin' mind?" His voice went high and tight. "They're bound to be watchin' after you there! Listen to me, I'm gonna get in me car right now, you pack up whatever stuff you need for the next week or so, and—"

"Gro, relax. I'm in a safe place."

"Hah." He was clearly exasperated. "You ain't at home, then."

She looked around. She was in the bed in Anthony's spare bedroom. This isn't where I live, not anymore. I don't belong here, not with Tio Bobby gone.

She reproached herself. He's not gone yet. Not that you know of, anyhow. "I'm at my girlfriend's house," she told O'Hagan, and she hoped Anthony had not heard her say it. "I'm gonna stay here for a few more days. When I start feeling a little better, I'll be back at it."

"You know, you are one hardheaded woman. Listen to me. I can get you some money. Maybe about ten K, I'll take it out of one of Caughlan's slush funds. Call it severance, why don't you? You can use it to buy time for yourself to find something better for yourself. Don't be so goddamned proud about this."

"I don't think it's pride, Gro."

"Call it whatever you want, Al, but I think I know you, at least a little bit. You ain't after being scared off. Al, I want you to walk away from this thing with a whole skin."

"Yeah, that's kinda what I want, too. Don't worry about me, Gro, I'm not gonna go on a crusade. There's just a few more things I need to check out, and if they come up blank, I've done all I can do. I can walk away with a clear conscience."

He was quiet for a moment. "Gotta leave on your own terms." She thought she could hear sorrow in his voice.

"Something like that."

"I wish you'd listen to me, Al."

"All the boys tell me that."

He snorted. "I can believe that. Keep your head down, Martillo. Will you promise me that much?"

"I'll be careful."

"I suppose I'll have to settle for that. When this is all over . . ."

"Yeah?"

"Can we meet for coffee, you and me? It was all business, that first time, and then the last time I was hungover out of me skull. Maybe the next time I can say what I need to say."

Al remembered standing on Caughlan's second-floor walkway, next to Helen Caughlan, remembered seeing O'Hagan look up at her, remembered seeing his somber face light up when he saw her. "That would be nice, Gro. I'll call you."

It was about a half hour later when her brain started to work. He never mentioned the dope coming through Caughlan's operation, she thought. And he said he heard about you from Caughlan. Didn't Caughlan say he heard from O'Hagan?

But then again, maybe it didn't mean anything. Rumors come and go, who knows where they start.

"I don't believe it." Rachael hovered over her, prodding, peering, listening with her stethoscope. There was more tension between them this time around. Alessandra could feel it. Maybe it was because she was less desperate than before, more resistant. Rachael had been a savior before, an angel of mercy. Now she was an authority figure.

"You don't believe what?" Unclench your fists, Alessandra told herself. Relax. Take it easy, she's on your side. Anger is your biggest weakness.

But sometimes it was all she had.

The doctor glanced up from what she was doing, looked into Alessandra's eyes. "Nobody heals this fast. It isn't right." Al thought she could see some resentment in Rachael's eyes. "You didn't stay in bed like I told you to. I was going to tell you that you could get up and get a little exercise, but I'm a bit late. Correct? You haven't been resting."

"I know my body." I can't lie in this bed all day, she thought. I'll go out of my mind. "I know when it's time for me to get up and get moving."

"Sure you do."

"Really," Al said. "I'm fine. Besides, I have been taking it easy. I've been resting a lot. For me, anyhow." And I missed morning practice four days running, she thought. Isn't that enough?

Rachael reached up and brushed the hair out of Al's face with her fingertips. "Your bruises are almost gone," she said. "Your face looks much better than before."

"Thanks."

"Have you given any more thought to what I suggested? It's not too late, you know."

"Not too late for what?"

Rachael grimaced. "Are you kidding? It's not too late to go to the police. I can testify . . ."

Alessandra shook her head. "Come on, you know exactly what's going to happen if we go to the police. They'll take one look at me and think, 'Hysterical Puerto Rican broad, boyfriend probably caught her jumping the fence and smacked her around, now she wants to get back at him.' They'll never take me seriously. They'll sit me down with a caring and sensitive lady officer from the cotton pony squad, and she'll make a great show of investigating. She'll make it look good, which is supposed to make me feel better, and everybody goes home happy."

Rachael took her hand. "Alessandra, the men who did this to you really should face some sort of . . . Al, you're hurting my hand."

Alessandra released her grip. "Sorry."

"Surely the police—"

"Rachael, the guys who did this are gonna get theirs, but first I need to know how soon I can get out of here."

"You're asking me? Does that mean you'll do what I tell you to do?"

"No," Al told her. "But it means I'll think about it."

"Fair enough." Rachael kneaded Alessandra's rib cage, feeling for the places where she had been kicked. "How much discomfort in here?"

"Not a lot. It's still sore, but no sharp pangs anymore."

Rachael looked disgusted. "There really should be a lot more pain. Well, I can't say for sure without an X-ray, but I'd say your bones are healing. You can get out and around now. You'll need to build your endurance back up gradually. You ought to avoid contact sports for about two more weeks. Can you do that?"

Alessandra thought about it. "Maybe," she said. "I can do a week, I think, but after that, it all depends on how things shake out."

"All right. Al, I misjudged you, I think. I really thought you were going to let these guys walk away from this. But you're not, are you?"

Al shook her head. "Not a chance," she said.

"You know, I gotta tell ya, sis, your taste in men sucks." Elizabeth Walsh, TJ Conrad's parole officer, was nothing like what Alessandra had pictured. She was a short, plump, middle-aged white lady with bumpy orange hair and a strong chin. They were sitting in her office, a small cluttered room in a musty government building in downtown Paterson, New Jersey.

"How do you figure that?" Al asked her.

"Oh, come on. You can't be that naïve. TJ Conrad is a drug addict and an alcoholic. He is chronically unemployed, he's a user, he's a womanizer . . . For God's sake," she said. "He's an irresponsible extended adolescent and he's one of the most arrogant human beings I've ever met."

Al decided to mess with her. "TJ is a gifted musician," she said. "He's an artist. You can't expect an artist to live by the conventional rules. Transgression is part of his job description. An artist is supposed to—"

Walsh interrupted her. "Artist, my ass," she snapped, and she jabbed a stubby finger in Al's direction. "I got that son of a bitch an interview with a very successful musical group, they

work just about year-round, believe me, these people are in demand. They need a piano player, Conrad plays the piano. And
do you know what he told me? Hmmm? He told me when
you're the best guitar player on the continent, but you're only
an ordinary piano player, you can't settle for ordinary. Even if
they wanted a guitar player, he said, he couldn't play with them,
because musicians who play weddings all the time wind up
playing everything like it was a wedding. What the hell is that
supposed to mean? Can you tell me? I'll tell you what it means,
it means he's lazy. I've got half a mind to fail his ass right back
into the can."

"Back into the can? You mean he's been away?"

"Oh, no, I guess he forgot to tell you about that. Simple
assault. Drunk and disorderly. Possession. Driving under the
influence. Assault and battery. Resisting arrest. And so on, and
so on."

White lady, Al thought, probably lived in the 'burbs her
whole life, never had the necessity to stand up to somebody.
You ever have to fight for what's yours, Al wanted to ask
her, you ever have to drop your dignity in the street and
fight off the rats who think they have the right to walk on
you? She didn't, though. It's an argument she knew she
could not win. No matter how soft they've had it, no matter how cush their lives have been, people always think
they've had to walk through fire and broken glass to get
where they are. Anyway, she told herself, you don't know
anything about this woman. What you're feeling right
now is prejudice. Maybe she's had it just as hard as you.
Maybe she's as tough as she wants you to believe she is.

Yeah, okay.

Sure.

"Listen," Al told her. "You might be right about TJ. He might be everything you say he is, but what he did the other night took guts. Things would have gone a lot worse for me if he hadn't stepped in."

"I never said he didn't have guts." Still, she didn't look convinced. "So what, these two guys jump out of an alley, is that right? You were just walking down the street, minding your own business? Come on, no bullshit. You weren't trying to cop for TJ? You gotta know, sis, anybody looks like you waltzes into some alley to cop is taking a hell of a risk. You sure you didn't take a beating trying to score for this guy? Walk me through what happened."

"TJ took me to the Met. We had driven back and—"

"The Met? The Metropolitan Museum? Oh, Christ, that's priceless. I gotta give TJ his due, he never stops looking for the right angle."

Al ignored that. "I had borrowed my uncle's van. I park it in a lot nine or ten blocks from my apartment. TJ volunteered to drop me off, park it, and walk back. That's how come he happened to be walking past the alley when he did. They had me in a bad spot. I thought . . ." You didn't think, she told herself. But that was not part of the story she was going to tell this woman. "Anyway, I heard TJ yelling from the end of the alley. He said he had a camera phone, and that he had pictures of them. You know, the two guys who dragged me in there. They left me alone then, ran off chasing TJ."

Elizabeth Walsh glanced at her watch. "All right," she said. "I suppose even a creep like Conrad can do something right once in a while, although it's hard for me to believe he'd stick his neck out unless there was something in it for him." She thought for a minute. "Did he have a camera phone?"

"No."

Walsh stared at her for a long count. "Listen, sweetheart, I'm gonna give you some advice. Dump this guy. You don't owe him a thing. You got the looks, you got a job, you got an apartment, hell, you can do a lot better than a bum like TJ Conrad. He's nothing but bad news."

"What the hell happened to you?"

Alessandra was so surprised to see her father sitting in a darkened corner of Tio Bobby's hospital room that her mind didn't register his question. "What? What did you say?"

Victor Martillo rose up out of his chair and stalked across the room. He put a hand to her chin, turned her face into the light coming through the doorway behind her. "What happened?"

Al gritted her teeth. She was getting sick of the question. Besides, *I'm not twelve years old anymore,* she thought. *It's a little late for you to start worrying about me . . .* She couldn't say it. She took a breath, tried to calm herself, dampen the fire inside. "Walked when I should have run," she said. "Nice to see you coming to see Tio Bobby after all."

"This isn't the first time I've been," he said a bit defensively. She allowed him to turn her into the light so he could see her better. She wondered if he was angry at her for catching him committing an act of compassion, or if he was steamed because someone had gotten past the defenses he'd taught her. "Who did this?" His voice was getting loud. "Who did this to you?"

"I'm handling it," she said. "Come back in and sit down. And quit yelling, you're gonna get us kicked out of here."

"You think this is yelling?" But he said it in a quieter tone, and he followed her back into Tio Bobby's room and went over and sat back down in his chair. He turned the chair to face her, leaned forward with his forearms on his knees. "Tell me who hit you."

"So you can go crazy on them? I told you, I'm handling it."

He thought about that for a minute. "Believe it or not," he said, "I still have some connections. Lots of retired military in the NYPD. I can do a lot more than fight. I can use the telephone as well as the next guy."

She was still half angry, and she reproached herself for it. She resisted the impulse to confide in him, because she didn't want him telling her what to do. You want him closer to you, she thought, but you don't want him up in your face. Martillo, she told herself, you sure do lay a lot of conditions on people. Talk to the man.

"We got this client," she said, and she started in.

After she finished, he sat quietly for a while.

I shouldn't have told him anything, she thought. No good can come from this. I should have told him I got drunk and fell out of bed onto my face.

"You never met your grandmother," he finally said.

"Which one?"

"My mother."

"No. Mom had some pictures, but she never talked about your mother. Neither did you."

"No," he said. She waited for him to explain why not, knowing he never would. He sucked in a big breath of air, held it, blew it out. "You look a lot like her," he said. "Sometimes when I catch you looking at me, for half a second I think you're her, come back to torture me some more."

"Torture you? You didn't like her?"

"She was my mother," he said, as though that should explain everything. "I loved her." He patted his shirt pocket, feeling for his cigarettes. He's not gonna light up in here, he's just buying himself some time, Al thought. Her father left his butts where they were, hesitated a bit longer. "I'm not sure how to say this," he finally said. "But you remind me of her a lot. She was the meanest woman I've ever known, and by a significant margin."

"Oh, I see," Al said, bristling. "And I suppose—"

He held a hand up to hold her off. "Easy, now," he said. "Easy." He looked over at Roberto, who lay silent and still in his hospital bed. Tio Bobby was no help. "She had the quickest hands I ever saw," he said, looking into the darkness over Al's head. "She was faster than any instructor I ever had, quicker than anybody I ever worked with, anybody I ever fought. She could smack you four times while you were trying to hit her once, and twice more before you hit the floor. And I don't mean love taps, either. That woman could swat. But she didn't always win, nobody does. She liked to drink, and sometimes she got knocked around. But it never kept her down. She might lay in bed for a day or so, but I always thought that was more from the hangover than anything else. Then she'd be back up and around like nothing happened. Normal person would still be in the hospital." He looked down at her, held eye contact. "You were always like that, too, ever since you were a little kid. And you got your grandmother's hands. But you got some of her temperament, too."

"You think I'm a mean person?"

"No," he said, hasty. "That's not what I meant. Not really. But as much as I hated my mother growing up, I can't judge her now. She lived in a different world. She did what she had to do to survive." He sighed again. "I know you didn't exactly have it easy, either. After your mother . . ."

Alessandra gave him a minute, then finished his sentence for him. "After she killed herself."

"After she did what she did. I didn't know what to do. I went back to work because I couldn't think of anything better. And then, after you ran away from Mag's house, those were the worst years of my life, because nobody knew what had happened to you. I thought it was my mother's spirit, coming back a generation later to punish me."

You ran out on me, you prick, you took that witch Magdelena's side . . . "Why would she want to punish you?"

"I came to New York in 'seventy-two. I didn't call home, or write or anything, I was just glad I got away. I thought she was probably happy to get rid of me."

"What happened to her?"

"I'm getting to that." He'd been sitting hunched over, his hands balled up into fists. He leaned back, held his hands out empty, palms up. "Nobody knows," he said. "She just disappeared, like you did."

"You never found out what became of her?"

"No," he said. "She liked her liquor, and sometimes it took her places where she didn't belong. And no matter . . . no matter how gifted you are, Alessandra, no matter how hard you can hit, you can still be beaten. Nobody wins every time. Nobody."

"You ever lose?"

"Why do you think the shore patrol always sends guys out in teams? You have a bad night, your partner picks you up. You're out on your own and you have a bad night, it might be the end of the story."

"I hear you," she said, and then it was her turn to sit quiet for a while. "This was my fault," she finally said. "I should have seen it coming, and maybe I did, but I didn't want to see it. I won't make that mistake again."

"Will you let me help you?"

"Maybe," she said. She wasn't sure she trusted him enough to let him help her, even after all this time. And she couldn't remember him ever talking this much before. She wondered how much more she would get out of him, if this was a real opening or just a momentary leak in the dam. "Who was your father?" He stared at her then, and she could feel the sadness coming in waves across the darkened room. He sounded very young when he answered her.

"When I was a boy she used to tell me he was a pirate," he said. "She said he'd come back someday, but he never did."

"You really have connections in the NYPD?"

"Yes," he said.

"All right," she said. "There's somebody you can check out for me . . ."

Nineteen

Anthony watched Al pack. He remembered when he and Roberto had been young, how little they'd started out with. Never, though, could he remember being so poor that all his worldly possessions would fit in one medium-sized duffel bag. "You sure I can't talk you out of this?"

She looked up at him. "I'm not going far, Anthony."

"Al, honey, I've known you a long time. I watched you grow up. I know what you're going to do."

He saw a change in her eyes. "Do you now?"

"You're going to start a war."

"Come on, Ant, don't be so dramatic. It's not gonna be a war."

"What would you call it, then?"

"The achievement of political ends by nonpolitical means."

"You've been reading. I'm impressed."

"I know I got a lot of gaps, Ant. I'm doing the best I can."

"So how bad is it going to be? This, this, political campaign of yours?"

She shrugged. "Hasn't been a lotta fun so far. Listen, as

long as they don't know where to find me, the odds are on my side."

"Are they? How many men did they use at your apartment?"

"Five," she said, "but—"

"And how many the other night, when you went back there?"

"I don't know, Ant, how did you—"

"You may think I was born yesterday," he told her, "but I wasn't. You're going up against organized criminals, and you're only one woman. And regardless of how capable you may or may not be, you're still one person, alone. And besides, you have responsibilities."

"What are you talking about? Who am I responsible to?"

He swallowed. "Al, you're my last link."

"Ah, Jesus, Ant . . ."

"It's true," he said. "When Roberto's gone . . ." It was the first time he'd spoken those words, and they stung, even though it seemed he'd thought of little else for weeks. "You know, it's funny," he told her. "You know how I feel about Roberto. But all these years, a tiny bit of me always wondered what it would be like to be free, completely free. I always discounted that, wrote it off as a harmless fantasy, more or less along the lines of 'what if I won the lottery,' or something like that. I never really wanted it. Roberto completed me, somehow. He made me a real person. Without him, I don't know what I would have been. But now that 'harmless fantasy' is going to be my reality. I'll be a free man."

"You make it sound like a prison sentence."

He swallowed again. "Al, as funny as it sounds, pretty soon you'll be all the family I have left. I don't want freedom. I want to be part of something. I want to belong to someone. It's bad enough I'm losing Roberto . . . Bad enough we're both losing him. But if something happened to you, too, I honestly don't think I could take it." He'd gotten to her, he could feel it, he could tell by the way she stood there looking at him. Guilt is dependable, he thought, guilt works every time.

God, I sound just like my mother.

"I have to do this, Ant."

"I understand," he said, keeping his voice low and disappointed. Anthony, he thought, is there no depth to which you won't stoop?

"Listen, I'll be careful," she told him. "Nothing is going to happen to me."

"Come home when it's over," he told her. "Come back."

"I'm supposed to be a big girl, Ant. I can't crash with you forever."

"This house is as much yours as mine."

She laughed at that. "Probably gonna belong to Magdalena soon enough," she said.

"You can help me fight her off," Anthony said. "Won't that be fun?"

She laughed again. He thought he heard something like relief in it. "Yeah," she said. "It'll be a gas. I'll call you, okay?"

"I'll stay up all night worrying if you don't."

She was on to him. "All right, Mom."

Laurie Villereal, from Gemini Records, lived in a building on the corner of Vernon Boulevard and 47th Road in Queens. Alessandra had never been in that neighborhood before. She stood on Vernon, uncertain of which direction she should go. It wasn't a bad street; she wondered what the rents were like, how tough the commute into Manhattan would be. You're always ready to move on, she thought. You're always ready to fade away.

She found the right building, rang the bell next to Laurie's name. A moment later, she heard a voice. It was Laurie. She was four floors up, leaning out of the window next to the fire escape. "The buzzer's broke," she yelled. "Catch!" A key tied to a purple yarn tail sailed down, and Al caught it out of the air, used it to let herself into the brick apartment building.

Laurie had her apartment painted brighter than a Caribbean whorehouse. There were no lights on in the place, though, and that made it a little easier to take. Al stepped through the front door and into the main room, which smelled like a mixture of patchouli and herb. Mary Jane maintenance program, Al thought. She gave another inward shrug. None of my business, she thought. "Thanks for agreeing to see me."

Laurie bounced down on the couch. "No prob," she said. "I thought you forgot about me. Have a seat." Laurie was wearing a Led Zep T-shirt, no bra, and a ratty pair of cutoffs.

Alessandra sat down in a big soft chair opposite the couch. "I didn't forget you," she said. "I been busy."

"Yeah?" Laurie had a big grin on her face. "Taking boxing lessons?"

Al wanted to be irritated, but it was a good line. She remembered how funny everything is when you're messed up. "Maybe I should," she said.

"You're so butch," Laurie told her. "Don't you worry 'bout scaring all the guys away?"

Damn, Al thought. Laurie is really a different person when she's stoned. She's direct, she looks right at you, breaks your chops. I think I prefer her this way. "Hey, you know what, they're scared off, they don't have what it takes anyhow."

"Lotta work though, bein' butch," Laurie said. "Gotta get up that attitude alla time. Fun just being a little more girlie once in a while. Know what I'm saying? Every time I seen you, you got the same outfit on. Jeans, T-shirt, sneakers. You got great hair, but you always got it tied back. It's like, I don't know, you got yourself strapped in or something. Christ, you wear a dress once, nobody will reckanize you."

Al looked down at herself. It was true. "Maybe I should change up a little bit," she said. Don't be taking "dress for success" tips from Laurie Villereal, she told herself. "So tell me, Laurie, how long you been working for Gemini Records?"

"I dunno. Couple years, I guess. Sandy got me the gig."

"Sandy Ellison. You're, what, his personal assistant?"

"Slave to the slob, that's me."

"What's he like to work for?"

"Are you gonna, like, put this in an article or something?"

"Not if you don't want me to."

"Not," Laurie said, nodding. "He's a spoiled thirteen-year-old baby. I practically gotta tie his shoes for him every morning. But it beats dog walking, which is where I was at when I met Sandy."

"How'd you get from dogs to Ellison?"

"I dunno. We hooked up, I guess. I mean, normally I'm not into men, but Sandy has this thing, you know what I'm saying? I mean, he's like this little boy, and I guess I dug that. But then, you know how it is, somehow the thing you like the most about someone turns into the thing you can't stand about them, and we split up. But he was crashing here for a while, and he got used to the way I, like, took care of him. I was kicking myself for doing it, you know, but it got me into Gemini, and, like, a whole different pay scale, so I guess it turned out all right."

"You've been in on BandX since the beginning, then, am I right?"

"Yeah. Since Sandy scouted them."

"So what do you think?"

"I dunno. I mean, I can never tell who's gonna make it and who isn't. It never makes any sense to me. Sandy had this girl band for a while, they were so hot you couldn't believe it, I mean, I would pay money to see them, right? So maybe I'm biased or whatever, but they went nowhere, and then they split up. I woulda bet my last nickel on them, and I was way off. So, I mean, I don't know. TJ is the real thing, and Cliff's got a great voice, but I don't know how much that counts for. Know what I'm saying? Sandy seems pretty sure they're gonna pop, though."

"Did you know Willy Caughlan?"

"Yeah." Laurie broke eye contact, started playing with her hair. "Yeah, I did." Her voice got quiet.

"What did you think of Willy?"

Laurie twisted her brown hair between two fingers. "He had that same thing that Sandy had, that, like, little boy thing, it made you want to watch out for him. Like, I needed to make sure he was gonna be okay."

"What did you think when you heard he was dead? Did you believe he OD'd?"

"I don't know. I mean . . ." She looked back up at Alessandra. "He didn't use, for one thing. You get guys like that sometimes, even in the industry. But, like, if it wasn't an overdose, that would mean someone killed him, and he was so sweet. I couldn't think of why anybody would want to hurt him or anything. I mean, he, like, got along with everybody. Cliff and Trent and the rest didn't fight as much when he was around, cause he would just, like, joke them out of it and stuff. So it was hard to think that someone did that to him on purpose."

"So you thought about this, right? You wondered if it was a drug thing, or if maybe someone got him."

She scowled. "Yeah. I did. I thought I was just being paranoid."

"How did he get along with TJ?"

"I dunno. I mean, Willy thought TJ was the second coming, you know what I mean? But TJ wasn't around much back then, so I don't know."

"What do you think would have happened if he had lived? Would BandX have kept him, or would they have taken TJ back?"

"No, they needed TJ. Trent would have fought, but I'm sure Sandy would have made them take TJ back. But I mean, there's no law you can't have three guitars. I don't think it would have been a big deal."

"Did you ever have a theory on who might have killed Willy? Is there someone you suspected?"

Laurie looked away again. "Well, you know . . . I kept calling the coroner's office. I got to know one of the doctors there. Over the phone, I mean. She told me that Willy didn't have any needle marks on him. She said he had ingested some strange form of opiate, and because it wasn't, like, processed or whatever, it took a shitload of it to kill him. So I wondered who would have something like that, you know, and all I could think of was that TJ had just gotten nailed for possession."

"Wasn't he supposedly in rehab when it happened?"

"Please," Laurie said, scorn heavy in her voice. "I know he was in-patient, and everything, but that guy could talk his way out of anything. Or anywhere."

"What about Willy? Did he have drug connections? You think he could have been dealing?"

"Nah, he was funny like that. I mean, a musician who doesn't do coke, get real, am I right? But not Willy. No way. If you even used around him, he'd give you this face, you know?"

"You had a thing for him, didn't you?"

"Yeah. I mean, like I said, I'm not usually into guys, and he and I weren't in love or anything, but we, like, got into each other for a while, yeah."

"He ever stay out here with you?"

"Yeah," she said. "Yeah, a few times. But he was a musician, you know what I'm saying? They're all the same."

"So he never moved in with you, did he? Didn't leave his stuff here." Like a guitar, or a laptop, or a pile of floppy discs . . .

"No. It wasn't like that."

"Did you want it to be?"

Laurie stopped fiddling with her hair and stared at Alessandra. "Let me tell you something," she said. "When you're balling a musician, you will never come first. Never. Do you hear what I'm saying? No matter how much you love them, no matter how much they say they love you, okay, you always come after the band, and after the gig, and after the coke, and even after some kink bitch they met after a show somewhere. So, like, go ahead and do what you wanna do, but don't kid yourself that it's ever anything more than fucking. 'Cause it's not."

It seemed to Al that she had run out of questions. She

looked around at the brightly painted walls. There's nothing you can do for this girl, she thought. And besides, who are you, anyhow? Laurie is going to make her own mistakes, not yours.

"Listen," Laurie said. "Sorry if I bummed you out or anything. I'm just gonna tune up a little, okay, and then I'm gonna go get lunch. You feel like Mexican?"

"I got something I gotta do this afternoon," Al said. "Out in Jersey. Maybe next time." Besides, she thought, you might wind up bringing home some of the mariachi players, or a waitress or two, and I would just be in the way . . . "Thanks, Laurie. You've been a great help."

She felt the twinge in her ribs as she twisted in the driver's seat to look into the back of the van. Still looked pretty weird, she had to admit, but at least it was clean. Her new toy was rolled up in a black bath towel and stashed safely out of sight underneath the couch. It was a Valtro PM5, a pistol-grip pump shotgun with a magazine that hung out of the bottom of the barrel just ahead of the trigger guard. Seven rounds in the magazine and one more in the pipe, and she had four extra magazines. It was made in Italy, but it was no thing of beauty, its design was brutally straightforward. Drive carefully, she told herself. Don't give anyone a reason to pull you over and see what you've got in here . . .

She'd gotten directions to the warehouse Marty had told her about off MapQuest. Norwood, New Jersey, was a quiet, prosperous little town in the woods about half an hour north of the George Washington Bridge. The place was a plain brown concrete-block building, thirty feet high, two hundred feet square, a glass atrium appended to the front in an attempt to give the place some office space and a little class. You couldn't see through the smoked glass, but Alessandra knew nobody was home, there were no cars in the parking lot. An empty green Dumpster stood lonely in the far corner of the lot, its black plastic lid hanging open.

She parked the Astro across the street and settled in to wait. Maybe they're out to lunch, she thought, maybe you got here too early. Bad guys don't work through lunch. Maybe they'll show up at one.

They didn't show up at one. She got out of the van and stretched carefully, feeling out the mending tissues of her rib cage. Almost healed, she thought. Another day or so, you'll be all better. The bruises on her face were already nearly gone. She got back into the van and slumped in the driver's seat.

She came to about an hour later when she saw a small panel truck pull into the lot and back up to one of the three large roll-up doors. Two guys got out of the truck and went inside the building, one black guy and one who looked Korean. She pulled on a vest that held the four extra magazines. She could feel the weight at the tops of her shoulders. She fished around in the boxes she had stashed under the sofa, added two sets of handcuffs to a vest pocket. One plastic foam plug for each ear, a thin pair of gloves, a pair of shades, and she was ready. She pulled the twelve-gauge, towel and all, out of its hiding place, tucked it under her arm, and walked across the street.

The panel truck's suspension groaned; Al could hear a fork-lift drive onto the truck bed, deposit its load, and back off again. There was a personnel door off to one side, the two men hadn't bothered to lock it behind them. Not that it matters, she thought, hefting the Valtro in her arms. I've got a master key . . . She dropped the towel, chambered the first round, yanked the door open, and stepped inside. It banged shut behind her.

The Korean was standing by the rear of the truck, a clipboard in his hand. The black guy was out of sight. Al could hear the moan of the forklift's hydraulics somewhere in the stacks. She pointed the shotgun at the Korean's chest, held a finger to her lips. He looked at the gun, not at her, swallowed once, nodded.

Large cardboard boxes on pallets, stacked in metal racks that reached all the way to the ceiling. Stark white walls, unpainted concrete floors, harsh, bright mercury-vapor lights, white security camera high in a corner. She took a step away from the Korean, shifted her focus, fired twice. The shotgun jerked in her hands, making a satisfying roar right through the earplugs. The ejected shells bounced across the floor as pieces of camera rained down from the ceiling. Damn, she thought, that feels good. All of a sudden I got the biggest dick in the room. The Korean's eyes were wide, his face white as she pointed the gun back at his gut.

The black guy came running from the interior of the place. "Jesus Christ, Henry, what the fuck was . . ." He skidded to a stop when he saw her, the business end of the gun now pointed in his direction. "Holy shit, lady, do you have any idea . . ."

She peered over her sunglasses at him. "I tell you to talk?"

He shook his head, clamped his lips shut.

"Good." She reached into a vest pocket, fished out a pair of handcuffs, and tossed them to him. "Put these on," she said. "Around that column, over there. Just so you don't get lost." He wrapped his hands around the vertical steel I-beam, fastened himself in. Alessandra pointed the shotgun back at the Korean. "Step this way, Henry," she said, and she backed toward the black guy. "Okay, that's far enough. Stand right there." She checked the cuffs. "You wait right here," she said to the black guy. "Okay?"

He didn't reply.

"Show me the rest of the security cameras, Henry."

"Three more," the Korean said. "In the corners."

She pointed the gun at his head. "You wouldn't want to hold out on me, Henry. It's probably not worth it."

He swallowed again. "Plus two more," he said. "In the middle."

"Show me." He led her around, watched as she took them out one at a time. No wonder we love guns, she thought. So much power in such a compact machine, hold one in your hands and you're Wonder Woman . . . They might get a few frames of her on tape somewhere, but she didn't mind that. "All right, Henry," she said, and she tossed him another pair of handcuffs. "Just like your friend, over there, but down this end. Over here." She relaxed a bit once he was secured, let the gun hang from one hand as she wandered around the warehouse.

She hadn't had time to look too carefully before. She examined the boxes as she walked past. Most of them held giant plasma television sets, surround-sound systems, and other audio and video equipment. The boxes, stacked on pallets, were parked in orange metal racks that took up about three-quarters of the floor space. Rows of plastic fifty-five-gallon drums occupied the rest of the space. The barrels wore colored paper tags bearing the word GLYCERIN.

The forklift stood silent in one of the rows between the pallet racks. It was the kind of machine you stood on to drive. Al climbed on and the thing clicked into life when it felt her weight, its electric motors whining. She played with the controls a minute until she'd figured out how it worked, then stepped off again. She took one more circuit around the edges of the warehouse, looking through the normal junk that accumulates in those places: a pile of broken pallets, some brooms, a bucket and mop, a battery charger for the forklift, a long piece of rusty metal chain.

The orange racks were not fastened to the floor, they were freestanding, depending on the weight of their contents to keep them still. Originally, Alessandra had planned on simply shooting the shit out of whatever was in the place, but as much fun as that might be, she thought she saw a more efficient way. She dragged the piece of chain over to the forklift.

It took a few minutes to set it up. She climbed up to the top of one end of the pallet rack, tied one end of the chain around the top corner, then climbed back down and tied the other end of the chain to the forklift. She drove the forklift slowly backward until the chain went taut. She wondered if her granny knots would hold. She was sure that you weren't supposed to use chains that way, but the chain tightened on itself as she backed away. She increased the strain. The racks were not entirely rigid, the top corner curled forward as she backed away, the forklift groaning and skidding its tires. That chain breaks, she thought, I'm probably toast . . . It didn't, though, it held until she'd gotten the pallet rack past the point of no return. Some of the boxes in the top slots of the rack fell out and crashed to the floor, but then the whole thing came down, not all at once, but slowly, from one end to the other, curling down like a wave as it crumps lengthwise on a beach. The sound was stupefying, she could feel the impact up through the floor, and the vibration set off a few of the sprinkler heads, raining water down on the mess.

She'd only pulled down the first section, the other two rows stood still behind the rubble and the sudden dust cloud. Didn't think of that, did you, she thought. If you'd pulled over the farthest rack, you might have gotten them all to domino . . . But what she'd done seemed like enough.

Her ears rang as she got off the forklift and walked back over to the column where the black guy was kneeling down, his eyes squeezed shut, his forehead resting against the cold steel. She got down on one knee next to him. "Dude," she said. "What's your name?"

"Malik." He didn't open his eyes.

"Mal, what's in the barrels?"

He kept his eyes squeezed shut. "I don't know, man . . ."

"C'mon, Mal, I'm trying to help you here." She put a finger under his chin, tilted his head back. "Look at me, Mal. I want you to." He opened his eyes, watched as she perched her shades up on top of her head. "You're gonna be all right, Mal. I'm not gonna hurt you. Who do you work for?"

"Jerry Tomasino." His voice was barely a whisper.

"Okay. Cool. Listen to me now. Jerry Tomasino sent some of his goons to fuck me up. I want you to tell Jerry who did this to him. You know what I'm saying? Rican bitch with some faded bruises on her face. Okay?"

He nodded silently.

"What's in the barrels?"

"Lady," he said, his voice tight with fear, "I'm just a driver, I swear to God—"

"Yo, Mal, come on. I could leave a key for those cuffs. I could put it right here on the floor so you can reach it with your foot. I could give you maybe ten minutes before I call the cops, you could get loose, you and your boy Henry could get gone before they show up. Or I could leave you stuck. Now I know Tomasino doesn't give a shit about glycerin. Safe bet he doesn't give a shit about you, either. What's in the barrels?"

"The ones with the blue labels . . ." His voice was a whisper. "I've heard, you know . . ."

"Spit it out, Mal."

He glanced in the Korean's direction. "Opium base," he said. "The other ones are decoys. They never move. They been sitting here as long as I been around."

Tomasino, she thought, I am no longer your biggest problem. "Okay, Mal. You got a cell phone?"

He nodded. "Inside jacket pocket."

She put one hand on his shoulder while she retrieved his phone with the other one. An intimate gesture, casual physical contact between friends. He felt solid, felt like a good guy. "Sorry about your phone, Mal."

"It's okay. Company phone."

"Tomasino has an Englishman working for him. Short guy, blond hair. What's his name?" She felt him stiffen under her hand. He took a deep breath before he answered.

"Parker," he said. "Wallace Parker."

"Great," she said. "One more, Hispanic, guy named Ramon."

"Sorry," he said. "The Spanish cats come and go. I don't remember a Ramon."

"All right. Don't forget, you tell Jerry who did this. You tell him I can reach out and touch him anytime I want. Got it?"

"Yeah."

"Good." She fished a small silver key out of her pocket, placed it on the floor.

There were only four barrels with blue labels, they shivered and danced when she shotgunned them open. An oily, viscous fluid spilled out on the floor. The other barrels had been there a while, you could tell because they were coated with dust. You should have noticed that, she told herself. She blew a couple of them apart, just for comparison. And for fun. They were filled with something that looked and ran like water.

She opened the door, stuck her head out. The parking lot was still empty, except for the panel truck and a half dozen Canada geese that were waddling up the grassy verge by the Dumpster. She retrieved her towel, wrapped up the shotgun, stepped out. It felt good to be back outside, in the sunshine.

Back in the van, she dialed Marty's cell, but he had his voice mail on. Must be busy, she thought. She left him a short message, told him the Norwood warehouse was Tomasino's, but she didn't tell him how she knew.

Twenty

Marty Stiles drove through the suburban streets of northern New Jersey. There was a Dunkin' Donuts right on the New York state line—the place pulled him in like a magnet. This is why you can't lose any weight, he told himself. You can't stay out of joints like this . . . But you're gonna need the energy, he thought. Who knows what you're gonna run into out here? And they were having a special, anyway, large coffee, light and sweet, plus two glazed sticks for four bucks.

Back out on the road, he crossed over into Orange County, New York. It was his first trip to that part of the state. It looked depressing as hell. As soon as you passed out of Jersey and into New York State, the whole ambiance changed. The border is not real, he thought, it's nothing but an abstraction, an imaginary line, but on the north side of that line, everything definitely started looking seedier and more low-rent. It was more commercial, too. He passed old factory buildings, railroad sidings, industrial parks, a shuttered drive-in movie, and a strip joint. He peered at the street signs as he drove, finally found the one he was looking for and pulled into one of the industrial parks. Once off the main road, he eased his car to a stop and looked around.

Norman Green

He found the right building. It housed, at least in theory, three businesses. One was a cosmetics warehouse, the second a Korean import-export company, and the third was Access Fine Chemicals. The building was slapped together out of prefabricated panels, looked more or less like something a six-year-old would build out of Lego blocks. Access Fine was at one end of the building. Marty crept slowly on past, watching carefully. The parking lot out back was about three-quarters full, but the few windows at Access Fine were dark, and on the front stoop a couple of soggy folded newspapers lay on the concrete, deteriorating slowly back into cellulose. Somebody's paying the rent, Marty thought, but it didn't look like they were conducting much business. He wasn't totally confident in his information. A lawyer employed by the guy who ran Access Fine—the one who had gotten stiffed on his fee—had told him the place was a drug lab. But with lawyers, you could never be sure what angle they were working.

A guy in a suit came out the front door of the cosmetics warehouse, which was in the center of the building. He looked blankly at Marty, then turned and headed for the parking lot. That tears it, Marty thought, and he stepped on the gas, motored on past, found a place to make a U-turn, then headed back out to the main road, where he turned south, back toward Dunkin' Donuts. Kill some time, he told himself. Come back later, after dark.

The place was mostly dark when Marty drove past it a second time. He parked his car next to some Dumpsters behind a truck garage right down the road from Access Fine. Why am I doing this, he wondered. Ain't I a little too old for this shit? I must have taken a wrong turn, somewhere back down the line, I must have did something wrong, I must have stepped off course. By now, I should have been out of this, I should be sitting behind a desk getting a blow job from my secretary, I should have sent Martillo out here . . . Not too late for that, he thought, I could go home right now, get Martillo to do this tomorrow night. What difference would one more day make? He thought about calling her, heard her voice in his head question his manhood. Knock it off, he told himself. You've done this kind of thing all your life. Why back out now?

I'm just tired, he thought. That's all it is. Shouldn't have eaten them two donuts. He got out of the car, grunted as he stood up. He slapped his jacket pockets, doing a quick inventory: flashlight, cell phone, camera. He'd brought a .38 because it was smaller and lighter than his nine millimeter. It was in a holster, strapped to his belt.

The camera was low tech, he'd had it for years. It took him a moment to load it with a roll of high-speed film. He knew Martillo used something digital, but he was used to his old Nikon, he had confidence that he'd get good, clear images from it. Martillo was probably right, the digital stuff was lighter and probably better, but he was sticking with what he knew. He shifted the .38 on his belt, looking for a place where it wouldn't dig into his belly, even though he knew no such place existed. You should just leave it under the front seat of the car, he told himself. Thirty years of this, you ain't had to shoot anybody yet. He felt naked without it, though, so he left it on his belt. Probably won't need half this crap, he thought. Mickey Caughlan ain't gonna need pictures, you could lose the camera, too. All the Mick wants is a name. Who's the son of a bitch who's playing me, who's the guy on my payroll that's doing me like this? That's all he cares about. Marty felt sorry for the guy, whoever he was. You shoulda found a softer target, he thought. Someone who would go whine to the cops, or his lawyer, or his wife. When Mickey finds out who you are, you're gonna feel like a building fell on you . . .

Access Fine lay about a hundred feet away. The building was silhouetted by the streetlights out on the main road and the few spotlights in the parking lot, but the end of the building facing him was in darkness. There were still a few cars in the lot. Probably the Koreans working late, Marty thought. No wonder they're kicking our ass . . . He'd have to make his way through a line of underbrush and small trees that marked the property line between the two buildings. He could go out around, walk down the driveway from the truck garage and around to Access Fine, but he didn't want to announce his presence, and besides, it was longer that way.

He paused when he got to the tree line, waited to see if anyone was out and around. He listened to the hum of tires from the traffic out on the main road, but the industrial park was a daytime destination, and the only sign of life was him. He pushed his way through the undergrowth, felt the soft ground suck at his loafers. God, he hated the country, it was all bugs and mud and small animals, buried PCBs and chromium and God only knew what else. Jesus. He smelled something distasteful. Maybe a skunk in the neighborhood, he thought, and wouldn't that be great, get sprayed by one of those sons-abitches? He unholstered the .38, wondering if a dead skunk smelled any less potent than a live one that was pissed off at you. But if he's gonna get me, Marty thought, I'm gonna get him, by God. He crossed the open space between the tree line and Access Fine at a fast waddle.

There was a back door to Access Fine, it was in the gloom

between two big roll-up truck doors. It had a dead bolt and a lock, but they were both of the cheesy hardware store variety, and they yielded to Marty's ministrations without too much resistance. He slipped inside the door, pushed it softly closed behind him, stood motionless, silent, all his senses wide awake.

He could hear water dripping somewhere. There was a strange tang in the air, something he couldn't quite identify, but it tingled at his sinuses and collected in the mucus at the back of his throat. After I get Mickey Caughlan's money, he thought, I am definitely finished with this shit . . . He fished out his flashlight, clicked it on, scanned half the room, then turned it back off again. The space was mostly empty, looked like the last legitimate business to occupy the space had moved out in a hurry, left behind a collection of dented stainless steel tanks, some rusting conveyors, and a bunch of empty wooden packing crates. He did it again, scanned the other half of the room for a second or two. It was somewhat more organized, looked like someone had set up some kind of a rudimentary production line over against the far wall. There was an enclosed space up at the front of the building, probably housed some offices. Marty stood still, focused on the darkness up front. After some time it seemed to him that there was a very thin band of light down near the floor. Light on in one of the offices, Marty thought. Either my guy is still here, or he forgot to hit the switch on his way home. He clicked his flashlight on one more time, noted the exit door in a far corner, over next to a big circuit breaker panel with its door hanging by the bottom hinge.

He put his pistol back in the holster, hefted his Nikon, and took a couple shots of the jury-rigged production line. The camera's shutter and auto-wind motor snapped and reefed, sounding too loud in the empty room. There was a noise up front, behind the door to the offices, then some muted voices. Marty turned in that direction instinctively, pushed the camera's button reflexively as the door opened, blinding him.

"Holy shit!"

Marty didn't really see the guy, he just had an impression of a white lab coat swirling as the guy dodged back into the office, slamming the door behind him. Gotcha, Marty thought, and he dropped the Nikon, let it swing from its lanyard around his neck. He clawed for the pistol, felt his way back toward the door, back the way he'd come. He still had the replica of his NYPD badge, felt the weight of it in his jacket pocket. It had gotten him out of situations like this before, because it was a rare soul who really wanted to kill a cop. Cops were like Hell's Angels: you fight one of them, you got to be ready to fight them all.

Marty was not quite all the way to the back wall when the door banged open again. A tall man stood silhouetted in the light from the office. This was a second guy, bigger than the one in the lab coat. "Police!" Marty shouted. "Put your hands up, turn around and face the wall!"

The guy in the doorway hit a switch on the wall next to him, flooding the big room with light. He's not going for it, Marty thought, and his knees buckled under him, sending him to the floor. He heard two booming shots, felt shrapnel from the cinder-block wall behind him. He rolled over on the floor, trying to stay in motion, knowing that a body in motion, even a fat one, is harder to hit than a body at rest. He paused for a second, pistol straight out in front of him, focused on his shot, fired three times. He hit what he was aiming at, which was the circuit breaker panel over next to the door, because it erupted in a shower of sparks and the room went dark.

"Did you get him?" The voice was high and querulous.

"Cayete!" the man shouted. "Shut up!"

That has to be the shooter, Marty thought, and he got to his knees, scrabbled as quickly as he could in the direction of the circuit panel, which burned momentarily and flared out. He'll assume I'm going for the door I came in by, Marty thought, and I'll get over there to the far one, and by God it better not be padlocked or chained shut . . . He ran into something metallic and heavy. He grunted involuntarily as he heaved himself over it, whatever it was, heard two more shots.

"Get a light!" It was the shooter, yelling at the first guy. "Goddamn you, go get a light!" Marty bumped into something else in the dark. This is taking too long, he thought, you've got to risk it . . . He inhaled, held his breath, clambered to his feet. He could smell the stink of burning wire insulation as he fumbled his way closer to his exit door. He found the wall, felt his way along, finally got to the door. He leaned against the crash bar. The exit door, long unused, opened a crack with a metallic squeal. Marty cursed silently, pushed against it harder, finally got it open. The lights in the parking lot lit him up from behind. He feinted right, but he needed to get out around the opened door and move to the left, back toward his car. He heard two more shots, hardly felt the one that hit him just above his waist. He kept moving, spun around and stumbled backward as he fired wildly at his pursuer, saw the man go down. Got you, you son of a bitch, he thought, hoping he had done it, shot his way out of a box. Now you just got to get back to the car, he told himself, and you're home free . . .

He ran across the blacktop, hit the grass, got almost all the way to the tree line before he realized he wasn't going to make it. He was on his face in the grass, puzzled because he didn't remember falling. He horsed himself to his knees, willing himself across the last few yards to the bushes along the property line. I'm ruining my pants, he thought, they'll never get them clean . . . He rolled over on his back, exhaled, feeling the shock and numbness down below his waist. Goddamn, he thought, this is bad, and then he wondered: am I going to die here? Out here in the goddamn pucker brush? I always wanted to go like Rockefeller, I always wanted to die in the saddle . . . He wondered who would get his apartment, what they would do with all his shit. Probably just throw it all away, he thought, my whole life is gonna get stacked up on the curb to wait for the garbage truck . . . He became conscious of voices in the distance, wondered how far away they really were. He laid his pistol down in the weeds, fumbled for his cell phone with shaking hands.

"You are not authorized to make this call." It was a prerecorded voice, but still it seemed to carry an undertone of disapproval. Alessandra shook her head. Maybe the guy don't wanna talk to you, she thought. He cut the service off . . . It was the phone she'd retrieved from the empty lot next to her building on Pineapple Street in Brooklyn. She turned it off, laid it aside, fished through her camera bag for the phone she'd taken off Malik back in the warehouse. She looked through the phone's directory, found what she was looking for, made the call.

"Yeah."

"Yo, Jerry," she said, when she heard the voice on the other end. "That ain't no way to answer the phone. Yeah? Not, 'hello,' or 'howyadoin,' just 'yeah'? People are gonna think you don't give a fuck."

"Who is this?" His voice was affronted, angry.

"You don't know me? You gotta be kidding. I remember you, Jerry, you were one of the stiffs at Caughlan's party the other night."

"Who the fuck is this? How did you get my cell number? I find out—"

"Shut the fuck up, Jerry." That worked, for a space of five seconds.

"What?" He couldn't believe she'd said it, she could hear it in his voice. "What did you say? You got any fucking idea who you're talking to? Do you know what I can do to you, you fucking piece of shit? I am gonna—"

"You ain't gonna do shit, Tomasino. You had your chance the other night and you didn't get it done, so why don't you shut up and listen?"

"All right." She could almost see him fighting for control. "All right. You're that fucking bitch that . . . I got you. You don't know how sorry you're gonna be, you are gonna beg, before—"

"We got a problem, Jerry."

"The fuck are you talking about? You're the one with the problem. You got off easy, when I get you this next time, I'm gonna—"

"Yeah, yeah." She felt curiously calm. She had expected to have to fight not to lose her temper, but she was almost serene. Maybe it was because of what she had to tell Tomasino. "Listen, Jerry, you hear from the guys at your warehouse in Norwood?"

He was silent, then, but she had his attention.

"Oh. Maybe they didn't call you. I figured, they work for you, they'll call right away, but maybe they didn't. Maybe they took off, left the mess for you to deal with. Can't say I blame them. I was them, I might think about a nice long Mexican vacation."

"What the fuck are you talking about?"

"Your warehouse in Norwood. Jersey. Norwood, New Jersey? I took it down a little while ago. Fucked up your shit, called the cops after, told them what you had in those plastic drums. I mean, even if the shit's all over the floor now, it's still technically in your possession. I got your attention yet?"

He was silent for a moment, then, in a soft voice: "If what you say is true, there isn't a place on this planet you can hide."

"Hide, my ass. Five fucking guys you hadda send for me? You shoulda sent six, Jerry. They the best you got? I got bigger balls than all of them put together."

His voice was almost a whisper. "You're gonna be sorry you were ever born."

"I want the name of the man who sent you after me, Jerry. And I want the Englishman, and I want Ramon."

Tomasino lost it. "You want the Englishman? Well, you're gonna get him, right up the fucking ass you're gonna get him! You are gonna get—"

"Limp-dick motherfucker." That was the final straw. There was no going back now. Al spoke into the sudden silence. "I am not done with you, Tomasino. You hear me? I am just getting started." She hung up the phone before he could reply.

Twenty-one

Sarah Waters had a big rear end.

Alessandra hadn't noticed it before, but the woman had been sitting down through most of their first meeting, back in Marty's office on West Houston. Waters hurried across the emergency room and hugged Al. "Are you all right?" Al asked her.

Sarah nodded. "They found him early this morning," she said. "They said he died twice in the ambulance on the way here, but the EMTs were able to bring him back. They had to take out one of his kidneys, and he lost a lot of blood. They don't know if he's going to make it, and if he does, they don't know if he'll be the same. He might be paralyzed, or, or, you know, um, damaged. Upstairs." She released her grip on Al, then took her by one hand and dragged her over to a pair of empty chairs on the far side of the room. "How did you know he was here?" she said. "I didn't know who to call. I don't know if Mr. Stiles has any family or anything."

He never had the heart for anyone but himself, Al thought, then felt bad for it. "I think he's got a sister someplace down south," she said. "Marty called me last night, after he'd been shot. All he had time to tell me was where it happened, so I called the local cops. After that, I just kept checking with the hospitals."

"They were asking about you this morning," Sarah told her, her voice low. "Earlier. I didn't tell them anything."

Al nodded. Sarah Waters may have come from the other end of Brooklyn, but it seemed that certain principles held borough-wide. Don't tell 'em shit. "Anyone told you what his chances are?"

"No."

"Do you know what happened?"

Sarah shook her head. "He was out of the office all day yesterday. He called in at five and told me to go home, said he'd see me in the morning. Then this morning I got a call at home from the police, they said he'd been shot. Sometime last night. They said some woman called last night, reported hearing gunfire. I guess that was you. It musta been a quiet night otherwise, because four cruisers showed up, and that's when they found him. They sent a car down to pick me up and bring me out here. I was starting to think I'd be stuck in Jersey forever."

"Marty didn't tell you what he was working on?"

"No. I mean, sometimes he did, he liked to tell stories. Half the time I didn't believe him. But when he called yesterday, he sounded, I don't know, far away, or tired or something. I don't know what it was. I just thought, you know, it was a lousy connection or whatever."

A white guy in a brown suit stepped through a set of swinging doors at the rear of the waiting room. He saw Al sitting next to Sarah Waters, walked across the room, and stood in front of them. "Alessandra Martillo?" he said, but he stared at Sarah.

"Yeah," Al said. "I'm over here."

The guy glanced at Al, then looked back at Waters. "I thought we agreed you were going to come get me if she showed up."

"She just now walked in," Sarah told him, smiling sweetly.

The guy reached into his jacket pocket, pulled out his police ID, and showed it to Al. "Miss Martillo," he said. "Would you come with me, please?"

"Al, honey?" It was Waters. "The phone is gonna be ringing off the hook. What do I tell the clients?"

Al glanced at the policeman. "Tell them he's out on a case. Tell them he'll call back as soon as he can. I'll be back."

It was pretty small, even for a suburban police station. It was a tiny redbrick building sitting back on a quiet, tree-lined street just off what passed for the main road in Old Tappan, New Jersey. It was a ten-minute drive from the hospital. They sat her at a table in the one-room basement, but it was clean, air-conditioned, and well-lit because it was the same room where they held their staff meetings. The two detectives who brought her there questioned her relentlessly, same questions over and over, one of them insinuating that she knew more about Marty's business than she was willing to tell, and maybe more about his death, too. She didn't let it bother her. She put all thoughts of time out of her mind. This will take as long as it takes, she told herself, and she answered their questions calmly, annoyed them with frequent inquiries after Marty Stiles's health. There was a third cop, a black guy who sat silent in the background. Al thought something about him was familiar, but she couldn't place him.

"So let's go over this again," the guy in the brown suit said. "Just for the record. How long have you worked for Martin Stiles?"

How many times had they asked the same questions? She'd lost count. Answer them the same way, she thought. Use the same words. "Couple years."

"What is the nature of your duties for Mr. Stiles?"

"Lots of typing. I take some pictures. I have dinner, sometimes, in a restaurant that belongs to one of his clients, and I report back."

"What about car repos?"

"Oh, yeah. That, too. Sorry, I forgot that part."

"Weren't you arrested just the other night? In Secaucus, am I right?"

"I wasn't arrested. I was questioned. There was an eyewitness to the fact that I was assaulted while in the lawful pursuit of my employer's business."

"Just doing your job."

"That's right."

"The Secaucus PD didn't quite see it that way."

"They weren't there."

"So in the pursuit of your job, as you say, you do, at times, inflict bodily harm when you deem it necessary. Or when your employer, Mr. Stiles, deems it necessary."

"No. I defend myself when I am assaulted."

"Were you aware that your alleged assailant is considering a civil suit?"

Oh, great, Al thought. Just what I need. "No."

"Did you know that Stiles was investigated by Internal Affairs no less than three times during his years on the force?"

Apparently, they didn't find shit . . . "No."

"And you never heard of a Mr. Gerald Baker, who was assaulted four months ago in Brooklyn?"

Al repressed a smile. "No."

The cop sighed. "You have a very colorful past, Miss Martillo. You were—"

"It's been a good life," she said, interrupting him.

"—thrown out of the academy," he continued, "for assaulting an instructor, a certain Mr. Baines, who was teaching hand-to-hand—"

"Get off it," Al said, allowing herself a small spark of anger. "You know as well as I do, Lou Baines is a douche bag who loves groping female cadets under the guise of 'instruction.' He deserved worse than he got from me. He grabbed a handful of your crotch and you didn't do anything about it, I would wonder about you."

"Mr. Baines required extensive dental—"

"Point taken." The speaker was the other white cop, and he stepped forward, sat down across the white plastic table from Al. He looked at the first cop, who got up and walked out of the room. "Ms. Martillo," he said. "I don't disagree with you about Baines, for whatever it's worth."

"Al."

He nodded. "Al. We're not after you, here, I hope you understand that. Our problem is that Marty had some questionable associations while he was on the force, and we have some information that he continued those associations on a professional level since retiring."

"You think Marty worked for the mob?"

"We think he had some questionable associations. Are you aware of the nature of Marty's business? Or are you really telling us the truth? I'm sorry, Al, but you don't impress me as the sort of girl who spends her days typing."

Al sighed. "He was teaching me," she said. "You know what Marty's business is. Wayward spouses, crooked bartenders, silent partners. You got some slime stuck to your shoe, Marty will scrape it off for you. He ain't the only ex-cop in the trade, either. You might wind up working for him yourself, someday."

"And that's your aspiration."

"I'm just trying to pay the rent."

"Do you know what Marty was doing on this side of the river last night?"

"I don't know what he was working on. You're going to have to go back over his invoices and phone logs. Listen, if I knew who shot Marty, I would tell you right now, but I don't. And what's worse, I can't think of anything we did recently that would provoke this kind of a response, unless it was an aggrieved husband or something."

"All right." He leaned forward, put his forearms on the table. "You ever hear of a group called BandX?"

Oh, shit . . . She tried not to look startled. "Yeah, I heard of 'em."

"You follow that sort of music?"

"I heard of the band," she said.

"You ever hear the name Sean Caughlan, aka Willy Caughlan?"

"Yeah."

"How about his father? Daniel Caughlan, aka Mickey Caughlan?"

"Heard of him, too."

"You have any knowledge of a B&E on a house in the Bronx that was occupied by members of BandX?"

"No."

"So you wouldn't know anything about a kit of burglar's tools that was recovered near the scene? I'm told your fingerprints are all over them."

Do they have my prints, she wondered, or is he just fishing? She had been printed twice as a juvenile, but those records were sealed. Supposedly. "I was responsible for Mr. Stiles's equipment. I packed tools for him all the time. What he did with them was not my affair."

The cop shook his head. "Hiding behind a dead man."

"Is he dead? Do you know that?"

"We're trying to give you an opportunity to cooperate with us, Ms. Martillo, but this is a onetime offer. If you walk out of here holding out on us, we will prosecute you for the burglary in the Bronx, and with your record, you could go away for some time. You could be looking at three to five . . ."

"And I think you could be blowing smoke out of your asshole. You want to know who shot Marty Stiles? Stop wasting your time on me. Go get his invoices, go get his phone records. Go do the work."

The cop turned red, started to speak, but he was interrupted by the black guy, who had been sitting silent in the corner the whole time. "All right," the guy said. "All right. I've had enough. I'm going to take Miss Martillo back to the hospital."

"Look," the white cop said, suddenly angry. "If she and Stiles have been interfering with an ongoing investigation . . ."

"The only things you guys 'investigate' out here are drunk drivers and kids smoking dope in the woods. Stick to what you're good at." He stood up. "Miss Martillo? This way out."

He showed her to his car, held the passenger-side door open for her. He got in behind the wheel, paused, held his hand out to her. "Miss Martillo," he said. "I'm Sal Edwards. I apologize for my associates, back inside. They're just trying to do their jobs."

She shook his hand. "Sal," she said. "Funny name for a brother. Short for Salvatore?"

He shook his head. "Salathiel," he said.

"Salathiel," she said. "I like it. Are you with the Jersey cops?"

Sal shook his head. "NYPD," he said, and he started his car and pulled out of the lot. "I worked with your father, once."

Alessandra wondered if that was good or bad. "Is that right?"

"Yeah. Years ago, in the service. He was kind to me. Taught me a lot of things they don't show you in school." He glanced over at her. "Anyway. My partner and I have been working on a case for a couple months. It started with Willy Caughlan's death. We know Marty Stiles worked for Willy's father on a number of occasions. The two of them, as a matter of fact, go back to Marty's days on the Job." He looked at Alessandra again. "You know Daniel Caughlan. We've got pictures of you at a party he threw last weekend."

She nodded. "I know him."

He turned his attention back to the road. "Daniel Caughlan is one of those guys whose luck always seems to run a little better than ours. We're pretty sure he's dirty, but we've never been able to nail him for anything."

"You ever consider," Al asked him, "that maybe he's just running a trucking company? Maybe all you've got on him is your own prejudice. He looks like a bad guy, so you assume he's bad. You think that's possible?"

The cop shrugged. "It happens. But here's my point: this case has taken us in some directions we hadn't expected, but we haven't forgotten about Willy. Now, I'm guessing that Caughlan asked his old buddy Marty Stiles to look into his son's death, and maybe, just maybe, Stiles got into trouble when he started turning over rocks. And it seems a reasonable proposition that Stiles would use your help. Let me guess: he had you checking out BandX. Tell me, Al. Am I off base here?"

"Not entirely." Funny, she thought, I was the one who was curious about Willy, Stiles and Caughlan wanted me to leave it alone.

"All right, fair enough. Next question: that was you, up at that house BandX rented up in the Bronx. Yes?"

"No comment."

"I'll take that as a yes. I could make a case against any one of those dope fiends. They each had plenty of opportunity to murder Willy, and probably motive, too, if you dig a little bit. But how do you pick one of them over another?"

"Be nice if you got the right guy. You guys get anything from the crime scene?"

Sal affected an excited, high-pitched voice. " 'Officer, there's a hair stuck to the bathroom mirror! It must have the perp's DNA!' You know something? You got to live on what you get from the crime-scene guys, you'll starve to death."

"Had to be somebody Willy knew," Al said.

Edwards nodded. "If it was anything other than a simple overdose," he said, "if someone did kill him, Willy opened the door and let them in. That leaves us pretty much back where we started. Except for one thing: Marty Stiles was looking into this, and now he's lying on an operating table. He might make it and he might not. The way I see it, that leaves you out on a ledge."

"You don't need to worry about me," she said. "So what if Marty wakes up and tells you who shot him? You think you've got your guy?"

"Marty's shooting and Willy's death are connected," he said.

"How do you know that?"

"My gut tells me." He glanced her way again. "I trust my gut. I trust it a hell of a lot more than I trust crime-scene techs. So if Marty wakes up, yeah, I would consider that a big break. We can probably put one bad guy away. And I'm guessing, whoever the guy is, we squeeze his nuts hard enough, we'll find out what happened to Willy. But if Marty bites it, you're in big trouble, Miss Martillo. Whoever this guy is, good bet he's killed twice now. Attempted it twice, anyhow. First Willy, now Marty. Twice is a pattern. You know what I'm saying? He's into it. As a matter of fact, he might try for you just for the hell of it. So I'm saying, you're gonna need all the friends you can get."

Al trusted her gut, too. "You wanna be my friend, Salathiel?"

"Hey, listen. I'm just looking for the bad guys. That's my job. I like to think I'm pretty good at it. I don't think you're one of the bad guys, Miss Martillo, but I think you might be hanging out in fast company. You might be on Caughlan's team, fine, it's not a crime. But don't make the mistake of thinking Caughlan is going to protect you. Mickey Caughlan takes care of Mickey Caughlan. There's more than one man among the missing who thought different. And if these local storm troopers out here think they can get any mileage out of sticking you with that B&E in the Bronx, or for anything else they can get you for, they'll do it. So, like it or not, you got some exposure here. You're vulnerable. Way I look at it, though, that's the least of your worries." He reached into his jacket pocket, fished out his business card. "You can call me anytime, day or night. I think someone killed Willy Caughlan, and I think the same someone tried to kill Marty Stiles. I got a gut feeling that you're next up."

"Sal, do you know what happened to Willy Caughlan's laptop?"

He looked at her for a moment. "No," he finally said. "And we looked, too. We talked to everyone who knew him, we canvassed all the computer repair joints in his neighborhood, but we came up with nothing. Is that what you were doing up in that house in the Bronx?"

"No comment. What's your gut tell you about Willy's laptop?"

"Do you have it?"

"No. But there's a couple places I haven't looked yet."

He looked out through the windshield. "There are rules to this game," he said. "I generally play by them."

"So what's your gut tell you about Willy's laptop?"

He shrugged. "Can't say for sure. But if we find it, I'm guessing it'll give us a little bit more to work with than we got right now."

"I'll keep your card," she told him. "I come up with anything, I'll give you a call."

He held the door for her when they got back to the hospital. "You're very smooth, Salathiel," she told him as she got out.

"I do my best," he said. "That your van, over there?"

"My uncle's," she said.

"I have a few things I would like to ask Sarah Waters," he said. "Shouldn't take but a few minutes. Would you mind giving her a lift back into the city when I'm done?"

"No problem," she said.

"You can't see this guy again."

"What?" Alessandra couldn't believe her ears. It had been a

long time since anyone had tried to tell her what to do. "What did you say?" She stood on the sidewalk in Bensonhurst, the solidly Italian-American neighborhood in Brooklyn where Sarah Waters lived with her two kids in the basement of her parents' house. She wanted to hang up, snap the little cell phone closed and end the call, but she didn't.

"Now you listen to me, Al, I'm your father, and I'm telling you this for you own good. You need to stay away from this guy, he's not what he's telling you he is."

"Look," she said, fighting a quick hot rising tide. "I don't have time for this, okay? Leave my private life alone."

"Al, you have to listen to me. I don't want you seeing this guy again. I don't want . . ."

Bensonhurst seemed to fade and disappear, and she was back outside the front door to her mother's apartment, the hallway like a yellow-painted concrete vault. She was trying to see past the fireman, trying to get a last look at her mother's body on the floor. She could still see the unearthly pale gray of her mother's face, she could still smell the gas, even after they'd shut off the stove and opened the windows. She remembered struggling to breathe in the suddenly stifling heat, she remembered voices in the background, arguing, she felt the fireman's hand gripping her shoulder. She remembered feeling completely and irrevocably alone. She remembered being frozen in fear, unable to move, or speak, or think, or cry.

Her cell phone had gone quiet. She stared at the sidewalk. He waited a moment longer.

"Al?"

She inhaled, and the spell was broken. Where were you, she

wanted to say, where the hell were you? But she didn't. "I don't give a damn what you want," she said, her tone harsh. "You said you could help me, and like a fool I thought you would. This is not helping. For once in your life, why can't you just give me what I need?"

"I have to see you," he said. "Today. Right now."

"No," she said. "I can't."

"What do you mean, you can't? Goddammit, this is serious, Al!" She could hear the affront in his voice. "What are you doing right now that's so important that—"

"I have a life!" She shouted it into the phone, her voice right up on the edge of breaking. All her buried resentment bubbled to the surface. "Why do I need to explain that to you?"

"You wouldn't have a life if it wasn't for me! I fed you! I clothed you! I—"

"You sent money!" she shouted. "And then, when I needed you the most, after I left Mag's house, you know what you did?" She paused, unsure of her balance, breathing into the silence. She fought to regain control, went on in a quieter voice. "You gave up on me. You sat up there on your altar, wearing your vestments, and you waited for me to crash and burn. And you were disappointed when it didn't happen. Weren't you?"

"Al, honey, I never—"

"You told me they'd put me in reform school if I ran away! Do you remember that?"

"Alessandra, I didn't want you running the streets. I wanted you safe. Magdelena would have kept you away from the criminals and the slimeballs."

"The slimeballs took better care of me than she did. Or

you." He'd gone silent again. "Do you remember that pool hall down on Bedford Avenue?"

"Loan sharks." She could hear the contempt in his voice. "Bookies. Pimps. Hustlers."

"Maybe," she said. "But they used to make sure I had something to eat. They made sure I didn't freeze to death. Someone in there told Tio Bobby where to find me." She wasn't totally sure of the last one, but she threw it in, anyway. "Maybe without them you would have been right. Maybe I would have gotten locked up somewhere."

She heard him exhale into the phone. "I never wanted that."

"You waited for it to happen." She looked at her watch. "I can't meet you," she said. "Not today. It's too late, anyhow, there's someplace I have to be early tomorrow morning. I need to get some sleep."

"Al, listen to me."

"Do us both a favor," she told him. "Tell me what you found out. Can you just do that?"

"All right," he said, after a moment.

There was a neon sign in the first-floor window. ARMANDO's, it said, as if that was enough. It was a restaurant that specialized in BBQ, collard greens, corn bread and cold beer. It was a fine place to eat, but the chances that it would be discovered by the cuisinistas were vanishingly small, due primarily to its location in the dark heart of Brooklyn. Hard to have much of an appetite when you're worried about your car . . .

The neon sign in the second-floor window was about half the size of the one downstairs. It also said, simply, ARMANDO's, and if you didn't know the nature of the business transacted inside, you didn't belong there. It occupied one whole floor of a building on Bedford Avenue, one flight up. You could find most kinds of trouble at Armando's, but if you were an aspiring pool player in New York City, you went to Armando's to be measured, without sentiment and without mercy.

Armando, whoever he had been, was long gone. The place was operated by a black man named Philip Giles. Al had known him since she was twelve and homeless. He had paid her, back then, gave her a few bucks to sweep up, and on rare occasions, when it was brutally cold outside, he would forget to throw her out before closing up. Al thought he had been the one who'd ratted her out to Tio Bobby, but she'd never asked. If there was a sentimental bone in Philip Giles's body, he kept it well-hidden. Al wasn't sure she really trusted him, wasn't sure if the two of them were really friends, but he and the other regulars at Armando's were protective of her. It wasn't anything they said, but they wanted her to be all right, she could feel it, and it was a sensation she treasured.

The main room was occupied by eleven pool tables. There were two more in a small room in the back, and that was where the serious games were played, the ones involving heavy money. Al had never played there. Giles had not allowed her back there as a child, and she had avoided it since. She remembered his dark face in hers, his skin the blackest she'd ever seen on a human being, his intense and somewhat hostile expression tempered by his soft voice and precise diction. "Gambling," he'd told her, "will send you straight to hell."

Al stood with a half-dozen others in the main room, watching a game in progress. White kid, college age, was playing a black guy, one of the regulars. The shooter was silent, but he had an associate nearby who talked nonstop. Philip Giles walked up behind Al. She pretended not to notice him.

"Hello, little sister," he said. "Come to work on your game?"

"Little rusty," she said, even though it was not true. As poor as it may be, she'd come for the company. "Who's the mark?"

Giles understood her question. Which one was the fish, and which one the fisherman? "Joe College," Giles said, "has a real fine hand. But he's got one big flaw."

"Yeah? What's that?"

"He wants them to like him."

"Ah. And they want to eat his lunch."

"Won't happen," he said. "They're not good enough."

Al turned and looked at Giles. He seemed untouched by time. The years had deepened the creases in his face but otherwise he was unchanged. "So they're just having a friendly game then."

"So far," he said. "You still wasting your time with Marty Stiles?"

She didn't know the answer to that. "It's a job," she said.

"A miserable excuse for a job," he told her. "You know you can do better."

It sounded like a conversation they'd had before. She looked around. "I can't play for a living," she told him. "This is not who I want to be."

"How do you know I was talking about shooting pool?" he asked her. "You have no faith in yourself, little sister."

It galled her, how everyone seemed to think it would be so easy for her to move up. Sure, she thought, I'll just walk into some corporate building, ask them if my office is ready. She was trying, she wanted someone to understand that. She was doing the best she could but it never seemed like it was enough. It seemed to her that she was hanging onto the bottom rung, and at times it took all of her strength not to let go. "Maybe you're right," she said. "But hey, you know what? I got to drive a Lamborghini the other night."

"What was it like?"

"Sweet," she said. "I never danced with Fred Astaire, but I imagine it would feel like that."

"Doesn't count," he told her. "Not if you had to give it back. You let me set you up with a few games, you could buy your own Lambo, if that's what you want. How is that not better than what you're doing now?"

"I don't know," she said. "Maybe I want them to like me, too."

"A terrible weakness," he said. "You should work on it."

"Maybe," she said. "Listen, can I ask you a question?"

"Business or personal?"

"Business," she said, and she asked her question.

"How much heat will come with this?" he said.

"You never know."

"What are you trying to do? And what did this guy do to piss you off?"

She thought before she answered. "I can't prove it yet, but I think he killed someone," she said. "And no, I'm not looking to knock him off. I just want to expose him for what he is. After that, you know, I'm gonna let go of it and let nature take its course."

He gave it a minute. "All right. Since you're family, so to speak, we're probably looking at ten grand."

"Haven't got ten," she said. "How about seventy-five hundred? I could give you cash."

"I tell you what. Keep your money, let me set you up with one game."

She swallowed. "One time only."

He nodded.

"Deal," she said.

"Beautiful thing," he said, rubbing his hands together. "All right, here's how this is going to work: if this is my one shot with you, it's going to take time to set it up properly. You'd better figure on playing in just about a month. In the meantime, I want you in here once a week to polish your game. I want you sharp, you hear?"

"Yes, Giles." Now that it was done, it didn't seem so terrible.

She made her call from the sidewalk in front of Armando's. She wanted to do it before she had time to reconsider.

"That doesn't sound like a plan," he said. "It sounds like a way to kill yourself."

It had taken her half a bottle of Portuguese rosé to screw up enough courage to call him. Asking a guy to help you, she thought, is like looking for milk in the liquor store . . . She wasn't all that sure of the scheme herself, but it was the best one she had, and better than nothing. She wanted to feel committed to it, she wanted to feel comfortable that it would work, but talking yourself into believing your own bullshit is a dangerous habit. She couldn't bear the thought of going back to square one, though. "Will you do it?"

"Al, is there any way I can talk you out of this?"

"No," she said.

"There's gotta be a better way. Can't you just—"

"Listen to me," she said. "I've got this covered. You have to trust me. Now answer my question: will you do it?"

It was a long, agonizing five seconds before he answered. "Yeah," he said. "I'm gonna wear my funeral suit, though. You're crazy, you know that?"

Twenty-two

There was a particular smell about the place, a penetrating odor that was almost a physical presence, some reeking thing standing next to you, instantly recognizable. They used to call them garbage trucks, Alessandra thought, now they're environmental service vehicles, but they still smell the same. There was a constant grinding racket, the roar of big diesel engines mixed with the whine of hydraulics and the staccato hammering of heavy air-powered tools.

They were ready for her this time, or at least they thought they were. The building was bathed in light, inside and out. It was in the center of a large, unpaved parking lot in an industrial part of Yonkers, New York, just north of the Bronx. The place was surrounded on three sides by an eight-foot brick wall topped with concertina wire, and by the river on the fourth. Security guards stood at both the entrance and exit to the yard, and a few more uniforms could be seen wandering around inside the building.

It looked like a giant airplane hangar, with huge garage doors standing open at both ends, and it was filled with garbage trucks and the men and equipment necessary to care for them.

Most of the trucks were back from their rounds, had already been serviced, refueled, and parked in green rows in the gloomy, poorly lit space between the building and the river. The drivers and their helpers were long gone, and now the mechanics and refuelers were leaving, too, their jobs done for the night. A cold rain fell straight down out of the black sky, and the guards posted at the gates stood still, miserable in their yellow rain jackets.

Alessandra wore a poncho, dark green to match the color of the garbage trucks. She had slipped into the back of the yard by way of the river, using a tiny plastic inflatable raft she'd bought at a camping store. She had a large, lumpy green knapsack, which she took off once she'd clambered up the embankment from the river. A week ago, she'd have carried it without noticing the weight, but now she had to stop and put it down when she got to the first row of trucks. She sat down on the ground and leaned back against a tire to rest. She was still weaker than she wanted to be. You shouldn't have stayed out so late last night, she told herself. You should have gone to bed like you said you were gonna. Screw it, she told herself, the hard part's done. Still, she gave herself a few minutes to sit there and recover.

There were forty-three trucks. Each new one Tomasino added to his fleet cost him in excess of a hundred and forty thousand dollars. A new engine cost about twenty-five grand, installed. Still, business had been good, competition was sparse, and Green World Recovery was growing as the surrounding towns began making efforts to reduce their landfill costs. The future was bright, if pungent.

Each truck carried a large, squarish, steel fuel tank under the cab on the driver's side, with steps welded on for the driver to climb up. The fuel cap was a round four-inch brass cap screwed loosely on the top of the tank. Alessandra levered herself up off the ground, opened the tank on the truck nearest to her, took a plastic bottle out of her knapsack, poured the contents into the tank, then replaced the cap. She slipped over to the next truck and repeated the process, kept it up until her knapsack held only empty plastic bottles. It was still fully dark when she got back to the river, got back into her inflatable, and paddled away in the dark.

The little raft, its job done, wound up slashed and buried in the mud behind a steel yard a quarter mile downriver. The empty plastic bottles went into a recycling container at a large grocery store warehouse across the street from the steel yard. The boots, poncho, knapsack, and the clothes she'd worn would be disposed of separately, later in the day.

She changed her clothes in the back of the van, taking her time. She told herself that it was probably a mistake, but she wanted to watch it happen. When she was ready, she climbed back into the driver's seat and fished out the breakfast she'd packed; coffee in a thermos, black and sweet, four PB&Js on dark bread. She was hungry enough for them to taste great. Caffeine, sugar, and fat, she thought. Got all your major food groups covered . . .

The compound she'd poured into the fuel tanks would mix with the diesel oil. When it was exposed to the heat and pressure of a diesel engine, it would turn into a thick gum that would adhere to the cylinder walls of the engine, progressively building up and hardening until the pistons could no longer move, and then the enormous torque of the diesel would snap the connecting rod that held the piston to the crank and the engine would seize. Each engine would have to be completely torn down and rebuilt, and the fuel system on each truck would have to be disassembled, cleaned, and flushed. On one truck, it would be a costly and time-consuming affair. On a fleet, it was a disaster.

There was a greasy spoon just down the hill on the side street where Alessandra was parked, it opened at four in the morning to serve the crews who would shortly be firing up their trucks and departing on their rounds. The first of the dark green behemoths rolled down the avenue about a half hour later. Al let it go by, counted six more before she pulled out to follow. The one she was behind made it all the way to Central Drive, about eight miles away, before it shuddered to a halt in the middle of the entrance ramp to the Major Deegan Expressway. The driver got out, waved his arms in frustration at the chorus of bleating car horns. There was nothing he could do but wait for the wrecker.

Alessandra pictured the same scene, repeated in thirty-seven other locations around Westchester County. Thirty-eight bottles, that's what she'd been able to carry in her knapsack. She felt a tiny spark of amusement. She pulled out around the garbage truck and headed back to Brooklyn.

Ephiphanio Neves pointed the Town Car south on River Road, headed down the west bank of the Hudson River. Caughlan liked the way the kid drove. He was smooth, unhurried. Grown up, Caughlan thought. More mature than his years. Doesn't drive with his glands. He hated the Town Car, though, thing was nothing more than a glorified taxi. Since the Bentley had been stolen, though, he needed a way to get around, and the Lincoln was going to have to do. He couldn't bring himself to look at another Bent, not yet.

That's the way it goes, he told himself. You were stupid to take delivery of the Bent before they had all the alarms installed. And what irked him more than the loss of the car was the fact that someone had taken it right out of his garage. Some son of a bitch came on my turf, he thought, walked right up my driveway, came into my house . . . What a set of balls. When I find out who did it, he thought, I'm gonna put him into the trunk of that Bent and I'm gonna bury him in it . . .

But you'll still be riding around in this fucking Lincoln, looking at the back of Epiphanio Neves's head. He leaned back in the seat, willing himself to relax. He wondered what had gotten into Tomasino. He'd gotten a call from Tomasino's lawyer an hour earlier, requesting this meeting. Demanding it, actually. It was puzzling, because it was the wrong move, tactically. I'm the guy who needs Tomasino, Caughlan thought. I need him to get me a zoning variance on my warehouse property down in Edgewater. The guy should be playing hard to get. He should be avoiding me, hiding, hoping that time will rattle me and drive the price up. If I get fifteen million for this warehouse, I'll go one and a half to Tomasino for making it happen. I'll give him ten percent of the selling price, but no more.

Edgewater, New Jersey, had been a dump back when he'd bought in, nothing more than a hardscrabble, blue-collar town stuck to a narrow strip of rocks and mud between the river and the cliffs on the Jersey side. River Road had been the single street in Edgewater back then, and traffic was so scarce the kids used to play stickball right in the middle of the street. The Jersey real estate boom had changed all that, though, and now there was hardly a square foot of dirt in Edgewater that didn't have a shopping mall or upscale condominium on it.

Caughlan's empty truck terminal was one of the last undeveloped plots.

Neves eased the car up to the gate in the chain-link fence that surrounded the terminal. He got out and opened the gate. Caughlan, spotting Tomasino's Mercedes already parked inside, got out behind him. "Wait here, Eppi," he said. "Block the exit. Understand?"

The kid nodded. "I stay right here."

Tomasino always traveled with a bodyguard, usually the same guy, some English dude. Sure enough, the feckin' Brit got out of the Mercedes while Caughlan walked across the pavement toward the car. "Good morning," he said.

Caughlan nodded at him. "Where is he? Inside?"

The guy shook his head. "Out back. Down by the river." He paused, looked unsure of himself, just a bit. "He's, ahh, he's very worked up. I've never seen him this bad before." He stared at Caughlan. It seemed out of character.

Caughlan nodded again. Show any sign of weakness, he thought, whether it be simple ill health or mental instability or even just fear, and the jackals begin to wonder how vulnerable you are. Martillo had planted a seed of doubt in Caughlan's mind, and now he wondered if Tomasino might be behind the drug shipments moving through Penn Trans. Anything is possible, he told himself, but he doubted it. Tomasino was generally too careful to get into something as risky as that. The feckin' Brit was still looking at him, though. Caughlan made a mental note to have a private conversation with the guy. Be hard to deal with a Brit, but if he was ready to sell out Tomasino . . .

Tomasino was standing at the embankment, up on a large piece of broken concrete, about four feet above the high-water line. The tide was out, which meant the place smelled even worse than usual. Tomasino didn't seem to notice. Caughlan kicked at the rocks as he crossed the cracked pavement behind the trucking terminal. Tomasino, hearing the noise, jerked his head around. Caughlan could see the muscles working in Tomasino's jaw. The man had never, in Caughlan's memory, appeared to be what you would call contented, and on this day he looked about as pissed off as Caughlan had ever seen him. Tomasino turned toward Caughlan, thrust his jaw forward. "I wanna cut to the chase on this fuckin' place," he said. "I ain't got time for the usual bullshit."

It made the hairs stand up on the back of Daniel Caughlan's neck. This is the way you blow a lifetime of work, he thought. It hit him—Tomasino had to be in a jam. He must need money bad, Caughlan thought, but if a man got greedy here, let himself be overheard saying the wrong thing by a pair of electronic ears, he could find himself in a hole very quickly. A true conservative, Caughlan was suspicious of change. What Tomasino was calling "the usual bullshit" was there to protect both parties. Why is he going out on a limb, Caughlan wondered. And why should I? "I don't know what you're talking about," he said. He was relieved, though, in a way. If Tomasino was having money troubles, that pretty much ruled him out as far as the drug scheme was concerned. If he had been importing dope, his only money problem would be how to spend it without attracting undue attention from the IRS.

"What?" Tomasino demanded, red-faced. "You think I'm wearing a fucking wire? Is that what you think? You want me to take off my fucking shirt? You want me to fucking strip? How long you and I known each other?"

"I really don't wanna see you naked, Jerry."

Tomasino jumped down off his rock. "Knock it the fuck off, will you? I got a straight business proposition for you, god-dammit. Nothing fucking illegal about it. How about you shut the fuck up and listen?"

Caughlan wasn't sure how much he should take. What swayed him, though, was curiosity. He wanted to see what kind of trouble Tomasino was in. "Go ahead," he said.

"I know you wanna sell this place," Tomasino said, his belligerence undiminished. "What do you got into this, like thirty grand?"

"Bought it a long time ago," Caughlan said.

"My real estate guy ballparked it for me," Tomasino said. "He thinks you could get maybe twenty million for it."

"You wanna buy it for twenty? Tell you what, because you and I are so close, I'll give it to you for nineteen."

Tomasino ground his teeth. "No, I don't wanna buy the fucking thing," he said. He ain't got the money, Caughlan thought. He must have gotten stung badly somehow. Caughlan felt his predatory instincts rising. "I'll sell it for you," Tomasino said. "You let me act as your agent, I'll get you the permits and variances. I'll even pay for 'em out of my end. You give me five percent of the gross selling price."

"I'm not taking less than fifteen," Caughlan said. "That's seven hundred and fifty grand to you."

"My guy says twenty million," Tomasino said. "I got confidence in him. But there's two things."

Here it comes, Caughlan thought.

"I need five hundred thou up front."

Caughlan thought about that. "What's the other thing?" he said.

Tomasino twisted his face into a grimace, reached into a pants pocket, pulled out a white card, and handed it to Caughlan. It was a business card from a bar in Fort Lee, the next town north. Caughlan turned it over. On the back was written the name Alessandra Martillo.

"That's my price," Tomasino said.

Caughlan stared at the card. He had been fully prepared to pay Tomasino ten percent of his selling price in return for the zoning variance his buyer would need to put up another giant condo. Say he's right, Caughlan thought. Say it goes for twenty. Tomasino's end would have been two, but he wouldn't have seen the money until the deal was done, maybe not until the building was up. Optimistically, call it about a year from now, maybe eighteen months. So he's trading me two million bucks, payable a year down the road, for a half million right now plus Alessandra Martillo's head. And no matter the selling price, if I pay him a half million up front, that's all he'll ever see, and he knows it. The question is, is Martillo worth a million and a half, minus a year's interest on the up-front money? He had warned her, hadn't he? It wasn't his fault the guy was so pissed off. And then he wondered why Tomasino needed his help nailing her. He looked up from the card. "Normally," he said, "this is the sort of thing you would handle by yourself." He let it hang there, watched Tomasino squirm. This guy's so worked up, he thought, he's practically shitting his pants.

"Look," Tomasino said, his voice rising. "This deal is good for today only. You hear me? I want this off my desk. Today."

Tomasino knew him well enough to be sure that Caughlan was not going to say no to a million and a half discount. "All right," Caughlan said. "Have your lawyer draw up a contract. I'll get the money ready."

"Fine," Tomasino spat. "What about the other?"

Caughlan stared down at the card. "I'll set her up," he said. "But you're gonna have to do the actual work yourself." I'm not killing anybody for this guy, he thought.

"You're goddamn right," Tomasino said. "You're goddamn right I'll do it myself." He brushed past Caughlan without another word, stomped off to his car. Caughlan followed at a slower pace, the card still in his hand.

They were headed back up River Road when it came over the news radio station he listened to. "Ex-cop shot in Orangeburg, New York," the radio said. "Martin Stiles, a twenty-year veteran of the NYPD, is in critical condition at Valley Hospital in . . ."

"Epiphanio, pull over." Two more sentences and they were done with it, had already moved on with traffic and weather. "Turn it off," he said. He was still sitting there thinking it over when his phone rang. It was Martillo.

"We gotta meet," she told him.

His paranoia got to him for a moment, but he decided to ignore it. "All right," he said. They agreed on a location. "I can be there in about an hour," he told her. He looked at his driver, then opened his door and climbed out, motioned Neves to do likewise. Epiphanio got out, stood looking up at him. Caughlan reached into his pocket, pulled out a wad of bills, counted off five hundred bucks, handed it to his driver. "Go home," he said, "and stay there. Don't answer the phone. Anybody asks you where I am, you don't know shit. Don't move until you hear from me."

"Si, Señor," Epiphanio said. "No habla Ingles."

"Good boy," Caughlan said. "You're gonna have to take the bus."

"Is he dead, then?" Caughlan stared across the white plastic table at Alessandra Martillo. He was irritated, but more at himself than her. It was easy to be mad at her on the phone, but almost impossible now that he was in her presence. They were at the food court on the third floor of the giant Palisades Center Mall in Nyack, New York. Martillo wore a short black dress, her long black hair was loose, held back out of her face by the shades she had perched on top of her head.

"Marty's in the ICU," she said, glancing at him, then looking back out at the people flooding past.

He still wanted to be pissed off, but he couldn't do it. What is it? he asked himself. What is it about this woman? It wasn't just her looks, he knew plenty of women who had looks to die for, but none of them got to him the way she did. "You in disguise here?"

She smiled, looked down at herself, crossed her long brown legs. "Tomasino's goons are looking for a gym rat," she told him. "They aren't looking for a girl like me."

"Everybody is looking for a girl like you."

She snorted. "That hasn't been my experience."

Get to it, he told himself. "So what is it you've come to tell me?"

She stared at him. "It's Tomasino," she said.

He stared back. "Can you prove it?"

She shrugged. "I'm no lawyer. But ever since I started working for you, Tomasino has been trying to get me. Those three guys in the Bronx, I'm betting they were his. Then the crew of phony Brooklyn Union Gas hardhats showed up outside my apartment building. I know they were his, because I mouse-trapped one of them, and he told me he was working for Tomasino. Said Tomasino was trying to scare me off. He also told me that Tomasino was doing this as a favor to someone, and Tomasino strikes me as a guy who does favors for nobody, not unless there's something in it for him."

"How do you know this guy was telling you the truth?"

"He was up on the roof of my building, and I was just about to throw him off," she said. "The man actually peed his pants, okay? So I don't think he had the presence of mind to make up a good story."

"Son of a bitch. All right. Is that all you've got?"

"No. Tomasino has a warehouse in Norwood, New Jersey. About twenty minutes' drive from here. He had four plastic drums of opium base in that warehouse."

Caughlan felt like he'd been punched in the stomach. "Are you sure of this?"

"Positive. I was inside that warehouse, and I left that shit spread out all over the floor. I called the cops after I left. I haven't heard anything about it on the news, but I drove past there on the way up, and there's a cruiser parked out front, and they got crime-scene tape all over the joint."

"How do you know the warehouse is his?"

"His driver told me. Gave me Tomasino's name. I didn't prompt him."

He could feel a fluttering sensation in his chest, like his heart was struggling to restart itself. "All right," he said, after a minute. "All right then, it's Tomasino." His stomach churned. The timing on this couldn't be worse, he thought. But then, you don't have to get the guy today. You can cut him his check,

then press him on the zoning variances. After that, you got all
the time in the world . . .

"There's one more thing," Martillo said.

Caughlan, his head swimming, fought hard to concentrate.
"Yeah, I know," he said. "Who's the Benedict Arnold? Who is
Tomasino's inside guy?"

"Well, first," she said, "here's how they were doing it."
Caughlan tried to pay attention while she talked about soft-
ware and bills of lading. He wasn't sure he gave a shit about the
nuts and bolts of it.

"Cut to the chase," he said.

"I think I know who it was," she told him, "but I need to
be sure. We need to be sure."

He could feel the acid from his stomach, right up in the
back of his throat. Again, he struggled to concentrate on
what she was saying, his attention compromised by the
thought of his zoning variances, and fifteen million dollars
slipping through his fingers. Maybe twenty . . . He listened to
her proposition. She was right, her scheme would probably tell
them what they needed to know. It involved some risk to her,
though, and in her place he would have used a safer location
and a more direct approach. Go along with it, he told himself.
Cooperate, at least for the time being, until you can figure out
a way to get what you want first. Revenge could wait until he
had his money.

He waited until she was done. "Take me through it again,"
he said. "Step by step."

She didn't bother to call Tomasino, but it only took him a couple
hours to get to her. The cell phone she had taken off Malik,
back in the warehouse, warbled, and she answered it. It was a

strange male voice, but she had no doubt who was pulling the strings. "Enough," the voice said. "We're prepared to give you the Englishman. We require a face-to-face meeting. There's an empty warehouse in Jersey City . . ."

"No good," she said. "I'm not letting you set me up. You'll hear back from me later, I'll give you the address. You can meet me at midnight tonight. Get us into the spirit of the thing." There was the sound of a hand over the receiver, muffled voices in the background, then the voice came back.

"Agreed." He hung up without another word.

Twenty-three

Caughlan climbed the stairs ahead of Tomasino. The Englishman, Wallace Parker, was last. "I don't like it," Tomasino was saying. "Why did she want to meet here, of all places? And why do you gotta be here?"

Caughlan stopped at the landing and groped for the doorknob in the dark. "What happened to that hard-on you had for her this morning?" he said. "Change your mind?" He had expected Tomasino to bitch, it was the man's nature. Fucking little prick, he thought, loves to play the tough guy, but all he does is whine.

"No, I didn't change my mind, but I can think of a million places better than this."

"Look, this is where she wanted to meet, and you have to do this part of it her way. This bitch is gonna be hard enough to take down as it is. You get her thinking, you only make things worse. You try to persuade her to do it someplace else, she'll smell a rat." He opened the door, stepped through. "We ain't turning on any lights in here, I don't want anything visible from the street."

"All right, all right," Tomasino groused. "I just wish we

could do her someplace remote. You know what I'm saying? Just for security. You don't think anyone will hear her screaming and shit?"

Caughlan stopped and turned. He could just make out Tomasino's shape in the darkness. "Look," he said, "I already told you, you ain't doing her here. You got that? She steps through the door, okay, your guy hits her with the Taser. When she's out of it, you take her anywhere you want. You do whatever you want, but you do it away from me. Are we clear? I don't wanna know nothing about it. I'm here for one reason only, and that's because I need your help with some zoning variances in Jersey."

"Whatsamatter? You going soft? We was gonna let you have her first."

Caughlan was careful to keep the distaste out of his voice. "You wanna keep shit like this nice and clean," he said. "If I didn't see anything, I can't say anything, can I?"

Tomasino seemed unconcerned. "Yeah, whatever," he said. "Is there any place around here that I can sit down?"

"Stay where you are, I'll go find something." He walked farther into the darkened room, trying not to listen to Tomasino talking to the fucking Brit, telling him how they'd use Alessandra's clothes to tie her up, then throw her in the trunk of the car.

It was a little past midnight when Alessandra Martillo drifted down Lafayette, headed for Bedford Avenue in Brooklyn. She'd taken a cab instead of driving her uncle's van, because parking in that neighborhood was not always easy, and maybe not a great idea. It seemed like a long ride in the cab, and she felt tired, but even so, she'd had the cab driver drop her some distance from her destination. Maybe, she thought, a little walk will give me a little more spirit . . . And maybe I'm just delaying.

Most of the streets had been repaved since she was a child. Back then, the rectangular pattern of the cobblestones showed through the asphalt in places, along with the buried streetcar rails like veins under the skin of an old man's forearm. They were gone now, or maybe just buried deeper, but the rest of the neighborhood hadn't changed much. She looked at the buildings as she passed, remembering her life as it had been. A homeless brat, she thought, a runaway, a truant, a burglar. A liar and a thief, those were the words her Aunt Magdelena had used, in English and in Spanish, and her father had believed them.

I did what I had to do, a small inner voice protested.

And how have you changed, she asked herself. Are you any different now, or have you just buried those bones a little deeper? Like the rails under the street, you can't see them unless you dig, but that doesn't mean they're gone.

You're overtired, Al told herself. You wouldn't be thinking this way if you hadn't had to deal with Stiles last night, and with Tomasino's trucks after that. She got to the corner, finally, stood looking across Bedford Avenue at Armando's. It was Friday night, she'd almost forgotten about that. They'd have live music at Armando's tonight. She could hear the muffled thump of bass and drums, the sound leaked out through the restaurant walls along with the smell of Southern cooking, competing with the odors coming out of the Popeyes chicken joint behind her and with the normal racket of a downtown

Brooklyn night. She took a moment to stretch, felt the ache in her neck, some lingering soreness in her ribs. Are you ready for this, she asked herself.

No, she thought. I'm not.

The light changed and she stepped off the curb. She felt his hand on her elbow before she saw him. "Hssst. Al. It's a setup. Caughlan sold you out to Tomasino." He tried to talk without moving his lips.

"What I figured," she said. "Hello, Gearoid."

"Then what are you doing here?" He kept pace with her as she crossed the street. His put his hand on her shoulder, stopped her when they reached the opposite sidewalk. "Are you crazy? How you gonna run in high heels? And I'm not saying that dress isn't short enough, but Jaysus, how you gonna, you know, do what you do?"

She turned to look up into his mournful face. "Doing what I do hasn't worked in a while, Gearoid. And I'm too tired to run."

"Come with me, then. I know a guy up in Boston, he could put you up for a while . . ."

"You're taking a hell of a chance, talking to me out in public," she said, cutting him off. "What if Caughlan sees us?"

"Never mind that." He finally looked away from her chest. It was freer than she liked it behind the black silk dress Sarah Waters had bullied her into buying earlier in the day. *Why don't you just buy a fucking muumuu?* Sarah had yelled, after her patience had finally run out. *Christ, if I had your figure . . . Why don't you just dress up in a potato sack with a bag over your head, like in the Middle East? What the hell are you afraid of?* Al shook the black hair back out of her eyes. She was overly conscious of the silver heart-shaped pendant that hung on a chain down between her breasts, warm against her skin. So was Gearoid. "Don't go up there, Al," he said. "Please. For God's sake listen to me."

"Tell you what," Al told him. "We'll stop downstairs first. You can buy me a beer."

"You are one hardheaded woman, do you know that?"

"So I'm told. Come on in, it's a nice joint, you'll like it."

"Ain't it just like a woman," Tomasino said. "Bitch be late for her own goddamn funeral." He laughed at his joke.

Caughlan sighed. "Might wanna keep it down just a touch," he said. "And sit the fuck down, will you? Relax. You're gonna hear her before you see her anyhow. You want her to see your goddamn face in the window?"

"So goddamn dark in here, she won't see shit," Tomasino said, but he returned to the chair and sat down. "How are we gonna know she's coming?"

"Got it covered," Caughlan said. "You never did tell me what got you so hot for her."

It was a minute before Tomasino responded. "She fucked me," he said. "She cost me money, and I can't let that happen. Bitch. When I get my hands on her . . ."

"Oh," Caughlan said, keeping his voice neutral. "Messing with your business?"

Again, Tomasino paused just a blink too long before answering. "Something like that."

"I hate that," Caughlan said. "Get so sick of watching my back all the fucking time. You think you got your shit covered, some son of a bitch finds a new way to fuck you up."

"Yeah," Tomasino said. "This bitch is done fucking me up, I can tell you that."

"I got a piece of this club down near Giant's Stadium," Caughlan said. "Place is a real gold mine, most of the year. Got the ponies, got the football, got some college games and shit. We been there a while, right, so we know what the take's gonna be, most weekends. But then we start coming up short, right, but only like one weekend out of five or six. We don't got anybody just working one weekend out of six, so we didn't know what to do. Anyhow, we hired this private dick, guy worked me for two weeks. I mean, I'm pretty sure he had the shit nailed right away, but he worked me a little bit. I guess you gotta expect that. I guess I didn't mind."

"So what happened?" Tomasino said.

"What happened to what? Oh. Sorry. Yeah, it was one of the dancers. She was going with this guy, fucking idiot couldn't stay out of the joint. He was supposed to be doing weekends, right, but he'd miss one and then they'd toss him for thirty days and then let him back out. He'd get fucked up and miss the next one. But he didn't have the money to handle his shit, right, so every time he gets out, some of my money winds up going up his nose."

"How'd your investigator find this out?"

"Beats me. It's his business, right? It's what he does."

"What happened to them?"

"The dancer? Drowned her in the toilet, right there in the club."

"Jesus. And her boyfriend?"

"What about him?"

"What'd you do to him?"

"Nothing. You gotta understand, Jerry, it's just business. I didn't do the dancer because I was pissed off. I mean, it was only money, right? And not a hell of a lot of that. I did her because you can't have someone putting their hands in your pocket. You know what I'm saying? You let that go on, everyone's gonna want some. The guy wasn't my problem, what do I give a fuck what happens to him?"

"But he was the guy she was stealing it for!"

"I ain't God, Jerry. I ain't a cop, and I ain't the guy's mother. I'm a businessman."

Tomasino hauled a big shiny pistol out of his jacket pocket and began fiddling with it. "Yeah," he said. "I got you."

"Check this out," she told him. She almost had to yell to be heard over the music. "Booth in the corner. We got lucky tonight." The place was packed, and he was jammed up close to her. She could feel his hip next to hers, smell his faint cologne. She tried to concentrate on sitting with her knees together.

"Al," he shouted back, leaning over to stare into her face. "Al, they're in the pool hall right upstairs. Why don't we get the hell out of here? I'll come away with you. Please, Al, don't do this."

A waitress came, stood by their table, mute.

"You hungry, Gro? My treat."

He just looked at her.

Al looked up at the waitress. "You got Guinness?"

O'Hagan shook his head, irritated. "Just make it two Budweisers, okay?"

The waitress looked at him for a second, then back at Al, shrugged, turned on her heel and left. "Friendly bunch in here," he said, and he glared in the direction of the band on the far side of the room. It was a trio, and the bassist and guitar player faced each other, ripped into an old Hendrix riff. There was no vocalist, but that didn't matter, everybody knew the words.

"Actin' funny, and I don't know why . . ." Both musicians turned back to face the crowd, suddenly silent as half of the restaurant shouted the next line. O'Hagan didn't, though, he just stared at the guitar player. Or rather, at his instrument. It was a beat-up old Strat, had the initials SRV glued to the body. It was instantly recognizable from a dozen Stevie Ray Vaughn videos. Gearoid turned back to look at Alessandra, the sorrow and concern draining from his face, leaving him looking sour and mean. Al felt the barrel of his pistol in her ribs. "I knew I shoulda got rid of that goddamn thing," he said. "How long have you known?"

She spoke softly, so he had to lean in to hear. "For an Irishman," she said, "you're a terrible liar. You told me you didn't do e-mail, you remember that? 'Computers are the work of the divil,' that's what you said. My father told me you were working in IT for a bank in Dublin when your girlfriend went missing. The Dublin cops liked you for it, but they couldn't make a case. And it made me wonder when you never told Caughlan about that night those three mutts came after us in the Bronx. But I wasn't sure until my father found out who you really are. Did Willy know you were brothers?"

"Half-brothers," he snarled back. "Yeah, he knew."

"What about Caughlan? Did he know he was your father?"

"Don't call him that!" he snapped. A thin black man sitting adjacent turned to look at them, then turned away again. "He was no fadder, he was nothing more than a stallion covering a mare, went home to Ireland on holiday, got drunk, got his nut off, and then just walked away when he was done." He lowered his voice. "He was nothing to me."

"Did he know?"

"Did he care? Why don't you ask that? Did he fookin' care?" He jabbed her in the side with his pistol. "Come on, we're going."

Alessandra didn't move. "Can I ask you one question, first?"

He gritted his teeth. "Go on, then."

"At Caughlan's party, when Helen Caughlan and I were standing up on that balcony, and you looked up. It was her, wasn't it? It was never me."

"You don't know what he puts her through!" he said. "Even the dogs on the street have it better than her!" He looked at her face. "I'm sorry, Al, I like my girls white. Nothing personal."

Ah.

"And then later on that night, those guys that followed us, they were yours, right? You called them 'three good men,' and I kinda wondered how you knew that."

"They were good men, all right, but they were Tomasino's, not mine."

"Tomasino. Your partner."

"Yeah, my partner." He prodded her with the pistol again. "You've had your one question, and then some."

Again, she didn't move. "Were you gonna kill me that night?"

"No," he said, his voice growing loud again. "That was back before we knew how goddamn stubborn you are. We thought we could scare you off."

"And those guys outside of my apartment. Did you tell them what to do to me, Gearoid? Was that your idea?"

"Goddammit!" he exploded, the other diners forgotten. "This isn't about you! This was never about you! Don't you get it? You've gotten yerself into something way bigger than you are!"

"Money," she said. "Tomasino's drug operation. You were his inside guy at Penn Transfer."

O'Hagan's eyes glittered with anger. "How did you tumble to that?"

"Was it you?"

"Yes, goddammit, it was me. The whole bloody scheme was my idea, if you must know. How did you find out?"

"Marty called me last night, after he was shot. He told me what he'd found. I was the woman who called the cops and told them I'd heard gunfire." She watched his face as he calmed himself. "He thought he was gonna die. Just your hard luck he didn't." The lights of the bar reflected in his eyes. If Marty dies, she told herself, that's what he's thinking, if Marty dies, he can kill me and nobody will know. He thinks he might still be able to save it.

"Well, here's your consolation, then," he said. "Stiles did for Ramon, put two rounds through his chest. He's laying dead in that warehouse right now, not fifty feet from where they found Stiles." He jabbed her with the gun again, more insistently this time. "Come on, Martillo. *Mova la culo.*"

"How long we known each other," Caughlan said. "Twenty-five years?"

"Something like that." Tomasino was still fondling his pistol, feeling the weight of it in his hands.

"All this time," Caughlan said, "you been a true conservative."

"No fuckin' way," Tomasino said. "I was born a Democrat, and by God—"

"No, I don't mean it like that. I mean conservative in the real world, not in politics."

"What are you talking about?"

"You been a real conservative. Just like me. I take care of meself first, you know what I'm saying?"

"Of course," Tomasino said. "Nobody gonna do it for you." He sounded a bit defensive.

"Absolutely not," Caughlan said. "I mean, think of all the guys you seen fall by the wayside. What did they do wrong? How come you're here and they're not?"

"Usually they trusted the wrong guys," Tomasino said. "Or else they get too brave. You win an election or two, the money starts rolling in, you start thinking you can't put a foot wrong. Next thing you know, you get caught with your dick where it don't belong, your picture's in the papers, it's over. Or else you get too greedy, someone thinks you're gouging them, they rat you out, it's over."

"That's what I'm saying," Caughlan said. "Look at all the Jersey politicians went to jail. Never happened to you."

"I see where you're going. I'm conservative, meaning I'm careful. I don't take chances, I take care'a business."

"A true conservative," Caughlan said. "Hooray for me and fuck you."

"Hey," Tomasino said, "plenty'a nice guys in the cemetery."

"Or in prison," Caughlan said. "An entire personal and political philosophy in six words. Pretty highly evolved."

"Six words?" Tomasino said. "What are you talking about?"

Caughlan repeated himself. "Hooray for me and fuck you," he said. "You know, I used to think it was just me. Saw guys like you on television, I thought you were really doing something. Thought I was a louse because I had to take care of myself."

"Yeah, we were doing something all right," Tomasino said. "We were doing the same shit you were, just in a different place."

"Probably learned the same lessons I did."

"Keep your hand on your wallet," Tomasino said. "Watch your back. Watch the guy watching your back."

"Never give a schmuck a break," Caughlan said.

Tomasino laughed. "That's a good one," he said. A moment passed. "What do you mean?"

"Oh, you know how it is," Caughlan said. "You feel sorry for some schmuck, you know you should really put him in the ground, but you decide to let him walk. You'll pay for that one every time."

"You gotta bury someone, you better fuckin' bury them. You remember the shah of Iran? He let the Ayatollah leave the country, let him go to France. He buries the motherfucker instead, it's a different world."

"Isn't that funny?" Caughlan said. "You know what that tells you? That giving someone absolution is the only unforgivable sin. You let somebody walk, they'll fuck you every time. But, Jerry, my question to you is this: why are you taking a chance like this? The Jerry Tomasino I know would never come here himself. He'd be at Lincoln Center or some damn place while Martillo was getting whacked. I don't get it."

"I gotta do this," Tomasino said. "The bitch put too many of my guys on the shelf. I got nobody I dare to send . . ."

"Got you," Caughlan said. "It's down to you and the Brit, here."

"Yeah."

"You didn't dare send O'Hagan."

"The son of a bitch already . . ." His voice died away as he realized what he'd said. He pointed his pistol at Caughlan's guts. "Wallace," he said to the Englishman. "Turn on the fuckin' lights."

Wallace Parker, over by the door, fumbled for the light switch. Caughlan was momentarily blinded. He squinted at Tomasino, who squinted back. The pistol never wavered. The three of them were in the room over the garage at Caughlan's house in Old Tappan, New Jersey. "You son of a bitch," Tomasino said. "You fuckin' bastard. She ain't coming, is she?"

"No," Caughlan said. "Why'd you do it, Jerry?"

"Gearoid brought the scam to me," Tomasino said, sneering. He looked around, but there was no one but the three of them there. "He said you were fat, dumb, and happy. An easy mark. It was too much money and it was too good to pass up. When the Feds finally caught on, they'd take one look at you and throw your ass in the can while we walked away counting the change. We couldn't lose."

"So how come you're down to this? How come you're losing?"

"That fuckin' bitch! Martillo is what happened, but when I get my hands by God on that—"

Wallace Parker stuck the Taser against Tomasino's neck and fired. The gun fell from Tomasino's boneless hand as he crumpled to the floor. Caughlan retrieved the gun while Parker hit Tomasino with the Taser again. "Got another entry for his list of life lessons," Parker said, straightening back up. "Never back a lame horse. Was that all right? That's what you wanted me to do, right?"

"That's what I wanted." The Brit stared at him, and he

stared back. The guy doesn't trust you yet, Caughlan thought. Maybe he never will. He took your money, though. But that's the way of it with turncoats . . . "Pick him up. I got a hole already dug, out back in the garden."

Parker hauled Tomasino semi-erect, got him over one shoulder. Good thing Tomasino's a little guy, Caughlan thought, and he followed the two of them back down the stairs. He did not want to have to touch the bastard. They walked out of the garage, around back, and through the wet grass of the backyard. "Over here," Caughlan said, treading carefully in the dark. "The hole is right in front of you. See that big pile of dirt?"

"Got it," Parker said. "You want . . ."

Caughlan found the shovel, swung it high over his head and brought it down on the back of Parker's skull. Parker and Tomasino both tumbled down into the hole. Caughlan stuck Tomasino's pistol in a jacket pocket, took the jacket off and laid it aside. He began filling the hole back up. Gave that whole goddamn speech about conservatives, he told himself, but the feckin' Brit must not have been paying any attention at all.

She stood up, and he stood up right behind her, pressed himself close to whisper harshly in her ear. "Don't try anything stupid. I'll pop you right here in the middle of this restaurant, don't think I won't." She ignored him, moved slowly across the crowded room, paused and turned to face him just as they got to an open space on the other side. He had his pistol in a jacket pocket, pointed more or less in her direction.

"Why did you do it? Your own brother."

"Half-brother," he said, angry.

"Did you have to kill him?"

"He got everything he ever wanted," Gearoid said. "Seen that guitar up at auction, the old man had to go and buy it for him. It was sickening."

"You killed him for that?"

Gearoid's eyes glittered. "No. The little bastard was smarter than I thought he was. He knew I hated the old man, and once he found out we were related, he never took his eyes off me. I don't know how he tumbled to our little import scheme, but he did. He was a better programmer than I thought he was. He was gonna rat me out. I tried to talk to him, but he wouldn't listen. Enough, now, go on outside."

"My turn next?"

"You sealed that one when you broke into my apartment and stole that goddamn guitar. How did you know I had it?"

"I didn't," she said. "But I had a feeling, you know what I mean? I figured, if you were the murderer, you'd flip when you saw it. Which you did. And that ain't even the real one."

"What are you talking about?"

"That one's a phony. I wasn't sure what you'd done with the original, so I had a friend make that one for me." It felt good, saying that.

"You played me? You bitch . . ."

"Worse than you think," she said.

Gearoid reached up with his free hand, grabbed Alessandra by the hair, and twisted. He pulled her up onto her toes, it felt like he was about to tear the scalp right off of her head. He had the pistol out in plain sight now. He scanned the crowd, which had suddenly grown silent. "Looks like you blew it again," he said. "Overconfidence. Isn't that what nearly got you last time?"

Philip Giles, the tall thin black man who'd been sitting at the table next to theirs, came out of the bathroom behind them and grabbed the Irishman's wrist, twisted the gun up toward the ceiling. O'Hagan bellowed, hauling even harder on Al's hair, began twisting the gun back down inch by inch, closer to Giles's face. There was a commotion behind them as someone tried to push his way through the crowd. He won't make it in time, Al thought, and she reached over, got O'Hagan by one ear, snatched it off.

O'Hagan bellowed again, louder this time, exploded in a kinetic frenzy of blood and furious motion. He dropped Alessandra, ripped his gun hand away from Giles, swung it in her direction, the blood streaming from the side of his head. I still got his ear in my hand, Al thought, and she dropped it, got both hands on O'Hagan's gun arm. She saw TJ Conrad out of the corner of her eye, heard a swish as he swung the wooden guitar like an ax. It flew past her ear and hit Gearoid in the face. He went down with Giles on top of him, banged his head hard on the wood floor. Giles kicked the gun away, got up wiping blood on his pants. "Jesus," he said.

TJ Conrad walked past Alessandra, retrieved the guitar.

"Little bit heavier than I like 'em," he said, turning back to her, grinning.

She looked at him. "Me or that guitar?"

His grin got wider. "You kidding? Ain't you got any mirrors at your house?"

She ignored that. "That's your funeral suit?"

"Changed my mind," he said.

Salathiel Edwards finally managed to push his way in through the crowd, followed by three uniforms. The uniforms began shoving the crowd back from the prone and bleeding Irishman. Alessandra reached up, took the silver necklace off, handed it to Edwards. "Get what you need?"

"Clear as a bell," he said.

Twenty-four

Al was back in jeans and a T-shirt. She walked through the front doors of Astoria Studios carrying the laptop under her arm. She had broken into O'Hagan's apartment in the early hours of the morning, found the real Stevie Ray Vaughn guitar and Willy Caughlan's laptop. She left the guitar for the police but she'd taken the computer. The cops didn't need it, after all; they had O'Hagan's confession on tape.

Security stopped her at the front desk. She gave them her name, sat down in a waiting room while they got the necessary clearances. It took about half an hour before someone came for her, walked her down some stairs, and through a dark corridor to a small room on the lower level. It was empty but for a long table and four chairs. Al sat down, opened the laptop, and fired it up.

Twenty minutes later the door opened and a man in a gray suit stuck his head in. "Are you Ms. Martillo?"

"Yeah."

"All right," he said, and then he went away. Five minutes later he was back again; this time he came all the way into the room, followed by God and two very large bodyguards. God, aka Shine, looked pale and drawn. They all came around to Al's side of the table and looked over her shoulder at the screen, but Al folded it down.

"Hold up," she said. "All you guys, get over there." The three men stopped, looked at Shine for instructions.

"G'wan," she said. "I'll be all right."

Al waited until they were settled in on the other side of the room. Two of them were seated and one of the bodyguards stood at the door. She opened the computer back up. She had one moment of consternation when she thought the file wasn't going to open, but then the video started. She turned the laptop so that she and God could both see the screen.

The opening footage was some shaky images of Tudor City, Willy Caughlan's neighborhood on Manhattan's east side, Willy grinning into the camera on an overcast winter day. Shine, sitting next to Al behind the table, sucked in her breath, then went silent. There was a woman's voice, off-camera, indistinct. She asked Willy something, Al could tell by her inflection. Willy shook his head, looking with some annoyance at the camera that occupied the space between himself and the woman. "Man, you really are in love with that thing." The woman holding the camera laughed, said something that seemed to reassure Willy, and he smiled again. "You wanna come up?"

Alessandra felt a sudden wave of sorrow as it hit her that she was hearing a voice from the grave. It was a boy's voice, lacking timbre because he had not fully grown into his body yet, he was still young, long-boned, and skinny. He would have been a big man, Al thought, he had his mother's height, but his father's genes showed clearly in the shape of his face and the breadth of his shoulders. And he's dead, she thought, murdered as he stood in the doorway of his adult life, just before he had any real chance to become something. He was so different in the video, so alive and so human, moving, breathing, talking. When he had only been an image, a sterile, two-dimensional face on a still photograph, he had been almost an abstraction in Al's mind. Seeing him alive on that winter day somehow brought home the enormity of his death, the magnitude of the loss of all the years he might have had.

The camera blinked, and suddenly they were inside Willy's apartment. Shine was a natural redhead, and one pale, freckled breast filled most of the screen as she fiddled with the camera until she had it where she wanted it. Then she backed away, crawled on hands and knees across an expanse of queen-sized bed to join Willy, who was very ready for her.

"Stop it, stop it, stop it!" Shine said, her voice rising rapidly. The two men who were seated on the other side of the room jumped up, but Shine was faster than they were. "You stay where you are!" she shouted, half-rising out of her own seat. The men froze, looked at each other once. "Goddamn you, sit back down!" she yelled, and they subsided slowly back into their seats.

Alessandra closed the file, and the video quit playing.

"What do you want?" Shine asked her.

Al shrugged. "I don't know. A better job. A guy I can trust. World peace."

Shine didn't look at her. "I mean, what do you want from me?"

"I don't know. I was just gonna wreck this, you know what I mean? I was gonna pull out the hard drive and throw it in the river or something. I never met Willy, but I figured I owed him that much. But then, the more I thought about it, the more I thought you ought to have a voice in it."

"You could have sold this," Shine said.

"I know."

"So why didn't you?"

"I'm not old enough to sell it. I'm still all idealistic and shit."

Shine stared at her.

"Couldn't do it," Al told her. "Felt too low-rent."

God's pale face looked haggard under the fluorescent lights. She looked at the computer, then at Al. "Can we still . . . Can we take out the hard drive and wreck it or something?"

"Why not."

"Jimmy," she said, looking at the guy in the gray suit. "Go find a hammer and a screwdriver." She turned back to Al. "Are you okay?"

"No," Al said. "But I'll get over it."

Twenty-five

Alessandra Martillo had asked TJ Conrad to handle the music at Tio Bobby's funeral. Her mind blunted by grief, she hadn't given it another thought, had no idea what he was going to play. She was in the front row next to Anthony, maybe a dozen feet from the coffin. She sat there watching Bobby's calm face while the preacher's words bounced off the hard shell of sorrow that surrounded her.

The church was full. Half of those in attendance wore heavy black leather jackets and boots, and the other half was more carefully suited in somber pinstripes and dark grays. These poor guys, she thought, the gays are all too well-acquainted with death, and the bikers dance with it, they court it in their own way . . . She was dry-eyed, shut down, as sere and unmoving as a bouquet of dried flowers until shortly after Conrad sat down at the piano. She didn't recognize any of the music he played, but it sounded medieval to her, slow, sonorous, building up gradually until it filled the entire space, booming and echoing off the stone walls, leaving everyone in the church sitting in an almost stunned silence, but then he segued into something quiet and soft, and a slender, gray-haired woman got up to sing a version of "Ave Maria" that Alessandra had never heard before. The crowd stood then, began filing out. Alessandra lost Anthony in the shuffle, his friends swallowed him up, wrapped him in a cocoon, and swept him away. He turned back once to look for her. She blew him a kiss, waved good-bye.

She stopped on the church steps, stood there alone as the tide receded, watched long black cars and glittering chrome-and-steel motorcycles as they coughed and stuttered into life. She felt curiously distant, as though she was watching something that was happening in some other place, until she felt his hand on her shoulder. She knew it was him just from the touch, she could feel the calluses on his fingertips, and she turned, lost her grip, wrapped herself around him.

He took her back to his place in Greenpoint, after. He didn't ask her if she wanted to go, he just put her in a cab, climbed in after her, gave the driver his address. He surprised her once again, because the place was relatively clean for a guy, decent, if small, sparsely furnished, with exposed brick walls, wooden floors. He hit a button on his phone as they entered. A disembodied voice told him he had sixty-seven messages.

"What?" she said, turning. "Sixty-seven . . ."

He turned the phone off. "I'm very popular, these last couple days," he said.

"What happened?"

"God gave me a co-writing credit," he said.

She was confused. "God . . ."

"Last week, in the studio. The day you were there, remember, I sat in with a couple guys that morning? Turns out it was God's track they were working on. As a matter of fact, she was there."

"Shine?"

"Yeah. I didn't see her, but she was there, she heard what we did, decided I deserved a credit."

"How about that. Does that mean you're rich and famous now?"

He shrugged. "Very hard to tell what it means when God does something. Can I get you something to drink?"

"What you got? And how are the guys in BandX taking this?"

He walked over to his fridge, opened it, and looked inside. "Not good," he said. "Not good at all, but we already got all the tracks down, so maybe it doesn't matter. I got beer, I got half a bottle of red wine—which I gotta warn you is pretty vile—and I got a bottle of Cutty Sark."

He remembered what I drink, she thought, and he stocked up. "Cutty," she said. She felt a bit unsteady on her high heels, felt awkward in the unfamiliar dress, felt the gulf yawning between the two of them, felt her heart hammering high in her chest. He turned to watch as she kicked off her shoes. He had the scotch in one hand, two glasses in the other.

"Forget the ice," she told him.

He stood, silent, looked at her.

"You don't know how bad I wanna run away," she said.

He spread his arms wide. "I'm a pussycat," he said.

"I'm not."

He nodded. "I get it."

"Can you deal with . . . Can you help me?" she said.

"Relax," he told her. He put the glasses down, opened the bottle. "Everything is gonna be fine," he said. "You'll see . . ."